THE
FOURTH
WAR

CHRIS STEWART

ST. MARTIN'S PAPERBACKS

This is a work of fiction. All of the characters, organizations and events portrayed in this novel are either products of the author's imagination or are used fictitiously.

THE FOURTH WAR

Copyright © 2005 by Chris Stewart.

Cover photos:
Flags by Getty Images
Fire by Paul Taylor / Getty Images—Tony Stone

Library of Congress Catalog Card Number: 2005043962

ISBN: 0-312-93975-2
EAN: 9780312-93975-5

Printed in the United States of America

St. Martin's Press hardcover edition / October 2005
St. Martin's Paperbacks edition / July 2006

St. Martin's Paperbacks are published by St. Martin's Press, 175 Fifth Avenue, New York, NY 10010.

10 9 8 7 6 5 4 3 2 1

OUTSTANDING PRAISE
FOR **CHRIS STEWART** AND
THE FOURTH WAR

"Chris Stewart's literary torque wrench cranks up the tension to an unbearable point in this stark tale of the war on terror. *The Fourth War* is more than a page-turner, it's a mind-blower as he tosses twists, turns, and surprises on every page. Bound to be a movie!"

—Walter Boyne,
bestselling author of *The Wild Blue*

"The novel's surprising details feel entirely authentic . . . Stewart is impressively skilled at presenting the entire tapestry of his war—the many threads of the terrorist, allied and American forces."

—*Publishers Weekly*

"A smash-'em-up, swift-flying Western."

—*Kirkus Reviews*

"Better than Tom Clancy. Knuckle-whitening flying scenes."
—Douglas Preston, bestselling author
of *Dance of Death,* on *Shattered Bone*

"Full throttle . . . laced with intrigue."

—Eric Harry,
author of *Arc Light,* on *The Kill Box*

Also by Chris Stewart

The Third Consequence

The Kill Box

Shattered Bone

To my dad,
who instilled in me the pure joy of flight.

And Pat and Shellee Dooley,
who sacrificed to make this possible.

BOOK
ONE

BOOK
ONE

It is foolish and wrong to mourn the men who died.
Rather we should thank God that such men lived.
—Gen. George S. Patton

Here rests in honored glory an American soldier
known but to God.
—Inscription on the Tomb of the Unknown Soldier

PROLOGUE

Tora Bora
Eastern Afghanistan
17 January 2002

The weave of natural caverns extended deep into the earth, more deeply than the rain of American bombs could ever hope to reach. But the smoke, black and acid, that poisoned the air had forced the few soldiers that remained to take refuge in the back of the caves on the south side of the mountain. There they listened in the darkness, waiting for death to appear.

The soldiers had pledged to sacrifice their lives to God, though few expected the opportunity would present itself so soon.

Still, the bombing confirmed what the Taliban had been told. The Americans—smooth-faced and soft like a fat woman's belly—were too cowardly to fight them man-to-man on the ground, and too callous to care how many they killed. So let them rain down fire and steel from the sky. If they brought death, that was fine; death only brought paradise, and other warriors were always ready to step into their place.

The soldiers cowered in the caves and listened carefully. Over the past weeks they had learned to tell which kind of attack aircraft it was—the slow and lumbering B-52s, with their monstrously noisy engines and long contrails of smoke, or the sleek and speeding B-1s, which streaked in very low, their bombs reaching their targets before the sound of their engines arrived.

On this night, on this target, B-52s were overhead. A flight of four passed over the caves and belched out their bombs. Two hundred and sixteen five-hundred-pound bombs fell through the night with a soft *whooshing* sound, a mild rushing of air pushed aside by their nose cones and small steering fins. Then the earth began to shake and the ground began to roll. The air shattered and compressed, smashing the eardrums of the men as the bombs created a mushroom of fire and overpressure that carried chunks of hot metal, broken rock, and pieces of human flesh. For almost seven minutes the attacks rolled in from above, the bombs dropping like angels of death from the sky. The acidic smoke carried through the caverns like a black, deadly wall, before finding the air vents and lifting into the night wind.

As the bombs fell, the al Qaeda soldiers hunkered and waited in their caves. Many of them died. Soldiers died every night. But the leader, the great warrior, lived through the attack. His men knew that he would, for he had been touched by God.

After what seemed like an eternity, the last explosion rumbled through the cave. Then the air finally settled and the night wind returned. The smell of smoke, burned flesh, and human intestines seemed to be everywhere.

Then the Great One, their leader, struggled again to his knees, turned to his warriors, and lifted his head. His eyes, clear and bright, reflecting the red fire and flame, moved dangerously around the small cavern, boring through every man.

"It is time," he announced in a voice filled with rage. "Let the devils tear down the mountain, it is time we moved on. The greatest battle awaits us. Come, let us go."

And with that he stood and crawled from the cave. He struggled through a small opening to set out across the desert, making his way through the night toward the border of Pakistan, walking alone and unafraid with only a small pack on his back. Two lieutenants struggled to keep up, following him across the dry sand. The moon was cold and white. Sunrise was seven hours away.

Late the next day the leader passed through the port of Karachi. Two weeks after that he was in his new home.

1

Eastern Dasht-e Lut Desert, Iran
Eleven Kilometers from the Afghanistan Border

The meeting took place on the edge of a high mountain desert, miles from humanity, but near the center of Asia. The terrible mountains of Turkmenistan lie not far to the north. The unmarked wasteland of the Afghanistan border was just to the east. It was a harsh land, foreboding, majestic, and severe, with no well-established borders to belabor the travel of beasts or men. Hidden under the desert were a thousand years worth of battle relics from the past—arrowheads, cankered armor, broken spears, and rusted guns—all of which served as a reminder that the area, though desolate, had been fought over before.

During the last century, the Dasht-e Lut had taken a turn toward relative peace, allowing the local nomadic herdsman to recapture an existence that hadn't changed for two thousand years. But rumors of war could now be heard again. Bandits, nonuniformed armies, and fugitives from international law could be found in the caves that spiderwebbed through the base of the mountains, and even up into the rocky buttes with their scrub-topped plateaus.

It was a perfect place to hide, for this was territory beyond the edge of civilization. There were no borders in the mountains and no nation-states, no governments or security, no communications or roads. And there certainly was no authority that recognized the West.

The designated rendezvous spot was along a rocky lip of the Garabil Plain, on the outskirts of a forgotten mining town that had been happily deserted soon after the First World War. The broken-down shanties, tiny dwellings that had been scraped together from tar paper and old shipping crates, had been arranged around a small spring that was now a dark, muddy hole. The opening to the mine shaft was somewhere up the side of the hill, lost in the cedars and brush that had grown up over the years. On this night, the moon was clear and round, bright white and surrounded by a thin halo from the ice crystals that had blown off the snow-capped Himalayan peaks to the east. The air was perfectly still, as the earth seemed to take a breath and hold it, waiting and listening, knowing something soon would appear.

The American watched from the mount of his horse, a long-legged Arabian that he loved like a child. He patted her mane gently, softly speaking her name. *The Harlot Isabel* he called her in tribute to his first wife, a blonde and blued-eyed heartbreaker who had taken most of his money and skipped off with her boss. Behind his legs, the saddlebags bulged with the latest in twenty-first-century technology—a rubber-coated computer, GPS, satellite telephone, encryption encoder, laser designator, and infrared sensor and night-vision display—all of which would have been worthless if it weren't for the horse, for there was no other way to travel in this part of the world. The terrain was too harsh, the mountains too steep, and the distance between water supplies was simply too far to get around any other way.

The saddle held another secret: Sown into the cotton saddle straps, wrapped under the sweating belly of his horse, was $200,000 in thousand-dollar bills. Over the past year the agent Peter Zembeic had passed out more than three million dollars to various warlords, terrorists, old men, and young girls—everyone and anyone willing to feed his intelligence operation. Entire armies were for sale, but they didn't come cheap, and flashing cash was one of the things the CIA did very well. Peter sometimes wondered which he needed more, his horse or his cash. The truth was, both were indispensable in this part of the world.

Peter worked for a CIA group known as the "Campers" (though the organization was so secret their code name was changed every six months or so). There were a hundred or so Campers working throughout the Caspian area. With infiltration routes, drop zones, stolen Russian helicopters, intelligence contacts, and assault points, the Campers were a key to the fight against terror. With the ability to hide in plain sight, they get in and get out before anyone can figure out who they were.

The American agent held the reins lightly, then carefully nudged his animal's side. The Arabian moved forward, her eyes already adjusted to the night, then instinctively stopped at the crest of the hill. Brushing against the needles of a juniper, the horse sought additional cover. She had been trained very well. He owed his life to this mount.

The American waited, knowing he wasn't alone. In the distance, in the shadows on a hill twenty paces behind him, four Tajiks and his Afghani guide watched through their night-vision goggles. Soldiers of fortune, they worked for the American and were only as loyal as his money could keep them. And there was also someone else. Someone down on the path, near the trees. The American had not seen her yet, but he knew she was there. He closed his eyes to concentrate on his ears.

He listened and waited, picking up the slightest sound. It was an extraordinary gift, his ability to know, his ability to hear things that no one else seemed to hear, his ability to sense things that his eyes couldn't see. And so he waited and listened to what the night brought. Behind, he heard the soft breath of his men. There was scratching to his right, soft paws against the dry dirt, and the wings, overhead, of a very large bird. And the sound of her crying. The woman was drawing very near.

Dawn was still more than two hours away when a small,

human shape approached from the end of the trail, emerging into the light of the full moon. The American dismounted silently and checked the time. He waited another twenty seconds then stepped into the dim light.

He snapped a chem-stick, which glowed with a dull, yellow light. Holding it up, he studied her face. She was young, slender, and stunningly beautiful, with Eurasian eyes, light skin, and black, silky hair. He smelled her exquisite body oil and was flooded for a moment with memories of a girl in Madrid. She wore the traditional *ghueto,* a long, flowing cloak that was pushed back over her shoulders and fastened at the neck, but underneath were a white cotton sweater, blue jeans, and dark leather boots. Tiny diamonds in her earrings caught the light of the moon and sparkled dimly, like the stars in the sky. Here in the desert, her beauty seemed completely out of place. Everything about her spoke of physical perfection, which was the reason, of course, that she was what she was. Since the age of sixteen, she had been her master's *Ji nu'.* She was perhaps twenty now, though it was hard to tell. She could have been younger, for she had the body language of a child, but her eyes showed the weariness of too many years in a dark world.

Approaching the American, she displayed little emotion, for the simple fact was she knew she was already dead. Her only hope, her only dream, was to leave this world alone, exit by herself, with little fanfare.

The American agent studied her face, growing anxious and tense. Something about her made him uneasy. Fifty meters behind him, on the side of the hill, he knew the low-light video camera was running. The encounter would be taped and played back for his superiors later on. He maneuvered to his right, allowing the camera a clear shot of her face, then glanced at his lapel, where the tiny microphone was hidden. Taping such encounters was standard procedure now, for much could be learned when a tape was reviewed.

"Ready, *Rasul,*" the American heard in his earpiece. As always, the Tajik had called him by his Arabic title. Peter

Zembeic was his real name, but the Muslim guides behind had never heard it before. Here, in the field, his men only knew him as *Rasul al-Laylat,* an Arabic phrase which meant Apostle of the Night.

The CIA agent, a former air force pilot who had been stripped of his wings, a former army Ranger who stayed in for only one year, was one of the new breed of CIA agents who operated continually "in-country." To call the agent hard core would fall short of the mark. He was wild and ruthless, and American through and through. Well studied and arrogant, confident enough to believe he was on the right side of this war, he was willing to fight dirty, to scratch, bite, and claw to make certain his side prevailed.

Maybe ten years older than the girl, the agent looked like a Hells Angel who had just dismounted his hog. He wore a tight beard, long hair to his shoulders, and a dirty baseball cap, the bill hanging over his neck. His black T-shirt was cut off at the shoulders exposing biceps that were taut from a combination of constant work and a high-protein diet. Leather gloves covered his hands, except for the fingers, which had been cut away at the first knuckle. A 9 mm was stuffed in a holster that hung from his belt, along with four clips of ammunition, a knife, compass, matches, radio, a small pouch for his tobacco, and a picture of his dad.

They had been operating in-country for almost four weeks—sleeping in the desert, eating dry rations and snakes, watching the roads, and consorting with the rebels who flowed back and forth between Afghanistan, Turkmenistan, China, Tajikistan, and Pakistan. His mission was simple. Listen. Watch. See what was going on. Talk to the warlords and sip *hemish* tea with the tribesmen while watching their men, befriend the tribal leaders with gifts of information on their enemies. The desired outcome, of course, was to gather information on the al Qaeda forces. The enemy was regrouping and it was now a real concern. Indeed, they were growing stronger with each passing day. The Russian generals had warned them, and now it appeared they were right.

Peter's father had enlisted in the United States Army just

as the Vietnam War was kicking into high gear, and his father's military experience had planted the seed in his mind. From the earliest memory, he knew that was what he would do. When he was eight, Peter broke a leg jumping off the garage, wearing a homemade parachute. When he was eleven, he built a submarine out of an old fifty-five-gallon drum, which immediately sunk to the bottom of a mossy pond in the city park. In high school, he was an outstanding athlete and the defensive team captain of his football team and, though he had been offered several scholarships, he had turned them all down, accepting an ROTC slot instead.

The summer after his freshman year at Purdue, when Peter was still young and embarrassingly naïve, he signed up for the Peace Corps and set out for Cairo, bent on bringing peace and love to the innocents of the world. But, that summer life stepped up and slapped him in the face. The realities of ethnic and religious hatred proved a powerful instructor, and Zembeic was now a strident convert to the old ways of the world. Power, strength, and information had become his new religion, and saving America was now his cause. Uncannily gifted at language, fluent in Persian, Arabic, and Urdu, a former military officer and Army Ranger, the CIA officer understood the culture enough to survive in this part of the world. He was one of the new breed of paramilitary operators who slithered throughout central Asia—hard, educated, smart as a whip, focused, determined, willing to fight, kill, and die for what they knew to be right. In his dark T-shirt and black jeans (black was his favorite color, as he only traveled at night) the young American was technically a spy with none of the benefits accorded by the Geneva Convention, a fact he resented but accepted.

The American smelled like burnt camel dung, the only fuel available in the desert. He was hungry, anxious, and weary to the bone. He was running a fever and hadn't eaten all day. His stomach groaned within him as he looked up at the moon. Hang on, he told himself, the task almost complete. In a few minutes the chopper would pick him up and take him back to Camp Horse, where he would deliver the package and spend a month debriefing and resting before coming back in-country again.

As Zembeic studied the girl, she bowed her head, refusing to meet his eyes. He took a deep breath, glancing toward the dark expanse of Afghani desert on the other side of the border, then back at his pack, with its communications gear. The two strangers were silent, for the rendezvous had been so hastily planned there had been no precoordinated introductions, code words, or authentication codes—no expectations of who would be waiting or what they would say. Just a time and a place. That was the rendezvous plan.

Zembeic held out his hand. "Do you have it?" he asked in Persian, having no idea what he was asking for.

The young women looked up and bit on the side of her cheek. She gazed at him thoughtfully, but didn't say anything. He took a step toward her and asked the question again, this time speaking in the local dialect of the Khorasan province.

The woman stared blankly as if she did not understand, then smiled in submission. The American narrowed his eyes. "Do you *have* it?" he demanded, speaking in Persian again. Beautiful as she was, he was in no mood to delay.

The young girl only nodded. Isabel snorted behind him, waiting for her master, untied, in the dark. The girl cocked her head, pushing her lower jaw to the right, then slowly opened her mouth while reaching up with her hand. A piece of broken tooth sat on the tip of her tongue. She touched the tooth cautiously, then held it out carefully in the palm of her hand.

The agent stared in surprise. "What have you there?"

"It's a cap," the girl answered. "It has been imbedded with a microchip. Take it. Keep it safe. It contains what you came here to get."

The agent took the piece of white porcelain. Fingering the dental work, he swore to himself. It wasn't what he had expected, but then neither was the girl. He considered a moment, then glanced over his shoulder again.

"Anything else?" he asked sharply, forcing himself to ignore the beauty of her eyes.

She hesitated a long moment, staring into his face, the

moonlight illuminating his features as he took a step back, holding the piece of broken tooth tightly in his palm. She looked at him pleadingly as Isabel snorted again. She glanced past his shoulder at the sleek outline of the horse, hesitated, thinking, then leaned toward him and put her lips to his ears. "She is a good animal," she whispered.

He stared, not understanding.

"Your horse," she explained quickly.

Peter ignored her. She was wasting time now, trying to bait him, trying to loosen him up. "Is there anything else!" he demanded abruptly.

She paused, then looked sadly away. She had said everything, done everything she had been instructed to do. "The messages have been delivered," she replied quietly. She looked at the ground, swallowing against her dry throat. *"Laoshih, Mei ou le,"* she concluded softly. "Teacher, there is nothing more."

She slowly lifted her head and scanned the ring of darkness around them, fearful all the time for what she had been commanded to do. She thought again of her family. Did she really have to choose! Did she love them enough? Did she have the strength to save them, to do what her master had told her to do? She knew that she did and her heart sank in her chest.

A light wind began to blow, cooling her neck, and she rubbed her bare arms in an effort to warm them. Her skin almost shimmering in the light of the moon, and the soldier noticed the scar near the crest of her shoulder, the mark of her master, identifying this as his girl. Only the most favorite *Ji nu'* received the family name. The girl had nearly graduated from concubine to wife.

Zembeic studied her face. She was so beautiful. So lovely. Yet also lonely and sad. A feeling of deep sorrow began to pull at his chest. There was something about her. She looked so lost and alone. Why was she here, on the edge of the desert, at the tip of the mountains, walking the most barren land on earth? Why did she meet him? Why did he choose to send her?

She looked at him and waited, trying to smile. He nodded and grasped the porcelain cap in his hand. She watched him carefully then lowered her head. "Will you take me with you?" she muttered quietly, as if afraid he would hear.

He stopped and looked up, then immediately shook his head. "I can't. I have my mission."

"Please," she begged.

He shook his head vigorously, fighting the thought. She reached out to touch him, placing her hand on his arm. "Please take me with you. You don't understand." For the moment she felt an overwhelming desire to live. She forgot about her family and the fate that would await them if she were to just disappear. She forgot about the small handgun that was strapped to her leg. The human instinct for survival was simply too strong to deny. "Please, American, please. Will you take me with you?"

The soldier turned away, unable to look at her any more. Everything within him wanted to take the girl by the hand, lift her up, and whisk her away. But he couldn't. He knew that. It wasn't in the operational plan. He couldn't bring her back, like a little boy rescuing a lost puppy. To leave her wasn't right, but he didn't have a choice. "I'm sorry," he said simply. Turning, he picked up his gear and began to make his way up the trail.

The shantytown and muddy waterhole were off to his left. A ridge of low, rocky hills was on his right. He set his course by the moonlight, making for the ridgeline, where the outline of the trees could be seen against the night sky. He didn't look back. He didn't want to see. He pictured her face, knowing he would never forget.

After thirty paces he stopped and looked back. The trail was empty. He took a breath and moved toward the extraction point.

Twenty minutes later he was on the side of the ridge, at the military crest, one-third the way down the hill, hunkered under an outcropping of sandstone and brush. He had just completed making his call to Big Dog. The chopper, a Russian Hind the agency had liberated sometime in early '92, was on the way. From his vantage point on the side of the hill he could look down on the trail. He watched it intently, suffering inside.

He could take her. He *should* take her. She wanted to go. Screw the rules of engagement. What else could he do!? She was clearly in danger, he could see that in her eyes. She was frightened, in danger—and she was begging him. She could ride on the chopper. There was plenty of room!

He should take her. He would take her. He couldn't leave her behind. There were refugee camps in Turkey. He would help her get there.

He started to move, pulling himself out from the brush. In the distance, to the west, he began to hear the sound of helicopter rotors. The chopper was coming. He didn't have much time. He scrambled out from the brush and turned to make his way down the hill. Hunkering over, he moved with powerful strides.

The sound of the gunshot shattered the night. He dropped to his chest, falling behind a low brush as his hand moved instinctively for the 9 mm handgun that was strapped to his thigh. He took a deep breath as the hairs on his neck stood on end. He listened and watched while his heart beat in his chest.

The sound of the single gunshot echoed through the narrow canyon walls before receding into the emptiness of the desert to the east. Then there was silence, sudden and still. Even the sound of the chopper had fallen away as the Hind dropped behind the back side of the hill.

"Status!" the soldier demanded into the tiny microphone that was strapped to his neck.

"She's down," his Afghani guide replied with little emotion. "Self-inflicted gunshot. I'm sorry, boss, there's nothing left of her head. We didn't have time to stop her. Negative hostiles in the AOR."

The soldier closed his eyes and took a deep breath. Standing, he listened, then turned for the top of the hill. Reaching into his pocket, he felt the porcelain cap and a shudder ran down his spine as he wiped the sweat from his eyes.

He pressed his microphone switch again. "Bury the body." He paused as he thought. "Give her some kind of prayer. And take care of my horse. I'll see you in a few weeks."

2

Shin Bet Auxiliary Outpost
Twelve Miles South of Tel Aviv

F̲ew people have ever heard of the Israeli counterintelligence agency known as Shin Bet, or their undercover detachments know as the *Mista'arvim* (marauders). And if few knew of the Shin Bet, fewer still knew of their brutal tactics or what they had done.

But those who worked with the agents or had suffered under their hands, having experienced the "special measures" the Israeli high courts had authorized, could testify the Israelis were as good at extracting information as any organization on earth. They were much better than the Egyptians, the proxy interrogators the CIA used, for the Egyptians were too slow and clumsy to rival Shin Bet. And over the years Shin Bet had only gotten better, more focused and intent. The war was too bloody. Too many people had died. They were caught up in the great battle that tested which nation had the strongest will to survive.

Since the war on terror had grown to a worldwide effort, the United States and Israel had been bound by multiple cords, all of them leading back to Islamist terrorist groups. And both intelligence agencies shared the same fear. The enemy hadn't been defeated, but had only slithered a little deeper into the dark. And the big one was coming. The black day was near.

Eleven hours after being extracted from the mountains of Central Asia, Peter Zembeic was asleep in the officers quarters of the Shin Bet auxiliary compound. He had been asleep for less than two hours when the intercom buzzed.

"Peter, you awake?" Even through the haze, Peter recognized the American colonel's voice.

The CIA agent rolled painfully onto his side. He was sore and exhausted, and he needed another fifteen hours of sleep. "Yeah, boss," he slurred, making no attempt to hide the irritation in his voice.

"Come down to ops. We've got a problem with the chip."

Peter stared at the wall, his mind suddenly clear and awake. He started to question, then swore to himself.

A problem with the chip!

He cursed angrily, then rolled off the bed.

Special Agent Peter Zembeic ambled wearily into the Shin Bet operations center. The room was dimly lit and lined with computers, telephones, fax machines, and secure data-transfer consoles. Along the front wall a huge plasma video screen was directly linked to the Shin Bet command center in Jerusalem. The room was deserted except for an Israeli escort and the American colonel, an air force liaison on temporary assignment to the CIA.

Col. Shane "Clipper" Bradley (he had once clipped his F-15 wings through some trees) sat, dressed in faded jeans, a blue shirt, and leather hiking boots at a small computer console. He hadn't worn a uniform since stepping off the government jet and onto the tarmac at the airport in Jerusalem, for the U.S. military officers working inside Israel *never* identified themselves. Might as well paint a red target on their foreheads and wander down to the nearest bus station and wait for the next suicide bomber, as be walking around the besieged country in air force blues. Further, the last place in the world either side wanted to see a U.S. military uniform was inside a compound run by Shin Bet. Such was a risk neither side would endure.

Colonel Bradley glanced up as Peter walked into the room. Zembeic had cleaned up, having spent thirty minutes in the shower before dropping into bed, and his skin was still pink from being scrubbed raw. His long hair and bushy beard smelled of shampoo and soap. He wore faded jeans, a white T-shirt, and black cowboys boots. The colonel smiled lightly. Peter was one of the few men he knew who dared wear faux black rhino boots. He eyed his good friend. "You feel better?" he asked.

Peter sniffed and wiped his nose. He didn't. Not much.

Bradley watched intently as the long-haired agent poured a cup of steaming, bitter coffee, an Israeli home brew. He looked like a hood, the kind of guy you expect to find hustling pool at some sleazy bar in El Paso, a small-town thug who did time for drunk-and-disorderlies and stealing old cars. But Bradley knew him better, he knew the truth. Peter was one of the best men he had ever met. Hard and intelligent, dedicated and strong, Peter wasn't the kind who waffled in the babble of relative good; he saw things as they were, not as some wished they would be. How many times had Peter lectured him. *"This thing is black and white, baby!"* Bradley could almost hear his voice. *"Screw everything else. Don't dribble psychoanalysis on why we deserve any of this! Just give me a mission and get out of my way! We're the good guys in this war, and don't you ever forget!"*

Peter sucked in a mouthful of coffee, bowed his head, and closed his eyes, savoring the bitterness before swallowing it down. Acidic and sour, it matched his mood. His stomach muscles were sore from heaving his guts the night before. He had caught something new in the water of Afghanistan and was paying the price, and he envisioned the parasites that were now growing in his bowels.

The colonel nodded to his escort. The Israeli frowned, then stood and walked reluctantly through a back door, leaving the two U.S. agents by themselves. The colonel looked around, wondering if the room was still bugged, then nodded toward the nearest computer display. "Take a look," he said.

Peter Zembeic turned to the screen and frowned.

```
D..A..R...
K...D..A..
R...K...D..A..
R...K...D..A..
```

The letters repeated and filled the entire silver screen.

Peter stared, then huffed. "So—?" he asked wearily.

Colonel Bradley stared down at him. At six-two, he towered over the squat man's head. Peter looked up and frowned. "You're the boy genius," he said. "Tell me, what does it mean?"

Bradley didn't answer. Handsome, solid, dark-haired and dark-eyed, he *was* young, it was true. Peter used to call him *Dyphemus,* Greek for "new star," until he realized how sensitive Bradley was to the perception that he was too young for his rank. Bradley had fought the impression of inexperience most of his professional career.

And the truth was, Bradley had been promoted so often and so early he outranked men who were almost twice his age. In the military, ugly was fine, soldiers didn't get points for good looks; indeed, mud, snot, and gunpowder had a way of making all men look like swill. But the colonel was handsome. And young. A terrible career combination.

Envy didn't die when his fellow officers had taken their oath of office, Bradley had learned. "Pretty boy," his detractors had said. But they didn't any longer. And even if they did, they were so far behind him he could no longer hear their sneers. For almost fifteen years Bradley had walked the walk, a beautiful amble through the pitches and pines of political and real war, until he had worked himself into a position where he didn't need to take crap from anyone anymore. Everyone knew his record, and it said it all.

Bradley smiled at the boy genius remark, then sat down

and crossed one leg on his knee, then nodded again to the screen. Peter followed his eyes and stared at the code. "The chip was imbedded with several internal security logarithms. We've worked through them all and that's all there is."

```
D . . A . . R . . .
K . . . D . . A . .
R . . . K . . . D . . A . .
R . . . K . . . D . . A . .
R . . . K . . .
```

Peter hated puzzles. He preferred sweat and muscles, head banging and blood. He stared at the screen of random letters. "That's it?" he said angrily.

"Yep. That's it. We just hit a wall."

Peter swore and stood up. "Don't tell me I lived like a rat in the desert for six miserable weeks to recover a *useless* computer chip!" he sneered. He glared at the letters. "What is it?" He jabbed a thick finger at the screen. "DAR—KDAR!! What does it mean!"

"I don't know," Bradley replied.

"You think the chip might be damaged?"

"No, Peter. We got everything. That's all that is there."

Peter thought of the porcelain cap the young girl had given to him. He frowned again at the screen, its silver light casting a pale glow in the dimly lit room. "I don't believe it," he said. "There's *got* to be something more there!"

"Believe it, Peter. There's nothing on the chip but what you see on that screen."

The agent turned a cold eye on his friend. "Did he set me up!? Is that what he was doing!? Testing the chain to see if we would still jump when he said to!"

Bradley shook his head slowly. "Might be . . . probably so. It's really hard to say."

"What do you think, Shane? You know Donner better than anyone. Was he screwing with us!"

Bradley hesitated, then answered, "Could be he wanted to

test our operations to see if we were still secure. It isn't an unusual procedure, to send a meaningless message to test the security and operational capability of the code before the real message is sent."

"Don't tell me I sat in the desert for weeks to recover a worthless piece of silicon! Do you know what biscuits taste like when they're cooked over camel dung? Do you know how cold it gets in those mountains at night? So, don't tell me I hit the rendezvous for nothing!"

Bradley didn't answer and Peter shook his head. "Sloppy work, Shane. I say we tell Donner to FedEx his message next time."

Bradley hesitated as he thought. "Tell me about the girl," he said as he rubbed his neck.

Peter looked away. He did not want to think of her. "Young, Eurasian," he finally answered. "Scared. She had the mark of her man."

"Could she have been one of his runners?"

"She wasn't a professional, I promise you that. She was scared as a rabbit, trembling inside and out." Peter paused and closed his eyes. "Have you watched the tape of the rendezvous?" he asked.

"Yes, I've seen it."

"You know then that she asked me to bring her out."

"I know." Bradley stared unflinchingly at his friend. "You did the only thing you could do," he forced himself to say.

Peter sipped bitterly at his coffee. He knew all that, of course, but it didn't help. Bring her out? Yeah, maybe; but how many others would then die? And it would have revealed their source, leaving Donner exposed. It was too high a price, one they simply could not pay.

He swallowed more coffee and shivered. What a lousy business this was. He wanted to shower again, to feel the warm water running down the small of his back, to feel it fall on him, washing away all the evil he'd done.

This was a business for a hard man, a man who was cold and ruthless. So why did he stay? Because he *was not* that man. There was no irony in that answer, it was as simple as that. If he left, maybe the next guy would be worse than him, more ruthless, more deadly, more unfeeling, more cold, his conscience even more deadened than Peter's had become.

Peter crossed his legs uncomfortably as his stomach rumbled again, the parasites settling in for a long winter's feast. "You gottta love this guy, Donner," he said miserably. "A real class act. Sending one of his women, then forcing her to kill herself."

Bradley's face flushed as he thought again of the video of the girl, and he silently added her face to the nightmares he would have in the long nights ahead. He shook his head sadly, then pushed himself up from the chair. He thought a long moment, staring at the computer screen. "Come on, Donner!" he pleaded across the thousand miles that separated them from their prize intelligence mole. *"Dark,"* he mumbled slowly. "What do you mean!? *Dark! Dark what!!* What are you trying to say!?"

Peter looked up suddenly, his face growing pale. He felt his heart sink, a cold rock of fear in his chest. "Dark!" he mumbled suddenly, his voice raspy and weak. He turned to the screen. Of course! How could he be so stupid!!

DAR . . . K DAR . . . K . . . DARK. DARK!!

An image flashed in his mind, hot and searing, as if it were etched in blue light. He pictured the girl leaning toward him. He remembered the feel of her lips on his ear and the intense look in her eyes.

"She is beautiful," she had muttered. *"Your horse,"* she'd explained.

Her words now seemed to stick like dry sand in his throat. His hands began to tremble as he saw two plus two.

Your horse . . . dark . . . horse. DARKHORSE! His mind cried.

He sat back suddenly, his coffee sloshing hot in his lap. *"Darkhorse!"* he muttered, his voice a tremble of pain.

Colonel Bradley stared steadily at him, but a pale gray was sweeping his face. "Darkhorse!" he answered as he stared at his friend.

"Show me the tape!" Peter cried as he pushed himself away from his chair. Bradley stared at him blankly, not understanding. "The tape of the rendezvous!" Peter exclaimed.

Bradley pointed to a nearby bank of computers. Peter reached for the nearest one, then held back, unsure of what to do. Bradley moved to his side, pushing him out of the way. Dropping a finger on the touchpad, he loaded the file. It only took seconds before Peter's image filled the seventeen-inch computer display. The low-light camera showed mostly green and dark hues, but the image was clear and tight; Peter's shoulders and the side of his face, the young girl before him, small, petite, wide-eyed, and beautiful. Peter sucked in his breath at the sight of her face. Bradley turned up the volume and a raspy hiss emitted from the screen; the sounds of the night, a horse's snort, a breeze through dry leaves, light footsteps from somewhere behind the camera. Then the sounds of the two whispered voices picked up by the microphone hidden under Peter's lapel.

"Do you have it?" Peter asked in nearly perfect Persian.

Peter watched the tape a moment, then reached down to fast-forward the digital file. He skipped ahead, then rolled back, then clicked the play button again.

Colonel Bradley watched as the young girl leaned forward, lifting onto her toes to whisper something into Peter's ear. He heard the sound of her voice, but could not make out the words. Peter punched the pause button, and the small girl's face froze on the screen; her eyes closed, her hair back, her cheeks glistening from unseen tears. Peter turned to Bradley, his face ashen. He started to speak, then clenched his fist as he thought.

Bradley waited, then demanded, "What did she say!"

Peter swallowed, looked away, then turned back to his friend. "She is beautiful," he answered.

"What!" Bradley cried.

"She said she was beautiful."

"What are you talking about!"

"My horse!" Peter replied.

The colonel took a step back. "Dark. Your horse! DARK-HORSE is here!" He paused, his face stern, then continued, thinking out loud to himself. "Why else would Donner break his silence after all of these years! Why else would he risk exposing himself? He broke the message into two parts; one verbal, one code. Simple. Effective. Yes, Darkhorse is here."

Peter thought of the young girl and the words she had said. *"The messages have been delivered. Teacher, there is nothing more."*

"How did we miss this?" he muttered in disgust and fear. "How could we not have seen it coming somehow?"

The colonel only nodded as Peter stared at the floor. "Can you say Apocalypse?" he muttered.

He looked up at Bradley, but the colonel was already on the phone. "I need a secure line to D.C.," he told the Israeli communications officer on the other end of the line. He paused as he listened, then gave a 212 area code. While he waited for the secure communications link to go through, as he waited for the Israeli and U.S. satellites to authenticate to each other, he motioned to Peter, waving desperately with his hand. "Get someone from tactics down here. Captain Stein, he's the best. I think he's upstairs, get him in here now. Tell him I want an overfeed to our Killbird. We'll need access through NRO, but I'll work that from here."

Peter didn't move until Bradley pushed him away with a brush of his hand. *"Go!* I want to see this. We'll have to monitor from here!"

Peter turned and moved quickly, heading for the back door.

Bradley gripped the phone tightly, his knuckles turning white. Fifteen seconds later the CIA director of operations picked up the phone. The colonel began to explain, his voice tight and quick. The director listened carefully from the other side of the world. The two men began to plot, mapping out a reaction plan.

But it was already too late. The wheels had started turning, though they didn't know why or where. If they had known even a few days, even a few hours before, they might have been able to act.

But all they could do now was watch. It was beyond their control.

3

As United States Air Force Col. Shane "Clipper" Bradley spoke on the phone, three thousand miles to the east, a brilliant and hateful plan was put into place.

Rawalpindi Air Force Base
Islamabad, Pakistan

The sun had just set, an orange circle on the smoky horizon, and the sky was cloudless yet brown from the dust that was blown up by the wind. A storm was brewing in the north, over the Himalayan range, but here, on the plain, on the dry river basin, it hadn't rained in four months and the air was gritty and arid. The days were growing short as winter came on, and with the smoke hanging low like a dense, ugly fog, darkness came quickly to the mountains of Northern Pakistan. As the sun set, the sky turned from pink to deep purple, and finally to black.

The two F-16s sat on the end of the runway, their engines at idle, their canopies down. The runway loomed before them, a long ribbon of black outlined by the blue runway lights. The cement strip crested in a long, gentle slope, then fell away a little over a mile ahead. The airport was quiet. All the other Pakistani fighters, few that there were, had been bedded down in their cement bunkers on the south end of the field, and the choppers had already taken off for the night. The radios were silent except for an occasional hiss of light static.

The F-16s sat in an echelon position, the number-two aircraft twenty feet behind the leader and off to the side. A small star and crescent moon, the traditional symbols of Islam, were painted on each tailfin in green and white. The fighters were the new D models, recent deliveries from the United States, just one of the payoffs for Pakistan's help in the war. With upgraded avionics, APG-68 radar, and the more powerful Pratt and Whitney 200 power plants, the fighters were the best aircraft in the Pakistani air force. Their engines screamed together in an ear-piercing whine as the intakes sucked in and compressed the dry, gritty air. Occasional vortexes of swirling dust and dead leaves formed several feet in front of the engines, for the runways were unswept and in general disrepair. In contrast to their stark surroundings, the fighters looked wonderfully new, with fresh paint, virgin tires, and spotless canopies.

Inside the cockpit of the lead aircraft, a young flight commander with a salt-and-pepper beard and deep, angry eyes pulled his oxygen mask up to his face and snapped it into position. He glanced over his left shoulder, giving his wingman a final inspection, ensuring his weapons had been armed and he was ready to go. The wingman nodded and the commander replied with a quick wave. The flight leader turned back toward the runway, adjusted himself in the seat, then spoke confidently into the microphone embedded in his mask. "Tower, Bengal two-one, ready for takeoff." The pilot spoke in his native Urdu, which was against the coalition rules. With U.S. flight supervisors monitoring airfield operations, all the flight crews were supposed to communicate in English, the internationally accepted language of air-traffic control. Most of the Pakistani pilots complied with this rule, but the commander did not. To him, the Americans were un-invited intruders, rude and arrogant, and he figured they could learn Urdu if they wanted to understand what he said.

After a moment's pause, the tower controller replied, "Bengal, stand by." The controller spoke in English and the pilot bristled in his seat. What a pitiful language, like the chatter of little girls. He glanced at the clock on his cockpit display. Forty seconds until takeoff. He swore anxiously.

Waiting for clearance, he pressed on his brake pedals and brought his engine up to 85 percent power. The aircraft shuddered below him, straining to move forward as the front strut compressed against the force of the brakes. He watched as his wingman also brought his power up. His engine-exhaust nozzles closed, indicating the second aircraft was near the afterburner range and a beautiful orange and blue flame began to glow in the afterburner cans. The pilot waited impatiently, his breath sounding in his mask. Ten seconds later, the tower controller finally came back, "Bengal, cleared for takeoff. Good hunting tonight."

Without acknowledging the controller, the pilot pushed his throttle to full military power. His engine accelerated to 100-percent RPM in less than two seconds. As the engine screamed behind him, the fighter began to inch forward and the pilot pressed more firmly against his brakes; one final check of his instruments and navigation displays, then he re-leased his brakes. The fighter almost jumped forward, push-ing the pilot back in his seat. He jammed the throttle forward to the afterburner range and a bright blue and yellow flame shot from the back of his engine. The two Falcons raced to-gether. A thousand feet down the runway they passed through one hundred and twenty knots. Stealing a look to his side, the commander saw he was moving forward of his wingman and cracked his throttle just a bit so the younger pilot could more easily stay in position.

As his fighter accelerated, it bounced across the cuts in the pavement, for it was heavy with weapons and fully loaded with fuel. An AIM-9 Sidewinder missile was mounted on the tips of both wings. Further in were an assortment of other air-to-air and air-to-ground weapons—two AMRAAMs, the most lethal air-to-air missile in the world, and four GBU-15 laser-guided bombs.

Pakistani Presidential Aircraft (Steal One)
Over Western Pakistan

As the two fighters lifted into the air, several hundred miles to the west the president of Pakistan, a four-star army general, leaned against the leather seat of his personal aircraft, an old Boeing 727 built in 1962. He looked at the landscape below as the aircraft flew toward the night, evening deepening quickly from dusk into gloom. He was tired and angry. And frustrated with himself. His mood, like the night, darkened as the aircraft flew east.

The president was tired of this military campaign—this war of revenge that never seemed to end. He was tired of the situation the United States had placed him in, a dark and dangerous situation that might lead to civil war.

The Pakistani president swore to himself.

He had to extricate himself from the Americans before they bled him to death.

The president was returning from a meeting with the American secretary of defense, a meeting in which the American spent most of his time making more demands of him. Impossible demands. More pieces of broken glass added to the box.

After the fall of the Taliban the enemies of the West had taken refuge in Pakistan, where they concentrated on rebuilding their forces and strengthening their numbers, seeking to reestablish themselves while hiding in the enemy's backyard. Forging ties with Lashkar-e Tayyiba and the Harkat-ul-Mujahideen, two of the most violent and militant groups in all of Pakistan, the Taliban militants had reestablished themselves. Different people, same caves. Not much had changed. In response, the Americans had been pushing for more access to the Pakistani bases. Worse, they demanded that the Pakistani president provide more patrols in the mountains, more control over his people and less trouble from them. Most difficult, they wanted more intelligence on emerging fundamentalist factions.

But with each new demand, the Pakistani president was weakened at home. His generals weren't happy, and he was losing his troops. Officers were being assassinated along the front lines. And the Taliban, having come home to roost in the house in which they were born, were now gaining strength along his western front, putting him in the same position as the Afghanis before. There were ceaseless rumors that a coup was but a few days away.

If there was one thing he had learned, it was this: His friends weren't always real, but his enemies were.

It was time to sort them out.

He cursed again to himself. He hated the Americans. He hated the Taliban. He hated his ministers, who had proven disloyal to him, and his army for being slow to defend. He hated his brother, his army chief of staff, who was sleeping with his mistress to extract information from her. He hated the mullas because they hated him. He hated the Saudi sheiks for their money and power, rich and arrogant men who were waiting for him to fall. Like vultures they circled, smelling his blood.

"Qwidla e' hashne," he muttered in frustration and fear. "I'm losing control. And those fools in the West, they think this is *over!* Those idiots actually think they have won! Fools. If they only *knew*. This is just beginning. It is just getting underway."

Yes, it was just beginning.

And it was time to get out of the box. Time to extract himself from the battle. Time to take some control.

He pushed against his seat and frowned as he settled on his plan. It was ugly. It was brilliant. And it had to be done. He had a day, maybe two, before he lost all control. It was just enough time. But he knew what to do.

Shin Bet Auxiliary Outpost
Twelve Miles South of Tel Aviv

Peter ran into the command center with a heavily mustached Israeli captain in tow. Three other Israeli officers followed after, then a one-star general, his eyes piercing and bright, his walk intent, his shoulders square, his face defiant and proud. He moved into the control room and positioned himself behind the central desk, where he stood, his arms crossed, the decision maker in the crowd. The American colonel glanced at the general and hung up the phone. Walking forward, he announced, "I need you to synch up a streaming download to our KH-21 satellite."

The general's eyes burned. "The KH-21?" he repeated in disbelief.

Bradley hesitated, then nodded. The KH-21 Killbird was far and away the most sophisticated reconnaissance satellite ever built. To suggest allowing access to the satellite through an Israeli control room was more than remarkable, it had never been considered, let alone done before. Not in almost fifty years of space-based reconnaissance had the United States allowed any ally to data-link to their download.

"You are going to allow us to access the download from your Killbird?" the general repeated with almost a smirk.

"Once, and for a short time, yes sir, I am."

"And you have authority to?"

"Authority will be coming."

The general hesitated. Naturally suspicious, he started to think. "We'll need to know frequencies and access codes," he said.

"General, you're going to need *much* more than that. The security around the Killbird isn't protected by frequency hopping and mere access codes. So I will need complete access to your remote retrieval program to synch our bird up to your system here."

"*You* want access to *our* system?"

"Yes sir. And now. It's the only way we will allow you to synch to our bird."

"It's not going to happen. No way I turn over *our* access codes!"

The colonel took a quick step to his host. "General, think! What is the tradeoff here!? I am prepared to allow you access to our satellite, the most highly classified piece of American reconnaissance equipment ever built, and you're worried about sharing your ground-based access codes. It's like I'm offering my daughter in exchange for your dog."

Still, the general hesitated and a long silence filled the control room. Peter felt himself tighten, his hands pulling into fists at his side. Did this screwball of a one-star actually believe he could tell them no!? Didn't he know who they were, who they represented here!? Didn't he know what was a stake? Did he have any idea at all?

No, of course he didn't.

There was no way he could know.

Bradley took a step forward and lowered his voice. Protocol was important, and the general was his host. The last thing wanted was to embarrass him in front of his men, but they didn't have time, and he would not screw around. "General, I don't think you understand," he said in an authoritive voice. "I *will* have access to our Killbird, and I *will* have it now. And the only way I can do that is through your system here. Now we can do this between you and me, or we can do it some way else. Either way, you will give me access to your system so I can synch up our Killbird satellite."

The general turned away angrily. He would not be bullied like this.

Colonel Bradley leaned forward and lowered his voice to a whisper. "General, let me tell you what's at stake here."

Bradley started talking. The Israeli general's face turned gray with fear. "I'll have to get authorization," he said when Bradley was through.

"Do what you have to to get me your access codes."

The general grunted and turned away, picking up the nearest phone.

Rawalpindi Air Force Base
Islamabad, Pakistan

The two Pakistani F-16s lifted off and into the sky, their dull gray paint merging into the darkness, causing them to disappear before reaching three hundred feet. As the lead fighter climbed away from the runway, the second aircraft moved into position three feet off his leader's wing.

Pulling his throttle out of the afterburner range, the commander raised his gear handle and retracted the flaps. The gear pulled into the belly of the jet with a solid *thunk,* a firm snap in the airframe he could feel through his seat. Using his Heads-Up Display as his primary flight instrument, the pilot pulled the nose up into a ten-degree climb as the aircraft accelerated to 350 knots. "Bengal, go button five," the wing commander said into his oxygen mask.

"Two, button five," the other pilot quickly replied.

The commander reached down and changed the radio frequency on his side-console radio controller. "Islamabad departure, Bengal is with you, climbing through eight thousand, five hundred for eighteen thousand feet."

"Roger, Bengal. Confirm flight of two."

"Affirm. Flight of two. Loaded with air and mud."

"Bengal, say destination."

"Bengal looking for Kama."

The controller studied his radar display, searching for the flight of Falcons. The skies were nearly empty. He didn't have the fighters on his radar yet. "Bengal, negative radar contact," he instructed, "Squawk four-one-one-three. Climb and maintain eighteen thousand. Avoid whiskey approach route. Advise when you are ready to be turned over to the forward controller."

"Climb to eighteen," the lead pilot replied.

The military controller studied his flight schedule. Kama checked out. The flight of two F-16s were scheduled for a CAP, or combat air patrol, over the disputed territory of

Kashmir. The Indians, the enemy, were at it again. For the past several days, the monkeys had raised their ugly heads and were shelling the Pakistani forward positions, just like they did every fall. It was an annual tradition both sides looked forward to, a final opportunity to kill each other before winter set in.

Inside the lead aircraft, the commander reached down and turned the numbers on his transponder code, dialing in 4113 as he had been instructed, then hit the coolie hat (a small four-way switch) on his control stick to bounce out a quick signal to the radar controller. The air-traffic controller picked up the hit as a momentary green flash on his radar display. The numbers 4113 illuminated under the hit.

"Bengal, radar contact," the control then said. "Expect a climb to thirty-thousand in twenty miles."

In front of the F-16s, a hundred miles in the distance, Mount Nanga Parbat loomed up to its height of 26,650 feet. The Himalayan and Zaskar mountain ranges ran on both sides of Mount Nanga Parbat, a line of hostile and barren mountains that extended east to the heart of Kashmir. The fighters would have to climb over the mountains to get to their combat area. Below the fighters there was only darkness, no indication of human life at all. As far as the pilot could see there was nothing but sheer granite walls, barren rock, and valleys so narrow a donkey couldn't make its way through. To avoid hitting the mountains, the fighters would have to soon begin to climb to get above thirty thousand feet.

Nudging gently on his stick, the commander turned northeast, setting a course toward Kama, the handoff point where he would switch over to the combat controllers. His wingman stayed carefully tucked off his wing, three feet and slightly aft, using the commander's formation lights as a reference to remain in position. Throughout the sortie, the pilot in the number two aircraft would mimic his leader in every way. Even his transponder was in standby, so as not to radiate a radar hit, thus allowing ATC to view the two fighters as one entity, which for practical purposes was exactly what they were.

The two F-16s climbed easily into the night sky. Even with a full combat load, it only took a few minutes to level off at eighteen thousand feet. The lead pilot then waggled his wings, commanding a trail position. His wingman backed into a position behind his leader, allowing space for the two pilots to complete their combat checklist. The wing commander went through his checklist very quickly, turning off his exterior lights, arming his weapons, tuning his radar to an air-to-air mode, then setting the correct combat codes into his Identification Friend or Foe so that he would be properly identified.

"Buddy Spike," he heard over his radio. His threat-warning receiver momentarily buzzed as his wingman threw a beam of radar energy over his plane. Now two miles behind him, the young flight lieutenant was checking his radar by tracking his leader.

"Buddy Lock," his wingman said as he locked up his lead. The commander's threat receiver became still. His wingman had completed his radar check.

"Bengal, go secure," the commander commanded over the strike radio.

Reaching down, the commander synched up his secure radio, ensuring the Indian combat controllers would not be able to intercept their radio conversations. Keying the mike, he muttered in Urdu, "Two, take the lead for a Buddy Spike check."

"Wilco. Say airspeed."

"Three hundred fifty knots."

"I have you at my twelve o'clock. I'll be on your right side."

The commander waited. The moon was less than a quarter and it was very dark. He saw a quick shadow pass beside him as his wingman passed fifty feet off his right. Glancing through his HUD, he watched the second Pakistani jet move out before him. He checked his airspeed and adjusted his altitude, then slew his radar to the right, moving the disk to look for the other F-16. As the second fighter passed through the seventy-degree arc, the APG-68 radar began to track its position, the little fighter showing very clearly on his multi-function display.

"Tally," the commander announced. "Two, you have the lead."

"Bengal flight, check," the new flight leader replied.

"Two," the commander answered. He was now the wingman.

The commander pulled back his throttles and slipped to a half-mile trail. The lieutenant, the new leader, moved out ahead. "Buddy Spike," the commander said as he threw a tacking beam on his leader. He watched the lead aircraft for a moment, then flipped a switch on his throttle to arm up a missile.

"Buddy Lock," he said as he locked onto the target. A warble emitted in his headset as a tracking pipper locked up the target on his Heads-Up Display. The computer-generated tracking box remained frozen over the lead F-16. The target flew straight and level. From this position, the commander could use either his missiles or guns. He thought for a moment, then flipped the switch to select his M-61 20 mm cannon. The tracking box shifted momentarily as the new computer software kicked in, then settled over the target as firm as a rock. It was too dark to see his target visually, but the commander didn't mind. The radar guided his actions, telling him where to fire the gun.

The fire-control computer emitted a buzzing growl in his ears. The pilot moved his finger, resting it on the trigger. His hands were sweaty, though within he was calm.

For a moment he paused. The young lieutenant was his friend. He had a wife and four children. He was a good man. But he couldn't be trusted, so what choice did he have?

The commander held his breath and pressed the trigger on his cannon, letting off a three-second burst. His F-16 shuddered as the cannon fired almost two hundred shells. The left side of his aircraft emitted a tiny cloud of acidic smoke that was washed away in the slipstream and sucked up by the night. The tracers glowed before him, a stream of

dull orange and red, snakelike, alive, reaching for the oblivious F-16. The pilot fired again, putting out another two-
second burst to shatter the air.

He peered through his canopy, watching the trail of light,
the thin, snarling line of 20mm shells. As he watched, time
seemed to compress—temporal distortion, they called it.
Every second took a minute and every thought came with
piercing clarity.

The target F-16 flew evenly through the night. Inside the
cockpit, the lieutenant was looking down, studying his
charts and his navigational display. The only indication he
had of his oncoming demise was a brief reflection of the
tracers against his canopy glass. He looked up very quickly,
but it was already too late.

Between fifty and sixty shells impacted the jet. The aft
engine bay was the first thing to go, the engine exploding
into a thousand pieces of burning debris, igniting the fuel
that sloshed in the blended-wing tanks. Eight thousand
pounds of jet fuel went up in flames. Pieces of wreckage
shot out from the center of the fire as the F-16 shattered into
a thousand smoldering pieces. The fireball grew and illuminated the sky, smoky and thick. Chunks of wing and fuselage tumbled in every direction, colliding together with
incredible force. Mixed in the debris were the pilot's remains. The torso and legs were still strapped to the ejection
seat, though the head and the shoulders were now tumbling
somewhere else. The pieces of wreckage twisted as they fell,
then settled into an elliptical pattern, which scattered over
the mountains for ten miles.

The commander watched the fireball with very little emotion. Reaching down, he checked his switches, then pushed
the jet over into a very steep dive.

"Mayday! Mayday!" he began to scream in his mask.
"Bengal is going down." He paused for effect. "Bengal . . .
midair collision! My wingman is gone!" Reaching down, the
commander turned off his transponder to make his aircraft
disappear from the controller's radar display.

"Bengal!" the controller called out in a panic.

"Mayday!" the commander shouted. "Midair collision, I've lost everything!" He paused once again. "Bengal's going down. I've got to eject!" The commander released the broadcast switch on the radio.

That was enough to keep them guessing for the next hour or two. And all he needed was a few minutes before this thing was through.

Switching his avionics over to air-to-ground mode, he pulled up the FLIR and ground-mapping radar to check his position against the rising terrain. He pushed the aircraft over into a fifteen-degree dive, watching carefully as the terrain screamed up to meet him. If there was danger in this mission, it was during this phase, as the commander flew at a low level to avoid the radar sites on the mountains north of Islamabad. Though he peered through the night, it didn't do any good. It was too dark. He was going to have to rely on his machine.

Turning sharply, he settled at an altitude of ten thousand feet, then slowly made his way down to terrain flying altitude. The aircraft screamed along at three hundred feet, following a narrow valley that led to the plains, then lurched suddenly, pushing the pilot up in his seat, as a bubble of turbulence threw the little fighter around. His forward-looking infrared turned night into day, showing the way, giving him a picture of the terrain that was falling before him. The pilot concentrated on the flying; night operations were difficult and he wasn't well trained. But it wouldn't be long before he climbed again.

The pilot turned the aircraft to two hundred and fifty degrees, flying toward his next target. He adjusted his course a few degrees to the north, wanting to pass over the secret villa on the lake. Flying over the enormous lodge, a brown rock-and-log building nestled between the lake and a clear mountain stream, he hit his afterburner, sending a thirty-foot flame out his engine exhaust. He glanced down at the villa, which glistened in the moonlight, and wondered if the Pakistani Foreign Minister was already dead.

Shin Bet Auxiliary Outpost
Twelve Miles South of Tel Aviv

The American agents watched the multiple displays from
KH-21. There was too much information, far more than the
Israeli control room was able to show at one time. While Peter studied the control displays, Bradley was talking on two
secure phones at once, his voice always calm, though his
eyes were sober, sullen, and intense as a man walking his final steps on death row. Through one receiver, he talked to
the control room at the NRO, through the other he spoke to
the operations director at Langley.

"Anything at the military complex north of Islamabad?"
Bradley asked into the phone in his right hand. He listened,
glanced at Peter, and shook his head no.

"Have them check the storage facility at Sukkur!" Peter
commanded. He knew where to look. He wanted to reach for
the phone—this relaying through Bradley was driving him
nuts. Bradley nodded impatiently at Peter and repeated what
he said, then listened while hunching his shoulders anxiously. Peter took a step toward him. "The Sukkur military
depot," he tried to explain. "Sind Provence. Eastern Pakistan. Last report, that's were they were!"

Bradley spoke to the controller at the NRO, then turned
to Peter and replied, "They've been there. Nothing happening in the vicinity. No activity of any kind."

"Tell them to keep looking. They have to show their faces
somewhere!"

Bradley shook his head as he listened, then covered the
receiver with his chin. "The Killbird is going to move out of
range in twelve minutes," he said.

Peter swore. "They know when our birds fly overhead!"

"NRO says no. No way they know that! No way at all!"

"Yeah, it's just a coincidence," Peter replied sarcastically.

Bradley shook his head. Peter turned away, pulling anxiously on his beard. He shook his head to brush back his

hair, then reached for a cigarette. He hadn't smoked for ten years, not since his college days, but the habit died hard and his fingers fidgeted nervously. He turned again to the satellite display. The Killbird was hard at work; searching, listening, and probing from above. Other recon assets were also being monitored from the States, but the only download to Israel came through the Killbird KH-21. And the controllers at the National Reconnaissance Organization had cast a very wide net; monitoring all air traffic, ground military vehicles, military-traffic control broadcasts, as well as other intelligence or military communications over Southern Asia. There was so much information, there was no way to absorb it all. It would take days, even months to wade through.

And they didn't have days. They didn't even have hours.

Darkhorse was riding. They had no time at all.

Peter heard a quiet warning chirp emit from the air control screen. A lieutenant moved toward him and nudged him in the side. The room fell in silence as the Israeli military and intelligence officers stared in awe.

"What is it?" Peter asked.

"See the blue triangle," the lieutenant explained.

Peter nodded quickly. "What is it?" he asked.

"A Pakistani F-16 out on military patrol."

"Okay, so?"

The lieutenant glanced to Bradley. "Fifteen seconds ago, there were two fighters there."

Peter watched a blue symbol on the enormous screen shift from deep blue to red. "You see that," Peter said as he turned to Bradley again.

The colonel looked up and nodded. "You saw the F-16 go down?" he asked the controllers at NRO. He waited and grunted, then swore quietly. "That's our first rider! Keep your eye on that bird!"

4

Lake Peshawar
Northwest of Islamabad, Pakistan

The Pakistani foreign minister, a fat, grumpy Christian with a bulbous nose and thick yellow hair, lay in his bed and sweated. He had heard the rumors. He knew that his time was near. And though the huge mountain villa seemed the best place to hide, still, he did not feel safe. His wife lay beside him, snoring, unaware of his fears. Down the hall, in the kitchen, the television was on, the announcer's voice drifting into the bedroom, the screen causing a flicker of light. A ceiling fan turned, gently stirring the air, creating a tiny breeze that tickled the hair on his arms.

The night air suddenly shattered as a military jet flew overhead. It was low and fast. He felt the walls of his villa shake. The sound rumbled in the darkness, then quickly died away.

The minister swallowed, trying to control the heartbeat in his chest. He stared up at the darkness, fighting dreadful thoughts. And though he was awake, though his eyes were adjusted to the dark, though his senses were wired and his mind near the edge, still, he didn't hear the assassin as he entered the room. He didn't see the shadow cross the window or feel the air stir. The man simply appeared suddenly at the foot of his bed, a shadow dressed in black, with bright slits for eyes.

The minister sat up with a start, his heart slamming into his chest. Grunting in fear, he almost heaved on his bed. His wife stirred beside him but didn't wake up. The assassin approached and breathed quietly. The minister rolled to the side, holding his hands in front of his face in a childlike gesture of fear. His wife woke with a start. She felt a hand on her knee and froze in cold fear.

The assassin moved quickly. Two slits of the six-inch razor and it was done. The blood pooled on the bed and soaked into the white sheets. The woman's foot kicked suddenly, though she was already dead.

Islamabad, Pakistan

The Pakistani chief of military staff had scheduled the meeting just a few hours before. His generals quietly filed into the brightly lit room and assembled themselves around the mahogany table. The command center was huge, with maps of Pakistan and the middle of Asia lining two walls. At the head of the table an electronic display showed the status of the military forces. A live feed from air-traffic-control radar showed the presidential aircraft inbound. The Pakistani president's 727 was a little over one hundred miles to the west.

The neon lights hummed as the generals filed into the room. The four-star chief of staff studied his commanders and swallowed the knot in his throat. Only six who were loyal! Out of his entire staff. Six generals he could count on. No, make that five.

They were just getting seated when there was a light tap on the door. A young major entered the room holding a small briefcase in his left hand. He glanced at the commanding general. "*Sayid,* I have been asked to bring this to you," he said.

The chief of staff scowled and took a step toward the young officer. "What is it?" he snarled.

"A package from Gen. Hyidda' Mohar Astti. He said it was extremely important and that I was to deliver it immediately."

The general narrowed his eyes. "Gen. Hyidda' Mohar Astti is in Afghanistan!"

"*Sayid,* he returned very early this morning."

Without invitation, the major walked to the center of the room. The chief of staff watched him closely, a worried look on his face. Something was wrong, he could see it in the young major's eyes. As the young officer approached the huge table, the air force commander stood suddenly, pushing himself away from the table. "No," he sneered to the major. "This isn't the time!" The major ignored him. "Fool!" the air force commander cried, staring wild-eyed at the briefcase in the major's hand.

And with that, the chief of staff knew. He took a step back, an empty look on his face. He moaned, his soul staggered, then he sucked in a breath.

Closing his eyes, the major muttered a prayer. *"Ashhadu anna la alaha illa Allah,"* he said in a low voice. "I testify that there is no god but Allah," he prayed.

Releasing his grip on the briefcase, he let it fall to the floor, triggering the firing mechanism hidden inside. Eleven pounds of plastic explosives exploded in the room, blasting out the walls with an inferno of heat and pressure. The north side of the defense building was blown into the street, filling the night with dust and smoldering debris mixed with pieces of human flesh.

Eighteen Miles West of Islamabad, Pakistan

The F-16 pilot was flying east when the bright flash and fire lit up the night. He couldn't miss the explosion and rolling fireball, and it came exactly on time. He nodded in satisfaction as he glanced at his watch.

Turning his attention back inside the cockpit, he continued to fly though the night, following the contours of the rolling mountains toward the target ahead.

5

The 727 was fifty miles from Islamabad and westbound, setting up for its initial approach into the airport. In front of the aircraft, the city lights burned through the low fog of dust, illuminating the layer like a huge saucer of dirty yellow light. Inside the cockpit, the flight crew was anxious to get on the ground. The flight from Spain had taken almost seven hours and required the crew to navigate some of the most challenging airspace in the world; from the congested straits of the Mediterranean Sea, to overflights of Syria, Iraq, Iran, and Afghanistan.

As they approached home base, the aircraft commander switched on his VOR, the antiquated navigational equipment used in this part of the world. The VOR would help the crew to safely navigate the mountainous terrain that surrounded Islamabad. Pressing his radio switch, the pilot announced, "Islamabad Center, Steal One is fifty miles southwest at one nine thousand feet, looking for direct to the field, and lower when able."

"Roger, Steal One, descend and maintain flight level one-seven thousand. Direct to the field. Report the initial approach fix."

The pilot lowered the nose and brought back the power. The aircraft began a slow and gentle descent.

"Steal will be looking for the visual. Will report at Shamir."

"Roger, Shamir. Make your best time."

The presidential pilot paused, immediately knowing that something was wrong. The air traffic controller, any controller, didn't tell Steal One what to do. Steal was free to make his best time or wander around in the night. They could fly any route, anywhere, and at any altitude. It was entirely up to them. Steal One was in charge. So the controller's instructions made the pilot stiffen in his seat. "Islamabad, say status," he asked.

"We are operating normal status, Steal. But we lost a flight of F-16 Bengals a few minutes ago. They were enroute to Kama. It appears there was a midair collision."

The pilot stiffened again, then motioned to the copilot, who pressed a tiny red button on the console near his knee. Immediately, a security agent appeared at the cockpit door, a member of the SAK, or Special Presidential Police, the bodyguards and soldiers sworn to protect the president of Pakistan.

The security agent leaned into the cockpit. *"Ashik, ne 'Omor?"* What do you have?

The pilot held up his hand, listening on his radio headset, then turned to the agent. "The Pakistani air force lost a couple fighters tonight. There was a midair collision just a few minutes ago."

"Location?"

"North of the field, maybe ninety miles from here."

"And?"

"That's all I have. Control is still calling operations normal."

The agent frowned and swore at the captain. "What kind of aircraft were involved in the midair collision?"

"Two F-16 fighters. But—"

"Were they armed?"

"I don't know." The pilot paused and then said, "Yes, of course, they had to be armed, they were heading for Kama."

"Both aircraft go down?"

"We don't know, but there is no reason to believe—"

"Fool!" the agent sneered. "Of course there is reason. Now get this jet on the ground!" He waved a threatening finger. "And tell the controllers to step up security. And keep our pathway clear!"

The security chief turned and stomped from the cockpit, determined but unsure of what he should do. Making his way to the back of the cabin, to his SAK brothers, he approached his commander and whispered in his ear.

Staying low, near the ground, following the contours of the earth, the F-16 pilot studied his multifunction display. He tuned the radar out to eighty miles, throwing out a beam of energy to search the skies to the west, and the target appeared suddenly on his color display. It lumbered toward him, descending through eighteen thousand feet, tracking a straight course, oblivious to the danger ahead. The pilot armed up his AMRAAM missiles, then turned his fighter south and pushed up the power. The Pakistani president's 727 passed through his three o'clock position, forty miles away. The F-16 pilot jerked on his stick, barely pulling his aircraft over a hill. His flying had turned sloppy and he swore to himself. He straightened up in his seat, and took a deep breath, then pulled the fighter around, banking into a tight right-hand turn. He stared through his HUD to track the horizon, careful to keep from flying into the ground. Jerking back, he pulled the nose of his fighter up, climbing into the night. The force of the g's pushed him into his seat, and it only took a few seconds to climb to fourteen thousand feet.

Rolling out, the F-16 was in a textbook position, behind and slightly lower than the target before him. He could fire his missiles at any time.

He leveled the aircraft, but kept the power up, accelerating to close on the presidential aircraft. His hands began to ache, and he relaxed his grip on the stick; he was tight, but that was good, it was the thrill of the hunt. He breathed even more deeply and felt his heart pound in his chest. From the beginning of time, from man's earliest hunt, from the first swing of a club or throw of a stone, the physiological reaction had not changed in the past million years. The killer instinct was internal, a part of the pilot's psyche; it wasn't learned, it wasn't taught, it was just part of who he was. And it was driving him now as he closed on the presidential jet. He pulled up behind it and for the second time that night he heard the gentle growl in his helmet as the radar locked onto the aircraft before him. Less than twenty miles now. Perfect firing range! But he waited, wanting to savor the emotion, the flush in his face and rush in his head, the clarity of thought and the thrill of a kill. It was easy, so easy, but still it was fun.

Fifteen miles behind the target, the presidential aircraft suddenly dropped toward the ground. It accelerated as it dove, jinking and turning violently in the dark.

The pilot smiled and switched his radio frequency to pick up the air traffic controller.

The air-traffic controller was screaming into his radio mike. "Steal, *bandit is at your six o'clock and closing!*" The controller's voice was high and almost laughably hysterical.

The fighter pilot snorted. So his F-16 had finally appeared on the controller's radar display. Surely it was pure panic now inside the control center. He envisioned the chaos. It would have been fun to see.

"Steal, *climb!*" The controller screamed his desperate instructions. The fighter pilot listened a few seconds more. "No—*dive.* Steal, *dive!* No—he's still there! Break right!"

The commander shook his head. Climb, dive, or break, it didn't matter at all. The 727 could stand on its tail and bark like a dog, either way that aircraft was dead! He placed his finger over the trigger, the growl sounding in his ears. He took a breath and fired, blasting two AMRAAMs into the night.

The flash from the missile engines almost burned his eyes. Twin bursts of fire rushed forward, trailing thin lines of white smoke.

"*Steal, fox, fox!!*" the radar controller screamed over the radio.

The fighter pilot studied his radar as the target began a frantic series of dives and steep turns. It pulled up and rolled over in a smooth barrel roll and the commander almost laughed. Who did the 727 pilot think he was, a fighter pilot? This guy had some guts.

As the missiles closed in on the target, the ground controller fell silent. It was painfully obvious his president was dead.

The F-16 pilot turned his fighter to the south and headed for the Arabian Sea. He was getting low on fuel and he still had three hundred miles to go. As he rolled into the bank, he saw a quick flash of white and looked over his shoulder to see the huge fireball. He smiled to congratulate himself, then descended again, getting below radar coverage.

Twenty-nine minutes later, the pilot crossed the rocky shoreline of the Arabian Sea. He picked up the small ship on his radar display, forty miles from the coastline and due south of Karachi. He did one low pass and saw the flare on the foredeck, which sparked brightly then faded quickly, leaving the ship once again cloaked in darkness. Completing his ejection checklist, he positioned his fighter to pass abeam of the ship, sat straight up in his seat, and pulled on the handles of his ejection seat.

He was in the water less than five minutes before an inflatable skiff maneuvered beside his small raft. Twenty hours later, the F-16 assassin was safely inside a base camp deep in the Saudi Arabian desert.

Shin Bet Auxiliary Outpost
Twelve Miles South of Tel Aviv

The control room had turned chaotic as more and more Israeli intelligence officers filled the room. What had started out with four officers quickly turned into twenty, then thirty, then more, all of them manning their posts, working their intelligence desks. Reports began to fill in, urgent messages from Shin Bet resources throughout the world.

An Israeli communications officer handed Peter a handwritten note. He read it quickly, then moved toward Bradley. "There's been an explosion in central Islamabad," he said.

Bradley looked over, his brow covered with sweat.

"We've got missiles inbound," one of the controllers called out. "Steal One is the target! Look out! Oh my . . . ."

A sudden gasp moved through the control room and every eye turned to the tactical display. It only took seconds to watch the Pakistani leader's aircraft go down.

Bradley pulled on Peter's elbow and the two men moved to a corner of the operations center and lowered their voices. Around them, they caught the glancing stares, the looks of fear and uncertainty as the Israeli officers wondered exactly what was going on. The Shin Bet general followed them, joining their circle.

"General, I guess you have some understanding as to what is happening here?" Colonel Bradley said.

"I have my ideas."

"Perhaps. But have you considered the Pakistani warheads?"

"We consider them all the time." The general paused. "But we have had your assurance, the word of your president."

"Yes, we have provided assurances. And that's where we are now. DARKHORSE is the code word signifying a clear and immediate threat to Pakistan's nuclear arsenal. We have known—like you—and we have feared for several years that the Pakistani cache might be vulnerable. A sudden coup, a single death from utter disaster. We can't have these weapons ending up in the wrong hands. So we have been making arrangements in case of such an event.

"You've seen what's happening over there," Bradley nodded toward the satellite screens. "The attack on the Pakistani president. The explosions through the city. Now, maybe this is something that will sort itself out, maybe this is something we can work our way through; perhaps there are forces behind this we can work with in the future, but I personally doubt it. And this much we know, the Pakistani president is gone. And we won't wait, we *can't* wait, to see who takes control of his country, we won't wait and we *can't* wait to

see what happens to his nuclear arsenal. I'm sure you understand the necessity of intercepting those weapons before
someone else does."

The Shin Bet officer nodded gravely. It was just as he
thought. And no one in the room was more determined than
he. No nation had more to lose; no nation felt this same
noose slipping over its heads. Nuclear warheads in the
wrong hands meant annihilation. The threat was intolerable.

And this time the Israelis would not go down alone. They
were prepared and determined to take their enemies, too. A
single nuclear detonation in Israel, and the entire Middle
East would explode, from Lebanon to Iran.

The general sucked in a breath, his face turning ashen.
"You know what Blackbird is going to say!" he said in a dry
voice.

Bradley paused as he consider the hardnosed general who
was the head of Shin Bet. General Petate (known as Blackbird to his men) would take the news of the coup in Pakistan
like a dose of rat poison. He wouldn't sit around hoping
things turned out okay. He would have to take action!

The general took a short step toward Bradley and looked
him right in the eye, his face but six inches from the taller
man's nose. "Take care of this problem!" he hissed in a
gravelly tone. "You know our position. We won't take this
lying down."

Bradley stepped back. "I need your help," he replied.

"What is it? What can we do?"

"I've got to get back to D.C.," Bradley said. "Can you get
me an escort to the airport where my transport is waiting?"

The general nodded. "Of course. Anything you need."

Bradley nodded, then turned toward Peter. "If I were to get
you out to the DARKHORSE camp, would you ride with the
special ops guys on the intercept mission? We need to have a
set of agency eyes and ears on the ground."

"How would you propose to get me out there? It's two thousand miles. The team will launch long before I could arrive."

"The Rangers won't be ready for two or three hours. We

can get you there if we have a little help." Bradley turned to the general. "Can you get this agent to . . ." He paused and considered before he continued. "We have a covert base camp in western India, along the Pakistan border."

The general scowled. He had never heard of this base camp. How could Shin Bet not know!? He did the mental math. "I just don't see how."

"We'll need one of your fighters."

"It will take time to generate a sortie."

"Don't give me that. Half of your air force is on alert. I need you to take one of your birds, one of your F-15s, strap on some long-range fuel tanks, and get my guy out to the camp! There's only a small runway, but it's sufficient if your pilot is good. We'll make the overflight clearances. Now, do we have a deal?"

The general thought, then nodded. "I'll make arrangements," he said and started walking away.

Bradley grunted thanks, then turned to Peter and lowered his voice even more. "Get those boys to the Sukkur storage facility before it's too late."

"Roger that, I'll do all I can."

"Washington wants me to brief the national security staff. By the time I get there I want to have some good news for him. I want to hear your boys have found the warheads and taken them under our control, that they are safe and secure in American hands."

Peter nodded grimly and the two men turned to leave. Moving through the crowded control room, Bradley shot a sideways look to his friend and wondered suddenly when he would see him again. He stopped and grabbed Peter by the arm. "I know you were hoping for a few days to get home," he said.

Peter pressed his lips and lowered his gaze. Bradley saw the look, the remorseful guilt in his eyes. "I'm sorry," he said softly.

Peter looked away.

"I'll tell your dad . . . if you want me to, I'll go . . ." Bradley started to offer, then paused as he searched for the words.

A painful looked crossed Peter's face, a shadow of emotion from somewhere deep in his soul, a broken responsibility that was painfully clear.

"Tell him . . . ," Peter said. "Tell him, if you need to, tell him good-bye for me."

"I won't have to tell him. We'll get you back to the States. Very soon, I swear."

The two men were quiet until Peter turned and walked from the room. Bradley watched for a long moment, then turned for the back door.

Tel Aviv International Airport
Israel

Twenty minutes later, Bradley was heading home. The engines were already running, and the small C-21 military executive jet started to roll before the air force lieutenant even had the door closed.

It took only minutes for the plane to climb to forty-one thousand feet. As the aircraft leveled off at trans-Atlantic cruise altitude, Bradley sat alone in the narrow cabin and stared out the window at the dark Mediterranean below.

Less than ten minutes later, an Israeli two-seat F-15 also took to the air. It too climbed to cruising altitude, but flew east, set on a course for southern India, more than two thousand miles away.

Leveling off and flying into the rising moon, the Israeli pilot adjusted his twin throttles to set his airspeed at just below subsonic Mach.

He had his instructions. And there was no time to spare.

Shin Bet Headquarters Compound
Tel Aviv, Israel

The man who commanded Shin Bet was a no-nonsense three-star general who had risen through the ranks of the intelligence community. Like the organization he headed,

General Petate had a reputation for toughness and efficiency that was well deserved. An extraordinary military officer of Russian descent, the general was born on a *moshav* near the infant nation's northern border ten years after the Second World War, where he spent his youth patrolling the hills and open rangelands around his small village, a watchman against raiders from the neighboring Arab villages. By fifteen he was initiated into the Palmach, the famed Jewish underground force, where he honed his skills in ranging and reconnaissance. By seventeen, he became the youngest officer in the legendary Unit 101, the nation's first formal antiterrorist organization; at twenty-one he was the unit's lead sniper, at thirty-two in command.

Unit 101, though highly effective and even more highly feared, was a nearly schizophrenic organization that vacillated in its approach between two distinct and completely divergent models of leadership: the traditional method, which stressed a strict chain of command, and the Wingate model (first taught by British officer Orde Charles Wingate), which emphasized individual initiative, speed, severe risk, high payout, and direct accountability. Petate was a huge believer in the Wingate model and made no bones about his appreciation for high-risk, high-value military and intelligence opportunities. The higher the better. No risk, no return.

Which was why he found himself in command of Shin Bet; these were dangerous times, and his nation needed him now. It also explained where he picked up the nickname he had. Blackbird, the famed American SR-71, was the fastest and highest-flying aircraft in the world, and Petate flew like the Blackbird when he got on a roll.

And though over time Shin Bet became somewhat known to the press, the general remained in the shadows, always working behind the lines; few of his countrymen would recognize his face, and for obvious reasons he rarely exposed himself. Instead, he spent most of his time at the compound, and traveled only when necessary. Indeed, his existence was not dissimilar to that of some of the prisoners he held, though he drank better whisky and slept in more comfortable beds. He was a fearsome and focused man, not religious but practical, a man who had resigned himself to only one purpose in life—protect the state of Israel, whatever the cost. He considered it his mission, and he felt the special burden of loving his nation too much. The emotion burned, a hot coal, giving him the strength to do the things that he did.

General Petate sat alone in his office staring blankly at a coffee table containing some of his personal effects; a picture of his wife and two children, beautiful daughters—early twenties, blond, smiling, their arms around their father's neck. An eighteen-inch bronze statue of a bucking stallion sat next to the picture of his family. Beside that was a fist-size piece of granite enclosed in glass, a gift from a close friend who had climbed Mount Everest. Beside the chunk of granite was a picture of a smiling Palestinian girl with a news clipping attached, a Knight Ridder dispatch from the West Bank town of Abu Qash:

> Rofayda Qaoud—raped by her brothers and impregnated—refused to commit suicide, her mother recalls, even after she bought the unwed teenager a razor with which to slit her wrists. So Amira Abu Hanhan Qaoud says she did what she believes any good Palestinian parent would: restored her family's "honor" through murder.
>
> Armed with a plastic bag, razor, and wooden stick, Qaoud entered her sleeping daughter's room last Jan. 27. "Tonight you die, Rofayda," she told the girl, before wrapping the bag tightly around her head. Next, Qaoud sliced Rofayda's wrists, ignoring her muffled pleas of "No, mother, no!" After her daughter went limp, Qaoud struck her in the head with the stick.
>
> Killing her sixth-born child took 20 minutes, Qaoud tells a visitor through a stream of tears and cigarettes that she smokes in rapid succession. "She killed me before I killed her," says the 43-year-old mother of nine. "I had to protect my children. This is the only way I could protect my family's honor."

The clipping reminded Petate that he wasn't only fighting for his daughters, but for other daughters too. The Palestinian girl deserved to live, just like his daughters did.

Staring blankly past his personal effects, the general shuddered, an angry determination building in his chest.

His deputy knocked and entered. "Sir," he said simply. Petate turned slowly as he held up his hand, unwilling to break his thoughts. The deputy waited quietly. The general brought his fists together and pulled them to his chin.

"We will not suffer this," he said after a full three minutes of thought.

The deputy nodded. "Sir, I agree."

Petate tapped his chin with his fists, then stood and leaned against the side of his desk. "Watch the U.S. agent," he said, his voice gravelly and low. "His real name is Peter Zembeic. He's one of Thomas Washington's men and has a serious nose for the fight. He's had a hand in some of the most significant intelligence operations of the past half-dozen years; but he's also a cowboy, the kind who has a hard time staying in the box. That makes him nervous, but Thomas still loves him and uses him every chance that he gets. So I want you to keep a man on him twenty-four hours a day. Never, and I mean *never,* let him out of our sight. Move our people around, use whatever assets we have, he is our only priority now. I want to know what he knows, I want to see what he sees, I want to smell what he smells and think what he thinks. If the Americans locate the warheads, he will lead us to them."

The deputy nodded. "But sir, he's just one man. Do you really think he will lead us to the—"

"Yes, I do," the general cut in. "And let me tell you something about this agent and what we are dealing with here. Remember the battle at Kirkuk in the early days of the Iraqi war? Zembeic was there with a dozen CIA and paramilitary men. They were in a convoy, heading out of the city after the rebels had taken over, when they came under attack. Half his men went down in the first thirty seconds. Two of their Humvees were taken down by RPGs, killing almost everyone inside. Zembeic and his remaining men fell back and called for chopper extraction. As they waited, a couple rebels fought their way forward, moving toward the burning Humvees. Zembeic realized it was going to be Somalia or Fallujah again—crazed teens prancing over some shot-up American Humvees, pictures of American bodies being dragged through the streets, video on al-Jazeera, you know the scene, Iraqi and foreign insurgents gloating over destroyed U.S. hardware while some hooded thug hangs a burned corpse from a bridge."

Zembeic decided he wasn't going to give the rebels another chance to get on CNN. He ordered his men to stay and fight, but they were ordered back. Nothing doing, Zembeic said. The extraction choppers came in, but he wouldn't get on. Absolutely refused to get on board the choppers. His second in command put in a call to headquarters. Thomas ordered Zembeic to get on the chopper, but he pretended satellite interference and cut the connection.

"For the next thirty-six hours, he holed up in the fourth floor of a bombed-out apartment building, shooting anyone who even came close to the bodies of his buddies or the burned-up machines. He was that serious about protecting the remains of his fallen comrades, that serious about denying them a propaganda tool. He used a silencer and shot from almost a full block away, so they never found him, never knew where he was. I guess they thought it was silent death straight from God. By some counts he killed half a dozen insurgents, some say it was more, but who really knows. Two days later, marines regained control of the area. The fallen soldiers were repatriated to U.S. forces, and Zembeic finally crawled down from his sniper outlook."

General Petate's aide bit his lip. "Sounds like he needs his head examined," he said.

"Yeah. Maybe. And what would I give to have a few more like him."

The deputy took a step back and said, "Alright, sir, we'll stay with him."

"You do that, Colonel, and he will lead us to them."

"And when we find the warheads?"

"You know what to do."

6

Colonel Bradley's aircraft was just passing over Cyprus when he got the call he was expecting on the secure telephone. Dr. Thomas B. Washington, Deputy Director of Operations (DDO), United States Central Intelligence Agency, spoke into the STU-IV. Bradley listened to his boss, holding the receiver away from his ear as the DDO cursed through the satellite phone.

As DDO, Washington specialized in HUMINT, or Human Intelligence. For almost twenty years he had been working with various intelligence contacts overseas—smugglers, spies, traders in human flesh, traitors, officers, and even the occasional king, president, or premier; men who for one reason or another—money, sex, power, hatred, or revenge—had been willing to trade what information they had for what they wanted most. Washington knew these men; he knew who they were and what they had done. The secrets in his head were worth many lives.

And because his professional life was a shadow of covert operations and lies, the elements of which he rarely seemed to be able to control, Washington compensated by demanding perfection from his underlings and staff. And the one thing he *couldn't* tolerate was being caught unaware. And the fact that none of Washington's informants, none of the dark work he had done, none of top-secret sources he had cultivated over the years, had provided him with an early warning of the pending catastrophe, only made the bitter news worse. Washington had sold his soul to satisfy these dark, evil men, and none of them had come forward to warn him in time.

Bradley calmly sipped at a bottle of water and watched the passing night clouds, while Thomas Washington ranted on the phone, knowing it would take another twenty or thirty seconds before his boss would settle down.

Despite the tirade, the men had a good relationship, though both would admit it was often strained. For one thing, their personal backgrounds were as different as their skin color; Washington, a black man from the inner city, Bradley, a white kid from the upper middle class. Dr. Thomas B. Washington, Ph.D., was a self-made intellectual raised in the ghettos of Detroit: slumlords and slum schools—he had seen nothing but crap since the day he was born. Indeed, he was one of the very few children in the United States who actually grew up hungry, sucking on dirty bottles filled with sugar water and playing among discarded beer bottles thrown in the corners of his mother's drug-infested bedroom. He was barely more than eight when he saw his first murder, by ten he was running acid and heroin, slipping tiny plastic bags under neighborhood doors. But, through it all, there was something inside him, something hot, rich, and angry, something that sensed the great waste that he had become, something that screamed with a fury, *"you are better than this!"* Sometime during his fourteenth year he made a decision. He was getting out. He would not die this way, twenty years old and destroyed by life. Guts and grit (he had not yet discovered his brains) were all that he had, and all he could hope was that it was enough, but he swore that one way or another he would scratch his way out of this dead, lethal world. When he started high school, Washington moved in with an aunt who, if she didn't quite live on the good side of the tracks, at least didn't reside in the human garbage dump either. He worked hard, driven by the hunger inside, and after teaching himself to read, graduated near the top of his high school class, not enough to get a scholarship, but enough to get admitted to NYU. Government grants and odd jobs kept him flush through his years of earning an undergraduate degree. From there, he worked days while going to school at night, earning his doctorate in International Studies. He spent a few years as a consultant to the Department of Defense before being recruited by the CIA, where he found his home, and he had been there ever since.

Bradley, on the other hand, grew up in the upper middle class, his father a well-known and hard-core army general. The old man, one of McNamara's masterminds, raised his sons tight and straight—tight like his crew cut, straight as the crease in his pants. To this day, if Bradley closed his eyes, he could still hear his old man's voice. *"Army! You hear me! Boys, there is nothing else! Not air force, not navy! They're nothing but spit in the wind! You walk the gray line and you sweat army green!"*

No, Washington and Bradley couldn't have come from more opposite worlds; but the result was the same: they were both determined men. But ambition and clandestine operations were a volatile mix. And through the years that they had worked together (years during which Bradley resented being called away from the cockpit and the flying he loved), they had butted heads more than once. But still there was enough respect that they enjoyed working together; and truth was, each considered the other a good friend.

After cursing and ranting about the situation in general, venting an anger that was born of frustration and gut-wrenching fear, all the time knowing it was ultimately his fault, Dr. Washington settled down and finally got to the point. "The risk is too great to not take action," he said. "The NSA staff is on board. We're calling POTUS now."

"Where is he?" Bradley asked.

"Up in New York. About to have dinner with the delegation from Oman."

Bradley thought a moment, then questioned hesitatingly. "Are you certain we have enough evidence to request a DARKHORSE operation?"

Washington only scoffed. "You're kidding me, right!?"

"No sir, I'm not. I think we need to ask the question before we jump off this cliff. Do we understand the situation enough to—"

"No, Shane, we don't understand! We don't understand anything, which is the *entire point*. We don't understand the situation, which is exactly why we *must* act."

Bradley waited, sucking on his cheek as he thought. "And you believe POTUS will authorize an operation?" he asked into the phone.

Washington didn't waver. "Yes."

After completing the conversation with Washington, Bradley made his own call to Col. Dick "Tracy" Kier, his vice wing commander, back at Whiteman Air Force Base.

It took several minutes for the call to patch through. "Colonel Kier," his friend finally said as he picked up the phone.

"Tracy, it's Shane," Bradley announced hurriedly.

"You okay?" Kier asked, a worried tone in his voice. If Shane was in trouble, then, baby, he was there. He was as protective of Bradley as any subordinate could be.

Bradley almost smiled. Loyalty and dedication were only two of the reasons he had selected Colonel Kier to be his second in command. "I'm fine," he answered quickly, "but we've got a problem here."

There was a short pause. "What's up, boss?"

"Stay close to your intel office. You should be hearing soon."

Kier grunted, an apprehensive reply. He was one of the few men in the air force who was aware of Bradley's responsibilities in the CIA, and he knew Bradley only worried when things were an inch from the fan.

Kier paused a moment. "Anything you can tell me?" he asked.

"Not yet. But stay close. And Tracy, I think I'm coming home."

"Good. When will you be here? I'm tired of doing your job."

"A day, maybe two. But meanwhile, I need you to do something, okay?"

"Anything you say, boss. You know I'm your guy."

"Take a look at the regulations governing Group 21. I think we might get a mission, and I want everyone prepared."

Bradley heard Kier swallow, a dry gulping sound. "No kidding," he answered.

"Wish I was," Bradley replied.

The Waldorf-Astoria Towers
New York City

The presidential protocol officer stood in the spacious dining room at the top of the Waldorf Towers, the U.S. ambassador to the United Nation's official residence for the last thirty years. He studied the table. The china was elegant: white plates ringed with blue and overlaid with an image of the presidential seal, the eagle facing the olive branch in a gesture of peace. The table centerpiece was made from pink roses and white baby's breath. The napkin's tight cotton weave was also edged in blue. The military waiters, young naval enlisted men, stood off to the side in their military tuxedos, pressed uniforms so crisp they nearly crackled when they moved. Four marine color guards walked through a side door and were sent toward the entrance. A dozen secret service men came and went, all of them intent and serious, listening to the wires in their ears. The official White House photographer slipped into the room and was quickly accosted by two security agents. Though they recognized him, having worked together for almost three years, they still asked the photographer to unzip his bag and leave it on the floor so a short-haired German shepherd could sniff it for bombs. "Let me see you operate that," a dark-eyed agent said to the photographer as he motioned to his cell phone. As the protocol officer watched, a steward began placing the name cards in their positions—the calligraphy radiating the power of the men who would soon arrive. The president would sit at the head of the table, with His Excellency, the President of Oman on his right and the secretary of state on his left. From there, the guests would be seated in pecking order; Gen. Shif' Amonnon, Oman's secretary of state, Omar Mushar, then the United States secretary of state and the U.S. ambassador.

The protocol officer studied the menu, which was embossed with the presidential seal:

Mixed Green Salad   *Goat Cheese and Herb Vinaigrette*
Fillet of Lamb with Rosemary Au Jus   *White Sauce with Split Beans*
Georgia Sweet Potato Tartlet

He knew the president had requested steak. Rare. With A-1 sauce, mashed potatoes, and maybe a beer. But he got white sauce with split beans and fillet of *halal* lamb, which meant it had been blessed, making it clean and pure. The officer suspected the president would have lifted his arms to the heavens and blessed the young lamb himself, if it would have helped to keep the Omanians happy. The world had grown complicated, and friends were in short supply.

Outside, a line of black sedans pulled onto Park Avenue. The ambassador's wife scurried in, harried and tense. "Larger water glasses," she demanded after surveying the table. "Less ice. Crushed, not cubes. And the napkins need to be folded like this!" she instructed the headwaiter while folding a crease across the nearest blue napkin. The headwaiter nodded, but didn't make a move. This wasn't her lunch, it was a White House affair, and he knew how to fold napkins, thank

you very much. The ambassador's wife waited, then huffed
and scurried from the room. Minutes later, the president's
voice could be heard from the foyer and a charge of electricity filled the air. "Gentlemen, this way," the president said as
he led the delegation into the room. Passing the marines, he
stopped to inspect the honor guard. "How old are you son?"
he asked the first soldier.

"Twenty-three, sir," the marine barked in reply.

The president studied him a moment more. "You look
sharp. Real sharp. Tell your mom she did a real good job.
And tell all your buddies that I'm counting on them. Tell
them I think of them every day."

The marine broke role and smiled, then forced a stern
look once again. "Yes sir, Mr. President. I will tell them, *sir!*"

The president slapped the marine on his back, then swag-
gered into the dining room. It seemed to ignite with energy.
The Man had arrived!

The president paced around the table, inspecting the name
cards, then motioned to the delegation, directing them to their
chairs. The gentlemen were just sitting down when a short-
haired army colonel slipped in from the hallway to approach
the president's chair. "Sir, if I could?" he whispered in his ear.

The president looked up. "What's going on, Frank?"

The officer swallowed. "Sir, *Mayer Smith* is on the phone."

The president froze, recognizing the code instantly. He
forced a quick smile and excused himself from the table.
"One of my mayors," he explained to the Omanian president. "They probably lost their power again."

The president followed the army officer out of the room
and the two men stopped and stood in the hall. "General Massarif is dead," the colonel explained in a low voice. "His aircraft went down a little more than an hour ago." The president
swore and furrowed his brow. "There's more, Mr. President,"
the colonel went on. It took him several minutes to explain
everything. "Sir, the national security staff recommends that
we send in an interdiction force," was the last thing he said.

"Do it!" the president commanded. "Get the team in the
air."

Camp Thor
Extreme Western India

Peter had barely climbed down the tiny built-in steps of the fighter and pulled his helmet off when a U.S. Special Forces sergeant ran up to him.

"Peter Zembeic?" he screamed, holding a finger in both ears. The F-15 engines screeched behind them, just fifteen feet away. Peter nodded while reaching down to unzip the g-suit from his waist.

"Come with me. We're ready to go," the sergeant said.

Peter heard the sound of helicopters, their rotors already beating the air. He glanced to his left to see six choppers running, their exterior lights off, the smell of burning jet fuel hanging heavy in the dry desert night. "You been waiting for me?" he asked.

The sergeant shook his head as he turned. "You aren't that important, sir."

Peter nodded, then followed the special forces soldier, leaving his F-15 flying gear on the tarmac. Behind him an American crew moved toward the waiting Israeli F-15. Its right engine was still running, and the ground crew worked quickly to refuel the jet and get it back in the air.

The burly sergeant ran toward the lead chopper where he nodded to an empty canvas seat in the rear of the MH-60, helped Peter strap in, then dropped a modified Uzi in his lap. "You know how to use this?" he yelled above the noise of the chopper.

Peter cleared the chamber, flipped the safe, and nodded his head. The sergeant pushed a headset toward Peter and he pulled it over his ears.

"I have a message from Colonel Bradley," the young soldier said over the intercom system. "I'm supposed to remind you that you're an observer, not an infantryman. You are stay low, keep your head on, and not jump into the fight. So keep aside, Mr. Zembeic, or you'll get in our way."

Peter nodded, leaned his head back and immediately closed his eyes. It was a long flight to Sukru, and he was tired to the bone.

Leaving their base camp in far western India, a camp that didn't exist just a few months before, the U.S. military choppers lifted off a little after midnight. Flying through the night, and refueling twice in the air, the choppers made their way west, across the enormous Thar Desert. Approaching Pakistan's Indus River plain, the formation turned sharply south. The combat troops, deployed in five twelve-men teams, were being carried by a combination of MH-53 and MH-60 special operations helicopters. With their long-range fuel tanks, terrain-following avionics, active defensive systems, and fifty-caliber machine guns, the choppers were capable of taking care of themselves. But the hope was the operation would take place without a shot being fired, at least until the soldiers had been placed on the ground.

The contingency operation had been in the making for almost three years, and the teams were as confident as they could be. The pilots had flown the route in the simulator and in the real world, flown it in daylight and darkness and with various combat loads. The delta teams had been through the most rigorous training they had ever experienced, with time spent in the California deserts, the plains of India's Jaipur Province, and southeast Pakistan. In preparation for the mission (which was under the direction of the CIA) and with the full support of the Pakistani government, a replica of the Pakistani weapon storage compound had been erected in a remote corner of Fort Erwin, California. With information provided by the Pakistani generals and the architects who had designed the facility, the replica of the Pakistani compound was identical in every detail. For six months, the delta soldiers used the replica to practice their mission. After months of training, they were confident and ready to go.

Then they deployed and waited for the orders they hoped would never come.

In planning the mission, it was always understood that it

was time, not the Pakistanis, that was the worst enemy, so when they finally got the execution call, it took fewer than three hours to gather the crews and get the choppers in the air.

Sukkur Military Facility
Sind Province (Eastern Pakistan)

It was almost dawn when the formation approached the Pakistani weapon storage facility. The sky was turning pink over the muddy brown Indus, as the morning twilight illuminated the sandy buttes that surrounded the compound. The six choppers, four HH-60s and two enormous MH-53s, turned to approach the compound directly from the east. If they couldn't come under the cloak of darkness, something they would clearly have preferred to do, they would at least take advantage of the rising sun in order to cloak their approach. The chopper pilots flew low, only a few feet off the ground. Skimming the desert, a brown rolling sea, they kicked up plumes of fine dust as they passed overhead.

The concrete and barbwire compound came into view in the dim morning light. Beyond it, in the distance, seven miles to the east, the gritty town of Sukkur cluttered the horizon, a series of black smokestacks and tin-roofed buildings situated along the brown Indus River. The weapons facility was situated behind a twelve-foot-high concrete wall. Atop the wall, a four-foot razor wire fence extended outward at a forty-five degree angle. Guard towers were positioned at the four corners of the compound, looking out on a mine field that extended in every direction. A single road approached the compound, weaving through a series of cement barricades. Inside the main wall was a double line of electrified fence, with motion detectors, laser sensors, and a series of fortified bunkers to provide the guards a firing position in every direction.

It was a fortress. A sparrow couldn't land in the compound without being detected, electrocuted, detonated, or shot.

The flight commander, the lead pilot, studied the storage facility as the choppers approached. At first look the compound appeared to be deserted; there was no movement, no indication of activity at all. The only sign of life was a thin spout of steam that escaped from the electric-generator building. Drawing closer, the pilot could see the compound was indeed empty. Then he saw the dead soldiers. He studied the scene, then swallowed hard. "Sir, it ain't good," he said over the intercom system.

Four feet behind him was the mission commander, a special forces colonel with a thick neck and brown hair. The colonel swore softly, slamming his fist against his knee. Peter Zembeic sat behind the colonel. He too shook his head. The army special forces colonel glanced at the CIA man, then turned away.

"Continue," he instructed, looking forward again,

The lead pilot pressed his radio switch. "Animals, take the towers," he commanded. Almost instantly the four MH-60s fired Hellfire missiles at the guard towers that watched over the compound, the missiles impacting their targets in a burst of white heat, sending dust, smoke, and debris scattering through the air. Nothing moved in the compound, as broken pieces of brick and wood scattered across the dusty ground. The smoke blew away in the morning wind and the four guard towers were gone. The lead pilot braced, expecting to begin receiving return fire, hoping and praying his expectations would be fulfilled. But nothing happened, and the sickness rose a notch in his gut.

"Thirty seconds!" the copilot announced to the formation over the secure radio. Already he was slowing, pulling his chopper's nose into the air. Behind him the five other choppers began to slow, too. They were spread in a V formation, with the heavier MH-53s off on each side. The young army colonel, the mission commander, moved forward to look out the cockpit window. He glanced at the burning guard towers, then scanned the compound below. But for the dead bodies, it was empty. He cursed once again, but this time to himself.

Turning, the colonel pushed his helmet microphone to his lips and gave his final instructions to his men, all of whom, like he, were dressed in black uniforms. "Be careful, guys," he said, "it might not be the way it looks. There could be hostiles or friendlies, or a mixture of both. Either way, we don't care. Get in, get the target, and let's get out of town."

The choppers lined up to set down together inside the perimeter fence. Beside the open cabin doors, gunners stood ready to fire the .50-caliber weapons mounted on the combat helicopter's floors. Dust began to blow as the choppers slowed down.

The pilot studied the LZ, looking for a place to land that wouldn't crush a dead body. Still no enemy fire. "Gun One, anything?" he asked over his intercom.

"Negative, sir."

The pilot knew it was over, there was no doubt in his mind. Though it had only been a few hours, they were already too late.

The lead MH-60 set down amid a whirlwind of brown dust. The Delta team was out the door even before the chopper put all of its weight on its wheels. Peter remained in the chopper a few seconds, then followed the lead team. Behind, the other choppers set down in unison. In seconds, sixty soldiers were inside the perimeter wall, the teams spreading out, moving rapidly.

Two teams moved south, toward the headquarters compound, two others took up positions on opposite sides of the outer walls, covering the field of fire for the other teams. Blue One, the commander, the colonel in his black uniform, moved with his men toward the main underground bunker. Four black Honda ATVs screamed out of the back of the MH-53s, each of them pulling a small green trailer with reinforced steel walls and fat, airless tires. The four-wheeled machines were driven toward a barricade along the north wall. As the soldiers scattered through the compound, the combat helicopters lifted into the sky once again to set up a defensive ring and provide air cover. As the choppers lifted, the sky turned brown with dust, which settled very quickly as the sound of the choppers faded away.

Then it was eerily still. No movement. No soldiers. No sound anywhere.

The commander passed a fallen soldier and reached down

to put his hand at the dead man's neck. The skin was soft, but not cold, the flesh still tender to his touch. It had not been long. He checked his wrist dosimeter, which was still in the green. No indication of radioactive contamination in the air.

"Snooper?" he asked into his neck microphone.

"Initial readings negative," came the reply. "No chemical or biological HAZMAT detected."

The net radio broke over the commander's earpiece. It was the lead chopper, orbiting now to the south. "Blue One, we've got a little problem," he said tensely.

"What's up, pilot?" Blue One replied.

"We've got hostiles approaching! A convoy of military vehicles coming in from the west."

"Makeup?" the colonel demanded.

"APCs in the lead. Tanks. T-72s. Four—check that, six covered vehicles. Maybe more. I lose the tail end of the convoy in the dust."

"ETA?"

"Not long, sir. Five, maybe seven minutes."

The colonel turned toward the river, then looked at his watch and started a mental countdown. "Okay, people, let's move!"

Waldorf-Astoria Towers
New York City

The president sat alone in the ambassador's office. He made no pretense of work as he leaned back in his soft leather chair, staring at the sculptured ceiling over his head. He was surrounded by gold—deep golden drapes, light gold wallpaper, and gold-and-white carpet at his feet—and the office seemed to radiate from the city lights that shone through the bay windows looking out on Manhattan.

He glanced at his watch and shifted nervously. If the team was on schedule, they would have reached Sukkur by now. They would be searching through the compound. They would know very soon.

The president's gut tightened as he stared at the secure telephone on his desk. The SECDEF had sworn he would call him the second he heard anything. So the president waited, sitting at his desk while he listened to the small mantel clock tick away, counting the seconds, then the minutes that the team was in Sukkur.

CIA Headquarters
Langley, Virginia

Thomas Washington paced back and forth in the operations center, surrounded by communications specialist and satellite technicians, then turned to the large screen before him, near the front of the room.

"Anything?" he asked.

"Still nothing, sir," the technician replied.

"Check the system," Washington demanded. "We should have heard something by now."

The technician shook his head. "The communications system is fine, Dr. Washington. It does a self-check every ten seconds. There is nothing wrong. They've only been inside the compound for six minutes. Give them a little time, sir."

Washington stared at the technician and frowned. His instincts were screaming. He slowly shook his head.

Typhoon 57
Over the Atlantic Ocean

Colonel Shane Bradley sat near the back of the C-21. It was a small aircraft with only one seat on each side of the narrow isle, but, because it was VIP-configured, the seats were wider than most. The aircraft flew northeast and, crossing the English Channel, a young airman in a tight air-force-blue skirt brought Bradley a sandwich and Diet Coke.

"Can I get you anything else, sir?" she asked him.

"No, thanks, Airman Ripley."

Reading his body language, she left the colonel alone. It was painfully clear he did not want to chat.

Bradley took a bite of the sandwich then turned and stared out the small oval window at his right side. The C-21 was flying higher than most airliners could climb, and Bradley could tell from the high whine of the engines that the pilots were pushing the aircraft. He knew they had their instructions. Get him to D.C. as quick as they could.

He watched the cold channel pass beneath him, the surf along the beach shining in the moonlight, then the southern coastline of England curving gently to the north, the lights of the small towns along the coast twinkling in the clean air. Approaching the Northern Atlantic, the weather clouded over to form a smooth carpet that stretched in the moonlight as far as he could see. Bradley reached up and pulled his window shade down.

Beeping the airman, she came back to his seat. "Get me a satellite feed and a monitor," he said. "I'd like to watch the news."

"Yes, sir, of course," she said as she turned.

The airman returned with a portable flat screen LCD and plugged it into the communications outlet beside Bradley's seat. "BBC is channel 341," she said. "FOX is 213, CNN 243."

"Thanks," Bradley offered as he slipped the headset on.

CNN was running a commercial and he never trusted the BBC, so he settled on FOX, which was broadcasting live from Islamabad.

"It appears to be chaos," a blonde reporter was saying as Bradley tuned in. "The Pakistani constitution makes it clear that Prime Minister Natelez is the next in line of succession, but our sources are telling us that General Ali Khan Sanghar, commanding general of the armed forces, is claiming this is a national crisis and that he is in power. He has declared martial law and dispersed military units around Islamabad. And though all of the radio and television stations have been taken off the air, we have reports—and these are still unconfirmed—that the army is taking advantage of this opportunity. Soldiers are moving through the Shiva neighborhoods on the south and eastern outskirts of Islamabad and taking into custody suspected members of the Popular People's Rebellion, the leading antigovernment party.

"From where I am here, on the roof of the Ambassador Hotel in central Islamabad . . ." the camera broke away from the reporter and panned to the side, showing a wide darkness with only occasional pinpricks of light, ". . . you can see that electrical power has been cut to the entire city. The roads are dark, though masses are gathering in the streets and there is more than occasional gunfire below. We have been advised to stay in our rooms, and security forces have cordoned off our hotel. Though the Ambassador has private security, we are not at all confident that things may not turn ugly for us. As you can see"—the camera panned at an awkward angle to show the streets below—"crowds are gathering below us and on almost every street corner. The Ambassador, unfortunately, is well-known to house Western guests, and gunshots have already been fired through the lobby windows."

The reporter fell silent and a slight pause followed because of the satellite delay. The anchor in New York, his face taking up half of the split screen, looked grim. "We've heard most of the Pakistani cabinet and many of the military leaders have been assassinated," he said. "Are you hearing anything—has anyone claimed responsibility for the attacks against the Pakistani president and his cabinet?"

The reporter stared into the camera while she waited through the pause, then nodded. "Yes, we've heard the same rumors about the cabinet, but right now I can't confirm anything. All I can tell you is that there were almost simultaneous explosions at both the Interior and Defense ministry buildings, as well as central police headquarters."

"What about outside of the capital?"

"Outside of Islamabad we have no idea what's going on, though there are reports of military units on the road leading down to Faisalabad and Karachi. And remember Peter, there are many parts of Pakistan that have hardly developed past the fifteenth century. The south is fairly stable, but the northern and western provinces are run almost entirely by local tribal chiefs and warlords. Remnants of the Taliban control several strongholds in the mountains, and the local tribes in the west have always been some of their greatest supporters. I would guess that, even now—"

The New York anchor cut in, "Jane, Jane, let me interrupt you. We've just been informed . . ." He hesitated, then continued, "Jane, we're being told that the Indian government has just placed their military forces on the highest alert. The BBC is reporting there have been military incursions across the borders in the mountains around Kashmir. Of course we know that both Pakistan and India, sworn enemies for many generations, have an unknown number of nuclear weapons, but in light of what appears to be a quickly deteriorating situation, do you know if—"

Bradley reached over and snapped the monitor off.

No, they didn't know! No one had any idea. It was a sickening mess! No one knew what was going on!

Sukkur Military Facility
Sind Province (Eastern Pakistan)

The main bunker sat near the center of the compound, behind the electrified fence and small guard tower. It was a semiburied cement structure, forty feet wide and one hundred feet long. The walls were six feet of reinforced concrete, the roof multiple layers of concrete and steel plate. There was only one entrance, a narrow circular stairway that led to a steel door, fifteen feet below ground level. A small elevator shaft had been built beside the stairs, but it could only be controlled from inside the facility. There were no visible airshafts or vents. The structure was completely sealed.

The main contingent of special forces moved to the central bunker, taking up protective positions behind the firing walls. A single team moved toward a small outbuilding, the power generation plant. An explosion was heard, then the smell of black smoke filled the air. Four soldiers entered the building, moving quietly and quickly, knowing exactly where to go. The information from the architects proved to be exact. The power relay was shorted and the electrified fence lost its power. The soldiers hunkered near the firing bunkers and listened carefully, waiting for the hum of electricity to dissipate as the power went down. Moving quickly, a soldier tested the fence with an insolated wire, then quickly cut the wires, letting them fall on the ground. The main team of twelve men moved through the downed fence toward the central bunker, crouched at the waist, providing each other with cover, then spread out in a line on both sides of the stairs.

"Four minutes, team!" the helicopter pilot counted down.

Peter ran, crouching, across the brown dust and dropped down beside the colonel. The colonel waited until his men were in position, then lifted his finger and held out his hand. A captain moved forward with a satchel charge, pulled the pin, and dropped it down the winding stairway. The explosion was enormous. Dust and acid smoke filled the air.

The combat soldiers listened, not moving. There was no sound from the stairs, no movement, no sign of resistance at all.

Peter nearly screamed with frustration, his eyes squinting in anger. All the planning and sacrifice. The stakes were enormous, and he was sure they had failed.

But they had to be certain. So, someone had to go down.

He turned his eyes to the eastern sky. "Bird, say ETA of hostiles?" he demanded.

"Three minutes," came the reply.

Peter could see the column of dust rising above the dry plain from the riverside. The enemy convoy was so near, he could feel the ground rumble. The colonel followed his eyes, and Peter saw the look of defeat in his eye. "Colonel, if we're going to send someone down there, we better do it now," he said.

The young colonel nodded brusquely. "You going down with them?" he asked.

"If that's alright with you."

The colonel nodded, then turned to his executive officer,

his second in command. The exec, a lieutenant colonel, wiped his hands across his face, which was camouflaged gray. "Booby traps?" the colonel asked.

The exec shook his head. "Doubt it, sir. They didn't have enough time. I'd say chances are three or less on a scale of ten."

The colonel nodded, then eyed his XO. "Send Talbott's men in," he commanded. "Tell them they have ninety seconds and not one second more." The commander motioned to his exec, who began crawling toward the six-man team to his right, then nodded to Peter, who followed the exec, crawling on his elbows and knees.

The commander hit his radio mike. "Birds, be ready to get us out of here!"

"Ready there, boss," the lead chopper pilot replied.

The XO and his soldiers moved toward the top of the stairs, pressing themselves against the side of the half-buried bunker. They waited, then moved forward and down the smoky stairwell, disappearing quickly into the gloom and smoke, Peter moving comfortably in their midst. As the men disappeared down the dark stairwell, the commander listened on the tiny earpiece in his ear. It was less than a minute before he heard Peter's voice. "Strike a couple dozen warheads. There's nothing here, sir."

The commander sat back against the mud and brick wall.

"Hostiles, one minute!" the chopper pilot said over the net radio. "Choppers moving in."

A long and swollen pause followed. "What do we do?" Peter demanded over the radio.

"You got pictures and readings?" the colonel replied.

"Best as we can."

"Then let's get out of here!" The colonel heard two clicks in reply. He wiped the dust from his face as Peter and the soldiers emerged at the top of the stairs. "Let's go! Let's go!" he cried to his men.

The helicopters were already setting down in the compound, blowing dust out before them, filling the sky with brown sand. As the last chopper set down, a T-72 tank crashed through the main wall, sending more smoke and choking dust in the air. The U.S. soldiers ran for the choppers and in seconds were on board. Peter scrambled onto the lead chopper, the last man inside. He was barely on board, holding onto a seat brace, when the helicopter lurched violently into the air, just clearing the compound's outer wall. Peter pulled himself into his seat, the cabin door open, the dusty wind in his face, as the chopper dipped and rolled onto her side. He stared down at the desert while reaching for his lap belt to strap himself in, then glanced back to the compound, which he could now barely see.

The military vehicles had moved through the breach in the wall. Armored personnel carriers were disgorging their Pakistani combat teams.

But if they had come for the warheads, they were also too late. Peter watched them, then cursed and sat back in his seat.

The chopper pilot set a course, moving back over the desert.

It was a long and quiet flight all the way back to Camp Thor.

7

Word that the interdiction operation had failed came a little after ten in the evening. Within minutes, the president was on his way from New York back to D.C.

Meanwhile, the story of the assassinations in Pakistan had completely taken over the news. Cable news showed a nearly continual loop of the Pakistani 727 wreckage and the bombed-out Defense building, which was on fire still, flames reaching high in the early morning air. A short time later the power went out in Islamabad, cutting off most transmissions to the outside world. The U.S. embassy hunkered down, fortifying its outer walls. India announced it was placing its military forces on the highest state of alert, and shortly thereafter, the White House issued a terse and obviously incomplete statement. *The president is aware of the situation in Pakistan. He urges all parties to remain patient and calm. The United States government is working to stabilize the situation. The president will make a public statement once he has consulted with his staff and other world leaders.*

Other than that, neither the White House nor the Pentagon would have further comment.

◆ ◆ ◆

As his caravan pulled away from the Waldorf Towers amid a sea of press, the president commanded the White House tactical communications director to have the national security team available to brief him by the time he boarded Air Force One. There were only two members of the national security group on board the aircraft with him, the secretary of state and the chairman of the joint chiefs of staff, an air force four-star with a ridiculous number of ribbons on his chest. The others were scattered around the world, but would be tied in through secure telephone.

Seconds after the president boarded Air Force One it took to the air. The president moved to the main conference room near the front of the highly modified Boeing 747-400 where he sat, grim-faced, at the head of a wooden table surrounded by computers, communications gear, television screens, coffee makers, and anxious staff. Only the chairman of the joint chiefs and secretary of state sat with him at the table. The lower staff members, both military and civilian aids, occupied small swivel chairs lining the four walls. POTUS was fuming, literally seething inside. His lips pressed together and his eyes were intense. They narrowed as he spoke, but his voice remained calm. "So the mission was a failure," he said to his staff. It was a statement, not a question, and everyone remained still. The president glanced at his chairman. "We did not recover the weapons?" he said to confirm.

"No, Mr. President." Gen. Lowe H. Abram, the chairman of the joint chiefs, answered the president.

"Just like that. *Poof,* they're gone." The president grasped his hands together then quickly spread them apart. It was a visceral reaction, but the sarcasm of his gesture was not lost on this team.

General Abram nodded reluctantly.

"General," the president asked, leaning forward in his chair. "How much effort, how much time, how much money and manpower have gone into this operation to ensure that exactly this didn't happen?"

General Abram answered slowly. "Sir, apparently not

enough." The president snorted and the chairman went on. "They were very well prepared, Mr. President. It was a brilliantly executed plan."

The president nodded brusquely. That was obvious enough. "How many weapons do they have?" he asked in a tense voice. He tightened his gut as he waited for the reply.

The general paused. "As best we know, the Pakistani government has completed development and construction of twenty-four warheads, sir. All of the warheads were kept at Sukkur, the only secure nuclear facility they had."

The air went out of the president and he visibly deflated. His face grew pale and his hands shook in his lap. "Two dozen warheads," he repeated, his voice trailing off. A chill ran down his spine. There was nothing in the world he feared more than this. Twenty-four nuclear warheads in the enemy's hands—an enemy who had sworn to destroy the United States, an enemy who believed there were glory and waiting virgins in death, an enemy as bloodthirsty and hate-filled as any his nation had ever faced.

They could reach any place, from the ports in L.A. to downtown D.C. Overnight, the world had been turned on its head. He thought of an image, somewhere from deep in his mind, a wild-eyed Sunday morning preacher he had seen on TV. The preacher had conjured up an image from some obscure scripture and used it to coax a few more dollars from his flock. He could hear the minister's voice as he described the coming horror, a picture of death and destruction that was hanging over the world. *"And there came forth a great dragon with seven heads and fire."*

The president shook his head. The dragon didn't have seven heads. It had twenty-four.

He felt physically sick. He rubbed at his temples, then fixed his eyes on the general. "How powerful are the warheads?" he asked.

"It varies, Mr. President," the general replied. "From the information that has been provided to us, it appears that a majority of the weapons are in the five-to-twenty-five-kiloton range. A few are larger, perhaps by a factor of two."

The president felt the ball tighten up in his chest. "And the delivery systems?" he asked.

The general shook his head. "That sir, is where the news gets really bad. You see, Mr. President, the Pakistanis designed all of their weapons for tactical delivery; mortars, small rockets, some of their more advanced missile systems. All they were looking for was to lob them over the border into India. In addition, mobility and secrecy were their primary means of protecting the warheads from a counterattack, so all were designed to be very small. We considered this a weakness, for it degraded their reliability, but it did allow the Pakistanis an enormous range of attack options.

"And that, Mr. President, is what scares me so. The Pakistani warheads are small enough to be dropped from a Cessna flying over the border or put in the trunk of a car and driven downtown. Indeed, most of the warheads are so small they could easily be smuggled across the border from Mexico. The options are enormous. And that is the heart of our fear."

"And the codes? The command and control procedures and precautions?"

"Sir, the Pakistanis have never been able to develop sophisticated security systems into the weapons themselves. They are what we call "raw." There are safeguards, yes, but cracking the weapons won't be much harder than cracking a common bank safe. And anyway, Mr. President, we have to assume that whoever has the weapons also has the arming codes. Yes, the facility at Sukkur was taken by force, but the warhead storage bunker itself showed no signs of forced entry. Whoever stole the nuclear warheads knew the access codes and procedures to the bunker's only door. So we have to assume that the person or party also has access to the individual weapon codes."

The president swallowed, his mouth dry, as an uncomfortable silence filled the room. He lifted his eyes and stared at the communications box on the center of the table. "Who did this?" he demanded in a determined growl. Everyone understood the question was directed at the CIA chief.

Richard Braun, the CIA director, didn't answer as he thought. He was in his office back at Langley, surrounded by his senior staff. The director, a former cowboy and Wyoming senator, was one of the few men in D.C. who was willing to tell the president the truth. Hard-nosed, though soft-spoken, he and the president went back. Way back. They knew each other's secrets.

Normally arrogant and outspoken, the director was quiet now. He cleared his throat deeply, the secure telephone humming softly.

"Who has the warheads!?" the president demanded again.

The director's voice came over the phone. "Sir, the truth is we really don't know."

The president scowled. "Nothing? You have no idea at all!?"

"No sir, we don't."

It was the worst possible answer. Yet it was truth.

But the president knew who had taken the weapons. And he knew in his heart where they would appear. New York City, D.C., Jerusalem, or Tel Aviv. Chicago or L.A. Where they hit hardly mattered, he knew they would come. "Okay," he struggled to keep his anger in check. "What *do* we know, Richard? What is going on over there? Is there someone we can work with to find where the warheads have gone?"

"Sir, no one has stepped forward to claim responsibility for the assassinations. And the situation in Pakistan has gone from indescribable to worse. Over the last few hours, anyone tied to Massarif's government has either been killed or gone into hiding. Even now they are being hunted. Radical groups, tribal leaders and their local militias, clans and their families, these are the elements that control the reins of power inside Pakistan now. And while it looks like the army has maintained control of the major cities, it is also fractioned and likely to break into tribes. And it appears there is no central government or means of transferring authority. We don't know who to contact in order to establish a relationship. No one has stepped forward. Only our CIA agents and a few military forces are providing us any information right now, and there are very real concerns about the security of our assets in-country.

"There is no government in Pakistan, Mr. President, no military leadership, no pro-Western forces. We have no one there we can deal with, at least not at this time. Someone will emerge, of that I have little doubt, but for now we have no indication of who that might be."

The president leaned back in his leather chair and stared into space, feeling the aircraft bumping gently under his seat. "Who stole the weapons?" he demanded again as he cast a cold glare around the table.

No one moved. Many eyes stared at the floor. The president shook his head. "I know who took them," he said in answer to his own question. "And all of you know who stole them too. This has been their entire focus since the towers went down. And now it has happened. We knew this would come."

General Abram cleared his throat. He was a lean and no-nonsense man with Indian blood in his veins, his mother a full-blooded Apache, his father a street kid from St. Louis. He was a product of their fighting spirit, and his blood boiled now. "Mr. President," he growled, "I do not believe that al Qaeda acted alone. This was far too broad an operation to have been carried out without some kind of assistance."

The president frowned in agreement, then suddenly stood from his chair. "I want them located and I want them destroyed. We don't negotiate and we don't screw around."

The staff stood and faced the president as he began to walk from the room. "We meet again in the morning," he said to his staff. "Brief at seven o' clock. By then I want to know who has the weapons and how you intend to take them down." The president paused a quick moment as he passed through the door. "Who is this—this Donner—this operative who called out the DARKHORSE? Is he a legitimate asset? Why didn't he give us more time!"

The CIA director's voice answered through the speaker phone. "Ah, Mr. President, Donner is a HUMINT priority code."

◆ ◆ ◆

The president nodded. Human Intelligence priority code. Access to this information was limited to perhaps three or four men. It wasn't a subject that could be spoken of here, not even among his most senior staff. The president took a small step toward the telephone speaker in the middle of the table. "Okay then, who is handling the asset?" he asked.

"A man named Colonel Bradley, sir. He's an air force officer on loan to the agency."

"A military officer? Why not one of your men?"

The director paused a moment. "Sir, as I mentioned, Donner operations are a priority code."

"Alright, fine! When can I be briefed?"

"Sir, Bradley is on his way back from Israel right now. He'll RTB early morning."

"Fine. I want to see him immediately upon his return."

"Yes, Mr. President. We'll be there, sir."

8

D r. Thomas B. Washington was waiting for Colonel Bradley in the VIP lounge. The C-21 executive jet taxied to the front of the base-operations building and stopped, its red and white lights strobing the early morning darkness. Sunrise was still a half hour away, and the moon and the stars were blocked out by a thick bank of clouds, dark and rumbling and low to the ground. It was raining in the district, a constant and bone-chilling drizzle, and it caused a deep gloom to deepen the dark. A red path had been painted on the cement from the front door of the operations building to where the C-21 had come to a stop; a permanent red-carpet treatment for visiting dignitaries. An airman opened the small door of the C-21 as the aircraft came to a stop and Colonel Bradley, dressed now in air force blues, emerged and walked down the short steps. He held his briefcase over his head and walked briskly through the rain toward the operations building. The glass doors slid open as he approached. Washington was waiting there. He moved forward and took Bradley's hand in a crushing grip.

Washington was a huge man, with a bowling-pin torso, powerful walk, and a quick mind. He was as direct as a sledgehammer and impatient with time. Eighteen-hour days were the norm for him, and the early morning brief was not unusual, so he appeared showered and fresh and ready to go. Colonel Bradley, on the other hand, looked bone-tired and disheveled, having shaved and changed clothes in the cramped quarters of the small jet.

"You ready?" Washington asked as he shook the colonel's hand.

Bradley glanced at his watch. Just after six in the morning. "Seven o'clock briefing, right?" he replied.

Washington nodded.

"Have I got time?"

"No. I've got a driver waiting. We'll talk in the car." The DDO turned and started to make his way through the operations building, glancing at Bradley's uniform as they walked. "I brought a clean shirt if you need it," he said.

"I'm okay," Bradley answered. "I had my bag on the plane."

A young airman trotted into the foyer, carrying the worn leather suitcase he had pulled from the rear baggage compartment of the C-21. As the sliding glass doors opened, Bradley turned and nodded for him to follow, then continued to walk.

A shiny black SUV was waiting under the covered entrance out front, it's engine running, both back doors open, a driver behind the wheel, another agent waiting at the rear of the car. Bradley motioned toward the back of the heavy Suburban and the airman placed his suitcase inside. Turning, the young airman moved toward Colonel Bradley and asked, "Anything else I can do for you, sir?"

"Thank you, Airman Johnson," Bradley said. "I appreciate your help."

The airman stopped and saluted respectfully. "Anything at all?" He waited like a puppy, ready to jump at his command.

"No, thanks," Bradley answered. "You always do good work."

"Thank you, sir. It's always a pleasure to have you on board." The airman moved toward the operations building, hesitated, then stopped and glanced back. "Sir, if I may?" he asked in a hesitant voice. Bradley nodded and he went on. "Something's going on, sir, I can see that in your face. Whatever you're involved with, I wish you good luck."

Bradley nodded. "Thank you, Bobby," he answered, "now get back to your jet."

The airman saluted again, then trotted toward the building. Washington watched in silence. It was always the same. There was something about the colonel, he connected with his subordinates in a way that bred a loyalty that was both obvious and rare.

Washington and Bradley climbed into the back of the dark SUV. The driver and other agent sat in front, on the other side of a thick bulletproof and soundproof sheet of glass. The Suburban pulled away from the operations building and drove toward Andrews' front gate. Passing through the main gate, two police cars were waiting. They flipped on their lights as they fell into position, one ahead of the Chevy and one behind. Though it was still early morning, traffic into the district was already heavy and would only get worse. Hitting the on ramp, the cars were packed together, and the road ahead was a trail of flashing brake lights reflecting off the wet pavement. The caravan moved into the extreme left lane, the police lights flashing, the commuters moving out of its way.

Bradley settled back in the deep leather seat.

"You get any sleep on the way back?" Washington asked.

Bradley shook his head. "Too much to think about. Too much to do."

Washington eyed his man closely. "You ever briefed POTUS before?" he asked.

"You know I haven't, Tom," Bradley replied.

Washington shifted nervously. "Listen, Shane, I don't mean to state the obvious, but this is a whole different ball game, a whole different thing. To call this the World Series would be to understate things."

Bradley raised an eyebrow to Washington. "Really?" he answered sarcastically. He was edgy with fatigue and it showed in his voice.

Washington watched him a moment. "You want some advice?" He then asked, "Or you want to do this alone?"

Bradley hunched his shoulders. "I'm sorry," he answered. "It's been, you know, kind of a long flight. Kind of a long day."

"I understand. Now listen to me. Don't waste his time. Get to the point. This is an informal briefing on our history with Donner, so there won't be anyone but you, me, the president, and Director Braun in the room. That will make the entire thing a bit easier; what you say won't be recorded, and no notes will be taken by White House staff. So relax, be direct, but answer only his questions, and don't offer any more."

"He wants to know about Donner?"

"That's the whole reason we're going there."

Bradley turned to look out the window as the SUV passed the slower cars. "He's not going to be happy with what we tell him, will he?"

Washington grunted and cleared his throat. "No, he probably won't."

"I'm just guessing he isn't going to be in a good mood anyway."

"From what I heard, I think not. His guns will be blazing. But remember, Colonel Bradley, if he shoots you down, it isn't personal. You've been thrown in the lions den because you're the first Christian we could find, so don't take it personal if he rips off your head. This whole thing about Donner, it isn't something you could control."

"Don't shoot me, I'm just the messenger, right?"

"Yeah, something like that."

Bradley paused and thought. "If he asks me, am I free to answer? Can I say what I really think?"

Washington reached into his pocket and pulled out a piece of gum. "Be careful. Be tactful. Show judgment. Beware. But no, I'm not going to script this for you. We're not going to be able to please him, we know that going in. There are just too many holes, too many things we don't know. So let's accept our beatings, tuck our tails, and get out of there.

We've got a lot of work to do, and this thing with Donner is the least of our worries. We've got to answer his questions, but let's cut bait and run at the first chance we get."

Bradley nodded sullenly. Washington reached into his briefcase and handed him a red-bound briefing folder. "I thought you might want to brush up on a few dates and such."

Bradley glanced down at Donner's classified personnel folder that Washington had placed in his lap, then set it aside. "I don't need that," he said.

Washington nodded. He knew that Bradley wouldn't. But he wanted to be sure.

Twenty minutes later the motorcade moved through security at the side gate of the White House. Ten minutes after that, after passing through three separate checkpoints, Dr. Washington and Colonel Bradley were waiting outside the Oval Office door.

Standing there, Bradley felt it and shivered. There was something special in the air. This was the *White House*. He took a deep breath, smelling the energy there. It was the first time in his life he felt the raw pulse of power. Supremacy. Dominance. Absolute control. The future of nations. The lives of countless men. All of it folded together inside these walls.

He shifted uncomfortably and Washington eyed him and smiled. "You can feel it, eh?"

Bradley didn't answer as he stared at the wall; a portrait of Ronald Reagan, blue suit, red tie, dark hair, head cocked, the crooked smile.

The two men waited patently. The president, as always, was running behind, and the two men stood quietly until Bradley leaned toward his boss. "I can't continue serving two masters," he said.

Washington only grunted.

"If Donner follows the same pattern, this is the last we will hear of him in a very long while. It will probably be years—if we ever hear from him again. You don't need me now. I've done all I can."

Washington stared at the blue wallpaper and grunted again.

"I need to get back, Tom. It's hard on the wing. It's hard on me when I'm away. I was just getting settled when Donner popped up again. Now I want to get back to my B-2s. I'm a good commander, sir, and it's what I love most. It's also where I can be most useful to you."

Washington nodded slowly. "I know that," he said.

"Then you are going to release me?"

Washington clenched his jaw. "That's my intention. But if Donner makes contact again, I won't hesitate to pull you back in to liaise with him."

Bradley leaned back and nodded. It was all he could ask. A quick shiver of excitement ran through him. One White House meeting and he was back in the air.

The two men fell quiet again. Ten minutes later the wide door was thrown open and the President of the United States was standing there. Behind him, the CIA director stood near a white couch.

"Dr. Washington," the president said as he shook Washington's hand. He then turned to face Bradley and the colonel took a step forward. The president was taller than he had expected, his face more lined, his hair a bit thinner, his eyes deeper blue. He was handsome and confident, and Bradley felt unexpectedly at ease. "Colonel, welcome to the White House," the president said, sweeping his arm toward the Oval Office. "Come on, let's talk. There are a few things I'm anxious to have you tell me about."

The four men sat in two identical white couches on opposite sides of a highly polished coffee table. Washington and Bradley sat next to each other, the president and CIA director opposite them. The president glanced at his watch and began, "I've got a national security staff briefing in fifty minutes. I need some time to get ready, so let's make this quick, if we can."

Coffee had already been poured in four small china cups

that were surrounded on a silver tray by warm Danish pastries, soft butter, and jam. The president lifted a half-full cup of coffee, his face friendly but intense.

Washington sat on the edge of the couch, his huge bottom hanging halfway over the edge. "Sir," he answered simply. "What can we do for you?"

The president turned his attention to Bradley and got right to the point. "Tell me about Donner," he said.

Bradley sat with his elbows on his knees, staring the president right in the eye. "Sir, Donner is a human asset we have inside the fundamentalist community."

"You have an asset inside al Qaeda?" The president raised a suspicious eyebrow.

"Perhaps, sir. He might be. We really don't know."

The president paused. "You don't know where he is?"

"The truth is, we don't know anything about him, Mr. President. We don't know who he is, what role he plays, or where he gets his information. All we know is he sends us warnings from time to time, gives us good information—intelligence that so far has proven to be very accurate. He'll make contact with us, hit us with intelligence, then drop off the radar, sometimes for a very long time. And we never know if or when he will pop up again. He's an anonymous phone call, an e-mail, an overnight express, nothing that can be traced, and believe me, we've tried. For good or bad, modern-day technology makes it easy, Mr. President, to communicate anonymously from the other side of the world."

The president sat back and swore. "You're kidding me," he said.

Washington, anxious to get into the conversation, shook his head and said, "No sir, we're not. But Donner has been very good, Mr. President. We can count no fewer then six occasions when he had provided warning of an impending attack. The attempted bombing in Riyadh, the attack against the U.S.S. *Vincent*, the enriched uranium from North Korea, all were incidents we were able to thwart because of information that Donner provided. He's the one who tipped us off regarding the security breaches at Guantanamo Bay. He has provided information on the location of al Qaeda agents inside Iran, as well as the mullahs who were protecting and financing them. His help has proven extremely valuable over the years. He has saved American lives, there is no doubt about that." The president turned to the director, his eyebrow still raised. "He's been very valuable," the director confirmed.

"Yet, you don't know who he is?"

"No, sir, we don't."

He turned again to Bradley. "You've never met him?" he asked.

"No sir, I haven't. No one has ever met with him."

"How do you contact him?"

"He makes contact with us."

"Are you saying you have no means of initiating communication with him?"

Bradley hesitated, then answered, "That's correct, sir."

The president sat back in the couch. "Let me see if I understand. You have an asset. He's somewhere inside the loosely knit band of terrorist brothers. He seems to be able to provide a wide range of information, from al Qaeda operatives to potential attacks against U.S. assets. But you don't really know where he operates. You don't know who he is. And you have no way to contact him? Have I missed anything, or is that about all?"

Washington positioned himself even more on the edge of his seat, crushing the edge of the cushion with his enormous weight. "Mr. President, we do have some ideas who he might be," he answered. "But he is very elusive, as good as any agent I know. Donner is a professional, he knows what he's doing, and until he wants us to know more about him we're not going to find out."

The president considered this while he stared at his coffee. It was cool enough in the Oval Office that a fine wisp of steam could be seen drifting up from his cup. A roll of thunder groaned, vibrating the bulletproof windows against their ancient wood sills, and the rain could be heard pelting the windows and roof. He thought a long moment. The mental machinery churned. He turned to the colonel. "Alright, Colonel Bradley, how did you get involved?" he asked, shooting a quick glance to Washington, then bringing his eyes back to the man. "Why are you working with Donner? Why not one of Dr. Washington's agency men?"

Washington shifted, moving forward so far he barely sat on the edge of the couch, seeming to suspend his weight on his thick legs and knees. Always inanimate, his body language now screamed, anxious as he was to jump in. The president shot him a glance, warning him off, then focused on Bradley. He wanted to hear it from him.

"When Donner first made contact with us, he asked for a military liaison," the colonel explained.

"A military liaison?"

"Yes, sir. He wanted to work through an intermediary. A military man."

The president nodded slowly. "Okay. But why you? You were flying jets at the time. You were the commander of a bomber squadron, as I recall." Bradley looked up, surprised. Clearly, the president had been asking some questions. "So how in the world did you get involved with this?" the president pressed.

"Reluctantly, sir," Bradley answered.

The president huffed, understanding. "Okay. But reluctant or not, here you are. And I don't understand why."

"Donner asked for me, sir. It was one of the contingencies of him working with us."

The president cocked his head in surprise. "He asked for you?" he questioned.

"Yes, sir, he did. He demanded to work through only me."

"He asked for you specifically. Not an air force officer? Not a military pilot? You were a by-name request?"

"Yes, Mr. President, that is correct. The man we now refer to as Donner said he would only pass us information if he could work it through me."

The president shot another look toward his director, and hunched his shoulders in doubt. "You've got former military officers in your agency?" he questioned the CIA boss. "You've got officers from every service embedded within? Why Colonel Bradley? I don't understand."

"If I could, Mr. President?" Colonel Bradley said. The president shifted his eyes back to him and the colonel went on. "After graduating from the Air Force Academy, before I entered pilot training, I volunteered for special assignment to the United Nations peacekeeping forces in Gaza and along the West Bank. I spent more than three years working with the UN, Israel, and the Palestinians there. During that time I made a number of contacts, I wouldn't say friends, but associations—in some cases close associations—with various men. We think, although we really don't know, but we suspect that Donner might be connected in some way to the time that I spent working with the UN. He was someone I worked with then, or more likely someone associated with someone I worked with back then. We have been through my notes and the dossiers of suspects a dozen times or more, trying to match Donner with the men that I knew, but we haven't come up with a match, though we have a suspect or two. Still, at the end of the day, the truth is we simply don't know who he is."

POTUS sat back and swirled his coffee. The CIA director followed suit, eying the president carefully over the brim of his cup. Bradley didn't move as the president thought. Washington moved his hands to his knees, ready to push himself up.

"And that's all we know?" POTUS concluded.

Bradley shook his head. "That's about it."

"He warned us of DARKHORSE?"

"Yes sir, he did. But the rendezvous in the mountains took too much time." Bradley's mind flashed with a sudden image of the young girl's face, the only person in the world who could link them to Donner. "It took almost a week to make contact with his runner," he continued. "Donner selected such a remote location, it took us several days to get our agent there. By the time our man made the contact and brought the warning out, the coup in Pakistan was already underway."

"Okay. Fine. But now we've got a big problem. I got an NSA brief this morning, and from what I am hearing, my staff will come in shooting blanks. We don't have any more information on the warheads than we had yesterday. Is there any way Donner will help us find them?"

Washington took a breath, drawing the president's eyes toward him. "I doubt we'll get any assistance from Donner," he said solemnly. "If he follows his pattern, and we believe that he will, once he has exposed himself, he will quickly disappear. If there's one thing we've learned, self-preservation is his primary goal. He will help when he can, but only he chooses when, and if there is any hint, any indication he would be compromised, he always drops out of sight. So I suspect, Mr. President, our dealings with Donner may have come to an end, perhaps for a very long time, possibly forever. Once he sees that you are preparing to take action in Pakistan, he will lay very low."

POTUS ground his back teeth together, then glanced at his watch. "Alright then," he said, speaking more to himself than anyone in the room. "All right," he repeated, accepting the disappointment and mentally moving on. So Donner was out. They would find other ways. He shook his head then turned to the colonel. "If you don't expect to hear from Donner, what are you going to do now?" he asked.

Colonel Bradley hesitated, then glanced at Washington. "I hope to go back to my command," he replied.

"The B-2 wing in Missouri?"

Again, Bradley was surprised. The president knew more about him than he would have guessed. "Yes, sir," he answered. "I've been away from my wing while I've been acting as liaison with Donner, and I'm anxious to get back."

The president nodded, then leaned toward him, his voice now low and intent. "The B-2s are part of Group 21, aren't they?" he asked.

"Yes, Mr. President. We train regularly for Group 21 missions. We are ready to respond."

"Good, that's exactly what I need to hear. So be prepared, Colonel Bradley, for I may be calling on you."

The colonel nodded eagerly. "We'll be ready, sir."

The colonel and Washington were escorted out of the Oval Office by the president's chief of staff. They made their way through security, then paused under the veranda on the east lawn.

"When are you leaving?" Washington asked as he turned to Bradley.

Bradley paused as he moved his eyes to the sky. The rain had let up, the storm clouds having moved east, but there was still a fine drizzle and he shivered from the cold. "I have a few things to do here," he answered. "I've got to turn in my security badges and have my final debrief with your staff. Then I want to stop and see someone." He quickly thought of Peter's father.

Washington switched subjects, getting back to the comfort of work. "You know that Peter was on the DARK-HORSE intercept operation," he said. "He went down into the bunker himself. In fact, he was the one who realized the bunker door had not been breached by force, but opened through the use of the security code. I'm glad he was there. I just feel better when he's involved."

"We are lucky to have him."

Washington nodded his head.

"Where's he going now?" Bradley asked.

"I'm sending him back to Pakistan. Back to the mountains. We'll need him there."

Bradley nodded slowly. No way Peter was going to get back to the States in time to see his old man. Not now. Not for months. There was too much going on. His heart turned suddenly heavy. It was a high price to pay. And few people would know, and fewer still care. It was the way of a soldier. Part of their sacrifice.

Washington turned and started walking toward the waiting SUV. "You know," he said. "Shin Bet is holding a couple people for us."

Bradley turned quickly and lifted an eyebrow. "Are they holding al Qaeda?"

Washington grunted, as if it shouldn't be a surprise. "Yeah," he answered. "People we obviously couldn't bring back to the States, nor send down to mingle with the prisoners at Gitmo. There are a few prisoners we would prefer not to acknowledge we have, and the only way we can do that is to not take possession of them. So we have an agreement with Shin Bet that they will take care of these special cases for us. It works pretty well. We both get what we want." Washington paused fifteen feet from the black SUV and the driver got out and opened the rear door for them. He turned to face Bradley and lowered his voice. "I want to show pictures of the girl Peter met in the mountains to a man named Nashiri," he said.

Bradley stopped beside him. "I don't know what good that will do."

"Nashiri is the highest ranking member of al Qaeda that we have in captivity. If he recognizes the girl, that information could lead us to Donner. If Donner is inside his operation, then Nashiri will know."

"If he knows, he won't tell you."

"Oh, I think he will."

Bradley hunched his shoulders, than placed his hand on Washington's arm. "You do what you need to do," he said in a low voice. "And I wish you luck. But I have to tell you, I am so glad to be getting out of this work. It smells bad. It hurts. I'm not cut out for this. Get me back to my jets."

Washington grunted, then turned and walked for the car. Bradley followed and the two men climbed in silently.

9

Everyone was happy with the arrangement. The Americans didn't have to answer some very awkward questions from her people and it deflected criticism from some of the fence-sitting Arab nations as well. Moreover, the Israeli courts, after years of bombings and bloodshed, had already approved the "special measures" that permitted their intelligence organizations far more latitude in their interrogations than the U.S. courts or military tribunals would ever allow.

The agreement specifically stipulated that the United States and Shin Bet would share information. Sometimes this happened. Sometimes it did not. The reality was, there was often a gray line between the theory of an agreement and the real-world application in times of national stress. The Americans hid things. Shin Bet hid things as well. Some things were best kept secret, even from the most trusted friends.

As the Shin Bet leader stared at the paper that he held in his hand, he knew this was one of those times to keep a secret.

The three-star general who commanded Shin Bet stood in silence at his window, gazing out on the rising sun. A green pasture lay before him on the other side of the compound, and he watched a stallion and two mares graze the thick grass, wet and glistening with morning dew. Petate wished he was out there, as he did every morning, husbanding his horses, feeling his boots heavy as they soaked up the dew, bracing the cool bite of the early morning air. Tall and lanky, the general had a sharp edge to his features, and though he always spoke slowly, his mind was not a word, but a full page ahead of his mouth.

Petate took a deep breath and held it, then read the request once again. He studied the photographs that had been secure-faxed to him. Who was this girl? He had never seen her before. But still, something nagged him.

Dr. Washington wanted some answers.

So he would see what he could do. If Nashiri knew the girl, they would know soon.

But he had his suspicions as to what was going on. And if he was right, his nation had its own plan.

The Americans weren't the only ones who had considered the possibility that Pakistan might one day lose her nuclear arsenal. And if the situation had developed along the lines he suspected, then much of what he learned from Nashiri would not be passed to the United States.

Abd al-Rahim al Nashiri, a burly and sour-looking man in his midthirties, remained in his chair as the two interrogators entered the cell. A fine-haired captain approached the prisoner, and a slender civilian followed behind. As the men approached, Nashiri's eyes remained tight and sullen under a closely shaved scalp. He smelled of soap and harsh lye. The Israelis forced him to shower every day.

As the two men drew near him, Nashiri scowled belligerently. The thin-haired captain he had dealt with. But the other one, the tall one, he had not seen him before.

Nashiri studied the civilian in his dark jeans and loose shirt as he sat down, then looked away. Without introduction, the captain pulled an envelope from his briefcase and extracted five pictures, grainy and monochrome photographs showing various profiles of a young and beautiful girl. As he spread the photographs across the smooth table, the civilian kept his eyes focused on the prisoner.

Nashiri looked down, then took a sudden, shallow breath. His hands began to tremble and he hid them between his legs. He tried to force a blank face but it was already too late.

The captain leaned against the table. He had seen it too. The look on the prisoner's face. Nashiri knew the girl. He leaned into the prisoner. "Who is she!" he demanded in Arabic.

Nashiri cocked his head and remained silent.

The captain leaned closer and sneered, "You know her, Nashiri. Your eyes cannot lie."

Nashiri turned away.

The civilian took a step forward, his face perfectly calm. "Work with us, Nashiri," he said in a soft voice. "We feed you, care for you." He nodded toward the interrogation door and forced a compassionate stare. "We keep the ugly ones off you. At least we have until now. But you've heard the stories, Nashiri, you know what some of them will do. You have heard stories about the animals they are. And it's true, Nashiri, everything—and worse. You will be buried in pig's blood when they are finished with you.

"Think about that, Nashiri. Consider your options. You can do this easy, or you can do it slow. You can do it comfortably, or through the most exquisite pain. You know her, Nashiri, your eyes have already betrayed you."

The prisoner's shoulders slumped and he dropped his face to his palms. He wept like a child, gasping in uncontrollable sobs.

The two men looked at each other and frowned. It wasn't the way they would have chosen to do it, for, given time, they could have gotten the information without roughing him up.

But the Americans had insisted that time was of the essence. Absolutely critical. And if the Americans were worried, then they were worried too.

The two men dragged the prisoner back to his cell and left him alone. "Think about it, Nashiri," they said through the steel door. "Think about it awhile, while we get the roughing crew."

CIA Headquarters
Langley, Virginia

Thomas Washington waited as long as he could stand it, then picked up the phone and patched a call through to his man in Tel Aviv. "What's going on with those guys in the basement?" he demanded to know.

His subordinate hesitated, wishing he had something to report. "Nothing yet, sir. Looks like it might take some time."

"Time? Who's got time!? How much time will this take!?"

The young agent hesitated. "Sir," he finally answered. "I really believe they're doing all that they can."

"Tell them to do more."

The young agent grew frustrated. What did the boss want them to do? "Sir, you've got to sit back and take a breath," he said. "You can't expect miracles, at least not overnight. The Israelis are good, but they have rules too, and even with court-approved special measures it will take a few days, maybe longer, to get anything. You know how tough this can be, some of these guys never talk."

"This guy had better," Washington snapped, "or we all might be dead."

Shin Bet Auxiliary Outpost
Twelve Miles South of Tel Aviv

Abd al-Rahim al Nashiri lay motionless on the top of his bed, a bare piece of metal positioned in the center of the cell. He closed his eyes and shifted his body, listening to the plastic mattress crinkling under his weight.

The picture of the girl flashed again and again in his mind. He knew who she was. He knew who she worked for. And that was the problem. He just knew too much.

He opened his eyes and studied his cell, which was brightly lit from the florescent light overhead. It was quiet and he guessed it to be early morning. He wasn't wearing a shirt, and his pajama bottoms hung loosely around his thin waist. His cell was smooth with bare walls, a simple hole for a toilet, and no windows or bars. His one blanket, a small patch of cotton, had a wire stitched around the edges to keep him from tearing it in strips and creating a rope with which he could hang himself. The camera in the top corner of his cell kept a focused lens upon him. They watched him every second. He was never out of their sight. Which made his task much more difficult.

But he was prepared.

He had taught others to do it. He knew what to do. And like the other al Qaeda leaders, the necessary tool had been implanted in his ear, the agreed upon method of keeping their secrets safe.

But he would have to move quickly, before they could rush into the room.

Pushing himself to his knees, he crossed his legs on the bed, reached up and placed his little finger into his right ear. He could barely touch the tiny glass capsule, a custom-fit vial, about the size of a pencil eraser, that had been surgically implanted under the skin. It had a very sharp edge pointing into his ear. He positioned his finger squarely on the very tip of the glass, feeling it carefully through the thin skin, then took a deep breath. He closed his eyes, thought of his family, wondering for the last time where they were, said a prayer that committed himself to God, then braced himself for the pain. Satisfied, he shoved the glass vial inward as far as he could.

The pointed end of the vial cut into his inner ear, then shattered, releasing the cyanide concentrate. His neck snapped to the side and his eyes flung open, but he did not cry out. He bit his lower lip, almost cutting it through, then lowered his head onto his folded arms.

The burn began in his throat, but soon spread through his chest, an enormous fist squeezing the breath from his lungs. It tightened more fiercely and he exhaled warm breath. The burn spread to his groin and then down his legs and he kicked involuntarily, spreading his feet. His blood was on fire! It burned everywhere! His lungs punctured like balloons, incapable of taking in air. Then the fire raced up his back and into his skull. He snapped his neck back and finally cried out, then stared with blank eyes, looking into the camera that he could no longer see.

Seconds later, two panicked guards rushed into the bare room. But the cyanide had already swept through him and there was not a thing they could do.

Petate took the news of Nashiri's death with little emotion. He nodded at his assistant, huffed, then dismissed him with a wave of his hand.

It was just as well, he thought as the aide left the room. He had already guessed everything Nashiri might tell him, and this gave him an excuse for not having to tell the United States.

Qy-5 Underground Bunker
Al Ram, Extreme Northern Pakistan

As Nashiri slipped into sleep, sucking in his last breath, thirteen hundred miles to the east the senior council of the conspiracy met for the first time since the coup. They called themselves *Alsaque el Allah,* or the Sons of God, and they were the new leaders of al Qaeda, dedicated to destroying the United States. The Great One, the Anointed One, Direct Descendent of the Prophet, the Giver of Laws, sat at the head of a makeshift table deep in an underground compound the Soviets had excavated during the Afghanistan war, and glared at his men, taking short, angry breaths. "The warheads are gone?" he demanded in an agonized tone.

The room was deadly silent. "Yes, my *Sayid,*" his chief lieutenant began to explain. "They were taken from the compound a few hours before we shot the president's aircraft down."

The leader glared at his deputy with fatal, dull eyes. His hands began to tremble and his forehead creased. His anger was rising, like a sudden storm, and his men turned away, bracing for his rage.

The Great One was a violent and unpredictable man. Wealthy and pampered as a youth, he chose now to live in a tent. Unafraid of eating raw meat, he washed his hands constantly. They said he that he had several wives and many children, but he never spoke of them, and it had been several years since he had made any attempt to go home. His family, long abandoned, had eventually made its way to Lebanon. Gentle to animals and a student of the stars, the Great One spent many quiet nights alone, staring at the night sky, yet he had a violent temper and thought nothing of death; condemning men to die as easily as he ordered lunch, though he gave more thought to the menu than to their innocence. And there was no logic to his emotions, which often raged out of control, as if some secret switch turned off and on in his head.

Sitting around the table, his men held their breath, hoping the rising storm would not focus on them.

"The Americans stole the warheads!" the Great One screamed as he jabbed at the air.

"No, my *Sayid*—"

"Of course they did, fool! Do you think that I'm stupid!"

His chief lieutenant hesitated, avoiding his master's eyes. "*Sayid*, the Americans do not have the warheads," he said.

"Of course they do, fool!! They beat us to Sukkur!"

"No, my *Sayid*." The lieutenant respectfully bowed his head. "The United States didn't get the warheads. We know that is true, for we had a man watching, hidden in the hills above the compound. The warheads were taken long before the Americans got there."

"Then where are they, Imad!" the Great Leader demanded, a salty bead of sweat running under his chin.

"Unknown soldiers slipped into Sukkur and took the warheads a few hours before the coup," the lieutenant explained. "Someone must have warned them. That is all that we know."

The leader stood angrily, cursing the news. He stomped around the table, slamming his fist into his palm. "They were ours! They were the first Muslim bombs! Do you understand how effectively we could have extracted our revenge! Now, I want you to tell me how you let this great gift slip away!"

The leader stopped and grew sullen. His lieutenant didn't answer. The other men were silent. No one even dared move.

"Someone warned the Pakistanis," the lieutenant repeated. "There was nothing more we could do."

"Then there is a traitor among us," the Great Leader hissed angrily. "But do not worry, my brothers, I *will* find who he is! I will tear out his guts and hold his heart in my palm. He will pay the price of betrayal, I promise you that."

"Yes, *Sayid,* yes, if you were only to instruct us, we could go after him."

"No! No time now! We have other issues we must deal with first. We *must* find the warheads before the Americans do!"

10

Peter Zembeic rode his horse into camp two hours before the sun would rise over the hump on the ridge. It
was cold and the moisture in his breath had matted his
beard. In the west, clouds were moving. It was soon going to
rain. His hands were cold and his knees ached from holding
himself in the saddle, but his body was warm and sweat
damped his back under his loose-fitting clothes. Behind him
his partners, a Tajik and a Kurd, followed on their horses, riding low on their saddles, good riders, but not as expert as he.
It had been a seven-hour ride from the chopper LZ, a mean-
dering journey through the high mountains designed to make
it more difficult for observers to locate their base camp.

Entering camp, Peter dismounted and patted his horse.
Isabel snorted softly and lifted her ears. She was a very good
mount, sturdy, yet skittish with any other man on her back.
He rubbed the sweat from her shoulders and patted her
flanks. She snorted and leaned toward him, looking for him
to take off the bridle so she could roll in the dirt. He loosed
the horse, then walked into the command post where a
young army Ranger was waiting, a blond man with a butch
haircut and muscles so tight he could rip the sleeves on his

shirt. The Ranger looked up and smiled, a relieved look on his face. "Welcome back, Peter. Good to see you," he said.

Peter glanced around at the too familiar surroundings. His three week R and R and debrief in Israel had lasted just a couple days. Still, it was good to be back, at least in some ways, here among his comrades and subordinates, his friends. He walked to an old ice chest, a plastic cooler one of the men had commandeered from a BX in Karachi, and reached in and pulled out a lukewarm beer.

"Didn't think we'd see you so soon," the Ranger continued as Peter wiped the water from the side of the can.

He popped the top and sucked on the beer. It was warm and fuzzy, but he didn't care. "Just love you guys too much to stay away," he replied.

The Ranger grunted. Word of the catastrophe in Pakistan had already spread through the camp. He eyed the CIA agent. "Hear it's turning ugly over there."

Peter swallowed and nodded.

"All of them?" the soldier pressed.

"Every single one," Peter answered.

"Twenty-four?"

"Yep."

The Ranger stared at the floor, swore silently, then glanced up. "I'm sorry, Peter," he said, his face softened with emotion. "All of us are. I know you were hoping to get back to D.C. But man, I have to tell you I'm happy to have you back here. It just isn't the same. I know that makes me selfish, but I'm still glad you're here."

Peter glanced at the Ranger. "Thanks, Bart—I think." He took a long drink to finish the beer.

"How was the ride?" the Ranger asked. Peter only grunted and the Ranger nodded to the predawn darkness outside. "I love riding under the moon," he said.

"Yeah, I like it too. You can sleep in the saddle, and it's peaceful and quiet, except at those times when someone is shooting at you. Gives one time to think. I like a night ride."

"I spent all night with Abu," the Ranger said as he turned to his propane-powered griddle where he was making pancakes.

"How is the old general?"

"Same as yesterday. Same as last year. The old man's like the mountains, he doesn't change much."

The Ranger began to recount his evening with a local warlord, one of many who had helped the United States fight the insurgent Iranians and regenerating Taliban. He talked as he mixed, making up pancake batter, describing a meeting in which twenty-minutes-worth of business was crammed into almost six hours of smoking, talking, and staring into the fire, of complementing each other and cursing their enemies, of listening to sheep bells and watching for falling stars—an omen of the spirits being with them that night. After declining once again the invitation to spend the night with one of his wives, the Ranger had left the tribal leader with a firm embrace, many kisses, and two hundred thousand dollars in cash. That would keep the general and his small army happy for the next six months or so.

The Ranger debriefed Peter over pancakes. He ate them one by one as they slid off the miniature grill. The men talked for an hour, then Peter headed for his tent for a few hours sleep.

"What's going to happen in Pakistan?" the captain asked as Peter pulled his parka on.

Peter thought for a moment, then shook his head. "It's scary," he answered.

"We've seen scary things before."

"We haven't seen this."

The Ranger nodded anxiously, then poured another pancake onto the hot grill.

Shin Bet Headquarters Compound
Tel Aviv, Israel

General Petate was eating a late lunch—fried cheese balls, steak, and red beans (he had serious doubts about living long enough to develop heart disease)—when he was interrupted by one of his staff. Petate glanced to his wife and shrugged. It was the first time in two weeks they had sat down together to eat and they had enjoyed twenty minutes alone before being interrupted, almost a record since he had taken this job.

Petate shot a look to the major who stood at their apartment door. "Excuse me, dear," he muttered softly as he pushed himself up.

"You want me to fix you a plate to take with you?" she asked.

Petate shook his head and shoved another cheese ball into his mouth. "Delicious," he told her as he turned for the door. "Save me some for tonight."

"I might see you later, then?" she asked him.

"Hope so," he said.

The major and a driver were ready to take the Shin Bet director to the command center on the other side of the compound. The command center had been constructed under a long, low brick building that looked like a warehouse, and it only took three minutes to get there. The vehicle passed through multiple cement barricades and security gates, then dropped down a steeply sloped drive that led under the building. Another aid was waiting, and he opened the door for Petate when his SUV came to a stop.

The three men walked immediately into the command center and down a long hallway with steel doors on each side, their boots clicking on the highly polished tile floor as they walked. Dropping down three more flights of stairs, Petate moved into his office and sat on the corner of his desk. His deputy was waiting, a smug smile on his face.

"Okay, what you got?" Petate asked him, though he already knew it was good. It took a groundbreaking moment to get his deputy to crack a grin, and he was smiling like a seventh-grader who had just kissed his first girl.

The deputy waited.

"Come on!" Petate demanded, though he was smiling now too.

"We've been watching the American," the deputy began.

"You're talking Peter Zembeic, Washington's man?"

The deputy nodded. "He's back at Camp Cowboy. But while surveying the area, one of our guys identified someone else."

"Who?"

The deputy dropped an eight-by-ten, black-and-white photograph on the desk. It was grainy and dark and showed a man walking through the crowded slums of Peshawar. Petate picked up the picture. "Who is it?" he asked.

"His name is Ali bin Estasharn Khanaqin. He's been hanging around the area for the past couple days."

The director stared at the picture. "Never heard of him," he said.

"Neither had we until a couple months ago. But we've done a little searching and we think we know who he is. More, we think we know who he works for."

Petate waited and the deputy explained. By the time he was finished, Petate was smiling too. "I told you!" he said, a satisfied look on his face. "Now keep an eye on Zembeic! Never let him out of our sight."

Camp Cowboy
Northern Afghanistan

Peter Zembeic walked through the camp to his tent, an eight-man NorthFace with double-ply walls and a small wood-burning stove. He took off his damp clothes and put on dry socks, then climbed into his sleeping bag atop his aluminum cot. By the time he slipped into his bag it was starting to drizzle; by the time he was warm it was pouring in sheets, a cold and bone-chilling rain, normal for this time of year. He listened to the rain running down the tent's overfly, gathering into muddy streams on the ground that ran down the hill.

He started to drift. But in the quiet moment, somewhere between the reality of the world and the comfort of sleep, he thought again of his father, the last time he had seen him.

◆ ◆ ◆

Peter stood for a moment at the heavy wood door, the hospital bustling around him, nurses and aides hustling up and down the halls. Patients, all old men, walked slowly in their immodest gowns, bare flesh and hairy legs embarrassingly obvious. Some moved with walkers; a few, the lucky ones, walked holding the arm of a family member or friend. He took a deep breath, clenched his jaw, then pushed back the hospital door.

The four beds lined the room, two on the right and two on the left. The TV in the upper corner was on, but no one was watching and the sound was turned down. He glanced at the patients, four old dying men. Which was his father? How could he not tell? Could the cancer have changed his father's appearance so much? He studied the patients, then finally recognized his dad. His eyes, drooping hoods, were closed in deep sleep, his face taut and bony, with splotches of red.

Peter tightened his shoulders and moved toward his dad, brushing back the thin hair while leaning over the bed. He stood without moving for a very long time. The room was quiet and he gently stroked his father's forehead. The skin, warm and tender, was stretched over the bone.

His father, Norman Allen Zembeic, a South African immigrant who had immigrated to the States when he was only sixteen, had been sworn an American citizen and enlisted in the army on the same day. He served in the Vietnam War, then worked the rest of his life in the steel mills outside of Detroit. His wife, a good woman whom Peter could barely remember, had been killed in a car accident when Peter was just four years old. It had been the two of them ever since, always having each other, but both of them feeling alone, knowing they were missing a very special part of their lives. As a kid, Peter sometimes wondered who missed her most, he or his father. As the years passed he concluded it was harder on his dad.

Peter's father coughed and shook the bed, rocking it gently on its squeaking wheels. Peter pulled his hand back and his father opened his eyes, staring for a moment before he recognized his son. "Peter. What are you doing here?" he finally mumbled. His speech was slurred and weakened and he wet his dry lips.

"They brought me home, Dad."

"I thought you were in . . . I don't know . . . over there." His father waved toward the east with a trembling hand.

"I was. They let me come home."

"Well, well, that's really nice." The old man's voice trailed off and he struggled to swallow. Peter lifted a small glass of water off the bedside tray and positioned the straw to his father's lips. The old man drank, taking two tiny sips before relaxing back into the thin pillow. "Did you see Doctor, uh . . . what's his name?" his father asked.

"Doctor Mortenson."

"Yeah. Dr. Mortenson. He's very nice."

Peter nodded. "Did Doctor Mortenson tell you . . . did he, uh, tell you anything?" he asked.

"He told me I was going to die."

Peter paused. "We're all going to die."

"I'm going to die soon."

Peter looked away, then answered, "I know you are, Dad."

The old man coughed again, then stared at the window. "It's okay, Peter. I'm not afraid any more. But you know, this cancer, it hurts. It really hurts sometimes. If you have an option, I'd recommend something else. Get run over by a semi, jump off a cliff. Do something quick. That's my recommendation to you."

"I'm sorry, Dad," Peter whispered.

"Sorry for what?"

"Sorry it hurts. Sorry for everything."

"That's okay, Son. I understand. What have I got, a couple months, a couple weeks? I'm sure you've talked to the doctors, you probably know more than I do." The old man brought a shaking hand to his lips, wiping feebly.

"Dad," Peter answered softly, "I'm in the middle of something. I don't have much time. It's kind of hard to explain. But I can't stay very long."

"What you are doing is important. You do what you have to do."

"Is there anything I can get you?"

"How about a cigarette."

"You haven't smoked in forty years, Dad."

"And a beer."

"I'm not so sure that's a great idea."

"Yeah. Okay. I'll slurp on some Jell-O instead."

Peter pulled back and straightened up, placing his hands on the chrome rail that ran down the side of the bed. The old man wiped his chin again. "When will you come back?" he asked.

"I don't know, Dad. A couple weeks. Maybe longer. Maybe shorter. It's really hard for me to know."

His father strained against the pillow, reaching for his hand. "I understand," he said, repeating his assurance again.

That was seven weeks ago. Peter thought of his father while listening to the sounds of the night, the wind through the bare trees and the rain coming down. Isabel neighed from the meadow, but the rain muffled her sound.

He missed his father, but he *had* to be here. He was ashamed to admit it, but he wouldn't have changed things, even if he could.

His father didn't need him, but his country did. And he needed the feeling of doing something good.

He was ten thousand miles from his boss, a thousand miles from a hot bath, weeks away from a good meal, and who knows how long from home. But his tent was dry and secure, and it had a raised wooden floor. It was comfortable and private, and he had room for his tools. His gear was well stowed and well cared for, and he had a meal in his belly. He had a mission. He was good at it. He was exhausted and tired, but also satisfied.

This was the only thing he knew. And sometimes in the quiet moments, when there was no one around, when he would stare at the incredible mountains reaching up to twenty-eight thousand feet and the sky, so dark blue it look like it had been painted by God—at those times it all came together to make him feel small. And in those times the questions came to him and he asked himself why? Why did he stay? Why not go back to the States? Get a job? Make some money? Add some more to his stash? Sleep in on Saturdays, mow the lawn, watch football on TV. Get married, have a kid. Would that be such a bad life?

And yet here he was, in this tent, on this cold, rainy day.

He knew it wasn't the absence of options that drove him to stay. It was the joy of a *mission,* something one man in a million would ever understand in his life. Other men endured their jobs, and to what purpose, he asked? Money? Power? Maybe a little prestige? Everything they worked for amounted to diddly-squat; more money, bigger houses, more and more empty air. None of them would ever know the feeling of having a purpose in life. And he couldn't stand the thought of living without the overwhelming satisfaction of doing something *right.*

He had a good horse, a good tent, and friends who would lay down their lives to fight for him, if it ever came to that. It was all he could ask for, all he would ever need.

Peter breathed deep, satisfied, letting himself drift away. He muttered a silent prayer for his father, then put thoughts of him aside. He rolled onto his back and instantly fell asleep, exhaustion allowing him to sleep the entire day.

Fifty minutes after dark, a bearded man slipped into his tent. The night wind barely whispered as he moved inside, gliding toward the cot where Peter was asleep. Peter felt him more than he heard him and was instantly awake. He kept his eyes closed in tiny slits, his breathing heavy and thick, as he slowly, almost imperceptibly, moved his hand for the weapon taped to the underside of his cot.

Sensing the motion, the Arab quickly spoke. "Mr. Zembeic," he whispered, his voice a rasp in the dark. "*Sayid,* please, I have been sent here for you."

With a flicker of motion, Peter had the weapon in his hand and trained on the intruder. There was a metallic *click* in the night. "Who are you?" Peter demanded, a deadly edge in his voice. "You have two seconds to answer before I make a mess in my tent."

"*Sayid.*" The intruder slowly lifted his hands. "If I had wanted to kill you, you would already be dead. Do you think me incompetent? How did I get past your guards? How did I get into your camp? How did I know where you sleep? So please, my *Sayid,* put your weapon away. Please, we must hurry. You must come with me."

Peter rolled his legs over, sitting on the edge of his cot. He held the firearm ready, locked on the stranger's head. "Who are you?" he demanded. "And quick with an answer. The fact that you didn't kill me buys you no goodwill."

"Yes, my *Sayid,* but first you should know. Donner has something to show you. Now quickly, get dressed. We have such a long way to go."

11

Twenty-five hours after crawling out of his tent, the CIA agent was stripped, searched, commanded to re-dress, handcuffed, and blindfolded. A thick burlap sack was jerked violently over his head. His feet were bound with wire linked by a short, rusted chain. Under the sack, he found it difficult to breathe and the moisture from his breath soon condensed on his face. The agent was placed in the back of an old army truck, a deuce and a half with bald tires and a green canvas stretched over the back. Though bound, he was left unguarded, free to escape if he chose. But he didn't. He waited. The army truck's engine roared to life and the vehicle started to roll. The night passed slowly as the truck bounced over rough Pakistani roads. At times the vehicle moved at highway speed along roughly paved sections, at times it crawled slowly over treacherous terrain. It wound through steep mountain passes, then along flat valley roads. For the first thirty minutes Peter tried to estimate where he was, but he soon knew it was hopeless, and by the time the truck slowed to a stop, he couldn't have estimated his position within two hundred miles. He could have been in Pakistan, Afghanistan, or Kashmir. He could have been north of Islamabad or south of Kabul. Which was, of course, the point.

After stopping, all was quiet. Nothing moved and the night was very still. Peter listened as the driver's door opened and slammed shut. He could hear the crunch of heavy footsteps across loose gravel, the sound of the wind, but nothing more. No one was there to meet the driver. As far as he could tell, the two men were alone. He listened carefully as the footsteps moved to his left, then leaned anxiously toward the back of the truck. The deuce's canvas top slapped from a sudden gust of wind and a draft of cold air blew through a gap at his side. It was cold. Very cold. The air was thin and bitter. They were high in the mountains, that much he guessed.

He listened as the footsteps fell out of range. Many minutes went by and he became more frustrated and angry. His legs were cramping up and his hands were swollen and sore. The sound of footsteps returned. The driver, still alone, stopped and coughed, then urinated against the side of the truck. The agent waited but didn't speak.

"Stand up," the driver ordered as he flipped the canvas top and dropped the tailgate. "Walk toward the sound of my voice."

Peter pushed himself up and moved to the back of the truck, taking tiny steps against the restraints that bound his ankles together. His legs were so cramped that he could hardly walk, and the darkness of the hood made him cautious and slow. Feeling the emptiness with his right foot, he stopped at the back edge of the deuce's platform and held out his hands. "Uncuff me," he demanded.

The driver reached up and pulled the American violently to the ground, steadying the agent before he could fall to his knees. He swung him around. "I hope you had a most pleasant ride," the Arab mocked.

Peter stood tall, brushing the Arab's hands off of his coat. He stretched forth his hands. "I have done as you asked.

Now uncuff me. Loose my leg bands. My hands have lost feeling. You have the handcuffs too tight."

The driver laughed sarcastically. "Alright, *Rasul al-Laylat*. I will do as you say."

It took only seconds for the Arab to remove the handcuffs and chains from his feet. The last thing he did was pull the black sack off the agent's head.

Peter looked quickly around while rubbing his wrists. It was very dark. High shadows of mountains reached upward in every direction—deep, craggy cliffs illuminated by the low moon. The stars were clear and bright. Peter instinctively searched for the North Star, which was off to his right. The mountains ran almost north and south, which would put them on the west end of the Ladakh range. Light snow lined the road, which ran around the edge of a south-facing cliff. At the base of the cliff Peter could make out the entrance of a cave. He glanced at the sky once again, searching the skyline for an identifiable mountain peak.

The Arab caught the American searching the sky and lifted his flashlight to shine the light in his eyes. "Move!" he commanded, motioning toward the entrance of the cave.

Peter remained still as he studied the stranger's face. "Who are you?" he asked.

The stranger was short and squat, with a deeply-creased face and black, wavy hair. His beardless chin was narrow, his eyes evil and mean. He glared at the American. "You call me Donner," he said.

"Yes. But *who* are you?"

"You will never find out."

"I need to know—"

"You need nothing but what I'm about to show you!" Donner sneered. "Who I am doesn't matter. All that matters is what I give you. So, shut up! Follow me!"

The Arab reached up and pushed Peter toward the cave entrance. Peter stumbled, then stopped and the Arab stepped closer to him. "Decide!" he demanded in a menacing tone. "Do you want to see what I have to show you? Or do I shoot you in the head and leave your dead body here? I can have it either way. But if you want me to work with you, stop asking questions and do as I say!"

The Arab stared at the agent, his lips curling back in a snarl. Peter studied his eyes—the eyes of snake, cold, dead, and lifeless, reflecting the dark of the night. He memorized his features, then turned for the cave.

The entrance was only four feet high, and rough with sharp rocks. Peter bent over and stepped through the hole in the mountain while the Arab illuminated the entrance with his flashlight. The passageway narrowed and climbed slightly upward, where crude steps had been carved into the rock. Fifteen feet back from the entrance, Peter came to a thick steel door. The door was half open, and when he pushed it moved easily on its well-oiled hinges. He stepped into a large cavern where the air was moist and warm. Artificial heat was being generated somewhere. He took a deep breath, then touched the wall with the tip of his fingers. It was smooth and evenly cut. There were no calcified deposits. This was a man-made enclosure, not a natural cave. The Arab moved behind him, then flashed the light into the enormous room. Peter looked quickly left and right, but the darkness swallowed up the small beam of light. "Are you ready, *Rasul al-Laylat?*" the Arab asked, his voice raspy from a life spent sucking on cigarettes.

Peter pressed his lips together and the Arab moved forward, holding the light before him, then came to a sudden stop. Peter followed. Then he saw them and he took a quick breath. His heart slammed inside him.

The shiny chrome containers flashed under the narrow beam of the flashlight. The steel boxes were tight and double locked, but small enough to be lifted by two or three men. Peter moved forward to touch one, feeling its warmth. The Arab reached into his pocket and extracted a small dosimeter. He held it in front of him, then took a step back. Peter could hear the electronic instrument clack rapidly. "I wouldn't get too close," the Arab instructed. "The weapons are functional, but they are not built to the same standards as you might expect. They leak radiation. And those containers—well, as you can see, I had to improvise. The original lead crates were simply too heavy to be moved by hand."

Peter stepped away from the weapons. "Are they real?" he asked.

"Of course!" the Arab sneered. "Do you think I would drag you out here to stare at howitzer shells!? Would you like to see the dosimeter readout yourself? Now, let's go. We can only stay in here a few minutes."

The American didn't move. "I need to know for certain," he demanded.

The Arab swore, then moved forward and opened a crate. The dosimeter chattered more rapidly as the CIA agent stepped forward, edging toward the box. Inside was a single cylinder, eighteen inches long, blunt on both ends, silver and perfectly smooth. The CIA agent leaned forward, but the Arab stepped back. Peter reached out to touch the warhead. It seemed to hum, almost vibrate, and he pulled his hand away. The Arab moved forward and hastily closed the container, then shoved the dosimeter into the agent's hand. "It has an internal memory function. That will confirm for your people what they need to know."

Peter dropped his head toward the warheads. "Who else knows they are here?" he asked.

"Only them." The Arab flashed the light into the farthest corner of the cave. Peter saw the bodies and took a step back. The dead men were stacked neatly, perhaps half a dozen in all. Arms and legs jutted from the pile in unnatural angles. Eyes, dry and empty, stared blankly at him. They were soldiers, all dressed in combat fatigues.

"General Chaman," the Arab explained, shining the light on a dead general's face near the top of the pile. "Director, special weapons. In charge of Pakistan's nuclear arsenal. He agreed to help me protect the warheads. This wasn't the outcome he expected, but it will have to do."

Peter turned to the Arab, disgust in his eyes. The Arab shrugged. "I needed his help. I needed his men. I am not a man of power. I could not do this myself. Unfortunately for them, I then needed them dead. For my plan to work, I need this information alone. So I took appropriate steps to ensure this information was secure.

"And now it is done. As we stand here and speak, I am the only living man on the face of the earth who knows where these weapons are. I know the exact location, the grid coordinates down to the inch. But others are looking. The warheads will be found. Al Qaeda is looking, concentrating their efforts, their entire heart and will bent on only one thing: finding these weapons and taking possession of them."

"How close are they now?"

"They have mobilized every effort. They already are concentrating their search effort not far from here. Two days, maybe three, before the warheads will be found."

Peter sucked in a breath. The Arab frowned, moving away from the crates. Peter watched the older man as he walked away. "Donner!" he called out. The Arab paused at the sound of his code name. He stood there a moment, but did not turn around. Peter examined the dosimeter, then glanced at the cache of weapons. "How much do you know about the coup?" he asked.

The Arab only grunted.

"Do you know who they are?"

The Arab sneered, "Let's go!"

Peter didn't move. "Who are you?" he pleaded. "What is your name? What is your position?"

The Arab ignored the questions and turned for the opening in the mouth of the cave, then came to a stop and turned back to Peter. "Listen to me, American. I am not your friend. You have no friends here, not in this part of the world. You—all Americans—you mean nothing to me. The only reason I am here is that I am not as short-sighted as some. The leaders are intent on destruction. A hundred million of our people will die. What do you think will happen if al Qaeda detonates a nuclear warhead in the United States? How will your president react? How many of our cities will go up in flames? And then al Qaeda detonates another warhead and another ten million Arabs die. Twenty-four warheads! When will it end!? So, yes, we bite at your ankles, but you will crush our heads. America will be wounded, but we will *cease to exist*.

"The Arab world must not be destroyed. And their plan, it is nothing but a self-loathing scheme."

The Arab turned his light on the crates before he continued. "You must destroy these warheads before all my people die. You are the only ones who can do that. I stole the weapons. Now it is up to you." The Arab lowered his voice and took a small step toward Peter. "There are a few moments in history where the future hangs like a dry leaf from a tree, ready to be blown where it will in the wind. This is one of those moments, one of those turning points of men. If al Qaeda gets these warheads, then my world is over and yours will be brought to its knees. And the enemy is looking. You must act *today!*"

Peter tightened his jaw. The air crackled with tension, tight, electric, and cold. He studied the Arab, with his yellow teeth and fat lips. And that was when he saw it.

Fear. Almost panic. The Arab was terrified.

The military truck pulled away from the cave after turning carefully on the narrow, dirt road. It drove away in the darkness, its headlights off, moving slowly and carefully down the steep mountain road. The driver sat behind the wheel, driving with the aid of his night vision goggles. The American sat beside him in the front of the truck.

Eight kilometers from the cave, the truck pulled onto a main road and turned on its headlights. South toward the capital, it gathered up speed.

The Mossad agent waited in the darkness three hundred meters north of the fork in the road, then pulled his small Nissan pickup from behind the small cluster of trees. He drove slowly, thinking he might follow his target, then changed his mind and turned his truck onto the dirt road.

Forty minutes later, at the mouth of the cave, he found what he had been so desperately searching for.

12

General Petate got the call at a little after four in the morning. He was already up, neatly shaved, dressed in a white shirt and tie, his daily security brief in one hand, a stained coffee mug in the other. After lifting the phone to his ear he listened, asked two questions, then hung up without saying good-bye. He then called his staff, some of whom, to his displeasure, were still in their beds. "Get in here!" he told them. It was all he needed to say.

Forty minutes later, his senior staff assembled in his private office, a small and simply appointed, wood-paneled room down the hall from the main work area. Petate watched his men assemble, his deputy, military advisor, and Arab specialist. These were good men, good as any his nation had ever produced; all of them in their fifties and at the peak of their game.

The men gathered around a small table. "We have the warheads," General Petate announced.

His deputy's eyes widened. "Where are they?" he asked.

"Extreme northern Pakistan. Tirich Mir. At the base of the mountain."

"Tirich Mir!" The deputy whistled. "And you are certain we have them?"

"Not a doubt in the world." Petate took a sheet of paper and handed it to his deputy. "The Geiger counter readings," he explained.

The deputy glanced at the readings. "The warheads are—," he started to ask.

"Unguarded, yes. And the enemy is close." Petate sat back and ran his fingers through his salt-and-pepper hair. "The United States has located the warheads," he mused, the wheels beginning to churn. He lifted his eyes past the men, staring over their heads as he thought to himself. "Washington, Washington," he mumbled, "what is your boss going to do?"

"Group 21," his deputy answered in an assuring tone. "Bombers or cruise missiles. Give them thirty hours, and the warheads will be destroyed."

Petate nodded. "You're right, of course, I've already talked to Washington. They are going to use the B-2s. He is setting it up as we speak. But, I've been thinking . . ." His voice trailed off again.

His deputy leaned to the edge of his chair and took a deep breath. His stomach tightened up. He had seen the look before. He glanced nervously at the others as the general sunk into deep thought.

The three men had been bowled over by the general's plans before, plans that had been conceived in the distance of that faraway look; the security wall around Israel, isolating Arafat in his bombed-out compound, the assassination of Sheik Al Muhammad, all were ideas born in Petate's unfocused eyes.

The deputy watched him, growing more anxious with each passing second.

"Yes, yes, the United States will destroy the warheads," Petate mumbled to himself. "Unless—I've been thinking— might there be a better way?"

His deputy scowled. "Sir?" he asked skeptically.

Petate focused on him. "There *is* another way. Something we could consider, something that might buy us time.

A few months. A few years. This could be the break that we need."

The deputy shook his head. "What are you talking about, Blackbird! The United States has located the weapons. In a day and a half they will no longer exist. That is the best outcome we could hope for. I see absolutely no downside to this situation."

Petate leaned forward, excited, and began to explain.

His three lieutenants listened intently. Petate spoke in even and well-measured words, considering every option as he thought his plan through. He finished speaking and the room fell so silent you could almost hear the men's hearts. "Bloody, eh!" his deputy whispered. His face had grown pale and his eyes burned with sudden fright.

It was a brilliant idea, dangerous and desperate. Terrifying if they failed.

But it might work.

The deputy began to make a mental list of the pitfalls and dangers, the reasons they should not even consider the plan; but, looking at Petate, he could see he was wasting his time. It no longer mattered. Petate had made up his mind.

"Do we have the equipment?" the general asked as he sat back in his chair. Lighting a cigarette, he pulled in a lungful of smoke.

"I don't know," the deputy answered truthfully. "Nothing like this has ever been tried before."

The general unconsciously rapped his knuckles on the table. "We couldn't use our own air assets—too easily recognized. But we have other options."

The deputy scowled. "Are you talking about our Aggressor birds?"

General Petate smoked again and then nodded, and the deputy gritted his teeth. "There are significant considerations with the Aggressors," he said.

"I understand that, but could we get them up?"

"Maybe—I don't know. It will take us some time."

"Time is the one thing we don't have, my friend."

"Sir, it isn't that easy—it's not like pulling your grandfather's old Chevrolet out of the garage."

The general leaned forward. "I need a yes-or-no answer," he pressed.

The deputy thought, then tightened his lips. "We could do it," he concluded. "But we will have to push hard."

Petate leaned back and smiled.

"And there are other matters we have yet to consider," his deputy continued.

The general nodded. "Do we have the technicians and experience to complete the technical task?"

"I just don't know, sir." The deputy thought, then reluctantly added, "But I promise you this, if we put the word out to our teams, we would have a hundred volunteers."

Petate took another drag. "Think of the payoff," he dreamed, soliciting the support of his men.

Some of his lieutenants frowned, but some smiled as they stared in silence at him.

They actually believed they could do it.

But there was one critical question that had not been addressed, and no one dared say it until the deputy leaned forward in his seat.

"Are we going to tell the Americans?" he asked slowly while staring at his boss.

"Of course not!" Petate snorted as he smashed out the glow on the end of his cigarette. "That's why we can't use our own assets. Otherwise they would know."

The room seemed to grow warm from the heat of the men. It smelled tangy and musty as they sweated with concern.

"But sir—," the deputy muttered darkly.

Petate lifted a hand. "Let me take care of the United States," he answered in a calm voice. "It's my job to worry about them, and our other allies as well. You concentrate on completing the mission. Let me worry about what happens then."

Al Ram
Extreme Northern Pakistan

We have him," the lieutenant whispered in the Great Leader's ear.

The Great One looked up. "Who was it?" he asked dryly, no surprise in his voice. There wasn't a doubt in his mind they would find who the traitor was. The right questions, enough pain, it was simple enough.

"Major General Ghaith," his young lieutenant answered.

The Great One's head moved in an almost impercepti-ble nod. Yes, that made sense. General Ghaith. Security, political operations, was one of the few who would have known of their plans. He was old school. And soft. And apparently unable to catch the vision, unable to see this wasn't about politics, religion, or God; this wasn't about building Pan-Arabia, cultural power, or pride. This was about killing Jews and Americans. Nothing less, nothing more.

The commander thought of the general, his eyes burning from the rage in his heart. He waved off the three young women who surrounded him. "Get out," he commanded, and they scampered through a side door. The master pushed himself up from the cushions that had been spread on the floor. "How did you find out it was General Ghaith?" he de-manded.

"One of his housemaids," the lieutenant replied.

The leader of al Qaeda almost smiled. Such a stupid mis-take. "Take him," he said. "And bring in Angra. But tell him to be careful. General Ghaith doesn't matter. It's the war-heads we want."

The lieutenant nodded and bowed to dismiss himself, backing away slowly while remaining bent at the waist. Passing through the doorway, he straightened up and began to turn around. "Abulda," the commander called out and the lieutenant froze. "General Ghaith is no fool," he warned. "He will try to kill himself. I want him alive. Is that understood?"

"We have already taken action," the lieutenant replied.

13

Colonel Bradley was alone inside his wing commander's quarters. It was late, and he had just arrived back
at Whiteman Air Force Base. He glanced around the
house, thankful to be back on his home turf again after eight
weeks.

The wing commander's house was a large and well-
maintained rancher with four bedrooms, two fireplaces,
three living areas, and an enormous screened patio. It was
built to accommodate a general officer with a wife, four
kids, three dogs, and a cat. Shane Bradley had none of those
things, though he was considering a dog. Being single, he
had furnished the house with a wild and eccentric mix of
furniture, turning one bedroom into an exercise area, another into a home theater with a massive HDTV filling an
entire wall. His toys lay everywhere—skis, a pool table,
mountain bikes, guitars, and amps. The entry housed a grand
piano, and there was television in almost every room. But
still the enormous house seemed empty with just one man
living there.

A wing commander who was single was unusual in many
ways. As the wing commander, it was expected that Bradley

entertain; Christmas parties for his staff, Easter-egg hunts for the kids. The fact he didn't have a wife to assist him in these social events ran directly against many long-held traditions. His staff had once asked him who would host the weekly coffees for the officer's spouses? Bradley had laughed as he answered. He didn't care, so long as it wasn't him.

Walking through the house, he thought of the nearly bare condo in Georgetown he had rented when working for the CIA, with its cinder block bookshelves and his father's old leather couch. He remembered Washington's first visit. His boss had looked around incredulously, struggling to hold his criticism in, Bradley following his eyes as he took in the cheap wooden furniture, rough bookcases, and old beanbag chairs. A couple F-16 pictures were the only things on the wall. The townhouse was expensive and in an exclusive neighborhood, but inside it had a frat house atmosphere.

"Jeez, Shane, you live like a friggin' monk," Washington had exclaimed. "I grew up in the ghetto, and we had more furniture than this. Have you taken a secret vow of poverty that I don't know about?"

Bradley had smiled and looked around sheepishly.

"Man, I'm sorry," Washington had exclaimed, "but I have to ask. What in the world do you *do* with your money!"

"Penny stocks and the Nasdaq," Bradley answered. "And you know, Dr. Washington, I'm only here three or four nights a month. I spend more time in Europe than I do in the States. I'm always on the road; you're the one who sends me out there, so, though it's nothing special, this place is all that I need."

Washington nudged a green beanbag chair. "I don't think cinder block bookcases and beanbags will cut it when you take over the commander's house in Missouri," he said.

"Guess I'll have to get some furniture."

"What you need is a wife."

Bradley didn't answer. He'd been told that before.

Bradley smiled as he wandered through his house. Truth was, he wanted to get married, and almost had a couple of times. But it just didn't seem fair, as much as he was away. But one day—one day things would settle down a bit.

He made a cup of lukewarm coffee, using hot water from the tap, then sat down on the back porch. The sun settled below the horizon and the prairie wind blew. Fireflies danced through the sprinklers that chattered in his backyard.

As the evening deepened around him, Bradley couldn't help but think of his father. Maybe it was Peter's situation, maybe it was because he was feeling melancholy, alone.

Would his father have been proud of him? If he could see him as the commander of the world's only B-2 Stealth Bomber wing, would he have been satisfied?

Shane's father, Brig. Gen. Jeremiah F. Bradley, West Point, '52, had been a harsh man, a black-and-white warrior who derived his identity from the rank that he wore, and was the last in a long line of army officers. Bradley's grandfather (West Point, '27, distant cousin through marriage to none other than Omar Bradley) had been given a battlefield promotion to colonel along with orders to hold the crumbling line in the Battle of the Bulge. A tank commander and twice-captured POW in the century's most honorable war, his blood had been spilt crossing the Rhine to take German soil. Bradley's great-grandfather (West Point, '05) had spent his time in the stink-filled trenches that lined the Chemin des Dames Ridge, fighting point-blank in the century's most pointless war. This man's father, the first Bradley to serve in the United States Army, was a young cavalry officer during the Indian Wars. It was suspected that there might have been one more Bradley soldier, a kid who had enlisted in the Confederate army, though the genealogy was unclear.

When it came to serving their country, the men in Colonel Bradley's family had been provided opportunity to rise up and soldier as the good Lord had intended them do, and each had risen to a rank above the generation before. They all had served in the army, becoming leaders of men, willing to die for the country they held so dear.

Shane knew from the time he was young he would one day walk the gray line. But his plans took a sudden, sharp turn when he turned seventeen. His sideburns and goatee drove his father up the wall, which was pretty much the point, and it was one of the few times he had ever communicated effectively with his dad. His rebellion had been subtle, always unspoken, and he harbored a far-reaching doubt. Could he equal his father? His grandfather as well? He didn't know. He really didn't. And he hated the doubt.

There was more. An utter fascination with anything that had wings. The first book he had ever read was *Jonathan Livingston Seagull,* which he consumed at age six, almost memorizing each word. He dreamed of perfect freedom, maneuverability, and speed. He dreamed of being upside down at forty thousand feet, looking down at the earth. He dreamed of loops, rolls, and clouds, and of seeing the curvature of the sky.

So, when it came time to apply to West Point, he announced that he had other plans. "I want to go out to Colorado Springs," he said to his dad.

His father's face grew pale. Had his son lost his mind? He wouldn't have been any more shocked if Shane had announced he wanted to start wearing makeup and dressing up like a girl.

"The Air Force Academy," he had hissed, as if the place were a curse.

Shane nodded slowly. "I want to learn to fly."

"Peter Pan flies. Moths fly. Soldiers do their work in the mud and smoke and bloody debris."

"I want to fly jets."

"I want a full head of hair and a Porsche. I don't have either one. Sometimes we don't get what we want."

Shane only stared at his father, who softened a moment. "You can fly the army Apache," he offered. "It's a great helicopter! One of the most deadly fighting machines ever made."

"I want to fly faster than that."

"Helicopters fly fast enough to kill you. Isn't that fast enough?"

"It's much more than that. I'll see hypersonic aircraft in my career. And the air force *owns* space. Who knows what we'll see there! The air force is the tip of the technological sword. Air power is the future of battle! It's where I want to be."

His father ignored him, returning to his original argument. "Aviation is now a strong and well-established branch in the army. It won't hurt your career to be a chopper pilot for a few years. Go and fly the Apache for a while, then get back to the fight on the ground, down where the men are, where the battle is won. I guess I could support that, since I don't seem to have any choice."

Shane paused. "No, Dad. I'm going to the Air Force Academy."

"You will walk the gray line!" his father bellowed as he took a step back. "Like me. Like your grandfather. Like his father did before him."

"I'm going to fly jets!"

"What's the sudden fascination with jets? What's important here, Shane, is *a hundred years of tradition*. Can you walk away from that, just so you can go *zoom?*"

"But I want to—"

"We're talking family history. Five generations of soldiers! How can you even consider turning your back on our fathers!"

"It's just that—"

"What!? Afraid of fighting from the ground, where the real men die?"

Shane stammered, clenched his fists, then turned and walked from the room. The old man called out, "Am I therefore your enemy because I tell you the truth?"

Shane slammed the door behind him and sulked from the house. It was almost three days before he returned.

That was the last time either man discussed young Bradley's choice of career. And on that June day, hot and swollen with moisture from the California rains, when his son had gone down to the airport to get on the flight to Colorado Springs, Jeremiah Bradley IV had refused to accompany him to tell him good-bye.

"I'm leaving now, Dad," Shane had said while standing in the doorway to his father's study.

"Enjoy hell week," his father replied, not looking up from his book. "If you can't hack it, don't come home. I don't want a quitter living under my roof."

The old man, the general, had been dead going on eleven years, after passing away from a massive heart attack that was fifty years in the making. One day, while reading the paper, his heart had exploded in his chest, sending him crashing to the floor, already dead. Young Bradley was but a young lieutenant when his father had died, and it was one of his great concerns that the old man hadn't lived long enough to be proud of his son.

His mother once made an effort to assure him his father would have been satisfied. "He'd be proud of you, Shane." she offered, though she looked quickly away.

Shane pulled her face toward him, looking her square in the eyes. "He should be proud," he had answered.

She nodded sadly, again diverted her eyes. It was the last they spoke of it. They rarely spoke of the old man.

He glanced at his watch. A little past ten. He had to be in the office by five, which meant it was time for bed.

Moving toward the back door, he stopped and turned, searching the night sky for hints of the next day's weather. The night was perfectly calm and the air was heavy with the scent of magnolias and honeysuckle, and, as he stared at the sky, he could see high clouds moving in, thin wisps of light gray reflecting the light of the moon. Scout clouds they looked like, high stratus and condensation from ice particles in the upper atmosphere.

Could be rain was coming. He hoped it wouldn't storm.

14

At exactly five A.M., Bradley entered the wing headquarters building dressed in a desert camouflage flight suit, black boots, and brown parka. The headquarters was empty and his boots echoed across the lobby's tile floor. It was his custom to arrive at work early; from five until seven was when he got most of his real work done.

He unlocked the glass doors and entered the command complex. His oak-lined office was just down the hall. Pushing back his door, he was surprised to see a man sitting in his chair, leaning back, his feet up, sucking on a thin brown cigar. As Bradley entered the room, the man left his feet propped up and smiled.

Bradley's heart skipped a beat, an instinctive reaction based on years of experience working with the CIA. He made his way to the leather couch while Washington remained in his chair. "How are you, Shane?" Washington asked.

"Good, Thomas, good. What are you doing here?"

"That isn't much of a greeting."

"What were you hoping for?"

"A kiss. A hug. A 'glad to see you, buddy!'"

"It's only been two days, Tom. That isn't long enough for my heart to grow fonder."

Washington smiled. "No it isn't. Who would've guessed that we'd see each other so soon?"

Bradley nodded but didn't answer. He was not surprised. "Tom," he asked, "how did you get in here?"

Washington didn't answer, but pulled the cigar from his mouth and pinched a piece of tobacco from his tongue. Bradley didn't press. He knew it was easy, one of the things Thomas really liked about his job, sleuthing and pretending he was working back out on the street. Bradley sat on the couch. "Okay, what are you doing here?"

Washington placed his briefcase on his lap and pulled out a copy of a classified report. He tapped the top page, then placed it on the desk. The classified document was printed on legal size paper. Neatly printed on the red cover, in bold and dark print, were the letters TS-SBI-AL 1. *Top secret. Special background investigation required. Access limited by the White House.*

The DDO sat back and rubbed the sides of his head. "We made firm contact with Donner," he announced.

Bradley's mouth opened slightly. He glanced at the window and stared at the dark sky. He swallowed, then sat back and momentarily closed his eyes. "No kidding," he muttered. It was the best he could do.

Washington nodded quietly.

"He's really back?"

"Would I lie?"

"Are you certain it's him?"

Washington's voice turned sour. "Would I make such a mistake?" Bradley shook his head and Washington went on. "He had a very interesting meeting with Peter."

"Face to face?"

"Yeah."

It took a moment for Washington to describe the meeting between Peter and Donner—the warheads, the dead soldiers, what Donner had required them do. Bradley listened, dumbfounded, his eyes staring wide. "I can't believe it!" he muttered when Washington was through.

"The gods have smiled on us briefly. Now we have to act."

The colonel didn't move. He was completely lost in his thoughts. He pictured the gruesome scene, the dead soldiers, the warheads, warm and humming, the dark cave, Donner's voice. "Who is he!" he muttered in frustration to himself.

Washington couldn't understand him, but still read his mind. "Peter is going through some pictures, trying to identify him, but Donner was recently shaven, and so far he hasn't found a match. And anyway, it hardly matters, we've got *much* larger concerns."

Bradley hunched his shoulders. A suspicion rose inside him, an uncomfortable gnawing at his chest. It didn't make any sense. It was completely unpredicted. Something was missing. He stared quietly, turning it over and over in his mind, examining every angle, looking for a distortion in the answer that had too easily appeared. Washington watched him, staying quiet, recognizing the look on his face, allowing him time to think, to sort it out in his mind. "Something's changed—something's missing. It just doesn't feel right," Bradley said.

Washington nodded slowly. Inside he felt the same way. But it hardly mattered. Their path of action was clear.

"I don't think I will ever understand Donner," Bradley finished. "Why has he helped us? Why is he willing to take such an enormous risk?"

Washington only grunted. That was only one of a thousand things about his work that he didn't understand. And now he no longer questioned, he just accepted what was. "Men do what they do," he offered. "Like a mortician or a plumber. No one wants to drain the dead or stick their hands into someone else's toilet, but we're glad someone does it and we don't question why."

Bradley shook his head. "No. That's not it. I swear, something's wrong here!"

Washington sighed. "Donner has offered to help us. I no longer care why. We've got a job now, a mission. And we don't have any time. We can speculate on Donner's motives after the warheads are destroyed."

15

Less than an hour after Thomas Washington showed up in Colonel Bradley's office, Bradley's senior officers congregated in the wing command center: Col. Dick "Tracy" Kier, his vice wing commander, Lt. Col. Jeremy Connell, commander of the 345th Squadron of B-2s, and Col. John J. Cominsky, his operations officer, all of them dressed in desert camouflage flight suits. The B-2 pilots represented the cream of the crop, and they carried themselves with a pride that bordered on arrogance.

The room was cool and quiet, with a stillness in the air that came from the deep darkness of the hour before dawn, and the officers were almost silent as they gathered in the room.

"There's coffee in the back," Bradley said to his men. John J. and Connell stood up and went for the coffee. Col. Dick "Tracy" Kier, the vice wing commander, sat down at Shane's right, a dose of black brew in his stained squadron mug. He was a bear of a man, thick-necked and unyielding, with more hair on his shoulders than the top of his head. He sipped at the coffee, letting it warm his hands.

Shane and Tracy formed a very tight team, their friendship going back many years. Captain Kier had been Lieu-

tenant Bradley's first flight commander at Holloman AFB
when Bradley was first learning to fly the F-16. The two had
become very close, as Dick Tracy, or "D. T.," mentored the
lieutenant through the many obstacles in the life of a young
fighter pilot; beer, ego-driven officers, Operational Readi-
ness Inspections, ugly women, sergeants and their secret
codes, more beer, combat flying, pretty girls with ugly sisters, military regulations and rules, beer, local girls hunger-
ing for marriage, and office politics. After a particularly
famous party that included black whiskey from Brazil and a
game of strip poker in the O's club swimming pool, D. T. realized that his time for redemption had finally come. He quit
the women and beer and concentrated on flying, becoming
the best pilot in the wing, at least that's what he said. Soon
after, on his twenty-ninth birthday, he met his future wife at
an early morning mass, a beautiful and sincere Catholic girl
he loved from the first time they met. Three months later
they married, a formal military affair with ceremonial
swords, mess uniforms, and a military band. Seven days after the wedding, Captain Kier and his young bride were
transferred to Germany. Through the various moves that accompanied their careers, Kier and Bradley remained confi-
dants and friends, getting together once a year for fly fishing
in Idaho.

Now Colonel Kier was nearing the end of his military career. Six years older than Colonel Bradley, yet the junior officer now, D. T. fit comfortably in his role, being one of
those rare men who was genuinely satisfied to watch his
friend succeed. Having gone as far as he could, and with six
kids at home (making up for his late start with a very strong
finish of twins) he was anxious to retire from the air force
and go to work for Delta, where the paychecks would better
offset the cost of braces and basketball shoes. Colonel
Bradley, on the other hand was just sprinting out of the gate,
and D. T. considered it his responsibility to ensure that his
friend made his first star while commanding the wing.

As he sat down next to Bradley he rubbed his eyes and
said, "Kind of early for a staff meeting, isn't it boss?"

Colonel Bradley glanced at his watch. "Maybe for lazy men."

D. T. faked a hurt look. "You cut me deep, man. Cut me to the heart. Could it be that you're jealous that I don't sleep alone?"

"Perhaps. How many kids did you have in your bed with you this morning?"

"I think two. Maybe three. Sometimes it's hard to tell. Doesn't matter, the overall effect is the same. I might as well be here as at home. I'll get more sleep in my office than I will in my bed." D. T. smiled, then took a sip of his coffee and asked, "What's going on?"

"Hold on, D. T.," Bradley answered. "I'll explain in a minute."

D. T. shrugged and stood up to refill his coffee just as Thomas Washington burst into the room. D. T. stared at him. Clearly the CIA deputy director had worked through the night. His dark suit, badly wrinkled, matched the shadows under his eyes, and he smelled of sweat, mints, and coffee. He was wired and intense, with a fire in his eye, and he powered his way through the doorway with magnificent strides. Three other men followed, two deputies and a young aide carrying a large briefcase under each arm. Despite his appearance, Washington's power and energy charged the dull morning air. "Alright!" he bellowed. "Let's get down to work."

Colonel Bradley stood up to greet Washington and the two men shook hands. "Thomas," the colonel gestured to his officers. "These are my men. Gentlemen, this is Doctor Washington, Deputy Director of Operations, CIA."

The introductions were short, just a name, rank, and duty title. Washington didn't introduce the other agents who had traveled with him but instead indicated for the men to sit down. He positioned himself at the head of the group and spread his huge arms on the table. His aide opened a brief-case and pulled out a set of bound papers.

"Let's get started. Time is of the essence, gentlemen, as you will see. But first, Colonels Cominsky and Connell, I need you to leave."

The two men stared at the director, then over at their boss. Both looked angry. Lieutenant Colonel Connell raised a hand to protest but Washington cut him off. "Sorry, gentlemen, no offense intended, but what I am here to discuss is on a strictly need-to-know basis. You may be involved later on, but for now I would prefer to keep the lid on as tight as I can."

The men remained still, waiting on Colonel Bradley. "Colonel Connell, you understand the ROE for Group 21?" Bradley asked.

Connell nodded and answered, "Yes sir, I do. Group 21 is the National Command Authority designation for special missions regarding the interdiction and destruction of weapons of mass destruction. Special units, designated Group 21, our B-2 wing included, have been tasked to train and be ready to strike potential targets at a moment's notice."

"That's right," Bradley answered. "And the conversation that follows regards a Group 21. As you know, access to such information is only on a need to know basis."

Connell complained under his breath as he stood up from his chair. The two men walked from the room and pulled the door closed. Washington turned to Bradley, then motioned to introduce his men. "You know Manny Herrera?"

Bradley nodded slowly. "We've met a few years ago, before I was sent to Morocco."

"Yes, that's right. You probably don't know this, but Herrera was your ghost for that mission. He never let you out of his sight. He knows how you work. He knows you inside and out."

Bradley glanced at Herrera. Washington turned to D. T. and explained, "Manny Herrera is now Director, South Asia Division. Mr. Strausenberg is chief military liaison. And young Jeffery over there is my executive aide." The men nodded as they were introduced.

Washington turned to Colonel Bradley and got straight to the point. "As I told you already, we have located the warheads. Under the direction of the President of the United States, you are going to launch a sortie and destroy them. You only have twelve hours to be in the air."

"Where are they?" Bradley asked.

D. T. looked perplexed.

Washington didn't notice D. T.'s questioning look. He reached back to his aide, who handed him a small map. "Northern Pakistan," he answered Bradley's question. "Very near the Tajikistan border."

"What's near the border?" D. T. interrupted. "What's going on!" He was not used to being left in the dark. Worse, he had taken an early dislike to Dr. Washington, didn't like his manner, didn't like the tone of his vice. "What is going on here? Did you say the *president*?"

Washington turned to him. "You are aware of the recent developments in Pakistan, I'm sure. But like everything else in that hole, the situation is even worse than it would appear. In this case much worse, as you are about to find out."

It took Washington several minutes to explain what had occurred over the previous days, since the assassination of Massarif and his senior staff. D. T. listened carefully. Washington's facts were concise and complete, the narration chronologically exact. Every time, place, and event came off the top of his head, and D. T. had to concentrate to keep up with him.

By the time Washington had finished, D. T.'s face was pale. "Twenty-four nuclear weapons," he stammered, "sitting unguarded in the side of a mountain!" He sat back, stunned, trying to take it all in. "You were saying that you know where the warheads are located?" he finally said.

"Yes," Washington answered, turning his attention back to Colonel Bradley. "We will have the exact coordinates by late this afternoon. But we do know the warheads have been concealed in a cave in extreme northern Pakistan."

"And the ROE for the mission?" Bradley asked.

"Rules of engagement dictate two aircraft, one as the lead, with a second as backup. Both aircraft will be loaded with weapons, but only one aircraft will drop. Number Two will stay with the formation through the entire mission to make certain we get a good jet over the target.

"You know, of course, that B-2s usually fly single ship?"

"Yes, I know that. But this mission is too important not to have a backup. We want to send two jets, just to make sure."

Kier lifted a finger. "Have you considered a full-up air assault package? Navy attack birds, fighters escorts—the whole bit?"

Washington shook his head impatiently. "No. Can't do it. It's not an option now."

Kier started to argue, but Washington cut him off. "There are several absolutely essential considerations to this mission," he said. "First is secrecy. At this point, nothing is more important than that. It's a game of cat and mouse, and we don't want those guys to know we have located the cheese. Far better to show up in the middle of the night and destroy the warheads from the dark than to send up a combat package that lets them know where the warheads are. And if we put a multiservice attack package together, if we put AWACS and KC-10 refueling aircraft and fighter escorts in the air, everyone from Italy to India will know we are coming. Right now, al Qaeda is stumbling through the haystack, searching for the needle, but the instant we put combat assets over the target area, they will know where to look.

"Also, if we go with a full-up package, we would have to coordinate with half the UN. We'd have to get overflight clearances from Afghanistan and Pakistan, even Syria and Lebanon. Do you think that will happen? I don't think so. Maybe in a month or a week, but it wouldn't happen today. In addition, we'd have to advise our allies in the region; Iraq, the Saudis, Qatar, and Kuwait, and we have learned through sad experience that many of the Intel and military services of our allies are crawling with fundamentalist sympathizers and spies. Simply put, we couldn't guarantee security would not be breached.

"More, we don't need a full package. The B-2 is designed for exactly this kind of operation. It's got the range. Extremely accurate targeting systems. Impervious to enemy detection systems and radar. No need for fighter escorts, for it can't be seen.

"And it's the only aircraft that is capable of destroying

deeply buried targets. A couple bombs dropped from an F-16? Come on, they would barely raise dust. Cruise missiles? Forget it. They wouldn't make a dent. Nothing else can ensure target destruction—not the navy, not ICBMs (and what a mess *that* would be!), and not U.S. fighters with their conventional bombs. So, yes, we've thought this out. And this is what we need to do."

Kier nodded, satisfied, and Bradley went on. "The targeting information?" he asked.

"Weapons will be set for penetration detonation. No airburst. That is very, very important. Penetration detonation only."

Bradley cocked his head in surprise. "Thomas, are you telling me—"

"Yes, yes, of course." Washington waived impatiently at the air. "A B61-11 will be employed. It's our only choice. Donner has assured us the Pakistani weapons are buried behind a sufficient depth of granite that any other weapon would be useless. To assure destruction, we must employ the B61-11."

Bradley's eyes widened. "But the B61-11!" he cried. "Are you certain, Thomas? Have you guys thought this thing through?"

"The decision was made by the president himself. He did not hesitate. If all goes according to the OPPLAN, there should be few casualties and minimal long-term impact on the area. And yes, the president understands completely what is at stake, but when you consider the alternative, what choice did he have? Wait until New York is destroyed or D.C. is a hole!"

The enormity of the decision brought instant sweat to Bradley's ribs. Clearly it was the only way to assure the destruction of the weapons, but still his head began pounding and his throat went bone dry. Yet, this was the moment, and he was prepared. He had seen the real world, he knew how it worked out there beyond the borders of the blue ocean and finc sky, beyond the coastline that defined the United States. Out there, the only thing that mattered was who had the biggest guns, who could shoot first, who tasted first blood. It wasn't nice, it wasn't clean, it was a bloody free-for-all, and the only way to survive was through power and fear.

So he would do what it took to see the warheads destroyed.

As Bradley thought, Strausenberg leaned forward, catching his attention and holding him with his eyes. His face, bony thin, was weary and tight. "This won't be a cakewalk," he said. "Defensively, there are only minor considerations. The challenge will be to correctly and accurately identify the target. It has to be right. I mean down to the inch. Weapons on target and in the first pass. No aborts—there's no time. It has to be done perfectly and right away. There will be no excuses, no hesitation, and certainly no delays." He paused a moment, then added, "Gentlemen, those are not my words. They come from the president. So I think you understand what I'm trying to say."

"Are there any friendlies in the area?"

"The few U.S. assets are being moved out. You will be cleared hot upon entering the target area."

"And the ROE for target identification?"

"You need two forms of positive ID. Radar or IR in the aircraft. In addition, we'll have a team on the ground to designate the target with a laser. But the timing is going to be a struggle, it won't be easy getting the team there. They have to move covertly and through extremely hostile terrain, so don't withhold releasing your weapons if it turns out the team can't get there in time."

Bradley shot a quick look toward Doctor Washington. "Peter Zembeic?" he asked.

Washington paused. "Maybe, maybe not, we haven't assigned a team yet, but if it isn't Peter it will be some of his men. Either way, a team should be in place to laser designate the target, acting as a backup to your internal targeting systems. In addition, they will act as your eyes and ears on the ground."

"How close will they be?"

"Close enough to help. Far enough to be protected. They will be shielded from the target by terrain."

Bradley shifted uncomfortably.

Washington saw the concern on his face. "Those guys know what they're doing," he said. "They'll be okay."

Bradley nodded reluctantly, then turned back to the military liaison. "What about combat search and rescue?"

"There are no combat search and rescue assets in-country," Washington explained reluctantly. "All of our SAR forces were pulled out of the theater when we ceased combat operations in Afghanistan. It would take us seventy-two hours, minimum, absolute minimum, to get rescue helicopter assets in place."

"Don't you have a stolen Russian chopper operating in that area somewhere?" Bradley asked. "Peter showed me some pictures of him sitting in a Hind."

"That!" Washington scoffed. "You've got to be kidding me. What a piece of garbage that Russian Hind is! Half the time it's broken. We can't keep it in the air. And it's so power-limited it can't climb above nine thousand feet, which pretty much makes it worthless in that part of the world."

Bradley shook his head slowly. "So we're on our own."

Strausenberg cleared his throat. "Yeah. I'm afraid that you are."

"And if we go down?"

"Don't get captured. Please, don't do that. The political and emotional value of an American prisoner, the psychological value—well, you know the score. Absolutely don't let that occur."

Bradley pressed his lips in frustration. As if it were as easy as just saying the words. "And the air defenses?" he asked. "What can we expect?"

The liaison referred to the map the aid had placed on the table. "Minimal, if not completely nonexistent. The targets are located on the side of a barren mountain in a valley so narrow a truck can hardly drive through. So far as we can tell, the nearest surface-to-air defenses are almost forty miles away, located here . . ." the agent pointed with his pencil at the small map, "in the Khyber Pass, which lies to the south."

"How much time do we have then?"

"The al Qaeda forces have been joined by local warlords and various rebel groups," Washington broke in. "Donner speculates his men might have been observed, since they've concentrated their efforts in the general area in which the warheads are hidden. The enemy has organized search teams and is sweeping north, moving into the mountains. We estimate that we have thirty-six hours before the weapons are found."

The room fell silent. No one spoke as each of them wrestled with their own fears. Then Washington pushed back from the table. "The president is placing the full trust and confidence of the American people into your hands," he said. "He expects, Colonel Bradley, to have complete and absolute mission success. You have twelve hours to plan the mission and be in the air. Takeoff is scheduled for 1800 tonight. It's a twenty-hour flight, give or take, which will put you over Syria about dark, and the target around 2400 local.

"So, get some pilots into crew rest and your flight planners on the job. I expect to be briefed on the flight plan by ten o'clock this morning, after which I will fly back to D.C. to brief the president."

Bradley stared out the window. Sunrise was soon coming and the sky had turned from darkness to pink hues. A bank of low clouds hung on the western horizon, bringing the promise of rain later on in the day. The clouds drooped dark and heavy, with black, bulging cores. Bradley felt tired and overwhelmed. It all was coming so fast.

Washington leaned toward him. "Are you going to fly this mission?" he asked.

"Tom, do you think I would even consider sending anyone else?" he replied. "Unless you want to go back and tell the president that we're sending a couple lieutenants to Pakistan?"

Washington nodded to concede, trying to suppress a smile. The truth was he was relieved Bradley would be commanding the mission. "And the other member of your crew?"

D. T. thumped his chest. Bradley studied him with a sorry expression. "Sorry D. T., but you are out of the running. Air force ROE forbid the two of us flying combat sorties in the same aircraft. Besides, you need to remain here to head up the mission command center." Bradley thought for a moment. "I'll take Captain Lei," he said.

"Good pilot?" Washington pressed him, an anxious look on his face.

"Most experienced in the wing. You can tell the president that I trust Captain Lei with my life."

"Okay. Good enough. Let's get going then." Washington pushed himself up, anxious to quit talking and get down to work.

Bradley also stood and turned to Colonel Kier. "Contact Captain Lei," he said. "Tell her we've got a Group 21 and we need her here."

16

The colonel's office was cast in a deep yellow glow from the early morning light. The air was cool, not warm. It wouldn't get warm today. Already the smell of rain was in the air, and the atmosphere seemed charged. Outside, the wind calmed, then suddenly shifted direction. Hearing the rustle of leaves, Bradley paused from his work, looking out on the day. His mood, like the western sky, was unsettled and dark. Inside, he felt drained and he didn't know why. He thought back on other mornings he had prepared himself for combat sorties, reflecting on the emotions that beset him those days. Always he was eager, perhaps edgy, but also confident. There was a job to do, he would do it, it wasn't much more complicated than that.

But he felt different this morning, uncertain and apprehensive.

He had had premonitions before; every good commander did, every good officer had a feel, a gut instinct for the future, an instinct born of experience and practice and bone-crunching preparation. Those who didn't foster this sense either quit or were killed. Still, Bradley had never had such a powerful feeling before.

For the second time in a day he thought of his father, and of a story he had heard while hiding at the top of the stairs.

His father was a young lieutenant on a combat patrol. It was raining. No—pouring—the chilling rain coming in torrents that soaked to the bone and stung the face with each windblown drop. It was night, and the platoon was moving through the heavy forest, away from base camp, scared and alone. As the lightning crashed, the forest suddenly came alive. The first sound to be heard was a terrifying *thwaat,* as a VC bullet winged past his father's head to impact the chest of his radioman. The platoon was surrounded. It was fight, flee, or die. Proud, tall, and defiant, Bradley's father stood in front of his men, commanding them, jeering at them, coaxing them on, poking them, prodding them, demanding more than they had, holding them, pushing them, the blood of his brothers soaking his skin. For the next eleven hours, the young lieutenant led his men on, until, too late for many, reinforcements were finally choppered in. Twice he carried fallen soldiers through the thick firefight, draping the wounded men over his shoulders as bullets whizzed overhead, struggling to keep what remained of his unit alive.

The platoon lost seven of twelve soldiers that night. They were lucky, blessed, that they didn't lose every man, for they remained disciplined and together under Lieutenant Bradley's command. Shane's father was credited with personally saving two men that night, while performing in a way that would lead him to the Silver Star. But he never spoke of it, and as far as Shane could remember, he had never seen the small medal on his father's chest.

Sitting in his office on that cold Missouri morning, Colonel Bradley had no idea why this memory came to mind.

But the memory and premonition did not go away. He shook his head to clear it, then heard a knock and looked up to see Colonel Kier standing in the doorway. "Captain Lei is here," he announced.

At five-six, Tia Lei weighed in at a whopping 112 pounds, and that was after drinking half a gallon of water to ensure she made the minimum weight requirement in order to pass her flight physical. Beautiful, Asian, a refugee from the Cambodian killing fields, her face was a perfect oval rimmed by dark hair and narrow eyes, and despite her light stature she walked fearlessly. The nights as a child in Cambodia had sucked up her life's allocation of fear, leaving her determined and strong as a scrub oak in the wind. A slender figure among burly men, she had proven herself so many times that no one doubted her anymore. Her dark eyes said it all. This was a woman of strong nerves and steel. She walked to Colonel Bradley and extended her hand in a no-nonsense grip. "Sir," she said simply.

Bradley gestured toward a large leather couch and Captain Lei sat down. She was wearing her air force blues—a blue skirt and high-collared blouse under a dark cotton sweater. The skirt fit her neatly and she leaned back, at ease. If being in her wing commander's office was intimidating to her, she gave no indication.

"Tia," Bradley asked, "I need to talk to you."

Tia leaned forward and asked, "What's going on, sir?"

He explained very quickly. As Tia listened, her hands started trembling and her eyes grew wide. "You're kidding!" she kept repeating.

Bradley only wished that he was.

17

Peter Zembeic had a thing for poker—not just a thing. Like beer to an alcoholic, it was an obsession to him. He could cut the cards with two fingers, then deal them with one hand, tossing the cards around the table with a flip of his thumb across the top of the deck. There wasn't a poker game invented that he hadn't mastered, and he would rustle up a game every chance he could get.

"Remember Wake Island," he'd say as he rallied his troops for a hand.

So far as it could be determined, the world's longest running continuous poker game was started on the tiny Pacific military outpost of Wake Island some time in May of 1962, just as the United States was beginning to send military advisors to Vietnam, and continued without breaking until June of 1973, when the U.S. forces in the region were drastically and suddenly reduced. The card game ran without interruption, twenty-four hours a day, with men dropping in and out as their schedules allowed. Most of the players were transient aircrew members—pilots, navigators, loadmasters, and such—who were on their way in or out of the Vietnam theatre and had laid over at Wake for crew rest, fuel, or repair. Wake had become one of the primary stopover destinations for air force transports and fighters, and at any given time there were sixty or seventy transient aircrew on the island. Thousands of aircrew members played in the game at one time or another, and as the game grew in reputation, it wasn't unheard of for aircrews to fly a thousand miles out of their way just to get in on the game.

Peter was inspired by the Wake Island poker record. It had become his model, his example, the Holy Grail of poker games, and he was always pushing the soldiers at Camp Cowboy to get a game going with him. It didn't matter what time—early morning, late at night—if there was lull in the action he would gather the troops and insist on a game. After four or five hours of play the other guys would start dropping out and he would hassle them mercilessly.

"Come on Peter, some of us have to sleep," they'd say. "We can't live on adrenaline and donuts like you do."

"But guys, we're just getting started."

"No Peter, we're done."

"You call that a poker game! Weak sisters," he'd cry. "Haven't you heard of Wake Island! Eleven years, man! That's a hundred thousand hours of poker. We've been playing for five, now come on, sit down! I don't care what time it is, there's cash on the table and this game isn't through."

But the other guys would wearily shake their heads and head off to their tents, and after cursing a couple times Peter would follow after them.

It was in the middle of one of these games, a little after one in the morning, when Peter glanced at his watch and announced, "Happy Birthday to me."

The man to Peter's left, one of Camp Cowboy's helicopter pilots, paused and looked up. "Your birthday?" he asked.

Peter nodded with satisfaction. Living another year was no small accomplishment in this part of the world. "Yessiree, baby, another big one for me."

"Congratulations," the chopper pilot said as he dropped his cards on the table. "Now give me two."

Peter dealt around the table and none of the other players

said anymore. Birthdays in Camp Cowboy were like bowel movements; everyone was glad they had them, but you didn't announce it to the world.

Peter dealt himself three cards, a wild one-eyed jack and two hearts, which gave him a flush—with twenty bucks in the pile!—then eyed his buddy, the pilot. "You know what I want for my birthday?" he said.

The pilot grunted as he stared at his cards. "A girlfriend," he muttered. It was pretty obvious that he didn't care.

"No," Peter answered as he slowly dropped a two-dollar chip on the pile. Play them slow, play them easy or they'd drop out too soon.

The bet went around and a couple players tossed their cards on the pile. Peter flipped another chip and sat back, relaxed. The chopper pilot watched him, then matched him. "Okay, Peter, we give up, what do you want for your birthday?" he asked.

Peter smiled and leaned forward. "A good steak," he said lustily. "That's what I've been dreaming of. A hunk of meat. Grilled. With lemon pepper and beer."

The chopper pilot grunted and watched the bet move around again. "That's great, Peter. Only problem is, we don't have any steaks up here. I haven't had fresh meat since I left the States."

"Yeah, and I think it's disgraceful! We can land a man on Mars, but we can't develop a good combat-ready freezer."

The man across the table looked up. "Peter, we've never sent a man to Mars," he said.

"Minor point," Peter replied. "But either way, my statement stands. No freezers, no meat. And I want something to chew."

None of the men answered. Peter stared at his cards, hesitated, then increased the bet again. They all saw his indecision, but they didn't buy his bluff. "Really wish I had a good steak," Peter repeated again.

The chopper pilot sat back. Peter was working on something, that was perfectly clear. "Call," he said, stopping the bet.

The players showed their hands one by one until Peter dropped his cards on the table and smiled. "Happy birthday to Peter," he said as he scooped the chips and moved them to his pile.

A couple guys swore. "You're cheating!" one said.

"Of course I am," Peter answered, "but until you can prove it, there's not a thing you can do." He smiled evilly, then passed the deck of cards to his right.

The chopper pilot watched the new dealer shuffle. "Okay, Peter, what are you thinking?" he asked.

Peter picked up his first card. "You ever seen any of the Gads that live in the mountains around us?" he asked.

"Gads?" the pilot wondered, still only half interested.

"Gads, you know, Gads. Big, fat, white mountain sheep."

The chopper pilot nodded. "Yeah, okay, I've seen a couple in the early mornings on those lucky days when I can get that worthless Hind I fly to get up high enough."

Peter whistled at his cards, which meant nothing, then said, "I've seen a couple north of us, high on those cliffs just under the Cryb Pass."

The pilot hesitated. "Don't know where you mean."

"Don't worry about it. I'll show you."

The pilot laid down his cards. "Are you suggesting . . ."

"Well, duh! How else am I going to bag one of those things? Think I'm going to climb that mountain? It'd take me a week. We'll hunt from the back of your chopper and have us fresh meat for lunch."

"I don't think so," the pilot answered.

"Okay, I know mutton isn't steak, but it's the best we can do. And wait till you taste it. A little oil, some pepper and chives." Peter almost started drooling as he pictured the meat on the grill.

"Peter," the pilot said as he leaned toward him. "Do you have any idea how many regulations I'd be breaking if we were to do that—hunt from the back of a military chopper!? And from a stolen Russian Hind no less."

"Come on, Mike. Ain't no big deal."

"Let me count the ways it's a big deal," the pilot shot back. "Unauthorized use of a military aerial vehicle. Shooting of indigenous species. Unauthorized use of military weapons for nonmilitary use. Creating or facilitating in a potentially embarrassing situation for the host nation. Harassing of wildlife. The list goes on and on."

"Come on, Mike! Don't talk to me about harassing the wildlife or embarrassing the host government. Having Pakistani rebels dropping artillery shells on our heads every other night, now that's what I call harassing. But the Pakistanis don't seem to care a whole lot about that! Half the country is illiterate and starving—now that's an embarrassment to the host country. But shooting a mountain sheep, that's no big deal, Mike."

"It's a big deal to me, Peter. It's my wings. And that's my chopper, not some custom 'cruisemobile' for your hunting pleasure. I'm sorry Peter, but it isn't going to happen. And a Gad, for heaven sakes! We'll probably find out the stupid thing is endangered and have the Sierra Club raid our camp."

"Nope, not endangered, I've already checked. Now they used to be, yes, but they aren't anymore. And you know what else I found out? Some big shots in Europe pay as much as twenty thousand dollars for guided Gad hunts. Now, here we are, gentlemen, in this veritable Garden of Eden of mountains and rocks. It's a cold and miserable place, but the Gads seem to like it, so I say we take advantage of the opportunity and go get us one. And besides, its my birthday and I want some meat."

"No," the pilot answered. "You're not going to hunt Gad, at least not from my chopper."

"I'll share the meat," the CIA agent offered.

"I'm okay with canned sausage."

"You haven't tasted *my* barbecue."

"No, Peter, no way."

"You'll be the only guy in camp with a Gad head mounted on his tent wall."

The pilot hesitated. "We really shouldn't," he replied.

Peter only smiled. He had touched the right nerve.

The chopper took off just a few minutes before dawn. Peter hung from a canvas harness, his feet on the right skid, an army M-16 in his hand. The morning was cold and foggy, with scattered low clouds hanging on the mountains and a wet mist in the air. The pilot had told his crew chief to download most of the chopper's fuel before they took off, for they had to be light in order to climb up to the cliffs. As the two men climbed in the chopper the pilot said, "We've only got twenty minutes of fuel on board."

"Plenty," Peter answered. "Ten minutes to find a Gad, one minute to shoot it, two minutes to land and haul our lunch on board. That leaves us five minutes to get back and land."

"Okay," the pilot answered as he pulled up on the collective to increase pitch on the blades. Peter grabbed his handhold as the chopper lifted almost straight up.

Fifteen minutes later, the sound of the chopper echoed from the canyon as the pilot followed the descending terrain back to the camp. Flying over the compound, Peter held the white sheep's head in his lap, his feet still hanging from the open cabin door. As the chopper passed over the camp, he lifted a white hoof and waved at the men.

The BBQ was delicious. And the mounted Gad head certainly looked good on the tent wall.

Whiteman Air Force Base
Missouri

Against a backdrop of secret urgency—with little talk among peers, but some quiet speculation—the mission planning began. Air refueling coordinators, weapons specialists, targeters, airspace managers, diplomatic clearance coordinators, and flight mechanics worked feverishly to put all of the pieces in place that are required to fly a combat mission halfway around the world, drop a series of weapons exactly on target, and get safely home.

On the flight line, two B-2s were positioned in their protective hangars and the enormous doors secured. Air vehicle number 93-1086 was selected as the lead for the mission, an aircraft that was officially listed in the air force documents as the *Kitty Hawk*. Unofficially, she had been named *The Lady of the Night* by her squadron. Under the aircraft's dark cockpit window was a tactically acceptable three-inch piece of nose art, a black-and-gray depiction of a female Grim Reaper with pale eyes, flowing black hair, and skeleton teeth. Among the superstitious pilots and mechanics, the *Lady* was considered to be the wing's best aircraft, having an extraordinary reputation for getting the bombs to target. In preparation for flight, the *Lady* was towed to the center of the hangar, then hooked up to external power cables and cooling hoses. Her bomb bay doors were opened, revealing the double half-pipe cavities within. Her black boxes were electronically checked and checked once again. She was fueled and serviced, then wiped down until she was kitchen-plate clean. The last step in the preflight process was the "clover," or Common LO Verifications System (CLOVRS), a special radar system mounted on a small track that encircled the aircraft and scanned it electronically to ensure there were no detectable blemishes on the skin, as even the tiniest imperfection might bounce back radar energy. Finally, the *Lady* was declared ready to go. At that point, a contingent of highly trained, well-armed, and very serious security forces took operational control of the hangar. Everyone but key personnel was forced to leave. A secure perimeter was formed around the outside of the hangar, with multiple layers of security created inside the building as well. Then the men waited. Authorization from the National Command Authority to load up the nuclear weapons had not yet arrived.

Two hangars down, a second B-2 was also readied to go.

At 0948, the mission planners finally completed their work. Twelve minutes later, exactly on time, the flight briefing began in the wing command post. The two crews sat together, Colonel Bradley and Captain Lei in the lead, with Lieutenant Colonels Sobrino and Goodman flying number two. The briefing was concise and to the point. Takeoff was scheduled for 1800 local time. The formation would fly a more or less direct route from Missouri to Maine, across the North Atlantic, then drop south to pass through the Straits of

Gibraltar before turning northeast to Sicily, then through the center of the Med to Lebanon. By this time, the pilots would have been through a period of night, though shortened by their high-speed flight toward the oncoming sun. The day would also be short, with evening coming on very quickly. Approaching the coast of Syria, nightfall would emerge from the shadows in the east, masking the aircraft completely under the cloak of night. Upon reaching Syria, the crew would fly directly east, over Iraq and Northern Iran. It would be over the target in Northern Pakistan shortly after midnight local time.

Air refueling would take place as the bombers passed abeam the southern coast of Nova Scotia, with KC-135 air-refueling *Maniacs* from Maine, then once again after passing through the Straits of Gibraltar, with KC-10s deployed from Aviano Air Base in Italy. After being refueled by the second tankers, the bombers would be on their own until they were on the way home.

After the flight planners completed their overview of the mission, Mr. Strausenberg, Chief Military Liaison, CIA, stood to update the intelligence brief. "Over the past twelve hours there has been a significant increase in activity in the target area," he began with an anxious expression. He pointed with bony fingers to a huge map on the front wall, then ran a red laser in a circle around extreme northern Pakistan. "So far, all of this activity has been in the form of ground troops and organized regiments that are sweeping in search parties toward the border. Based on signals intelligence and communications traffic, it would appear the number of military units in the area has nearly tripled over the past twelve hours. Lots and lots of people are moving into the area—it's like a Wal-Mart in Arkansas on a Saturday night. The latest reports put the search parties only fifteen klicks away from the target . . ." His voice trailed off. The implication was clear. "Still," he concluded, "there is a bit of good news. So far, the search efforts have been far, wide, and scattered. There are lots of people looking, but they have not concentrated their efforts. It seems they know the warheads are hidden somewhere near the border, but they don't have information more specific than that. They are digging through the haystack, but the needle remains hidden. Assuming we have no delays, and assuming the mission is a success, we expect that we have time to launch the sortie and destroy the weapons before they are found."

Washington glanced at his watch, then shifted impatiently.

"As far as surface-to-air threats," Strausenberg continued, "you already are aware of the four SA-10 and SA-12 missile sites along the disputed border of Kashmir. Additionally, there are several mobile Pakistani ZSU-23-4s assigned to the area, but of course all of these assets have to stay in the lowlands and shouldn't be much of a factor. Additionally, none of them are capable of targeting the B-2. But be careful, there's always the possibility of a golden BB."

Strausenberg began to discuss the general features of the target area terrain while flashing a series of satellite photographs in the overhead display. The first showed the main road, which ran east and west from Islamabad to Peshawar, then through the Khyber Pass to Kabul. North of this a spur ran to a small town named Mardan, then north to the soaring Himalayas. Tirich Mir, part of the Hindu Kush range, reached its craggy fingers up to almost twenty-six thousand feet. The Pakistani nuclear warheads were hidden in a cavern at the base of this mountain, which sat square on the border between Pakistan and Afghanistan, and only a stone's throw from Kashmir and Tajikistan. Tirich Mir itself was a massive cluster of granite pyramids, dark gray and deeply fissured. The snowline began one third of the way up the mountain, the tops were covered with glaciers and were as barren as the dark side of the moon. South and west of the mountain, a snake of a road ran through a narrow valley, east to the Khunjerab Pass and China beyond. The formidable K2 and Mount Karakoram jutted from the same mountain range on the other side of Kashmir. Mount Everest, the father of all mountains, lay farther east.

The region surrounding Tirich Mir was bleak, with harsh, wind-blown peaks, barren valleys and snow-capped mountain tops. Every piece of terrain seemed to jut skyward at a vertical angle. The summers were short, the winters bitter and cold. The only natives were the tough-as-leather herdsmen, and bandits who ranged between Turkmenistan and the border. Vegetation was scarce; rock-like mosses and lichen were the predominate species. "You'd be hard-pressed to find a more hostile place to eject from an aircraft," Strausenberg concluded. "If you go down out there, you'll likely become the next Andes Iceman. So don't do it. There just ain't a good way to get you home."

"Emergency landing fields?" Bradley asked.

"None to speak of, sir. Baghdad International is way too far to the west. You've got Mardin to the south, and there are a few marines there, but nothing to provide anywhere near adequate security. And there's Lyangar in southern Tajikistan, but the runway is too short. It'd be hard to land a Cessna up there. And again, Lyangar is not secure. The truth is, you might as well land the B-2 in Kabul and leave the keys in it. From a security standpoint, if you have problems over bad guy territory, it would be better to eject and let the aircraft crash than try to make an emergency field. That's ugly, I know, but it's the ugly truth."

The crew nodded. They understood. Let the jet crash before you emergency land anywhere.

The weapons officer was next. His briefing was concise and to the point. "These are the target coordinates," he explained as he passed out a single, red sheet of paper. "The weapon for this mission is, as you all know, the B61-11." The weapons officer paused then glanced away. The room fell silent in a sudden and emotional response.

The B61-11 was the newest weapon in the nuclear arsenal and the first warhead developed since nuclear weapons production was suspended in 1989. Through the 1990s it became clear that many of the enemies of the United States were successfully protecting weapons of mass destruction storage and production facilities in underground tunnels. The B61-11 was designed to eliminate this threat. Produced by Sandia National Laboratories in New Mexico, the B61-11 was a hybrid that merged the adjustable-yield warhead from the B61-7 with a hardened steel, needle-nosed casing and stabilizing fins. The weapon could penetrate up to forty feet of solid rock, transferring most of its nuclear energy into ground shock. In theory (most things concerning nuclear warheads revolved around theory), by selecting a minimum yield and deep penetration, the heat blast would melt the warheads—the firing pins, the detonators, even the fissionable cores—a microsecond before the ground shock would collapse the underground facility, leaving very little above-ground radiation. And there was no chance the Pakistani warheads would detonate in the explosion, for they would be melted away before their firing mechanisms could be triggered.

At least that was the theory. They would soon know if it worked.

The weapons officer continued. "The target coordinates have already been programmed into each of the aircraft's weapons computers. The attack profile calls for the formation lead, piloted by Colonel Bradley and Captain Lei, to descend from high cruise altitude and deliver the weapons from thirty-four thousand feet. Number two, with Colonels Sobrino and Goodman, will stay high. Number two aircraft will not engage the target unless something goes wrong and lead is unable to drop.

"Your objective is to hit the mouth of the cave with a single B61-11. It won't be Hiroshima, but it will do the job. Each aircraft will be loaded with three bombs, so you have five weapons in reserve. We've got backups to backups this time. I can't image any circumstance that would preclude a successful weapons drop.

Finally, the chief weather officer stood. Weather was forecast to be clear through the Atlantic, with heavy overcast and intense rain showers through the Med. The aircraft would be well above the cloud layers, cruising at fifty-three thousand feet, which would conceal the mission from interested eyes on the ground. Meteorological conditions off the Sicilian coast would create contrails at cruise altitude, and the pilots would need to eliminate them by initiating the Contrail Management System, which would inject an alcohol-surfactant mixture into the engine exhaust. Once the crew hit land over Israel and Syria, the crew could expect typical Middle East weather—dry, hot, windy, and boring. Even the mountains of Northern Pakistan were forecast to be clear.

"The only problem," she concluded, "is going to be here in Missouri. A cold front has just moved in from the Rockies, and it will generate scattered afternoon storms. We will keep an eye on it and keep you apprised."

And that was it. The briefing ended and Washington stood up and said, "You've done a fine job so far." He turned to Colonel Bradley. "Do you need anything else from me?"

Bradley shook his head.

"Okay then," Washington finished. "Good luck." Washington and his staff left through the back door. An agency aircraft was waiting to take him back to D.C.

Bradley then stood and walked to the front of the room. "Are there other issues we need to discuss?" he asked. No one said anything. "The crews are going to go into crew rest. We will reassemble at 1700."

The briefers split up. The four pilots headed for the crew bunker to get a few hours sleep. The airmen and officers went back to work.

At 1112 local time, a highly classified and secure data transfer device inside the wing command post spit out a three-line, coded message directing the 409th Bombardment Wing to load up two B-2s with the B61-11 tactical nuclear bombs. This message was followed almost immediately by a series of coordinates, reconfirming the exact location where the Pakistani warheads were hidden.

Inside the weapons storage maintenance building, six torpedo-shaped bombs were extracted from their storage cradles. The silver weapons were thin, needled-nosed, and warm to the touch. Two small computers and stabilizing gyros were built into each warhead. The nose cones were made of multiple layers of depleted uranium, enabling the warheads to penetrate through solid rock. The sudden deceleration hitting the target would initiate the firing mechanism.

The initial chain reaction would generate a nuclear-driven fireball of twelve thousand degrees, which would melt the rock around it into a pool of lava. The overpressure would then lift a piece of the mountain before collapsing it down onto itself, crashing down the cavern where the weapons were hidden under half a million tons of rock. Half a second after detonation, the warheads would cease to exist.

The selectable yield on the warheads were set for 11.537 kilotons, the minimum detonation the targeters calculated would be required to destroy the target. The chief of the weapons branch reconfirmed the detonation yield, then carefully checked the settings against the calculations in his hand. The six weapons were then driven across the black tarmac and loaded into the bays of the waiting B-2s.

Everything was in place.

By midafternoon, thunderstorms began building over the base. It rained for a few minutes, with lightning and brief hail, but without the heat of the summer the storms quickly exhausted themselves. By takeoff time it was partly cloudy, with most of the storms having blown off to the south.

At 1700, the four crew members appeared with their flight gear for the final mission brief. They were driven to the flight line, where *Lady* and *Lone Wolf* were waiting. Their engines were running and they were ready to go.

At exactly 1800, the first B-2, call sign Kill 31, accelerated down the runway and lifted gracefully into the evening sky. It climbed straight ahead until it had sucked up its gear, then turned on its wingtip until it was heading northeast. Twenty seconds later a second B-2 lifted into the air and followed the leader in a half-mile trail.

D. T. watched from the control tower until the two aircraft disappeared. He glanced at his watch. It was smooth start to the mission.

He thought of his last words to Tia. "Good luck. See you later, after you've saved the world."

She had thought he was kidding, but he had meant every word.

18

The Arab climbed in blind terror, scrambling up the rocky knoll overlooking the city, reaching the jagged top in just twenty minutes. When he got to the top, the sun was sinking quickly and only half was still exposed above the western horizon. The desert air was still, as the evening's peace settled over the land and in the distance the mournful wailing over the loudspeakers called the faithful to prayer. Nearer, he could hear the calls of soldiers and the barks of their dogs. They were coming. They would take him.

And then they would know.

It would take only hours to break him. Then the warheads would be found.

The Arab turned from the sound of the chasing soldiers and ran over the crest of the hill. There he heard other soldiers below him, on the back side of the mount. Trapped. Nowhere to go. He looked around desperately, a cold terror in his eyes, then scrambled toward an outcropping of rock. The sun settled more deeply and darkness quickly fell. From his hiding place he could see a convoy of trucks on the highway three kilometers to the east, additional soldiers assembling, their vehicles blocking the road. He heard their dogs baying, anxious to get in the hunt, the sound of their cries carried by the light wind.

The desert fell into darkness.

If he could just get through the night, if he could just find his way down the back of the hill!

Then he heard a falling rock below him. They were drawing very near. Voices called out in the darkness not more than fifty feet away.

He wasn't going to make it. His capture was almost assured.

The Arab slid on his belly down the steepest part of the rocky hill, scratching his arms and legs, leaving a trail of blood that would drive the hounds mad. He found another outcropping and crawled underneath. He glanced around in desperation, his pulse slamming like a hammer at the sides of his head.

He caught his breath, then took out the cell phone that had been provided to him. Dialing the number, he initiated the call.

CIA Headquarters
Langley, Virginia

Dr. Thomas B. Washington was alone in his office, working at his desk. All around him was chaos—books stacked on the floor, papers piled high, his wastebasket overflowing with reports that he had never read. He sat hunched, his brow furrowed, his eyes narrow and intent. Everything about the him indicated he was in a foul mood.

The phone on his credenza rang and he looked up instantly. An amber light blinked, warning him the communications center was directing an emergency call to his desk. He grabbed the receiver and placed it to his ear, hearing a hum, then a click as the satellite call was put through.

"Is this Washington?" a husky voice cried.

The DDO nearly choked. He instantly recognized the gravelly voice. "Donner!" he exclaimed.

"I'm sorry," Donner answered. "They've taken my weapon. I am going to be captured! There's not a thing I can do."

"No!" Washington cried. "If you will tell me where you are I can get soldiers there!"

"It's too late," Donner answered. "My destroyer is here."

"Donner, listen!" Washington blurted. "We can get you out! We can—"

"No! Now shut up. You have to listen to me, American! They are already here! They will break me, you know that. I will try—I will try—but they are going to find out. Justify what I will suffer. They must be destroyed!"

Washington heard the sound of barking dogs, and shouting voices in the background. He heard gunshots and cursing, then the telephone went dead.

He stared in terror and amazement at the receiver in his hand. Then a great depression, a great blackness, settled over his soul.

Peshawar, Pakistan

Within hours of his capture, the general was strung up while they waited for Angra to come in and to do his job.

At 1220, Angra walked furiously into the holding cell. If the Great Master was angry, he was not nearly as angry as the Black Angel, who was so furious he hadn't slept in two days.

Angra, a huge Arab, wore a thick beard to cover the scars that curved under each ear, a reminder of the time he had spent in an Israeli prison. He wasn't old, but he was bent and many lines creased his face. Kabul was his home, though it had been months since he had been there; since the American invasion, access to home was only one of many luxuries that had been taken from him.

As the senior advisor on internal security for Alsaque el Allah, Angra did the dirtiest work. For more than twenty years he had been perfecting his trade, until there was very little about torture that he had not tried or conceived. After years of inflicting pain, there was no pretense to him now;

his eyes were dead, lifeless coals; he was a killing machine. Angra meant Black Angel, or Satan, but where he got the nickname, he could no longer recall.

The warheads had been stolen, but he would get them back.

A couple hours with Ghaith and Angra would know where they were.

He started his work and the general cried out in pain.

As the torture went on, Angra become more than impressed, for the prisoner was proving stubborn; very stubborn indeed. Already, he had suffered more than most men could bear. Now Angra had to be careful to not push him over the edge; no matter the will that resided within, the human body could only take so much pain and abuse before it shut down.

Which meant it was time to try something else.

Angra stood up from the table and went into the next room, a long and narrow chamber with no windows and only one door. A single low-wattage bulb provided a dim light. The floor was slippery and wet and smelled of blood and death.

The little girl was waiting, the prisoner's youngest child. Angra smiled at her warmly. It just wasn't her day. He took the child's hand and pulled her into the next room, where her father, General Ghaith, the man the United States called "Donner," had been strapped to a low stool, his hands tied together, his bare feet nailed to the wooden floor. In the corner of the dark room, behind a thin veil, a shadow watched quietly, his eyes grim, always moving, taking everything in. Angra nodded to the shadow then turned to the girl and she whimpered quietly, turning away from his stare. Walking toward her, he pulled on leather gloves which were stained, almost crusty, with old skin and dried blood. He pulled out his tools and nodded to one of his men.

"Come!" he said slowly, as he moved toward the child.

Through the torture of his daughter and more beatings than Angra had ever administered before, General Ghaith remained nearly silent, uttering but a few words. "Tirich Mir," he muttered once at the height of indescribable pain.

Tirich Mir. That was a start. But Angra wanted more. He wanted directions and descriptions, he wanted every detail.

Minutes later, Ghaith muttered incoherently through his clenched teeth. *"Rasul al-Laylat,"* he mumbled in pain. *Rasul al-Laylat.* The name was familiar. Apostle of the Night. Yes, Angra had heard it before. He growled again at the prisoner. *"Rasul al-Laylat* is your handler!" he asked.

The general bit on his tongue and did not reply.

"Who is *Rasul al-Laylat?!"* Angra demanded again as he twisted and put pressure on the tool of torture, pushing it deeper into the man's spine.

Ghaith screamed and spit blood, but didn't say any more as he closed his eyes to his suffering, trying to block out the pain.

Angra turned his questioning back to the mountain and the warheads, his primary concern. Twenty minutes later, he sensed he was getting close once again. The prisoner was breaking, teetering on the edge. One more prod and Angra would know exactly where the warheads were concealed. He turned his back on the general, reaching for one last special tool. He fumbled a moment, carefully choosing the right instrument; not too small, not too sharp, just enough to get the result.

Turning from his toolbox, Angra faced the prisoner again. He almost cried out in horror upon seeing the blood, a steady stream of red running from the prisoner's gaping mouth. Angra stared, then ran toward him, cursing under his breath.

Ghaith had bitten off his tongue and spit it out on the floor.

And *that* was something Angra had not seen before.

The traitor was bleeding profusely. And Angra knew what that meant. He swore in frustration, but there was nothing to do.

It only took a few moments before the prisoner was dead, slipping away in bloody silence, having only uttered two words.

Angra stared at the body, bruised and broken and red, then turned to the tall man who emerged from behind the thin veil. The Great Leader's face was flushed and Angra saw the hidden pleasure there. His hands trembled lightly and his forehead was matted with sweat.

He nodded angrily to Angra. This wasn't the outcome the he had been looking for. But Angra didn't flinch. There would be no apology from him. The Great One had insisted that he press ahead. Interrogations always resulted in death when the Great One watched on. So the traitor was dead. And there was nothing they could do about that now.

Angra pulled off one glove. "So we know where to start."

"Tirich Mir's a huge mountain. We needed much more from him."

"But the search area has been narrowed. Let's get our men there! We can have the warheads in a day if we organize properly!"

The Great Leader scowled. It would not be that easy, he knew. "Who is this man —this 'apostle' of which he spoke?" he asked.

Angra slapped his bloody gloves on his thigh. "I hear the name in Pakistan and sometimes near the Afghanistan border. CIA, maybe military, I don't know for sure."

The Great Leader waited, expecting more. "That is it?" he demanded.

"Yes, my *Sayid,* that's all I know."

"He got to our man, Ghaith. He is no amateur."

"Maybe. Maybe not. We don't know for sure."

The Great One took a step toward Angra. "Find him and kill him," he said.

Angra paused, then looked up. "But *Sayid,* this American, he doesn't matter any more. Whatever information he had, he has surely passed on. There is no reason to waste any effort on him now."

"He worked with the traitor Ghaith, and that is reason to me. So find him and kill him. I want every trace of Ghaith's work to disappear from this earth. I want no trail of his treachery to exist in this world. Ghaith is dead, and that's good, but I want to take the next step, I want those who worked with him to suffer the same fate as he. So, do what I tell you and don't argue with me. Find this 'apostle' and kill him for me."

19

Before heading out on a mission, Peter had developed a habit of calling on his friends who flew the Predator, for he had learned not to trust a map in this part of the world. The topographical maps that the National Mapping Agency provided the military of this area were notoriously unreliable. Entire mountain ranges went unnoted, villages were misplaced, and roads were depicted that had never been built. Worse, the target area around Tirich Mir was extremely remote and inhospitable, and Peter wanted to know exactly what he was getting into before he found himself following his map off the side of a cliff or into a glacier field.

The door to the Predator commander's trailer opened, and Peter moved quickly inside. The major glanced up and smiled. "Hey, buddy," he said as he stood up from his desk. "What brings you down here?"

"Business. Always business. I hope you got the word that I was going to drop by."

"Oh yeah, I got it. But you'll have to wait in line. My guys are jumping through hoops. We don't have any Predator time to give you, I'm afraid."

"Understand, Russ, but I've got my own hoops. I'm heading out on a road trip. Got a chopper waiting. So, I was hoping I could nudge myself to the front of the line. I only need a few minutes of one of your bird's time."

The major shook his head. "Ain't going to happen. Something big is going on. I have never, and I mean *never,* seen anything like it before. All our birds are in the air, spread out from one end of this forsaken hole of a country to the other. I don't know what it is, but believe me, Peter, this isn't a good time. If you could come back in a few days—"

"Can't wait, Russ. And I wouldn't ask if it wasn't important."

"Peter, I'm sorry."

Peter didn't answer, but reached in his pocket and took out a folded sheet of paper. He handed it to the major, who read it. "This isn't real," Russ said, a quizzical look on his face.

Peter only nodded.

"So, *you* know what's going on up north? You're part of the operation?"

"Afraid so," Peter said.

"But this is signed by—"

"Yeah. So, *now* will you let me borrow one of your birds?"

The major smiled and started walking. "Certainly," he said.

Snowman 91
Over Northern Pakistan

The Predator loitered around the base of Tirich Mir. The challenge for the pilot was to fly the aircraft as low as he could, so that he could observe the roads and intersections, while staying clear of the peaks that jutted up on the north, east, and west. Sometimes the pilot flew less than a hundred feet from the cliffs, tensing up every time he banked away from the rocks. It was an extremely challenging mission in this unforgiving terrain, and the reconnaissance pilot was growing weary from the twelve-hour flight. His arms were growing heavy and his leg muscles were cramped. He was hungry and tired and needed to pee.

The door to the ground control station in the van opened, letting in a wave of dry heat. The afternoon sun slanted through the half-open door, brightening the darkened control room with a harsh glare. The pilot looked up from his remote control screen as his commander and the CIA man stepped into the van. The major pulled off his flight cap and laid it on top of the nearest work table. Peter followed the major and dropped to his knees between the flight station screens. The captain looked over. "'Sup Peter?" he asked.

"In a bit of a hurry," Peter answered. "Another road trip."

The captain sniffed noisily. The CIA agent needed a shave and shower. "Didn't know you were coming down," he said, "or I would have drawn you a bath."

Peter shook his head. "Don't need a bath until sometime next week."

"Next week, huh? Now I know why you got a divorce."

"*Au contraire,* my good friend. Had nothing to do with it. Isabel had her faults, but she always smelled good."

"Good like your horse?"

"Not that good, I guess."

The captain laughed, leaning sideways in his seat as he banked the Predator on her wing, an instinctive reaction to the shifting displays. Peter watched, then continued, "Like I said, I don't have much time. How much fuel you got on that bird?"

"Enough," the captain answered. "What are you looking for?"

Peter nodded to the steep mountain range. "I'm heading up there tonight. Going to chopper in as far as we can, but will have to go the last ten or fifteen miles by foot. I'd like to scout out a trail. A few minutes of your Predator might save my team a lot of hard work."

The captain shrugged. "Sure thing. Where do you want me to go?"

The CIA man pulled out a plastic-covered map and pointed with his finger. "We're going to move in from the west, up this trail here." He tapped the map lightly and the drone pilot looked down.

"That's on the other side of the range?" the pilot said.

Peter confirmed by nodding his head.

"No problem, buddy," the pilot said as he turned the drone west.

The main screen showed the image from the Predator's forward-viewing video camera, a thirty-degree field of view taken from the nose of the aircraft. A wall of rock and snow passed in front of the unmanned aircraft. The remote control pilot, a former F-16 jock, maneuvered the aircraft aggressively, banking it up on its left wing. As he pulled the drone around, he adjusted the power to compensate for the increase in drag. Peter watched as the drone rolled out heading west.

Peter glanced at the cockpit displays, taking in the general condition of the aircraft's systems. The manifold temperature was a little high, but that was probably a result of the pilot hotdogging around—the captain had a reputation for flying the drone like a cheap F-16. The fuel was down to one hundred twenty, but the flow was steady at fourteen pounds. All of the other systems were green. He noticed again that it took an uncomfortably long time for the pilot's inputs to move the drone's flight controls.

A little more than two hundred miles to the north, the unmanned Predator reconnaissance drone was buffeted in the winds that blew up the face of the mountain, rolling almost constantly in the choppy air. Under the nose, the sensors continually moved, pivoting on their gimbals as they looked around.

The Predator was a new and rising star on the air-power stage. A strange-looking airplane with a bulbous nose, pusher engine, straight wings, and downward-sloping V tail, it was essentially a powered glider, with a forty-nine-foot wingspan and a gross weight just over a ton. Mounted in the rounded nose of the drone was a four-hundred-fifty-pound sensory payload that consisted of two electro-optical video cameras, an infrared sensor, and a synthetic aperture radar capable of seeing through clouds. The telephoto lenses on the video cameras could read a license plate from twenty-five miles away. Incredibly, the reconnaissance aircraft could stay airborne for up to forty hours. At a cost of 3.2

million dollars it was a steal of a deal, for the information it relayed was often more current than what a billion-dollar satellite could provide. The only downside to the aircraft was it was excruciatingly slow. Powered by a tiny four-stroke snowmobile engine, the aircraft cruised at a mere eighty knots.

Most of the pilots who flew the Predator felt they had died and been banished to hell; flying from the back of a van, sitting at a remote control station instead of a cockpit in the air. But what they did was important, everyone of them knew, so morale remained high despite the lack of real stick time.

The pilot spent thirty minutes giving Peter a bird's-eye view of the world, each sweeping panorama the same: steep mountains and box canyons, snow and rock and very little else. Peter watched intently, taking notes in a small book and placing marks on his map.

Flying up a glacial canyon, the captain stole a quick glance toward Peter. "You really going up there tonight?" he asked.

Peter only nodded.

"You know that most men couldn't survive a single night in that kind of terrain."

"Believe me, I know how hard it can be."

The captain grunted and turned back to his displays. Knowing where Peter would sleep the night made being a frustrated F-16 pilot suddenly seem less important.

Peter took a final look at the screen, flipped his notebook closed, and began folding his map. "Thanks guys, that's it," he said as he shoved the map inside his thigh pocket.

"Let me show you something else before you go," the captain suggested. "There's all sorts of bad guys just over the ridge from where you are going to be. If I were taking the scout troop on a hike, I'd want to see the enemy positions up close if I could."

Peter hesitated, then nodded and leaned toward the screen. "Show me," he said.

Peter watched the Predator's screen as the captain flew

over the ridge, where the ground fell away sharply until it met the tree line. Boulders as large as houses were piled in the canyon like children's blocks on the floor.

"There appears to be some kind of search going on," the captain explained as he flew.

Peter almost laughed. If the captain only knew!

"I haven't seen so much activity in a very long time," the pilot continued. "They are organizing into groups and sweeping through each of the canyons that lead up to Tirich Mir. And more troops are coming up the road every hour. They're everywhere, but disorganized. It's like watching ants run around."

The agent watched a moment. There was nothing new here. He knew the enemy was out there, and he was anxious to go. "Thank you gentlemen," he said as he pushed himself up.

"Hang on," the captain replied. Something had caught his eye. Something moving above the road.

"Choppers?" the pilot asked.

Peter had seen it too, and he leaned toward the screen. "Looks like Pumas," he said.

The pilot swore under his breath. "Pumas! No way!"

Peter stared, open-mouthed. Pumas. Here? It didn't make any sense! Pumas were sophisticated choppers, and very few nations flew them. He thought in confusion. "Get a closer visual," he said.

The pilot flew toward the choppers, his camera trained straight ahead. The men watched as the choppers came to a hover, then set down in a narrow valley on the south side of the mountain. The Predator moved toward them, watching their rotor blades spin to a stop.

Then there was a sudden white flash and the Predator pilot jumped in his seat. Every one of his sensors and flight displays went suddenly blank.

The pilot turned to his commander. "What happened?" he asked.

The three men stared at each other. The screens remained black. Without explanation, the U.S. Predator was gone.

Shin Bet Operations Center
Southern Tel Aviv

Petate waited in silence against the back wall of the tactical command center. Around him, his men worked in hushed voices. Acutely aware of his presence, they stayed out of his space, giving him wide berth, and avoided his eyes. Watching his troops, Petate could see the strain in their faces. He could also see doubt and fear.

If this worked, he was brilliant. If they failed, they were dead. Playing poker was one thing, but this was more like playing God.

At twenty-two minutes past the hour, Petate's deputy approached. The general watched the younger man moving toward him, desperately trying to read the look on his face, but the deputy remained stoic, giving nothing away. Walking up to Petate, he stared him right in the eye.

Petate swallowed hard.

The general leaned forward and whispered quietly in his ear. Petate listened, frowning, his heart racing as he nodded his head.

The fate of their nation had been placed in the balance, the future of the region suspended by a mere thread.

Reno Predator Security Compound
Islamabad, Pakistan

It took several minutes for Peter to get his satellite call patched through to Washington's desk.

"We lost a Predator," he quickly explained.

Washington was silent. "What happened?" he finally said.

"Don't know, boss. The air force guys are looking at it now, but that's one of the obvious problems with drones, when something goes wrong, without a pilot in the cockpit, it's lots harder to figure out why it went down."

Washington swore as he groaned.

"There's more," Peter said. He wet his lips before he continued. "Just before we lost the signal from the Predator we saw some Pumas down there."

"Pumas!?"

"Yeah, boss. It looked like they were predeploying to the mountain, finding a hiding place, then shutting down."

"Pumas," Washington muttered, his voice bitter and cold. "Pumas in the mountains! Who flies those birds?" The two men were quiet until Washington said, "Don't go up to Tirich Mir. Send one of your teams, but there's something else you've got to do."

20

Col. Shane Bradley awoke with a start, sitting up quickly from where he had slouched in his ejection seat. He was momentarily confused, not knowing where he was, then settled back quietly as he regained his bearings. He checked the instruments in the cockpit as he straightened himself. The aircraft was cruising peacefully at sixty-one thousand feet and five hundred and twenty knots, five miles above the highest civilian air traffic and eight miles above the tops of the clouds that hung over the cold northern sea. From this altitude he could easily make out the curve of the earth, and the stars were so bright they seemed unnaturally near. Dawn would break soon, but the sky was still dark and the northern horizon no longer sparkled with St. Elmo's fire.

Inside the cockpit, the instrumentation lights had been lowered, casting his face in a pale green-and-silver glow. He glanced at his watch, mentally adjusting the time: 0525 over the North Atlantic, 0025 back in Missouri. He had slept for almost forty minutes and felt surprisingly refreshed.

The aircraft hummed smoothly along, three billion dollars flying peacefully through the sky. He felt the aircraft vibrate beneath him and considered the jet.

Born in controversy, and incredibly expensive, the B-2 had proven in the end to be a remarkable success. Essentially invisible, a huge payload, and intercontinental range; the only problem with the jet was congress had funded so few.

Through the use of radar absorbing material and a seamless body design, the B-2 bounced back no more radar energy than a sparrow, making it essentially invisible to radar outside of five miles. Its IR signature was also incredibly small. The use of wing-top exhaust ports, flow mixers to blend the exhaust with cold outside air, and heat-absorbing paint, allowed the B-2 to leave no infrared trail in its wake. The aircraft flew so high it was impossible to detect using audio sensors, and because it attacked at night, it was impossible to see. For those portions of the mission that required it to be flown during daylight, special paints on the underside of the wings scattered and reflected the sun. Light sensors even allowed the pilots to change altitude to match the sky illumination, making the aircraft nearly invisible.

And the avionics inside the cockpit were as advanced as the technology used in the stealth design. The aircraft incorporated an astro-inertial navigational system capable of tracking celestial bodies, even during daylight or through cloudy skies. Its APQ-181 radar incorporated low probability of intercept (LPI) technology which adjusted the radar to the least amount of energy needed to detect and track a target.

Bradley was extremely proud of the aircraft, for it was without question the most sophisticated machine ever to take to the sky. He looked around the glass cockpit, then reached up and stroked the instrument display. "You're beautiful, baby," he told her. "I'm trusting you tonight."

He felt a touch on his shoulder and looked over to see Tia holding an unopened container of bottled water for him. He took it and thanked her.

During cruise flight neither pilot was wearing a helmet, just a small headpiece with a tiny microphone that extended to the front of their mouths. Bradley pushed the microphone under his chin and took a long drink. "Cheers, sir," Tia said above the low roar of the aircraft's powerful engines.

"Tia, you don't always have to call me 'sir,' " he said after taking a drink.

"It's okay, sir. It's more comfortable for me."

Bradley shrugged then swallowed another mouthful of water.

Tia looked over. "We haven't had the predicted tailwinds crossing the pond," she said. "We've got a forty-knot head-wind, not the ninety-knot tailwind the forecast predicted. So, even though we pushed up our speed, we're still falling be-hind. And pushing up our power has greatly increased our fuel flow."

Bradley had also been watching the fuel and time projec-tions. "When we hit the tanker we'll ask for more fuel," he answered.

"My greater concern is the time. Every minute, every second is crucial now."

Bradley nodded as he wondered for the thousandth time what was going on down "on earth." But he didn't reply to her comment, for there was nothing to say. They could con-trol many things, but they couldn't control the headwinds. "Station check," he said, glancing down at the flight plan he had strapped to his thigh.

Tia went through her cockpit checks quickly. "A little more than one-hundred-sixty-thousand pounds of fuel. Last contact with Snowbird was a bit more than an hour ago. The SAT-COM is down at this latitude, but we'll pick up the satellite communication link again when we get north of the Azores. I talked with Colonel Kier over the HF while you were asleep. He is coordinating the updates with the tankers out of Aviano."

"Any additional Intel?"

Tia shook her head no.

"How's number two?"

"So far, so good." The communications plan required there be no radio conversations between flight lead and the number two aircraft. No news was good news and, unless there was an emergency, the two aircraft wouldn't talk.

Tia sat back and stared out at the night. She glanced at her console clock. More than eight hours to kill. "Your dad was General Westmoreland's deputy?" she asked in an attempt to pass time.

"Yeah," Bradley answered, "for most of the war."

"What's he doing now?"

That was an interesting question. Bradley paused, then answered, "The general is dead."

"Oh, I'm sorry. I didn't know."

"It's okay. He passed away quite a few years ago."

"You called him 'the general.' "

"I didn't notice."

"You were not very close."

"Is that a comment or question?"

"A comment, I guess. Or am I reading too much?"

"No, you are right," Bradley answered. "He was 'the general' to me. He was a wonderful man, perfectly loyal to my mom."

"Did your father push you into volunteering to work with the UN peacekeepers?" Tia asked.

"It was something I wanted to do."

"You put off flight school to walk the streets of Ramallah?"

"It just seemed like a good idea at the time."

Tia looked away as she sipped at her water. "Is that why you work with the CIA?" she asked.

Bradley lifted an eyebrow. "That is not a good question," he said.

"I'm sorry, sir, but I mean, let's face it, you come from a—how would you describe it—an unconventional background. Peacekeeping on the West Bank. Fluent in Arabic."

"Mundane staff work. Writing papers. Reading reports. Nothing interesting, I promise you."

Tia eyed him quickly. She wasn't a fool.

"And your family?" Bradley asked, anxious to talk about something else.

Tia stared at the moon. "My dad was a pilot with the Cambodian air force. I've wanted to fly since before I could walk. My only disappointment is that the Communists are not our enemy any longer, for I've always had dreams of bombing them. But hey, we accept life's little disappointments, don't we."

Bradley had to laugh.

The air-traffic-control radio crackled quietly as a Delta 747 reported its position over the ocean. Bradley compared its location against the B-2. The airliner was almost three hundred miles to the north, following the well-used jet route from London to JFK. There was no radar coverage over the middle of the ocean, and the only contact with ground controllers was through the position reports the pilots called over the high frequency radio. After the Delta pilot completed his report, it grew quiet again.

Tia looked over to Bradley and pointed to the center display. "This weak tailwind is killing us. We're still losing time."

Bradley grunted anxiously, then looked straight ahead out of the cockpit. The target was out there, a little more than four thousand miles away.

21

The pilot settled into the tight cockpit and looked at the controls and displays, which, although familiar, were not comfortable to him. He ran his eyes down the out-moded Soviet cockpit, taking in the haphazard position of the primary flying instruments, engine indicators, and weapon displays. It had been too long since he had flown this jet, and even in the old days when he flew it regularly, acting as an attacker against his fellow pilots to train them in the aerial combat tactics they would see if there was open war, the old fashioned cockpit had never felt comfortable to him. The fighter's dartlike nose canted slightly downward and the Plexiglas cockpit wrapped around his shoulders, limiting his field of view. Worse, the rudder pedals were too small and the control stick too sloppy. But, though the fighter was slow and heavy until it got out the gate, it was incredibly fast and agile once it reached altitude.

As he settled in the cockpit and pulled his ejection seat straps over his shoulders, the pilot realized with frustration that he was finding it difficult to concentrate, his mind continually wondering what he was doing there. What kind of mission was this? It didn't make any sense!

He considered the first rule of combat. *Identify friend from foe.*

His gut tightened up. Had they done that tonight?

The pilot paused again, staring at the empty windscreen before him.

He had serious doubts about the wisdom of his orders, but when he had dared question his superior, the response had been stone cold. "Who are you to question?" his commander had said. "You have been given an order. Now go do your job."

Taking a deep breath, the pilot finished strapping himself in, then pulled out his checklist and strapped it to his leg. Moving his hands slowly through the cockpit he hesitated, careful not to make a mistake as he prepared the aircraft for flight. Looking around him, the cockpit seemed to blur, for he was already fatigued, having spent the last nine hours locked in a secure room. Knowing what he did now, he was a security risk; and even though he was a man of many talents, one of the very few pilots they had, he could not be trusted with such an enormous secret. Quarantined from the others, he had stared at the walls while waiting for his orders to walk to his jet.

And now here he was. It was time to go.

Reaching the point in the checklist when he was ready for engine start, the pilot signaled the ground crew and the hangar lights were turned down to a dim glow, allowing just enough light for the ground crews to work. Then the rear hangar doors rolled open behind his engine exhaust. After starting the two powerful engines, the pilot began checking his weapons and bringing his avionics and navigational systems on line.

Finishing these tasks, he glanced to his right at the other Soviet fighter. The second pilot was stirring his stick to check his flight controls, and the heavy fighter bounced lightly as the hydraulics snapped the elevators on the tail of the jet, then the rear-engine exhaust ports opened slightly as the pilot moved his throttles out of the idle detent.

They were beautiful fighters, these old Soviet machines. Steel and aluminum, they were heavy but capable; and despite the awkward cant of their nose cones and the archaic controls, the pilot had to admire the Soviet design.

Similar in size and performance to the American F-15 Eagle and F-14 Tomcat, the Su-27s were heavier than their American counterparts. With two enormous fuel-sucking engines, the Su-27 could climb like a rocket to sixty thousand feet, accelerating upward at nearly ninety degrees. Though the recent version of the aircraft had been upgraded, the earlier models, like the one this pilot sat in, carried the first-generation AA-10 and AA-11 air-to-air missiles as well as a very reliable cannon. (Soviet fighter pilots loved an old-fashioned, fang-to-fang dogfight, and the cannon was the weapon of choice when two fighters got close.) In addition to the cannon and missiles, the Su-27s were equipped with a Flash Dance radar, RWR IRST and a Balistic bombsight, as well as a highly-sensitive, digitally magnified TV sensor located in the nose of the aircraft. But despite all this equipment, if he was going to find the target, the pilot knew he would have to do it the old-fashioned way. Like his father before him, fighting over Gaza in the Six-Day War, he would have to use his eyeballs. He hoped he might catch a glimpse of the moon shining off the target's wings or a flash of it's windscreen under the light of the stars.

An impossible task to find it? He thought.

Maybe so.

But he had a significant advantage in the game of cat and mouse. For one thing, he knew where the target would be flying tonight, a pretty good idea of the time it would be appearing, and where it would be. He knew the approximate altitude at which it would be flying, as well as the direction it would be coming, and the approximate time.

After starting the engines, the pilot worked quickly through his checklist; he had a hard takeoff time and he couldn't be late. Loading his flight coordinates in the INS, he checked his navigational chart, then the coordinates of his refueling airfield—a tiny strip of cracked cement in the western Afghanistan desert—an emergency landing field nestled in a narrow valley that was no longer used. It would take him almost fifty minutes to get to the field (about two-thirds of the time of most any other fighter), then another half hour to re-fuel and get back in the air.

He glanced at his watch. They were cutting it close.

Turning in his seat, he communicated with his wingman, using hand gestures to signal he was ready to go. The second pilot nodded and the formation leader motioned to his ground crew to pull his chocks, then pushed up the power. The heavy fighters moved forward, kicking up dust and debris and sending a trail of gray smoke and dirt through the open doors of the hangar as they moved into the dark.

The fighters taxied quickly from the hanger and turned to the runway, their landing lights off and their wingtip lights set to dim. Two minutes later they took to the air, shattering the night with a thunderous noise, their twin engines sprouting blue-and-orange tails of flame as the pilots lit their afterburners and turned sharply east.

Kill 31
Over the Mediterranean Sea

The coming day proved to be short, with less than seven hours between sunrise and sunset. The two crew members took turns sleeping briefly in their seats in the mid-afternoon. Breakfast, lunch, and dinner were the same: sandwiches, orange juice, granola bars, and nuts. They drank plenty of water, keeping themselves hydrated to fight the elements of fatigue that were exaggerated by the dry cockpit air. In the late afternoon, with the sun passing behind them, the two B-2s prepared to refuel from a pair of KC-10s from Aviano, a military installation situated near the base of the Italian Alps.

The bombers hadn't talked on the radio since they had taken off from Whiteman AFB. As per the rules of engagement, the second air refueling was also conducted under radio silence.

Tia was at the controls and in the lead. The second B-2

tightened up the spacing, moving in on lead until he was right off the wing.

Two KC-10s were already level at twenty thousand feet. The B-2s descended to nineteen thousand five hundred and the rolling pastures and terraced vineyards of Sicily passed peacefully below as the four aircraft came together in a carefully orchestrated maneuver. With the huge tankers five hundred feet above them and one mile ahead, the B-2s began to climb and move forward. Tia moved into position expertly, fifty feet behind and below the first tanker. She cleared off her wingman, and the second B-2 moved in on the second KC-10. The two bombers would refuel simultaneously to reduce the time.

The lead tanker's air refueling position lights, a double line of green and red lights on the underside of the aircraft, began to blink, the signal for the bomber to move into the contact position. Tia moved the four throttle controllers forward almost imperceptibly and the aircraft began to creep forward and upward. Bradley reached to the console above him and exposed the air refueling receptacle, which was on top of the aircraft and nearly in the center of the body. He felt a quick *clang* as the air refueling receptacle rotated one hundred eighty degrees to reveal itself from underneath the aircraft's skin. A "ready" light illuminated on the center console between the two pilots. Bradley opened the rudder brakes slightly in order that the high performance B-2 might more closely match the flight characteristics of the lumbering KC-10. The B-2 moved forward through two separate downbursts, one from the KC-10's engines and one from its wings. As the bomber moved under the tanker, the bow of compressed air that was pushed out in front of its nose began to fight against the tanker, causing the aircraft to interact with each other. The tanker moved up and the bomber moved down.

Tia held the control stick lightly with her fingers, sensing more than thinking, flying by feel. She moved herself exactly into the proper refueling position.

The tanker's air refueling lights went suddenly off, the signal to halt the maneuver. Tia backed the B-2 away from the tanker, sliding back into the precontact position. The bomber crew waited. Almost a minute passed. Something was wrong. The refueling lights flickered, then illuminated again. Tia moved forward and upward until she was in a position right under the tanker again. She stopped the aircraft and held it steady, matching the tanker perfectly as it flew at three hundred twenty knots. The boom operator extended his boom, careful not to touch the delicate skin of the bomber, knowing even a tiny scratch would expose the Stealth aircraft to radar and cost untold millions to repair. The boom operator finally pushed the air refueling boom toward the bomber's receptacle. Bradley felt a solid thunk, but the two aircraft didn't latch. He felt the boom probe once again, hearing it knock against the refueling plate. The boom seated into the receptacle, but again, the aircraft didn't latch. The boom jabbed a final time, then pulled back, lifting away from the tanker. Tia remained in position, holding the bomber steady. The boom extended again. Bradley felt himself tense. The boom scraped the top of the bomber and Bradley visibly cringed. Tia sucked in her breath. "What's going on up there!" she said angrily. On the third attempt, the two aircraft latched and the air refueling finally began. Bradley let out a breath. Tia slowly shook her head.

"Good job," Bradley said over the intercom in his mask. Both of the pilots had their combat helmets on now.

"Do you think he got us?" Tia asked.

"I don't know. He pulled the boom across the top, but it felt pretty light."

"A tiny scratch is all it takes for us to radiate like a 747.

"We'll be okay," Bradley said, though he wasn't sure. He began to monitor the flow. The fuel was coming on very slowly. "There's a problem with the boom," he announced.

Tia didn't take her eyes off the tanker. "What's the fuel flow?"

"Two thousand pounds a minute."

"It should be six thousand."

"I know, but let's not push it. We could unlatch and have the tanker reset the boom, but I'd rather keep the connection than go through that again. It will take a little longer to get

our full offload, but I'd rather have that than give them another chance to ram the boom through our front window."

Tia nodded agreement, concentrating on flying the jet.
The enormous KC-10 bumped lightly as the aircraft passed
through a thin stream of clouds, and Tia adjusted the throttles to stay in position. Bradley glanced at the tanker through
the top of his windscreen. Tia remained within a few inches
of the center position. The minutes passed and, as the
bomber became more heavy, Tia slowly increased power to
compensate for the increase in drag. She glanced at the fuel
readout. Bradley followed her eyes.

"It's slow, but we're getting gas. We've taken on forty
thousand pounds. Another fifty-five thousand to go."

Bradley glanced off to his right. His wingman, the second
bomber, had already completed refueling. Bradley watched
as the bomber dropped away from its tanker and slid straight
back. After clearing the KC-10, the second B-2 slid left and
down, moving toward the lead jet, where it would take up a
position fifty feet below and a couple hundred feet back.
There it would stay until the refueling was complete.
Bradley watched the second bomber, the afternoon sun
glinting off its black skin, sliding into position until it had
disappeared below him.

"Two is complete and in position."

Tia clicked her microphone in reply. The boom was beginning to wobble and she was fighting to stay connected to
the air refueling receptacle. It was a battle. She was winning,
but it was hard work, Bradley could tell. He didn't say anything to distract her, letting her concentrate on the boom. His
eyes scanned across the cockpit. Everything was in the
green.

Suddenly Bradley heard a *crack* and looked up with a start.
Another *crack,* this one louder, then a shudder ran through the
jet. The refueling boom broke away, sending a jarring vibration throughout the B-2. Bradley stared in amazement as the
boom gyrated wildly directly in front of the cockpit, slicing
through the air in an uncontrollable dance.

Tia flinched and pulled back as the boom swung inches

from her windscreen, thinking it was surely going to smash through the glass. Another *crack* sounded and the left control winglet tore away from the boom. Jet fuel sprayed from the nozzle, washing over the upper fuselage of the B-2. It was impossible to see. Tia gripped the controls.

"Breakaway!" Bradley shouted as he reached for the controls. He jerked the throttles back and Tia dropped the nose. The breakaway lights flashed on the bottom of the tanker as the B-2 dropped away.

The boom suddenly jammed to the extreme right of the tanker, then broke away entirely from the tail of the KC-10. Broken pieces of metal scattered wildly in the wind. The main boom, eleven hundred pounds of metal, dropped toward the bomber, tumbling end over end, like a falling telephone pole. The main section of boom smashed into the side of the Stealth's cockpit and slashed along the top side of the jet. A broken piece of nozzle hit the bomber on the beak then rolled across the wing's leading edge. Pieces of steel and aluminum pattered the aircraft like hail. Tia gripped the control stick fiercely and pushed the jet down. Bradley grabbed the controls, helping her to hold it steady. The windscreen smeared with jet fuel like a dirty, oily rain. The jet fuel rolled back on the windscreen, then began to blow clear.

"I got it," Tia shouted. Her voice remained calm, though she held a death grip on the stick. Bradley nodded, then reluctantly pulled his hands away from the controls.

The B-2 descended steeply and the tanker accelerated away. Tia leveled off a thousand feet below the tanker. She kept it in sight and held a position about a mile behind. Seconds later the radios came to life. For the first time since taking off, the combat aircraft broke radio silence.

"Kill 31, say status," the tanker pilot asked, his voice tight and distressed.

Bradley ignored him while he ran through his checklist. He closed his air refueling receptacle, placed his rudder/brakes to their cruise flight position, visually cleared the tanker, monitored Tia as she leveled the aircraft, then initiated the automatic fuel balance system.

"Kill 31, say status," the tanker pilot demanded again.

Bradley switched his radio. "Boxcar, this is Kill. Stand by," he said. He released his broadcast switch, turned to Tia and asked. "How does it feel?"

"I've had a slight buzz in the pedals, but it's dissipating now. We must have broken some skin off of one of the control surfaces."

"The jet feels okay though?"

"Yes, I think so."

The radios crackled again. This time it was the other B-2. "Kill Lead, this is Two." The radio transmission was weak and barely understandable.

Bradley paused, glanced at Tia, then answered, "Go, Two."

"Yeah, what the . . . what happened up there, Lead?"

"We're checking it. The boom broke."

"Yeah, well, ah . . . I would say so. And we've got a little problem back here."

Bradley grew more tense. With those words, he knew the mission lay in the balance. He shot another look to Tia. "What's up down there, guys?" he asked.

"Part of the boom—it came out of nowhere. We took a piece of metal up our intake. Looks like we're going to lose engines three and four."

Bradley swore in frustration. "You going to make it back there?" he demanded.

"Yeah, we're okay, boss. But give us a minute while we sort this out. We do know that engine three is a goner, and four doesn't look good."

"Standing by," Bradley answered. He fumed, then turned to Tia. "All right," he asked, "how is our jet?"

"It feels okay," she answered. "Certainly mission-capable." She nodded toward the main computer display. "How do our systems look?"

Bradley scanned his CRTs, bringing up various displays to check the health of his jet. The integrated computer system ran a check of every valve, hose, relay, engine, black box, pressure, and system. The computers indicated several systems were down; including the adjustable intake scoop on the number three engine and the communications antennae relay.

"The number three bypass scoop has been damaged," he announced. "That will give us a higher infrared signature, and that isn't good when we're going into combat. How significant it will be, there is no way to know. And our flush mount antennae relay was also hit."

"Which means we have no HF and satellite-radio capability," Tia said.

Bradley nodded unhappily. The HF and SATCOM were used for long-range transmissions. They were the only way to communicate with their command post or American forces on the ground.

"We should still have UHF and VHF capability," Tia said. "The central computer should automatically route those radio antennae signals through the other relay."

Bradley shook his head as he recalled the electrical schematic. "I don't think so, Tia," he said. "The relays sit side by side and are flush-mounted to the skin. If one was damaged, chances are, they both got hit."

Tia glanced at him. "How do you know that?"

Bradley paused. "I can picture the schematic in my mind."

Tia nodded, impressed as Bradley worked his data input display. "I was right," he said, looking up from his computer. "The integrated computer is indicating damage to both antennae relays. And without the antennae boost, not only do we lose SATCOM and HF, but both UHF and VHF radios will be broadcasting on raw power only. They will have a very short range, perhaps just a few miles."

"That isn't going to help us much, is it?" Tia said ironically.

Bradley nodded, then their radio broke in again: "Kill, this is Two." The radio signal was so weak, it was barely understandable.

"Go, Two," Bradley answered.

"Yeah, Lead, status report. It looks like we sucked up a couple pieces of the boom and it has cooked number three engine completely. Four is overheating, but hanging in there right now. It might give us a few minutes, but that's about all. Looks like we're done for the day. We've got to nurse this baby home."

"Rog," Bradley said.

"We copy," the tanker pilot also replied. "We can escort Kill Two to Aviano."

"Okay, guys, stand by," Bradley answered. "We've got a few things here we need to sort out. Meanwhile, tanker, continue on track. Two, stay with us. We'll get back to you with the plan."

Bradley turned to Tia. "Okay, we've got to make a few decisions. First things first. Except for the radios, do we have a good jet?"

Tia stirred the controls and the B-2 responded in kind. She pulled the nose up, then pushed down, completing her controllability check. "It feels good," she answered, then nodded to the main console and said, "Try the radios."

Bradley punched at his control panel to broadcast over VHF radio. "No good on Victor," he said.

"COMSAT?"

Bradley tried the satellite communications and data receiver. "No good. I'm getting a partial signal, but that's it. Without the antennae relay, we won't have a range beyond one or two miles."

"FM?" Tia asked. She was down to their last radio.

Again Bradley played with his communications panel. He dialed up several FM frequencies. Tia concentrated on following the tanker and flying the jet. "No good," Bradley announced in frustration. "Five freakin' radios in this jet, and not a single one of them is good for more than two miles."

"Guess there might be a design flaw in grouping the two relay boxes together," Tia answered sarcastically.

"Yeah. Go figure why the engineers didn't consider the possibility of an air-refueling boom sliding down the top of the jet at four hundred miles an hour."

"At least the boom wasn't sucked into one of our engines."

"Or smashed through our windscreen."

Tia swallowed. In her mind she saw the enormous boom

falling toward them, a dark metal pole flipping end over end. She pictured it swinging by their cockpit window and swallowed again. "What do we do?"

Bradley glanced through the windscreen. He watched the two KC-10s, maybe one mile ahead and a thousand feet above. The sun was beginning to set and the tankers reflected the horizontal light. He punched his radio broadcast switch, "Boxcar, Kill 31, how do you read?"

"Kill . . . Boxcar . . . you weak and extremely broken . . . status and . . . intentions."

Bradley swore to himself. Without the com relay, his radios had even less range than he had expected. He motioned for Tia to close in the tanker. She moved the throttles forward and quickly closed the distance between the two aircraft. Bradley pressed his broadcast button again and spoke very slowly. "Kill 31 is in the green. But our antennae relays have been severely damaged, so we will be NORDO, except for when in extremely close range."

"Roger. Confirm mission capable—possible NORDO." The radio was more clear now that they had moved in on the tanker.

"Affirm. NORDO. No Radio," Bradley replied.

"NORDO, yes sir."

"You heard the status of number Two?" Bradley asked.

"Roger, Kill. Two has lost number three. Four is going down. Confirm you want us to escort Kill Two back to Aviano?"

"Is that what you want to do, Two?"

"Rog, Lead," the second B-2 pilot replied.

"Understand, Two," Bradley answered. "Boxcar, you copy?"

"Copy that, Kill."

Bradley paused then punched his radio again. "Boxcar, what happened up there?"

"You got me, 31. We've never seen anything like that before. The boomer tried to unlatch the boom to reset it, but he couldn't pull away from your receptacle. The latch lock then broke away, pulling the boom loose from its hydraulic seat.

It only took seconds before we lost one of the steering fins, and once that was gone, the asymmetrical lift broke the boom completely away. We figure you got about two thousand pounds of metal in the face. We're awful sorry, sir. We were sucking seat cushion too."

"You guys okay?"

"Nothing a little duct tape and superglue won't fix."

"Good."

"One more thing, Kill. The boomer reports your refueling receptacle is definitely cracked. You are Tango Uniform for more refueling, I'm afraid."

Bradley glanced at Tia and they both shook their heads. "Rog," Bradley answered. "Broken refueling receptacle. Negative ability to refuel."

The radios were quiet for ten seconds while the crews absorbed this news. "With your radios down, do you want us to relay for you?" the tanker pilot finally said.

"Stand by," Bradley answered. He looked at his fuel control panel. "We only got half our fuel load," he said to Tia.

She was already figuring how far they could make it. She tapped quickly at her flight computer. "We've got a little over 105,000 pounds. That will get us to the target, with a two-hour-forty-eight-minute reserve. But that isn't enough fuel to get anywhere safe after that."

"What options do we have?"

"Abort the mission and head for Aviano."

"Negative. With Two dropping out, we absolutely will continue."

"If we are bleeding radar energy or suffered damage to the RAM, we might not be able to complete the mission safely anyway."

Bradley turned to Tia. She was already staring at him. Both of them were thinking of the nuclear warheads hidden under Mount Tirich Mir. "Let me say it again," Bradley answered. "As long as this jet will fly, we will continue the mission. If it means we fly until we run out of gas, we will continue to the target. Regardless the cost."

Tia nodded in his direction. She understood. "I wasn't

suggesting otherwise, sir," she added. "But you asked for
our options. I'm only pointing out the things we have to
consider."

"Understand. Continue."

"With the fuel we have left, we could hit the target, then
turn west. A tanker could deploy and meet us over northern
Iraq."

"No good. The tanker would likely be shot down over
Syria, Iran, or Lebanon. And with a cracked refueling receptacle, we couldn't refuel anyway."

"Next option, we forge ahead, hit the target, then try for
Diego Garcia."

Bradley worked his navigational computer, figuring the
distance to the tiny British island in the Indian Ocean. He
shook his head. "We'll flame out five hundred miles short."

"Islamabad? Kabul?"

"Negative. That is the very last option we have. I'd ditch
before I'd land this aircraft at any airfield in southern Asia.
We will not land at an unsecured field. We will not expose
this aircraft to an unsecure environment."

"Kill . . . Kill," the tanker pilot broke into their conversation. "Ki . . . intent . . . relay." The radio transmission was
almost completely lost in static. Bradley looked out of his
windscreen. The tanker had moved out before them. He
glanced at his radar. The tanker was a little more than three
miles away. "Kill . . . state . . . Kill . . . intentions."

"Stand by," Bradley growled over the radio again. "Push
up the speed," he then commanded Tia. "Stay within half a
mile or we will lose communications with them completely."
Tia pushed up the throttles to close on the tanker again.

"We could hit the target, then try for Manama Air Base?"
Bradley suggested after some thought. Manama was on the
tip of Qatar, along the eastern edge of the Saudi Arabian
Peninsula. It was the nearest secure airbase in which they
could land. But with only 105,000 pounds of fuel in their
tanks it was going to be very close. "With a two-hour-forty-
eight-minute reserve, we should be able to hit the target,
then get back to Qatar," he said.

Tia thought as she flew. "Manama is a Qatar military installation, but it is secure. There's a United States Marine unit and deployed F-16s. It's the only place within a thousand miles of Pakistan that I would dare put this aircraft down." She turned to the data entry panel on her right side. "What are the coordinates of the field at Manama?" she asked.

Bradley pulled out his Flight Information Handbook and quickly, almost nervously, flipped through the pages. He found the information he was looking for and read the airfield coordinates for Manama to Tia. She punched the information into her computer, then looked at the result.

"We can make the airfield with a twenty-one minute reserve," she announced. "If the headwinds don't pick up. And if we have no delays."

"Twenty-one minutes!" Bradley shook his head in frustration. "And that's only if we fly over Iran, which we want to avoid at all cost, if we can." He reached over and picked up the aeronautical chart. "What if we go from the target south to the Gulf of Oman, and from there to Manama? That way we wouldn't have to over fly Afghanistan and Iran on the way to Qatar."

"No way. It's too far. We would run out of gas."

"Okay. But what if we charted a course for the tip of the United Arab Emirates. We could skirt the border of Afghanistan and most of Iran. That would keep us clear of most hostile airspace."

"It's longer that way, but probably worth the risk. The last thing we want is be over hostiles after we have completed the attack. But that would get us to Manama with only"—Tia punched at her data panel—"a twelve-minute fuel reserve."

Bradley pressed his lips in silent desperation. Calling it razor thin was a gracious understatement. It was less than a razor. It was near suicide. But he didn't have any choice. Bad as it was, it was the only option they had. "Okay," he said with a tight swallow. "We know we have damage to our RAM and we don't know how detectable to radar we might be. In addition, we might be bleeding infrared energy. We can probably sneak over before the attack, when the bad guys won't be looking. But everyone will launch their air-defense fighters to watch their flanks once they get word of the mission. There's no way we want to fly over those countries when we're on the way home.

"So we'll hit the target, then fly south for the Gulf and, once off the coast of Iran, head to Qatar. We'll do what we can to avoid hostile airspace and get to the Gulf as quickly as we can. That way, if we end up ditching the aircraft, at least it will be over international waters, not Iran. I want to go down somewhere where there will be U.S. or British naval assets who could assist in the rescue."

Tia didn't answer. She couldn't get it out of her mind! They were planning on landing with only a twelve minute reserve! It was almost ridiculous. Her chest tightened up. "I'll say this," she finally said, "cutting it that close will make it a lot more exciting."

"That it will. That it will. But it's the best option we have."

"You know, we'll be famous if we drop this three-billion-dollar aircraft in the ocean."

"I don't want to be famous."

"Neither do I."

They were silent, each lost in thought until Bradley finally punched his radio switch and broadcast, "Boxcar."

"Kill, this is Boxcar. Go ahead."

"Boxcar, we need you to take note and relay our intentions to command post. Kill 31 is mission capable and intends to continue. We will strike the target. However, with only the partial offload of fuel and no ability to refuel, we can not complete the mission as planned. Our intentions are to divert into Manama. Divert route will be direct Al Khasab, direct Doha, direct Manama."

"Understand. Complete mission. Divert to Manama, via Al Khasab and Doha."

"That's affirm. We anticipate being NORDO until mission complete. Estimate our time to divert field at 0325 local. Have them stand ready. You copy?"

"Roger, Kill. Your intention is to continue. Expect NORDO. Estimating Manama at 0325 local."

"That's affirm."

The tanker pilot waited, then said. "Kill, are you certain? You're cutting it pretty close!"

"Roger, Box, we'll be fine."

Another long pause, then, "Alright, Kill. Anything else?"

"Negative. You escort Number Two."

"Wilco, Kill. And once again, we are sorry."

"Roger, understand. Nothing you could do."

"Fly safe, Kill 31. Good hunting, sir."

Bradley watched as the two tankers started lifting away in a climbing, left-hand turn on their way back to Italy. He saw the shadow of the second B-2 fall in a mile behind the tankers. The aircraft climbed together and accelerated away.

Tia pushed up the power and pulled up the nose of her aircraft. "Guess that's it then," she said.

"Yeah," Bradley answered.

"We'll keep our eyes on the gas. We hit the target, then head south. Worst case, we run out of gas somewhere off the coast of Iran and we take a swim in the Arabian Sea. Rescue won't be long in coming."

"Of course, without our radios no one will know where we are. And they won't know if we go down. So we might be in the water for a while."

"But they have our route and ETA. Worst case, we get sunburned while we wait in our rafts. Best case, we have breakfast at the Manama Naval Officers Club."

"You get me there, baby, and I'm buying the beer."

"For breakfast?"

"It would be dinner time back in the States."

"It's a deal then. Beer and breakfast at Manama. It's not a bad plan."

Bradley smiled bitterly. "You know, of all the times, of all the things, I can't believe this happened—not on *this* mission."

Tia sucked on her lip. "It's a little ironic," she laughed miserably.

Bradley only stared.

"It's not impossible," she said as she turned to him.

Bradley nodded in answer. But inside he knew better and his gut tightened up.

22

The Stealth climbed, leveling at sixty-two thousand feet. Bradley took the controls, wanting to feel the jet. It was stable and smooth. So far as he could tell, there was no damage done. Tia turned to the avionics and weapons systems, running them through their self-checks. It was growing dark quickly as evening came on. Cyprus passed under the aircraft, a nondescript piece of landmass more than ten miles below, then the coastline of Syria began to come into view under the light of the stars, the shoreline shimmering in the dim moonlight. Tia shot an update with the radar to update the Internal Navigational System, taking a fix off a road intersection along the coastline.

"How do the weapons systems look?" Bradley asked.

"They check perfectly. The most difficult part of this mission is going to be identifying the target among all those caves, and we can still do that."

"If we have damage to our RAM, we might get lit up by radar."

"I don't think it will matter. The damage is along the top side, where it can only be detected by a fighter, not a ground-based missile. And neither Pakistan nor Afghanistan has any fighters that could hurt us this high. The only time we'll be vulnerable is during the bomb run, when we have to descend to fighter altitude."

"All right then. Let's go to war."

Tia flipped the master cockpit control mode switch to the "Go to War" mode. The rudder/brakes, which were normally open five degrees to provide better control response, immediately closed, thus eliminating their radar reflection. Differential engine thrust, a highly classified element of the B-2, would now provide directional control.

The crewmembers continued their combat checklist. Twenty miles from the coast, they were ready to go. By then it was dark. The B-2 crossed Syria and Iraq without being detected. Their route then took them almost directly over Tehran. The city lights shined unnaturally bright, seemingly close enough to touch them, even from sixty-two thousand feet. It was surreal to be flying over a hostile country's capital without any fear. The Caspian Sea shimmered off to their left. The mountains in the east loomed nearer, deep shadows against the darkening night. Bradley watched them, then noticed the brown moon on the horizon.

"Take a look on the radar," he instructed Tia. "It looks like there might be dust storms building along the Garagum Desert."

Sandstorms over the desert kicked up frequently, generated by the powerful winds sweeping down from the mountains. These storms carried tons of sand and debris in a billowing wall that sometimes reached up to seventy thousand feet. And the air force had learned from experience during the first attacks on Afghanistan that the dust would play havoc on the delicate skin of the fragile B-2. Bradley studied the brown clouds against the moonlit horizon. "We can't afford to divert around any sandstorms," he said. "We don't have the time, and we don't have the gas."

Tia worked the radar, selecting weather mode. Her heart skipped a beat. The weather scope cluttered with a solid green mass. She tuned the radar down, searching for the tops of the storms, then took a deep breath. "It doesn't look great, but I think we can make it. The storms are topping out at about fifty-five thousand feet. We should be able to get over the top, even if we stay on this course."

"How far out are the storms now?"

"Looks like two hundred—check that, one hundred eighty miles."

Bradley didn't reply. Tia continued to work her radar display. Something had caught her eye on the other side of the dust clouds; multiple hits on her radar, some high and some low. She looked carefully, switching to air-to-air mode. "Look at this!" she said, overlaying her radar data onto Colonel Bradley's center CRT.

He looked down and frowned. "No way!" he exclaimed.

"It's right. I've checked the signal. That's a Flash Dance radar. Definitely Su-27 fighters. Two of them. And they're loitering over the target, I mean right over it, sir. And look at *this*. Puma helicopters! Low. Near the target."

"Russians?" he asked her in a disbelieving tone.

"No way, boss. Wrong radar wavelength. The Russian 27s have the newer radar that operates on a slightly higher frequency."

"Syrians? Iranians?"

Tia didn't answer.

"Who else flies the Su-27!" Bradley demanded.

Tia shook her head.

"It doesn't make any sense," the colonel muttered angrily.

"I'm telling you, sir, those are Pumas down there. And Su-27 radars. Look at the wavelength. How can you argue with that! And they're directly over Tirich Mir!"

Bradley thought for a moment, then swore bitterly. Tia looked at him, her face growing pale in the dim cockpit light. Lot's of countries flew Su-27s, and none of them were friends. "Someone knows we're coming," she whispered. "And they're waiting for us."

23

Washington fumed at his desk, his temples throbbing. Less than fifteen hours into the mission, and things had turned upside down! Fifteen hours into the mission, and he had a rock in his gut.

Dropping the boom onto the B-2! Some genius was going to pay for that one. Someone, he didn't care who, but someone was going to stand up to the firing line and take a bullet for that, nearly sinking the mission before it even left friendly airspace. Now they were down to one bomber. And they had no communications with it! They had a three-billion-dollar aircraft strolling around central Asia with a bay full of nuclear weapons, *and they didn't have an ability to talk with the crew!*

Washington shook his head in disgust.

He glanced at his desk and the initial flash report of the Predator going down, then thought of the call from Peter Zembeic telling him how the air force had lost the signal from the Predator somewhere over the target. It wasn't clear what had happened, but Washington had an idea, and the fact that there were Pumas in the area only made his suspicions worse.

So he had sent Peter to investigate—to have a word with the old man. So far, he'd heard nothing, and that gnawed at him inside. Like a knife scraping an old wound, he waited for the bad news that he was certain was going to make him bleed.

Worse, and a more immediate problem, was the fact that it would be two hours before they could get another Predator over the target. *Two friggin' hours!* Washington almost moaned. Two hours was a lifetime! The Predators were too slow!

A thick darkness gathered around him, a sixth sense he had developed over the thirty years with the agency, a sense he had cultivated as a kid in the ghetto trying to grow up without being taken down. After a lifetime of fighting, he trusted his gut, and his gut told him now that things were falling apart.

Donner. Captured. Probably dead. The enemy tightening their search, scrambling around the mountains of Tirich Mir. No communications with his bomber. The Predator down.

His dread deepened. Something was happening, something he couldn't touch, see, or feel. Something was working against them. He had never believed in coincidence and he didn't believe in it now.

Islamabad, Pakistan

The taxi was a beat-up and rusted-out '89 Buick with a broken window on the passenger's side that had been taped over with plastic that was now dry and cracked from exposure to the sun. The rear seats were torn and smelled of mice, and the floor was covered with newspapers and crushed cigarettes. The sedan spewed oily exhaust and the entire engine rattled from the missing spark plug in the third cylinder, but no one noticed the spewing exhaust. Automobile parts were only one of the thousands of everyday items that were impossible to get in Pakistan.

The cab belched to a stop on the side of the street, pulling over just far enough so that the other traffic could pass, but few cars were out, not many souls had dared venture onto the streets just yet. The sidewalk was dirty and brown, with graffiti and old Hollywood movie posters posted everywhere and dry weeds and grass pushing through the cracks in the cement. To the right was a depressing bar and brothel that catered to the UN soldiers and contractors from Europe and Malaysia. Though illegal, the local police had been instructed to let the brothel be; the prostitutes were not Muslim, but girls from Cambodia, the Philippines, and (best of all) India and the establishment provided a steady stream of payoffs for the local party boss, but this afternoon the bar was empty, with all of the shutters closed. Further down, near the corner, was a small grocer and open air market that was just opening up. Lines of inpatient and fearful women waited, pressing forward, moving toward the grocer's door at the sound of the turning keys, fretful to get a share of the frozen fish and fresh meat they hoped had been delivered inside. On a normal day, goat, lamb, dog, and horse could have been bought in the store, but today there was only *braug,* a local mixture of cow gut, herbs, and oatmeal, and even not enough of that. It would take less than fifteen minutes for the small store to sell everything and again close its doors.

The southern end of the block had been taken up by an old tool shop which rebuilt electric generators for use in the Southern Caspian oil fields. The main door to the electrical shop was a thick slab of oak that opened directly onto the street, and the windows had recently been covered with thick steel bars, then painted from the inside with heavy black paint.

The taxi didn't come to a stop, but rolled slowly by the shop, the driver hesitating, the engine coughing blue smoke while the wheels crunched the gravel and broken asphalt under its tires. The driver's eyes darted left and right underneath his dark glasses. He waited ten seconds, then, checking his rearview mirror, pressed the accelerator and moved away from the curb.

Peter Zembeic emerged from the shop and quickened his step, slapping the trunk of the cab as it started pulling away.

The cab stopped and he jumped in the back seat before the cab accelerated to merge with the thin traffic.

"Nice place you guys got there," the driver said scornfully, referring to the electrical shop, which was a CIA front.

Peter didn't answer, adjusting himself in the seat. The driver moved his head slightly as he checked his mirror, and Peter watched him carefully, wishing he could see his eyes. He sighed wearily. His head pounded like a hammer. He needed a good fourteen hours sleep. He was tired and worried, his fears gnawed inside. The forty-minute car ride across Islamabad had left him in a very foul mood, seeing the soldiers and radicals roaming the streets, packs of wild dogs, snarling and ready to strike. It had been a dangerous drive, which required full military escort through the outskirts of the city, then a half-mile walk alone through the industrial part of town. The capital of Pakistan was momentarily calm, but anything but secure, and Peter knew it could boil over in an instant into urban war.

But Thomas Washington had insisted that he meet face-to-face with Petate's section chief in Pakistan. So he had made his way across the city instead of heading up to the mountain as he had originally planned.

"Where's Kalid?" Peter asked quickly, referring to the Israeli agent he usually worked through.

"You said you wanted to talk to the boss," the driver replied.

"Is that you?" Peter demanded.

"As boss as you're going to get."

"You can speak for Petate then?"

The driver hesitated, then answered, "I can."

Peter was sitting on the passenger side and watched the driver's profile as he looked left, then honked and pulled into the traffic on a much busier street. The smells and sounds of the downtown district wafted through the plastic covering the broken window and Peter breathed deeply, then leaned forward, feeling the broken springs giving under his weight. "We want to know what happened to our Predator," he said in a dry voice.

The driver's face remained stoic. "I don't know what you mean."

"Come on, my friend, give me a little respect. I've driven through half a dozen check points to get here, okay? I paid more bribes in the past hour than I've paid in a month just to work my way across town. Now don't waste my time. I'm just not in the mood. We've only got ten minutes before I have to head back to my camp. Are you going to help me, or am I wasting my time?"

The Israeli smiled faintly. "The general instructed me to be helpful," he said in a too-simple tone.

"Then tell me about the Pumas."

"They aren't our machines."

"Something brought down our Predator."

"I'm sorry, Mr. Zembeic, but I can't help you there."

"You can't or you won't?"

"Isn't it the same thing?"

Peter wiped quickly with his hand, brushing the light sweat from his brow. "Listen to me," he answered slowly, "as personal representative of Doctor Washington, as a representative of our government, I'm here to ask you directly: Have you got an operation going? Are those your Pumas hiding at the base of Tirich Mir?"

The Israeli hesitated before he answered. "You promised us your government would take care of this mess."

"I don't believe your organization has ever trusted my government to take care of anything."

"You are right, Mr. Zembeic. We never have. We never will."

"Then tell me about the Pumas. Tell me what happened to our drone?"

The driver jerked the car suddenly, pulling it to the side of the street. Removing his dark glasses, he shifted in his seat. "It wasn't us," he said simply, looking Peter straight in the eye. "I have nothing to tell you. You are wasting your time."

Peter stared at the Shin Bet officer, reading the look in his face. "You're lying," he murmured in a weary voice.

The driver didn't answer for a very long time. The car grew hot from the sun as the two men stared at each other in uncomfortable silence, then the Shin Bet officer leaned toward Peter and stared into his dark eyes. "Life can be uncertain," he whispered, "there is no doubt about that. Now get back to Camp Horse. It might be a long night."

24

Peshawar, Pakistan

It was a hot and muggy night, the air calm and wet and apparently unwilling to give up the heat of the day. The city streets were sludgy from rain and piled garbage, and there was a strong smell of rot and human waste in the air. Most of Peshawar was a slum, as poor as any place on earth, and the only men that seemed to prosper in the city were the smugglers who ran heroin west and the warlords who moved weapons and ammunition between China and the Muslim states. Few of the men in Peshawar worked; jobs were scarce and, once found, hard to hold, for the local economy was as unstable as the winds that blew down from the sandy plateaus that surrounded the small town. It was the perfect environment for envy; a rotting petri dish of poverty, oppression, ignorance, and tradition that sustained an almost acid hatred of the United States.

Like the people in the city, the terrain around Peshawar was hostile and unfriendly; the mountains rose in the east, north, and west, craggy fissures of rock that were capped with snow atop the bony, granite fingers. To the south, the mountains fell away to the Indus Plateau. Somewhere to the west, beyond the dim light of the moon, a thunderstorm crackled with lightning, promising a coming storm.

The men met in the residential part of the city, the most desperate part of the slums, where the tiny houses and ramshackle apartments were hardly more than cardboard shacks. They didn't speak as they walked toward each other, though the smaller man bowed, then gestured toward a brick-and-mud house to his right.

Angra paused outside the door of the house and listened to the sounds of the city; the cry of a baby in the second-floor apartment beside him, a gunshot off to south, the wind lifting a loose piece of tin roof before dropping it down. He sniffed the air, then pushed the door back and strolled purposefully into the house. The Great Master followed, his lanky frame and long arms flowing under his flowing robes. The men inside the main room looked up in stunned silence before a low gasp moved through the crowd.

The Master, the Great One! The Great Leader was here! The men hardly dared look at him, keeping their eyes on the floor.

No one had defied the United States like this man had done. No man had stuck such a dagger into the Great Satan's soul, sending him to stagger, almost bringing him to his knees. No man since the Great Sultan had stood so proud and so tall, standing for Allah and the very Prophet himself. This man was a fable, a legend straight out of old days.

The Great Leader followed Angra, but said nothing as they moved through the crowd. Standing in silence, he moved off to the side. Angra stood in the center, surrounded by a ragtag group of men.

These weren't their best soldiers. Indeed, quite the opposite, it was a group of misfits, but the only men they could spare. A few had some potential but were too young to be trusted; some were old soldiers who had been cast off. Others were mercenaries looking for a quick meal. But all of them were hungry and hoping for a chance to prove themselves.

There were eleven in all, and they stood awkwardly as

Angra walked to the front of the room. There were no lights, only candles, and his presence cast a shadow along the front wall. He cleared his throat, bowed to the Great One, then motioned to his men and all of them sat, crossing their legs on the floor. Angra, as always, got straight to the point. "Brothers, blessed be His Name, Gracious God has brought us together tonight. For some, it has been a treacherous journey; but you have been blessed for your effort, for our Great Leader is here."

Angra paused and looked back and the Great Leader nodded in a gracious gesture to his soldiers. Everyone knew he wouldn't speak, not to such lowly men, but the honor of having him among them was clearly enough.

Angra spit a small wad of tobacco, then continued, "We must disperse before morning, so we don't have much time, but I have been given a task by our Master, and it is important to him."

The men straightened and leaned forward. A task from the Master! What an honor indeed!

"There is a man," Angra said. "An American soldier who goes by *Rasul al-Laylat*. He might be CIA, maybe military. I want to know who he is."

The men stared at their commander, a dull stir in the air.

"Rasul al-Laylat," Angra repeated. "Does it mean anything to you?"

A young man—he couldn't have been more than seventeen—raised a thin hand and pushed himself to his feet. "I have heard the name," he said with such pride it looked like he might burst.

Angra turned to him. "Where?" he demanded.

"The Americans have an outpost along the Afghanistan border, way up north, near the mountains, where the rain falls cold on the rocks of the Badakhshan."

Angra stared, impatient, then waved his hand.

"They call it Camp Cowboy," the young soldier went on. "It is a hard target, fully protected, but the soldiers come out for patrols. Some of them ride horses. This one you are looking for, he is one of these horsemen."

"Are you certain?"

"Oh yes, *Sayid.* Many of us who listen and watch in that part of the country have heard the name before. Apostle of the Night. He is very well known. He has many friends, many traitors he has bought and sold over the past several years. He casts a long shadow, with his gifts and his gold. He could buy a whole army with the money he spends. I know eight, maybe ten, tribal leaders who have worked for him; warlord Lashkar Gah, Gen. Chekar Morejak—God willing, I could name many more."

Angra's eyes lightened. "What more can you tell me?" he demanded as the young soldier fell silent.

The young man shook his head. "*Sayid,* I don't know any more."

"Have you ever seen him?"

"No, master, no."

"Do you know what he looks like?"

"He is large and dark, like a bear. He looks like—well, like we do, at least that's what I have been told. He is dangerous and evil. They say he has killed many men."

Angra grunted. Of that, he had serious doubts. "You say Warlord Lashkar Gah has met with him?" he prodded.

"I have heard that he has, yes, my *Sayid.*"

Angra glanced back at the Master, who eyed the young soldier. "You would please me," the Great One muttered, "if you could find this soldier and bring me his head."

The soldiers grunted in pleasure. A word from the Master. Then a long silence followed. Their mission was cast.

Angra watched them, growing fidgety, his hands turning cold. He listened to the drumming on the tin roof as the rain started to fall. A sour feeling welled inside him. He knew that going after the American was a distraction from the far more important work that was taking place to the north, a hornet's nest of trouble that he would have left alone. But the Great One had insisted and he could not tell him no. General Ghaith's treason had been a slap in the Great Leader's face, a personal insult that could not be ignored, and killing the

American who had helped Ghaith was the only salve he could put on his wound.

So he would do as the Master ordered. He would send these men out and see what they brought back.

Kill 31
Over Eastern Afghanistan

The massive black bird was descending. Its engines were at idle and the sound of the wind blowing over the cockpit grew more noticeable as the aircraft descended into the thicker atmosphere that lay below sixty thousand feet. The air was dry and smooth; the night almost perfectly clear behind the dust storms that were still billowing out in the west and the moon was beginning to ride high in the sky. Mountains loomed ahead, unspeakable shadows with talons of stone reaching toward the aircraft, the snow-capped peaks brightly illuminated by the three-quarter moon. Craggy fissures streamed downward like thin veins of black coal against the white snow. Tia couldn't help but stare. Never in her life had she seen mountains such as these. The moonlight made the sight even more majestic, for the snow-capped peaks sparkled against the dark valleys twenty-five thousand feet below. She motioned toward them. "Wow," was all she could say.

Bradley was also staring through the windscreen. "Takes your breath away," he answered.

Tia watched a moment more, then turned to her radar display. "I've got a good fix point off the bridge over Harirud. The INS is tight. I mean really tight. The *Lady* is serving us well on this long, lonely night."

"She's a babe." Bradley reached up and stroked the side of his cockpit. "Hang in there, girl."

Tia turned her concentration on the fix point again, the bridge showing clearly on her radar display, a dark mass against the green monochrome screen. She watched as a small truck moved over the bridge. She tightened up the picture. The screen shifted, changed perspective, then tightened on the bridge and the truck came more clearly into view, the radar so clear it was like watching a movie. Though it was over seventeen miles away, Tia could easily make out the details of the vehicle, even seeing the antennae on the front of the fender. She snapped a picture of the southwest corner of the bridge, then fed the coordinates into her navigational computer. The INS compared the coordinates to update its position. "INS drift is less than three meters," she said.

Colonel Bradley leveled the aircraft at thirty-three thousand feet and pushed up the power. "Take the aircraft," he said. Tia reached up and took the controls.

Bradley studied the radar. "One hundred eighty miles to the target."

Tia searched the sky before her. "Where did those Su-27s go?" she said as she shook her head in frustration.

Bradley had asked himself the same question a dozen times. The fighters were out there; two sharks, lying in wait, ready to strike at the first whiff of food, ready to spring at the first target they found. His gut was tight and a trickle of sweat ran down his ribs. He turned the radar to air-to-air mode and commanded a slight increase in power. His sensors got a sudden sniff of Su-27 and the ALD-65 defensive system chirped in his ear, but the signal wasn't strong enough to pin down the direction and range. The enemy fighters had to be low, near the mountains, keeping themselves hidden on the other side of the peaks. Bradley studied his defensive system display, overlaying the readout over his moving map display. A yellow circle was depicted off to his right, indicating the last known position of the enemy forces. He hit *update* on his data panel but the threat ring remained fixed, unable to update without the satellite link.

Bradley glanced at the time. More than five hours since they had lost their SATCOM relay. Five hours was forever; a lifetime on the battlefield. Wars had been won and lost in five hours. Battles had turned, the future of nations decided in five hours or less.

Five hours was far too long to be without communications from the home base. He huffed in frustration. It was like flying blind.

His defensive system chirped again and he moved quickly in his seat, leaning toward the CRT display. Tia glanced at him, sensing his urgency. "Got a whiffer, low, eighty miles, ten o'clock," Bradley announced.

Intermittent radar target, low level, eighty miles to the left.

"It is out in the valley—at the base of the mountain. But I can't get a strong enough return to nail it down," he explained.

Tia held the stick loosely as she scanned up north, an instinctive reaction ingrained from years of air-to-air training. "Just one hit?" she asked anxiously.

"Check that . . . two . . . now three. NOE. Gotta be dogs."

Three choppers, flying nap-of-the-earth, barely above the terrain. The B-2 radar saw the helicopters clearly, despite the ground clutter.

"Choppers?" Tia wondered. "Where are the fighters?" she asked.

"They appear to be circling overhead, the dogs."

"But that doesn't make sense. Unless . . ." Tia paused. "Unless the fighters are following the choppers, providing air cover."

"Looks that way, Tia."

The captain shook her head. "Choppers. Su-27s. Working together." She wiped her gloved hand across her face as Bradley watched the choppers begin to slow on his radar display.

Tia watched them also. "Look at that," she moaned. "They're coming to a hover right over the target!"

Bradley shook his head in fear as the two pilots looked at each other. "They've found the warheads. They're going to move them in the choppers!" he said.

"We are too late," Tia answered in angry dismay.

Bradley's face paled. "No," he shot back. "There's still time. We're only a few minutes out. If we get the bombs on the target—"

"But we don't know who's down there! It could be friendlies, Pakistani forces."

"Or al Qaeda," Bradley shot back. "You're right, we don't know who's down there, which is exactly the point. We don't know who's down there and we can't take the chance. Without further orders, we will continue the mission and take out the target, including the choppers, whoever they are."

Tia fell silent. "Of course, sir," she said.

The colonel stared out his window, then glanced at the radar, which showed the choppers hovering over the target, ready to set on the ground.

Who were they?! Who were they?!

He took a deep breath. "We have to strike the target before they move the warheads," he said. Pushing up the power, he increased their speed. "Start on the bomb checklist," he commanded as the aircraft sped up, the rush of air over the windscreen increasing in pitch.

"Yes, sir," Tia answered as she turned to her displays.

"Target zero six five degrees. We'll begin our turn at the IP in just under a minute." Bradley's voice was intense. "Prebomb checklist complete. I've selected weapon stations two and four. Going to air-to-ground mode."

"Before you do sir, take a last look for those fighters."

Bradley worked his defensive display. "Nothing now. I've got nothing at all. The Su-27s must be on the other side of the mountain. Going to bomb mode. Target eighty-five miles. Weapons armed and selected."

Fifty-nine miles to the north, circling over a narrow valley with steep mountains on the north and rocky-topped buttes on the south, a flight of two Su-27 fighters flew in combat formation. The pilot in the lead aircraft, a thirty-seven-year-old colonel, pulled at his oxygen mask, releasing the pressure from against his tight beard. Sitting in the cockpit of the Soviet-made Su-27, surrounded by instruments and soft glowing lights, he was no longer tired, but intense and alive, showing none of the previous hesitation he had been feeling before. The target was coming, and he felt his back ache. His hands held the flight controls in a tight grip as he tensed for the fight.

Below him, the three helicopters were slowing, staying very near the ground. The pilot glanced at the time and then checked his fuel. He was running low on gas. "Snatchers, Bogey Dope?" he asked over his tactical radio. There was silence for a moment until the wingman replied, "Negative, Lead."

"Okay, tally south to the Bulls Eye. Let's take one last look before we have to bug out of here."

"Two," his wingman grunted in reply.

The two Su-27 fighters moved south, sweeping the skies with their radar. Turning, they had to climb aggressively to keep themselves clear of the mountains. The colonel pulled up the nose of his aircraft, trading airspeed for altitude, popping his fighter to thirty thousand feet. His fighter, light on gas, climbed like a rocket, and he popped above the mountaintops effortlessly to where the moon burned from over his shoulder, shining very bright. He swept his eyes across the horizon, studying the night, then scanned with his radar and got a quick hit. His heart jumped, his throat tightened, and he sucked a quick breath.

A hit. It was out there. The target had arrived.

He waited and prayed, pleading desperately with his God.

But the bogey disappeared very quickly, leaving nothing but empty, dark sky. His radar showed nothing and the warning tone fell silent in his ears. He cursed and he muttered, slapping his hand on his knees. He stared through his heads up display, then his radar growled again in his ears.

"Two, check ten," he asked in a desperate voice.

"Roger. I've been getting something, but I can't get a lock."

"Stay with me," the colonel said as he pushed up his speed.

The radar beam from the Su-27 fighters washed over the top of the wounded B-2. Behind the cockpit, parallel to the aircraft's contour flow, several dents marred the surface of the delicate bomber from where the air refueling boom had slid down the side of the jet. The dents were hardly more than dimples, but they weren't the only damage that had been done to the plane. Along the trailing edge of the beaver tail, a sixteen-inch piece of control surface had also been broken away.

The imperfections bounced back only traces of radar energy, but taken together, it was enough for the Su-27s to get a hit.

Inside the B-2, the crew was busy. They had decided in the preflight briefing that Bradley would fly the aircraft during the bomb run, leaving the more challenging task of target identification, selection, and aiming to Tia. She was focused on her work, mentally blocking out the other elements of the flight as she scanned with her radar, updated the INS, searched for the target, compared coordinates, rechecked the weapons configuration, confirmed the ingress route and timing, and searched for infrared clues to confirm the location of the target. The rules of engagement required that the target be confirmed through two independent and positive sources, radar and infrared. Without their communications, they weren't going to get any help identifying the target from the team on the ground.

At twenty-three miles Tia had target confirmation. The aircraft was on time, on course, and well within the release envelope. The weapons were prearmed and responding to her internal commands. The target coordinates had been fed into the warhead's internal computers.

"Twenty miles," Bradley announced.

"Ready," she replied.

Bradley let the aircraft's automatic flight control system fly the aircraft as he searched the night sky. His defensive display chirped once, then emitted a steady warble as it detected air-to-air radar, ten o'clock, and twenty-one miles. Bradley glanced at his defensive display. There they were, two Su-27s.

Tia glanced over, a worried look on her face.

"I got it," Bradley assured her.

The second Su-27 was behind his leader, two miles in

trail, climbing to the same altitude. The fighters didn't maneuver, but continued on a straight course, circling the airspace where the Pakistani warheads had been hidden in the
cave at the base of Tirich Mir.

Tia ignored the fighters, concentrating on her task. "Two
minutes to release," she announced in a flat voice.

Bradley tore his eyes away from his defensive display.
"Confirm bomb checklist complete."

"Affirm. Good offset and aim point. Weapons waiting to
arm. Confirm coordinates."

Bradley studied the central CRT and checked the target
coordinates for the fifth or sixth time. "Confirmed," he announced.

"Bomb checklist complete." Tia looked up from her radar
screen. "Fighters?"

"Bandits are blind."

"Codes," Tia said.

Bradley's mouth went suddenly dry. He looked down at
the red-topped security box situated between them. Together, the two pilots reached into the metal container and
extracted the authentication code cards. Slightly larger than
a credit card, the nuclear codes had been wrapped in clear
plastic, then sealed and stamped.

Bradley read the coded number stamped across the front
of his card. "Confirm. Alpha, Zulu, three, niner, niner,
Bravo, seven, six, one, five, Whiskey."

"Roger," Tia replied. "Alpha, Zulu, three, niner, niner,
Bravo, seven, six, one, five, Whiskey."

They had the same war codes. Both pilots broke the seal,
bent the cards over to split them open and reveal the eight-
digit code within. The pilots then turned to their data control
panels and entered the codes carefully.

"Complete?" Bradley asked after entering his code.

"Affirm," Tia answered. She turned to him.

"Ready to initiate?" Bradley said.

"On your command."

"Ready, three—two—one." Both pilots turned their ini-
tiator switches.

Inside the belly of the aircraft, the nuclear warheads accepted the codes. The weapons were armed and ready for release.

The cockpit was silent. Tia returned her attention to her radar. Twenty seconds passed in silence and Bradley turned to his defensive system display, which was growling in his headset, a jagged spike emitting in the 300 megahertz range. "Bandits collapsing," he said. "But they're blind, they don't see us." The fighters were getting closer, but it did not appear they were yet aware of the Stealth. "Continue," Bradley instructed as he watched the fighters draw close.

"Range of bandits?" Tia asked him.

"Three miles. Closing. Thirty-one and thirty-six thousand feet."

"Three miles! That's pretty close, boss!"

Bradley didn't reply.

"You got 'em!" Tia demanded.

"Roger that. Two thousand feet below us. Continue bomb run!"

"Thirty seconds to release."

"Active jamming ready. I'll light the fighters up with jam if they give us so much as a peep."

The Su-27 pilot studied his radar display. *There was something there!* There *had* to be something there. But it was like tracking a ghost or a mist in the wind; he would see it, a spike on radar display down in the 75-megahertz range, which indicated a very low power source, but it always disappeared before his system could define an azimuth, altitude, or range. Like a blind cat chasing a mouse, he could smell it, he could feel it, but he didn't know where it was. He studied his radar. There! He got a quick peek again.

"Snatchers, check left twenty," he commanded and the two fighters snapped left precisely twenty degrees. "Come off high. Angels thirty-eight. Echelon left," the flight leader cried.

The second fighter pulled its nose up into the sky, climbing in seconds to thirty-eight thousand feet and maneuvered forty-five degrees to the lead fighter's left side.

"Target Bullseye, seven eight zero, twelve, faded."

The target was directly west of the mountain, twelve miles out, but his radar couldn't lock up a solid return.

"Stay with me now," was the colonel's final instruction.

The Su-27 pilot lifted his head and jerked it to the right as something caught his eye, passing in front of the moon. Instinctively, he pushed up his throttles to close the distance between the shadow and his fighter. He strained, trying desperately to pierce through the night while cursing the fact that his squadron had never "acquired" the newest U.S. night-vision goggles. If an American Stealth bomber was out there, the goggles might have made the difference between finding the bandit and letting it get through. He unloaded the aircraft, pushing over momentarily to zero Gs, then rolled onto his back to see what was underneath. He hung upside down, his shoulder harness holding him in position as he scanned the darkness below. The blood rushed to his head, but he didn't notice as he scanned north to south, breaking the sky into four or five equal segments, scanning the sky by the light of the moon. Rolling the aircraft upright, he pulled into a tight turn back toward the tallest peak in the nearest mountain range.

Fifteen seconds," Tia announced.

"Cleared hot," Bradley replied.

"Picture?"

"Spike, two miles. Turning. It looks like they don't see us."

Tia shook her head, then turned back to her weapons displays. Ten seconds to weapon release. Bradley checked his airspeed and pulled it back to five hundred eighty knots, just below the bomb bay spoiler redline. Six seconds prior to release, the bomb bay doors would swing open on their hydraulic pistons. A spoiler would then descend in front of the bay to allow the weapons to clear the aircraft before being thrown back by the wind. With the spoiler deployed, the B-2 would bounce back more radar energy.

"Fighters climbing," Bradley announced after watching his screen. "They're going to be close, maybe two hundred feet overhead. Let's get this release and get out of here."

The Su-27 pilot saw it again, a deep shadow in the night. He jerked his aircraft into a tight three-sixty circle and the G meter racked instantly up to seven g's. Catching his breath, he held it while squeezing his abdominal muscles to stop the flow of blood from his head while his g suit billowed tightly, compressing the veins in his calves and thighs. His vision narrowed slightly as he took another breath then grunted again, forcing the blood back into his eyes as he pushed the button on his secure radio.

"Say status on the Pumas," he demanded in an even voice.

"Ten, maybe fifteen minutes until we're finished here."

"I've got a possible target, twenty miles, inbound."

The radio was silent before the voice shot back. "You know what to do."

The pilot hesitated. "Confirm I have an *arrow*," he insisted as he craned his neck.

"Affirm on the *arrow*. Do what you have to to bring that aircraft down."

The pilot grunted and clicked his microphone twice. Twisting in his seat, he banked his fighter again. The night was full of shadows from the moon reflecting off the mountaintops. He turned and he swore as he twisted and stared.

And then he saw it. A huge, black silhouette in the night. It flashed in the moonlight, like the shiny skin of a snake, passing almost directly behind him. He jerked his head and twisted up one hip. He lost it! Where was it? Off the left or the right? He tightened up the turn then let the nose drop in a very steep descent, all the while looking over his right shoulder at the blackness behind him.

Then he saw the bomber. He barely had time to shoot. He selected his cannon and let off a three-second burst, the 20 mm barrel sending a jarring vibration through his seat. He aimed as carefully as he could, avoiding the front of the bomber as he sent his shells through the heart of the aircraft, focusing on the engine bays and flight controls.

Despite the pilot's aim, the shells sliced the B-2, cutting a line from the cockpit to the tip of the tail, the white-hot shells cutting through the thin metal like they were passing through water. The cockpit shattered in pieces, sending steel and composite pieces scattering with the force of a bomb. As the shells moved back across the airframe, fuel, fire, and metal exploded in the air.

25

Peter Zembeic stood by his horse, feeling her breath as her chest muscles stretched the leather saddle strap behind her front legs. She took a long breath and snorted and Peter pulled close to her side. The night was dark, with no moon yet above the high hills, and the stars were too weak to provide enough light. So he listened and sniffed, his senses pulling in what he could.

The smoke from the fire was bitter. Green wood. Not well-cured. The recent rains had made dry firewood more difficult to find. Behind him, along the base of the mountains, a single falcon screeched in the night, hunting for rodents among the sage and low brush. The wind came down from the mountains. No more rain tonight. It was cold and getting colder and the hair on his arms tingled with goosebumps. An early winter was coming; he could feel it in his bones.

The American listened and waited for almost twenty minutes, then slipped Isabel's reins over her ears and dropped them on the wet grass. He didn't bother to tie her, she wouldn't go anywhere, and he patted her neck as he stepped away. Whispering in her ear, he slipped down the hill. Emerg-

ing from the shadows on the edge of the camp, he stepped
into the light of the fire in the center of the small camp.

The warlord was there, king of his world, surrounded by
his harem and his men. He waited near the fire for the American, sitting on a low log. The warlord Lashkar Gah was a
huge man, thick as a tree, with stumpy legs and round arms
and hands so thick and calloused they looked like small
baseball mitts. Peter approached and bowed slowly while
bringing his hands to his chest. "Lashkar Gah, good to see
you. Thank you for inviting me here."

The old warlord nodded to the American, then motioned
to a small log beside him and Peter sat down. The two men
sat in silence while a fat lad (all of the people in Lashkar
Gah's village were huge; the women and children as well as
the men) set a wooden plate of steer loins and sheep-gut
sausage between them. Peter waited until Gah nodded to the
food, then reached for a greasy sausage and smelled the
mixed meats and spices. He took a huge bite, stretching the
thin membrane until it broke and the warm meat and hot
spices burned like fire in his mouth. Though hard and dis-
trustful people, the Afghani herdsmen certainly knew how to
eat. Sheep-gut sausage and Shi tea—Peter would miss them
both when he got back to the States.

Gah watched him chew on the sausage, seemingly anxious, shifting back and forth in his seat. He glanced at a tent
on his right, then back at the fire. Peter watched him, but
didn't question. The warlord Gah was always nervous. It was
a dangerous life that he lived. He concentrated on his meat,
then sucked down a mouthful of sweet tea. Gah watched
him, satisfied, then lifted his own piece of meat and shoved
it in his mouth. The two men ate in silence, then stared at the
fire. The stars glittered above them and the fire soon grew
cold, until Peter stood and walked to the logs stacked behind
them, split one of them with a long ax, and threw a couple
pieces on the fire. Sitting down again, he turned to his host.
"What do you have, General Gah?" he asked.

The warlord grunted and wiped his greasy hands on his
pants. "You are in danger," he said in a straightforward tone.

Peter stared at him, his eyes flickering in the light of the fire. "We all live in danger. It is part of our job. Me. You. Are any of us safe?"

Gah shook his head. "This is more," he said. Though he spoke in a whisper, his voice was low and powerful. "There are men—new men—men I have not seen before. They are asking about the *Apostle*. You need to be careful. That is all I will say."

"Who are they?" Peter demanded, but Gah shook his head. He had said all he would, and Peter recognized the determined move of his head.

He tried one more time, but the village leader refused. "That is all I will say," he repeated, and Peter knew it was true.

The two men sat by the fire in silence again, eating and smoking for twenty minutes or so until Peter pushed himself up. He tried leaving the warlord a couple hundred dollars for the warning, but the tribal chief shook his head. "It wouldn't be right," he said as he threw the money back to the soldier. Peter nodded, slapped his shoulder, then slipped into the shadows. Finding Isabel where he left her, he mounted his horse.

The warlord waited and listened as the sound of the hooves disappeared along the rocky trail. He remained by the pit, staring at the flickering flames, until the fire had died down to nothing but glowing black and orange coals. As the moon fell behind the tree line, the clouds settled lower and the night turned very dark. He smoked and he stared until the stranger silently emerged from the tent to his right.

"Was that him?" the stranger whispered as he dropped to his knees by Gah.

The chieftain watched the mercenary a moment, his face nothing more than a dark oval in the night, then turned back to the dead fire.

"Was that *Rasul al-Laylat*?" the stranger demanded again.

The warlord turned back to him, then nodded. "Yes, that was he."

"You have been working with an American?"

"I have betrayed neither friend nor religion, I will tell you that."

The thin fighter snickered. "I wonder if that is true?"

The chieftain glared. The stranger didn't see his burning eyes in the dark. "I don't answer to you about my business dealings," Gah finally said.

"We will see, we will see," the mercenary muttered again. "But I'm thinking the Great Master wouldn't be happy to learn of your American friend."

"I have nothing to hide."

"Perhaps that is true. But you have an obligation to your people. The Great One wants this American. Now, are you going to help?"

Gah didn't hesitate. Though he liked the Apostle, this was business now. And his situation was precarious. "I will help you," he said.

The mercenary grunted as he answered, "Of course you will."

Peter Zembeic watched Gah's camp from a small knoll to the west. Buried in the low underbrush, his breath came heavy and deep from his hard sprint uphill to get to his perch above the camp. Two hundred yards behind him, Isabel had been tied to a tree and he felt naked without her and the gear hidden in her saddlebags.

From his hiding spot in the brush, Peter watched the warlord as the night wore slowly on. Time passed, the fire grew cold, and the moon and stars disappeared until the night grew far too dark to see anything. So he listened and waited, then pulled out his nightscope and peered at the camp, but the light was insufficient and the distance too great to see anything but shadows around the cold fire. He waited another five minutes, then stood and turned. Hiking in silence, he moved down the hill to his horse, his knees aching, his body shivering, his hands stiff and cold.

The mercenary glanced around him, then leaned in the dark toward Gah. "I need a runner," he said with a hunch of his shoulders. "Someone I can trust to send a message through."

The warlord Lashkar Gah nodded, then pointed to one of his men who stood on the outskirts of the fire and the mercenary walked toward him and leaned to his ear. His message was simple. "I have found the *Apostle*. Give me two days, and I will deliver his head."

Peshawar, Pakistan

A little more than three hours after the runner had left Lashkar Gah's camp, the young Afghani was meeting with Angra in the crowded lobby of a run-down hotel. A throng of humanity hustled around them; beggars, hustlers, prostitutes, and guests, and the two men sat at the small wooden tables near the back wall of the lobby. They eyed each other suspiciously and kept their voices low. Angra looked around comfortably, this was his territory and there was no reason to fear, but the runner kept his eyes moving, constantly glancing here and there.

The runner delivered the message as quickly and accurately as he could. Angra listened carefully, then nodded and leaned toward the young man and said, "Go back and deliver this message to your master for me. I don't want gunshots or explosions and certainly no roadside bombs. This can't be a combat fatality. I want an assassination, a political hit. I want a graphic beheading. And use a dull knife. And pictures, we want pictures, something we can show to the West."

Kill 31
Over Eastern Afghanistan

The force of the collision knocked Bradley back in his seat, sucking the air from his lungs and compressed his heart in his chest. His oxygen mask was ripped from his helmet and sucked through the slicing hole that ran across the side of the cockpit. The screaming wind, cold and biting, was a tornado in his face. The bitter cold froze his eyelashes, making it impossible to see. Blinded and disoriented, and struggling to breathe, he fought with the aircraft as it slipped into a dive.

White mist exploded in the cockpit as it depressurized. Everything that wasn't strapped down was sucked through the hole in the jet—pencils, papers, water bottles, flight plans, communication cards, flight books, panel covers, debris from the floor—everything was instantly pulled from the cockpit. Bradley wiped his gloves across his face, clearing the dirt and blood from his eyes. He glanced over to Tia. She lay slumped, her body limp, her head blown about by the wind. He reached over and grabbed her wrist and she slowly reached up to clasp his hand.

Bradley struggled to breathe, his thoughts growing rapidly dim. The depressurization had instantly metabolized the oxygen in his blood and his brain was beginning to starve. He had to get down. He had to descend. Without his oxygen mask or cabin pressure, it was a matter of seconds before he lost consciousness. His fingers had already lost feeling and his feet were growing numb. He glanced toward Tia, checking that her oxygen mask was tight against her checks, then slammed his throttles to idle and banked the jet on its side, rolling over and forcing the nose to slice toward the ground. The wind was like a freight train. It beat his face and crashed in his ears. He squinted against the onslaught. His fingers were nearly frozen and his teeth chattered in his head.

Bradley peered straight ahead. He was on the north side of the mountain, where the highest peak reached up to twenty-five thousand feet. He pushed the aircraft east, descending along the slope of Tirich Mir, the rocky ledges a mere four or five hundred feet under his jet. The bomber's descent matched the slope of the mountain.

Warning lights flashed in the cockpit; red, yellow, and orange. The aircraft vibrated, then bucked as his number three engine blew itself apart, terminally wounded from bullets and debris. Bradley threw out the rudder/brakes, then cross-controlled the bomber to slow the aircraft down. His digital altimeter was almost unreadable: *twenty-four thousand, twenty-two thousand, twenty thousand feet*. His fingers were aching and his head started to spin. The air seemed to grow hot and he started to sweat. He gulped like a diver coming up from the deep. The aircraft rolled on its side and the horizon tilted around him. The cockpit grew dark as he neared the edge of consciousness.

Eighteen thousand, fifteen thousand. The altimeter was impossible to read. It was hot. He was sweating. His brain was nearly starved now. He saw the ground rising. Such a beautiful night. He glanced up at the stars. Why were they burning so bright? He felt calm, almost peaceful. Why had he been so afraid?

A warning chime sounded in his ears. Fast rising terrain! The ground screamed at him now; rocks, boulders, craggy fissures, trees, and steep mountain cliffs. He flew toward the main valley leading up to Tirich Mir. He was heading for China. He didn't have any choice.

Thirteen thousand feet. The spinning slowed and he realized it was only his head. But he was descending too fast! Eleven thousand feet passed and his lungs pulled more oxygen from the thin air. His vision came into focus. He breathed deeply again and again.

He pulled back on the stick, raising his bomber's nose in the night. His aircraft came level just above eight thousand three hundred feet. His airspeed bled off quickly as his wings caught the air. Three hundred fifty knots, three hundred, two eighty-five. The aircraft started to wallow and he brought his rudder/brakes in. He took a quick glance over to Tia. She hunkered behind the broken windscreen to stay out of the wind.

The aircraft continued slowing. Two hundred, then one-eighty knots. Bradley pushed up the power. The aircraft shuddered violently as his number two engine started to fail. With a gut-wrenching *boom!* its compressor blades spun off the main spool, sending pieces of metal cutting through the main firewall. New warning lights flash in the cockpit. Bradley brought number two engine to idle and the vibration decreased. A soft glow began to illuminate from behind his head and greasy smoke poured into the cockpit through the pressurized vents.

The ENG FIRE light began to flash in his face.

Bradley punched the fire button, shutting the number two engine down, then hit the fire suppression button to spray retardant into the engine bay. He studied his master caution panel. His primary generators and the main hydraulic systems were gone. He moved the flight controls and the aircraft rolled sluggishly under his hand. Tia stared wildly at him and he reached for her hand. "You okay?" he was asking. She squeezed twice in reply. It was the only way they could communicate above the roar of the wind.

She motioned toward the controls. "Do I take it?" she meant.

Bradley shook his head, pointed north, making a level motion with his hand, then simulated pulling the ejection handles that were positioned near his knees. Tia nodded, understanding. He would get over flat terrain, then they would eject from the crippled airplane.

Tia pointed to the center panel. The number-one engine exhaust gas temperature was climbing into the red. The engine was dying, literally cooking itself. They had to shut it down before it blew apart. Tia reached for the number-one engine cutoff switch, but Bradley grabbed her hand. They were down to two engines. He would keep number one going as long as they could, to make certain they had time to eject. He lifted four fingers sideways, then made a fist twice, telling her to let the engine get to nine hundred degrees before she shut it down.

Bradley frantically rubbed his hands over his eyes. He turned toward Tia, a new fear on his face. "Weapons!" he screamed above the roar of the wind. He signaled toward his data control panel, lifted three fingers, and began to count down. Tia reached for her data panel, then followed his command. Together, they flipped the master arm switch. The nukes powered down. Bradley motioned for "safe" and Tia flipped the red-guarded switch. The internal computers inside the warheads scrambled the arm codes.

"Jettison!" Bradley screamed.

Tia hit the jettison switch and felt a deep rumble as the bomb bay doors opened into the slip stream. The ejection pins fired and she felt a solid *knock*. The weapons tumbled away and the bomb bay door closed again. Bradley glanced below the nose of the aircraft, seeing a pale dirt road shining in the moonlight along the side of a small hill. Then another road passed underneath him and intersected the first, forming a tight V at the crest of the hill.

The aircraft buzzed under their seats, then suddenly lurched to the right. The differential thrust mechanism failed from the lack of hydraulic power. Bradley selected TAKEOFF/LAND on the flight parameter switch, then pushed at the throttles to eke out more power. The aircraft began to buffet violently and the WING FIRE light flashed in his face. The thick smoke swirled in the darkness, burning his eyes. Bradley pointed to the altimeter. They were less than two thousand feet above the terrain. The valley loomed before them. He glanced at his console as the airspeed was bleeding below 162 knots.

They had done all that they could. It was time to get out of the jet.

He glanced toward Tia. She was looking up in anguish at the damaged panel directly over her head. He followed her eyes and his heart sank in his chest.

Her ejection sequence lines dangled from the gash in the cockpit. The pneumatic lines had been severed.

Tia's hatch wouldn't blow.

She could not eject.

Tia studied her hatch, then glanced over at him. She sat back in her seat, braced herself, closed her eyes and pulled her ejection handles. Bradley heard a low pop, but the seat didn't move and he saw the glow of terror begin to build in her eyes. Yellow flames licked around them and Bradley recoiled from the heat. A rocky peak passed to their right. The aircraft was losing altitude.

Tia turned quickly to Bradley, motioned for him to eject.

He shook his head and turned his attention back to the wounded jet.

"Go!" Tia screamed.

"No," he shouted as he fought to maintain control.

"Don't be stupid!" she cried.

Bradley shook his head. No way he was bailing out of this jet!

Tia reached over for Bradley's ejection handle.

26

C ol. Shane Bradley pushed Tia's hand away from his ejection seat handle. "No! he shouted angrily as he pushed it away.

"Go!"

"There's an airfield."

She looked at him blankly, unable to hear, the initial blast of the depressurization having left a shrill ring in her ears.

She reached for his ejection handles again and he pushed her hand away. Straining against his shoulder straps, he leaned toward her. "Lyangar," he shouted, pointing to the east.

Tia pulled back and tried to remember. Lyangar? She knew the name, but her thoughts came so slow. Lyangar? Yes, Lyangar. It came to her now. Like her hearing, her mind was beginning to clear.

Lyangar lay two miles on the other side of the Tajikistan border, beside the narrow finger of land that stretched toward China, deep in the Baroghil Valley between Kashmir and Tajikistan. The airfield was tiny, isolated, and dangerously close to the mountains. No way they could land a B-2 down there.

"No!" Tia shouted, "The runway's too small."

Bradley didn't answer and Tia screamed again. "Don't be a hero, Colonel, just get out of here."

Bradley ignored her as he searched the night. He motioned to his left, then banked the aircraft up on her side. He pointed with authority, lifted one finger, then five. One five miles to the airport. He had the rotating beacon in sight. "Checklist!" he commanded above the scream of the wind.

More smoke billowed into the cockpit, greasy, toxic, and thick. Tai reached again for Bradley's ejection handle, but he had already inserted the red safety pin, locking the handle in safe. The fire heated the cockpit as the aircraft lost more altitude. The FIRE warning lights illuminated their faces in red.

"Sir!" Tia shouted. "Get out of here!"

Bradley leaned toward her and screamed in her ear. "I'm not leaving you, Captain. Now you can either help me land this aircraft or you can sit there and whine. I would appreciate your help. So what are you going to do?"

Tia sat stunned, the aircraft bucking under her seat. The fire was spreading through the right engine bay. It burned through the primary flight control systems and the backup system kicked in. The fire was spreading, engines failing, systems dropping off line. They had only three or four minutes to get the jet on the ground.

She shook her head, then moved her hands through the cockpit, setting up the aircraft for landing while configuring the wings.

The runway at Lyangar was only six thousand feet long, half of the distance the B-2 normally required to land. It was narrow as a ribbon and almost hidden in trees. Situated deep in the valley, with steep mountains rising up on three sides, the airfield was barely adequate for a WWII transport, let alone a three-hundred-thousand-pound high-performance jet whose landing speed was faster than the old bombers used to fly.

Built by Indian slaves during WWII, Lyangar had been used as an emergency airfield for Allied transports humping over the pass, supplying arms and munitions to the

American–Iranian Command on the southwestern front. During the last half century the airfield had fallen into crumbling disrepair. The concrete was cracked and the tarmac was rubble. All the buildings, simple wooden barracks set on cinderblocks, had been deserted until the Afghan–Russian War. Then, late in the fall of 1981, members of the 191 Air Speciale, 41st Mobile Regiment, the elite Russian troops that had come to Afghanistan to get their teeth kicked down their throats, had attempted to reclaim the airfield. They spent four months resurfacing the runway and repairing the buildings, then abandoned the base in a hasty retreat.

Lyangar fell in the center of what was known as the Crimson Basin, the bloody, and lawless valley that lies between Tajikistan, Afghanistan, Pakistan, and China. The inhabitants of Crimson Basin utterly refused to recognize authority of any kind, and operated outside the influence of any police or military force. As a result, the valley provided sanctuary for Muslim militants and common criminals, as well as the most bitter political outcast and dangerous insurgents from the Muslim territories. The only regular occupants of Lyangar were Taliban leaders and Mongolian warlords who smuggled weapons and opium.

The runway was unmanned for most of the year, from November to May, when the winters snows fell. It didn't have any runway lights or navigational aids. Under ideal conditions, landing at Lyangar would have been stupid at best. Landing there at night, in a stricken bomber, was asking for death.

Toxic smoke poured into the cockpit, greasy and thick. It burned Bradley's lungs and made it nearly impossible to see. He pulled back the throttles on engines one and four, the only good engines he had left. The bomber slowed too quickly and he shoved the power back in. Tia turned on the landing lights and configured the jet. "Dumping fuel!" she called out. The colonel nodded in reply. High-octane JP-8 began to stream from the wingtips, creating dual streams of vaporized fuel. Tia started to pull down any unnecessary electronic equipment to reduce the drag on the remaining generators. "Defensive systems coming down," she announced as she looked up very quickly. "Have you got the airfield in sight?"

Bradley squinted against the wind, then shouted, "Yes!"

"Okay, I'm bringing down the radar. The ZSR-63 is coming down, too." Tia finished powering down the energy-draining systems, then glanced around the cockpit, looking for a chart that would have the coordinates for Lyangar. It was bare, having been sucked bone dry. She recalled the latitude and longitude as best as she could and plugged the coordinates into the navigational computer. "One fifty-eight is your approach speed," she called above the sound of the wind. Bradley pushed up the power. The aircraft wallowed at one hundred forty-five knots. Bradley stopped the descent and flew toward the rotating beacon. Was he lined up on the runway? It was impossible to tell.

They were flying too slow. "Power!" Tia called. Bradley shoved the throttles forward. It took full power on the two good engines to maintain level flight. Tia desperately searched the darkness for the runway threshold. The valley was so dark. Black mountains rose up on both sides. The aircraft buffeted in the wind, rocking from side to side. Bradley struggled to keep it level, fighting the backup flight controls. Smoke was so thick that he raised a hand to his face, using his glove to filter the air. The smoke billowed in through the air vents like water through a hole in a dam. And it was hot. Very hot. The fire was growing very bright. Would his fuel tanks blow? His radar altimeter read nine hundred feet. He felt a tug on his shoulder and saw Tia sweep her left arm in an arc, then point toward the field. Bradley banked the aircraft gently. Tia pointed outside again. The runway was there, a dark ribbon off to his right. But he was high. Really high. Bradley pushed the nose down. The airspeed picked up quickly as the aircraft dropped toward the ground. He pulled back the power to compensate for the descent.

"Airspeed," Tia called and he felt her pull back the power. Bradley concentrated on the runway. "Gear?" she called out.

"Not until we are over the runway!" Bradley stared through his windscreen at the dark ribbon of cement. He could see the outline of the taxi lights, but the runway was dark. And it was short. Very short. He was going to have to plant the jet on brick one, then get on the brakes and ride them all the way to the end. The trees crowded him on both sides. Would his wings even fit? He adjusted the power and lifted the nose. The radar altimeter read two hundred feet, and still he was high! He let the nose drop, feeling the aircraft sink under his seat.

"One hundred feet," Tia called. "Let it down, sir. Get it right on the numbers."

"Got it," Bradley answered. Black smoke billowed in. Another caution light flashed as the number one engine temperature screamed through one thousand degrees. It was essentially on fire, though the heat had not yet erupted into flame. The aircraft shook, the left wing dropped, and the nose rose in the air. Bradley's main computer screen shattered, sending shards of glass into his lap.

"Shut the engine down!" Tia demanded. "It's going to explode!"

"No! Keep it going! I need power *now*."

Bradley adjusted his aim point. The wing dropped. "Airspeed," Tia screamed again.

Bradley pushed up the power, commanding every ounce of energy out of the jet. Flames curled into the cockpit through the gap in the hatch. Bradley fought the dying aircraft as the flames singed his skin.

"Gear!" Bradley shouted.

Tia dropped the landing gear handle and the wheels fell into place. The bomber dropped like a stone from the additional drag. Hydraulic pressure collapsed and the aircraft's nose pulled into the air. The left wing dropped again and the aircraft fell from the sky. The bomber hit like a rock, almost bending the gear. Bradley slammed his throttles to idle and threw his rudder/brakes out, then stomped on the brakes with all of his weight. Tia shut down number one and hit the fire suppression system, but left the number-four engine run-

ning to provide hydraulic power for the brakes. The end of
the runway was approaching with terrifying speed. A pine
tree rushed by Bradley's left side and was cut down by the
tip of his wing.

Halfway down the runway, the three-hundred-thousand-
pound bomber decelerated through a hundred knots. With
two thousand feet remaining, it decelerated through eighty.
Then the brakes exploded in flames as the wheels locked up.
The main tires blew apart, spitting strips of burning rubber
behind the jet. A thousand feet to go, and the *Lady* was still
traveling faster than fifty knots.

Bradley saw the end of the runway pass under his nose.
He closed his eyes and bent over, still holding the brakes. Tia
shot the final bottle of fire suppressant to shut the last engine
down. The aircraft crashed over the runway threshold and
into the overrun, a patchwork of asphalt and uneven cement.
The bare wheel rims sunk into the soft asphalt and Bradley
was thrown forward in his seat. The right landing gear collapsed and the wing dropped onto the cement. The aircraft
jerked to a stop. Bradley took a deep breath.

Tia unstrapped from her ejection seat and moved toward
the hatch as Bradley reached up to turn the battery off. Tia
blew the emergency crew entry hatch door and the egress
hatch in the floor behind their ejection seats, and the egress
ladder slammed into the asphalt below. She grabbed Bradley
by the arms and pulled him out of this seat. The pilots stumbled from the aircraft and onto the ground, then ran under
the wing and clear of the jet. A hundred feet from the aircraft, they stopped and looked back. The *Lady* sat on one
knee, a broken shadow in the night. The fire was dying now,
though it still billowed smoke. With no fresh fuel to feed it, it
soon would die out.

Bradley fell to his knee as he coughed from deep in his
chest. He filled his lungs with air, then placed his hands over
his face.

Tia knelt down beside him. "Amazing," she whispered.

Bradley glanced at her, then back at the aircraft. "We
should get a medal for that." He smiled. Tia started to laugh

to hide the tears in her eyes. She brushed them away. Bradley took another deep breath.

Behind them, they heard it. Bradley's heart slammed in his chest. He slowly cocked his head. Tia watched Bradley's eyes.

The soldier moved toward them, grunting an unknown command. His brown robes flapped in the wind, and his beard reached almost to his chest. More soldiers emerged from the darkness, all of them dressed in desert attire.

Bradley started to stand, but the soldiers pushed him to the ground. Tia looked over and cried out, her face frozen in fear. A soldier grabbed her by the throat and pushed her face to the dirt. Bradley felt a cold knife against his neck. He pushed back, pressing upward, trying to struggle to his feet but another soldier knocked him over with a knee to his spine. A steel-toed boot smashed into his head, then he heard Tia scream. He moaned and fell back, then cursed and pushed himself up again, lifting the men, almost making it to his feet. The soldiers yelled at each other and knocked him back to his knees. Another kick to the head, and he fell on his face. A stab of pain rolled between his eyes and all the way down his spine. Then he felt himself falling into a bottomless pit.

BOOK
TWO

BOOK
TWO

We will always remember. We will always be proud.
We will always be prepared, so we may always be free.
—Ronald Reagan at Omaha Beach,
Normandy, France (1984)

27

The President of the United States sat alone at his desk in the Oval Office. The evening was quiet and very few of his staff were around, the word having spread through the White House to leave the president alone. He waited in the growing darkness, staring at the clock on the mantel, his eyes unfocused as he lost himself in his thoughts.

The national security advisor stood unnoticed for a moment in the doorway, then knocked quietly against the dark frame. The president turned to face her. He already knew from her face, from the minutes that had already slipped by, that something had gone desperately wrong. "What do you have?" he demanded, a worried edge in his voice.

"A little problem with the B-2," she answered simply.

"The second aircraft?" he stammered, an unbelieving look on his face.

"Yes, sir. It should have been over the target twenty minutes ago."

"And you haven't picked up any sign of detonations?"

"Nothing, sir. If the bombs had been dropped, our detectors on the border would have known instantly."

The president swore silently, then eyed his advisor. "The warheads are still in the mountain?" he asked.

"No sir. I'm afraid they are not. Ground troops are swarming into the area, moving up the road to the cave. The enemy has found the warheads. It's time we moved to worst-case."

Wing Command Center
Whiteman Air Force Base, Missouri

Col. Dick "Tracy" Kier wearily rubbed his tired eyes. He felt cranky and mean and his mind had slowed down. He sipped at his Coke, which was warm and flat, and swirled it between his teeth to wash out his mouth. He had been awake now for going on forty hours, since he had been called in for the five o'clock briefing on the morning before. He glanced at his watch; it was 1632 local time. Just over twenty-two hours since the Stealth had taken off. Four hours, seven minutes since the last communications from the crew.

The Stealth should have hit the target almost thirty minutes before.

Kier turned to the master sergeant manning the communications console. "Local time in the Gulf?" he asked again.

"It's 0032, sir."

Kier paced four steps, then stared again at his watch. His stomach rolled and he swallowed to push the acid down. He walked to the command console at the back of the room that had been his main desk, his home base, for the past thirty hours, and studied the notes in the command-center log.

> 1617 Zulu time. Air refueling tanker reports blue-flame incident. Kill 31 damaged as result of boom separation. Kill 31 reports mission capable. Partial fuel onload complete. Kill 31 to continue under No Radio (NORDO) ROE. Anticipate dropping weapons on target, on time.

D. T. read the log for the eighth or ninth time. Bottom line— the Stealth crew had elected to continue the mission, but the target had not been destroyed. In fact, no U.S. weapons had been deployed in the area. That was confirmed beyond a doubt from the seismic listening post located in Turkey. There were no explosions, nuclear or otherwise, anywhere in Central Asia.

No explosions. No communications. The aircraft had simply disappeared. Invisible to radar or any other means of detection, half a world away from its home base or any aerial support, flying over a region almost entirely uninhabited by man, the aircraft had taken off, slipped away, then vanished into the night.

Kier pulled on his chin, then took a deep breath, a darkness settling over him. Try as he might to deny it, he knew in his heart that the bomber was down. Yet, it didn't make any sense. Bradley was the single most talented pilot Kier had ever flown with in his life, and he considered it more likely the sun would turn cold and fall from the sky than Col. Shane "Clipper" Bradley would make a fatal mistake. And Captain Lei was Bradley's equal, a younger version of him.

So where was the aircraft? And where were his friends?

CIA Operations Center
Langley, Virginia

Dr. Thomas B. Washington eyed his military liaison. He was too drained to curse. Too drained and too sick. "How long now?" he asked.

"The aircraft is overdue by almost thirty minutes, Dr. Washington."

Thomas took a deep breath, then eyed the thin, balding man. "Is the director en route?"

"He is. He will meet you at the White House. He is meeting with POTUS at twenty-three hundred. He wants you to brief him in the Situation Room before the meeting takes place. You will only have five or ten minutes. You've got to leave now."

Washington pushed away wearily from his desk. He put on

his hat and wide-lapelled overcoat. It was raining outside, coming down hard. He headed for the door, hearing the chopper as it landed outside, the sound of the rotors thumping the glass of his third-floor office. Outside, he walked toward the helipad with drooping shoulders and heavy legs. An aide tried to cover him with his umbrella, but he walked away, letting the rain patter off his shoulders and run down the brim of his hat.

Shin Bet Auxiliary Outpost
Twelve Miles South of Tel Aviv

The deputy commander of Shin Bet turned to his boss. "The B-2 is down, sir," he began to explain, then quickly told the commander everything he had learned from his officers in the field.

Petate listened and frowned. "No survivors?" he demanded in an unbelieving tone.

"No, sir, no survivors, at least as far as we know."

Petate thought a moment, his face turning sour. "Not good," he muttered in a bitter tone.

"No, sir," the deputy answered simply. It was an understatement at best.

"It wasn't my intention to kill the American crew."

"We knew it was a possibility, sir."

"Do they have search and rescues assets in place?" Petate asked.

"Not much, General. They didn't have enough time. We've been listening, but all we've picked up are some broadcasts from a ground unit in the area."

Petate pressed his lips. "Keep snooping," he instructed.

"Yes, sir. We will."

Petate nodded slowly, then the two stared at each other in silence. The room seemed to grow cold and it was utterly quiet, the soundproof walls and thick steel door insolating the sounds of the busy office outside. "So it's finished," Petate finally concluded with relief in his voice.

"Yes sir," his deputy confirmed. "Our Pumas have landed

on their naval ships off the Pakistani coast. We are moving the *Rabin* and *Yafa* to escort the *Bethlehem* home. We still have to decide whether we dare bring our ships through the Suez Canal or do we take them around the Horn of Africa and through the Mediterranean Sea, and none of us will sleep soundly until the *Bethlehem* is safely in port. But sir, that aside, this is an incredible success. Few men will ever know, and fewer still understand, but you and I know what a victory we have accomplished this day."

Petate nodded grimly. "The battle isn't over, but we have bought ourselves time."

"The battle will not end in our lifetime or the lifetimes of our children. But that sad fact aside, this is still a step toward bringing us peace."

Petate nodded as he lit a cigarette, scratching the wooden match on the corner of his desk. He pulled in a drag, holding the smoke in his lungs, then let it drift from his nose in a light veil of white. "Good things are about to happen, you can mark my words. Watch what takes place over the next couple days. Watch what takes place over the next six months or so. Write down my predictions and see that I'm right. Beautiful things are going to happen, I promise you that."

Camp Cowboy
Northern Afghanistan

The morning after the runner met Angra in Peshawar, the rains started coming down in bitter sheets, heavy, and wet, and bone-chillingly cold. The sun was up there somewhere, somewhere above the rain clouds there was warmth, but Peter couldn't even picture it from where he sat in the soaking, cold rain. Down here in the deep shadows of mountains, in the cold and the mud where the sun didn't shine, the clouds were so dark and bloated they had completely swallowed the dawn, and Peter almost needed a flashlight to see along the steep trail. Despite his best gear, he was soaked to the bone and he couldn't have been wetter if he had jumped in a lake.

So he kept his head low, tucking his neck against his shoulders, and waited while breathing lightly in order to hear, his warm breath forming vapors as he stared through the rain.

He heard the barest movement behind him, nothing louder than a rabbit moving slowly through the brush, and waited for the touch on his shoulder and the sound in his ear. He felt it before he heard it, the warm breath on his neck, then the sergeant's voice.

"You see them?" the sergeant whispered.

Peter nodded yes.

"You've got a bead on all three?"

Peter lifted his hand slowly, pointing to his left, then to his right and in front.

The sergeant nodded and rested back on his feet.

The two men were hunkered in the brush three kilometers to the south of their camp. Below them, the ground fell away quickly and the forest was thick. Both of the Americans were fully camouflaged, their faces and hands, even the lids of their eyes, had been smeared black, gray, and green to blend in with the brush. Their camouflaged ponchos fell to their feet when they squatted and they wore wide-brimmed, floppy hats to keep the rain off their necks.

Peter waited, then turned and whispered over his shoulder. "Are the snipers in place?"

The sergeant nudged his shoulder and Peter followed where he pointed until he saw it, dull gun-metal blue sticking out from the brush forty meters off his left. "Garcia?" he asked.

The sergeant nodded.

"And Armstrong?"

"Higher up, twenty meters. Find the gray rock then look four or five meters left."

Peter began to search and it took him almost thirty seconds to see the muzzle of the weapon move, then the whites of the second sniper's fingernails. He grunted and turned back to descending terrain.

"Who are they?" the sergeant muttered quietly in his ear.

Peter shook his head. He didn't know.

"Do we take them?"

"No. Not yet. Let's see what they do."

"There might be more of them. A patrol. We should take the scouts while we can."

"Wait," Peter shot back.

The three Afghanis moved forward another fifteen paces and Peter lifted his arm. Pointing to the man in the center he said, "I think . . . yes, I know him. I've seen him at General Lashkar Gah's camp. He's one of his runners."

The two soldiers studied the runner as he moved slowly through the brush. He wore mountain green fatigues and black leather gloves. As they watched, the runner suddenly crouched, holding his Soviet machine gun in his right hand, then turned quickly and motioned to his comrades, telling them to get down. Pointing to the mountain, gesturing toward where Peter and the sergeant were hidden; but Peter knew he didn't see him and shifted his weight uncomfortably to his sore knees. The Afghani moved his eyes up and down the trail, squinting through the heavy rains, then, standing from his crouch, he placed his weapon on the ground.

"He knows the rules," the sergeant whispered in Peter's ear. "He shouldn't be here, so close to our camp. This is a kill zone! Is he some kind of fool?"

Peter didn't answer, but watched the runner intently.

The Afghani turned in a full circle, always looking around, then pulled out a black rag and stuffed it in his front pocket, leaving two or three inches of the cloth hanging from the front of his pants. Laying his weapon on the ground, he began walking very slowly up the trail, holding his hands above him while clasping his fingers behind his neck.

Peter watched, then stood up. "He has a message," he said.

The sergeant remained squatting. He had seen the signal but he still wasn't sure, and his lips curved nervously in a frown. The men were too close! They shouldn't have come so near their camp. And they seemed to know where they were going, which meant that they knew far too much. "I'll keep the snipers on them," he said as Peter pushed himself up.

"Rog," Peter replied as he grabbed his own weapon and began to move down the trail.

◆ ◆ ◆

The two men met thirty paces below the sergeant's position. The trees were heavy and drooping around them and the raindrops filtered through the trees to form huge, soaking drops that pattered on their heads and shoulders. Thunder rolled in the distance and the clouds draped the mountains in a blanket of gray. Peter came to a stop on the trail and the young Afghani approached. The two men stared at each other. "Come no closer," Peter said.

The dark man stopped and then gestured with his shoulders and Peter nodded his head. Slowly, the stranger lowered his hands to his side. "Lashkar Gah sent me," he said.

"He told you to come here?"

"He said it would be okay."

"He almost got you shot, do you know that? We've been tracking the three of you since you left the river."

The runner looked nervous and his eyes moved left and right.

"Yeah," Peter said. "We've got your buddies too. One bad move and they're dead. So be careful, comrade, and speak quickly."

The runner didn't hesitate. "My master wants to see you," he said.

"He knows how to contact me. We have agreements for such things."

"No. He can't wait. He wants you to come to his camp."

The American shook his head and looked around angrily. "Tell him I'll come when the rain breaks."

"No, my *Sayid*. He begs that you see him this morning."

"This morning?"

"Yes. Right now. He wants you to come with me."

Peter hesitated and scowled. "I'll come when the rain breaks," he repeated.

"No. He must see you right now."

"Why?" Peter challenged. Something grew tight in his gut.

The messenger looked around, glancing anxiously over his shoulder again. A sudden gust of wind blew, pushing a sheet of rain before it and he wiped the cold water from his face before he turned back to Peter. "He has information," he answered as he turned his head.

"About what?" Peter demanded.

The runner lowered his head. "Tirich Mir," he muttered.

Peter's heart slammed in his chest.

"Tirich Mir," the Afghani repeated as he started to turn. "Now come. It's important. My master said you would understand."

Twenty minutes later, Peter Zembeic was in the Camp Cowboy command post, talking on the satellite phone to his superior at the CIA.

"Lashkar Gah's got something for me," the agent said coolly into the satellite phone. He waited through the five-second delay as his message was encrypted, bounced from one satellite to another, then sent down to a reception center outside of D.C., where it was relayed to Thomas Washington's office at Langley. The electrical energy in the clouds broke the satellite reception with static and his earpiece constantly crackled as he waited for Washington to respond.

Washington's voice finally came back. "He actually said Tirich Mir?"

"Yes, sir, he did."

"You think Gah knows about the warheads?"

Peter thought a moment. "Doubt it," he then replied. "But he'd have to be blind and stupid to not know that *something's* going on. Half the soldiers in Pakistan have been transported up there. Unless he's spent the last few days on the moon or circling Mars, he'd have to have heard something."

The phone was silent as Washington thought. "This man, General Lashkar Gah, how long have you worked with him?"

"I don't know for certain. Since sometime last fall."

"But you trust him?"

"As much as I trust anyone."

"You don't trust him then."

"Not particularly."

Another moment of silence. "Alright," Washington answered. "Call me after the meeting. I want to know what he's got."

"Roger, boss," Peter said, "Signing off now."

"Wait," Washington interrupted before Peter could break the connection. "Who are you taking with you?"

"No one," Peter answered. "I'm going alone."

"Don't," Washington instructed.

Peter hesitated. "I can take care of myself, Thomas."

"Take someone with you," Washington repeated.

"I don't tell you how to schedule meetings or eat donuts, so please don't start now telling me how to do my job. Anyway, Gah wouldn't allow it. He never has. It's always been me and him, that's just the way that he works. He's kinda funny about U.S. troops in his camp; you know those tribal warlords, they are a skittish bunch. Besides, he and I have an agreement. I don't bring strangers to our meetings and he doesn't kill me while I'm there."

Washington didn't answer for a moment and the satellite phone crackled as he thought. "Be careful, Peter, I'm nervous. Something doesn't feel right about this."

"I'm nervous too. But I'm always nervous; that's why I'm still alive. And though I appreciate the thought, you've got bigger things to worry about than little ol' me."

The White House
Washington, D.C.

The national security meeting took place in the president's private office on the residential floor, a small room with thick walls and a creaky hardwood floor. Only a small floral couch and two leather chairs provided seating. A single window looked out on the office towers north of the White House where lightning flashed, illuminating the tall buildings in strobes of white light.

The director of the CIA, the NSA, and the chairman of the joint chiefs entered quietly and sat, each of them formal and intense. Four stories below them, in the basement of the

White House, there was panic in the air. Hundreds of staff members worked in the dim light of the Situation Room, where secure phones constantly chimed and chaos rang everywhere. At Andrews AFB, Air Force One had been placed on a STEPONE alert, the flight crews briefed, and the aircraft readied to go. The Homeland Security National Alert System had gone from yellow to orange and the military had increased its DEFCON to Two. Throughout the Middle East, U.S. embassies were on the highest alert.

The president sat in one of his favorite wingback leather chairs. His face was stricken, but calm, though his lips had turned dry from chewing on an old stick of gum. "Okay, why didn't the Stealth drop its weapons?" he asked in a no-nonsense tone.

"Sir, we don't know," General Abram answered quietly. "We can speculate on several possibilities—targeting malfunction, hostiles in the area, the aircraft going down—but without more information we'd just be wasting your time. And why they didn't drop hardly matters right now; the fact is they didn't and the warheads are gone."

"The warheads have been taken then?" POTUS demanded.

The CIA director nodded. "Yes, sir, they have."

"What happens next, then?"

The director squared his shoulders. "Sir," he began, "even as we speak, al Qaeda is dispersing the warheads throughout the region to protect them. We have counted as many as four dozen trucks moving through the area now. We suspect that most of the vehicles are only decoys, but some of them certainly have been loaded with bombs."

The president shook his head and swore, his jaw drawing tight. "And there's nothing we can do." It wasn't a question but a statement. He already knew.

Still General Abram answered. "Sir, as you know, we simply haven't had time to move any ground assets into the area. We are talking about, sir, what is unquestionably one of the most remote and inaccessible spots on this earth. It will take us days to get ground forces of any significant numbers into the area. By then, of course, it will be far too late. It's too late already. The warheads are gone. By morning they will be hundreds of miles from the area, and completely dispersed."

"And then?" the president asked as he sunk back in his chair.

"They could show up anywhere. Our bases in Turkey, Saudi Arabia, Oman, or Kuwait. A city along the east coast. Anyplace, anywhere. These warheads are literally so small they could be packed in a box, labeled oil rig parts, picked up by a FedEx contractor in Morocco and shipped to an airport in the United States."

The president turned to look through the large window behind him and the director saw him tremble as he stared at the back of his head. The president was silent for a long time, lost in his thoughts.

As the director watched, he tried to imagine what must be in the president's head. He thought of the venom spewed by their enemies, a constant and filthy river of hatred and rage. He thought of the attacks the United States had already endured, then the continual promises to destroy the United States.

The president turned around and the director diverted his eyes. Staring at his hands, he swallowed, then lifted his face to meet the president's stare. "There is not a doubt in my mind that one or more of those warheads will find its way to U.S. shores," he said. "I defy you to find me anyone who doesn't believe that is true."

"Then, short of invading and occupying the entire Middle East, how do you propose that we locate the weapons?!" the president demanded, his voice acid with rage.

The director pressed his lips. For the first time in his career he didn't have the answer. The truth was, he had no idea at all.

The president was silent, reading the fear in his advisor's eyes. "Okay," he announced, his decision made. "You don't have a suggestion, so let me tell you what we're going to do." He pushed himself up and placed his fist on the table, leaning angrily toward his staff. He looked each one in the eye, his face determined and proud. "From the first day I took office, I have felt in my gut that I would face this day. And I want you to know, I'm prepared for what I must do.

"The issue is clear. We have seen the work of radical Islam far too many times now; from the nightclubs in Bali to the schools in Beslan, from the U.S.S. *Cole* to our own soil. We see it every day. Every . . . single . . . day. Bombings and destruction of innocent lives. And now they have the potential to wreak the most evil carnage of all.

"So we can't wait. Our nation, our very existence hangs by a thread. I have a constitutional obligation to defend this country, and make no mistake, I will honor that pledge. And so, gentlemen, this is what we will do:

"First, I am immediately calling up every unit in the National Guard as well as activating the ready reserve. In addition, I am federalizing state militias, rescue assets, and emergency management organizations to help secure all of our borders. Until such time as we have found and destroyed these terrorist organizations and their nuclear weapons, I am ordering our military and civilian forces to seal our borders from all shipping and transport, whether by air, land, or sea. Now listen—I know—I realize the economic impact will be enormous, but when you look at the alternatives, what choice do we have?

"Second, it is time that we had some help. We have carried the burden of fighting terrorism far too long by ourselves. Too many of our allies stand on the sidelines, playing both sides of the fence. No more screwing around, it's time we found out who our friends are. I want to find those warheads and I want to find them right now. To do that we need help, and if our allies won't stand with us then they will stand out of our way.

"The First and Second World Wars were won and sealed with American blood. Then we defeated communism in the Cold War, the third war we fought. And now the fourth war is upon us and we will finish this task! So, listen to me when I say this, for this is my final word! And I want you to take this message to every country in the world." The president turned slowly to his secretary of state. "You go to the Middle East and give them this message from me. If our enemy strikes us, then we *will* respond. If an American city is attacked, they will see a crushing blow. Give them that message, and make it perfectly clear. They *must* join in this search to find these nuclear warheads if they want to survive. They cannot sit back and watch as we are destroyed. An attack on U.S. soil will result in their destruction as well. One way or another, they are in this war too!"

The president paused and took a breath and a cold chill settled over the room.

Was the president really serious? Would he retaliate? Looking in his face, there was no doubt in their minds.

The president finished speaking, the passion cracking his voice. Then, turning to his CIA director, he held his eyes. "You have twenty-four hours, Rich, not one second more. You have twenty-four hours to bring me a plan to go after those warheads. I'm telling you, Rich, to tear the world apart! You have my authority. You are free to bust heads. There is no law or regulation that would preclude any action you take. You *will* locate those warheads. Now, do you understand?"

The director nodded. It was perfectly clear.

The NSA cleared her throat. "Mr. President, there are a few other things that you need to decide," she said. He looked at her anxiously and she went on. "We have the primary target list where we want to begin the search. But we need your approval before we can execute the—"

"Give me the top three."

"Es Suweida, south of Damascus, Aqaba, and Tehran."

"Are our forces in place?"

"Sufficient. Not optimal, but we can start on the job."

The president waved his hand. "Get at it," he said.

The NSA nodded expectantly. "But sir, the Saudis. The French. The others on the list?"

"Put the screws to them! Hammer them to the wall!"

"Mr. President, are you then authorizing—"

"Yes! Yes! I'm authorizing any action. Have I not made myself clear?"

The NSA scribbled quickly on a legal pad, then glanced over to the CIA director. The operation they were going to order would require both of their signatures and she needed to confirm that he understood the president's instruction. The director hunched uncertainly and the NSA pressed. "Mr. President, forgive me, but I need you to be very specific. Are you authorizing our in-country agents to move against the Saudi King?"

"Do it!" the president answered.

The NSA nodded and the room fell silent again. "What else?" the president demanded, but no one replied. "Okay," he said, "let's get to work then."

The group stood as one, each of them breathless, and silently filed out of the room.

28

Peter followed General Lashkar Gah's runner down the muddy trail. The rain had broken for the moment, but the heavy clouds behind him promised more would soon come. Lashkar Gah had moved his camp down by the river, which was swollen and roaring from the morning rains, the water running cold and clear over the boulders and rocks. At the edge of the clearing, on the side of the camp, the runner came to a stop and stepped out of the way to let Peter pass by. He pointed to a single canvas tent and grunted. Peter understood.

The warlord's clan normally lived down in the valley, twenty kilometers east, nearer to the Pakistan border, but this prewinter romp through the mountains was something they did every fall. By summer's end, the valley grasses had been grazed away, and so the herdsmen that supported the chieftain drove their herds to higher ground, where the animals could forage among the grasses that grew along the steeper terrain. But the heavy rains were precursors to the snows that would come, and the clan would soon be driven to the valley again.

Two dozen tents had been pitched in a circle around a community fire on a sandy bank along the river. Peter could hear the tribal goats and sheep bleating on the grassy foothills behind him, and he smelled the tangy smoke of the smoldering fire. The camp seemed to be empty. He knew the children had been tucked away inside their canvas tents while the warriors and herdsman were in the rough shelters in the trees, from where they could keep their eyes on the camp while grazing their animals.

Peter approached the tent carefully and stopped until he heard the warlord say. "Come! I am here." Peter pulled the flap back.

Three men were waiting, the warlord and two strangers. He waited at the tent flap, dripping wet, until the warlord stood up and gestured him in. Shaking off the rain, Peter stepped inside. Gah grunted and pointed to his poncho and Peter took it off, folded it carefully before placing it on the floor. A black leather holster was strapped over his shoulder and around his waist. Seeing three other handguns in their holsters placed by the tent door, Peter unstrapped his weapon and placed it beside his poncho. Standing, the warlord twirled his finger and Peter lifted his arms and turned, showing there was no weapon at his side or tucked behind his shirt. Satisfied, Gah nodded and sat down heavily on the floor.

The tent was warm and comfortable from a small propane heater that vented through a slit in the tent wall. The canvas floor was well swept and clean, and it was surprisingly large. Wool blankets had been piled along one wall, with foodstuffs and a low folding table along the other. The men sat facing each other, their legs crossed, eyeing each across the floor.

Peter bowed to Gah, then turned to the other men. The nearest one was large and middle-aged, with downturned lips and a cold stare. The rough hands, worn boots, and dirty combat jacket with cluttered pockets betrayed him as a man who lived on the move. And there were only two reasons men moved around in this place. Running or chasing. Peter wondered which one it was. Then he glanced to the other. Hardly more than a kid, he stared quiet and wide-eyed. Peter saw the resemblance and realized he was the older man's son.

• • •

The two strangers watched him carefully, then shot a subtle
glance to each other. Their eyes darted nervously. This was,
after all, the *Apostle of the Night,* the American horseman,
the prince of the darkness who seemed to know everything.
He was well known in the mountains. Everyone—thieves,
terrorists, drug smugglers, tribal chieftains, jihadist, and
thugs—everyone had heard stories of the *Apostle* and the
men he had killed. Still, the older man almost smiled. It was
three against one. They were armed and he wasn't. And they
were ready. He was unprepared. It shouldn't be difficult to
kill him, the legend of his prowess aside.

Camp Doha
Qatar

It was dark, the wind blew, and sunrise was an hour away.
The sky was black and rolling, a thick ugly blanket hiding a
dull yellow moon. As the rain crashed in thick sheets, the
thunder rolled in from the seas. The wind howled violently
across the open water, creating whitecaps tall as buildings,
walls of frothing white that crashed in on themselves.

Two U.S. Army MH-60 combat helicopters sat at the far
end of the runway. Their cabin doors were open, exposing
two .50-caliber guns mounted on the floors, lethal out to two
miles, and multiple bundles of equipment and ammunition
stashed under the main cabin seats. The choppers were unmanned and their rotor blades were tied down, but they had
been preflighted and cocked for combat alert.

Inside a small building, the crews huddled around the operations officer, the second in command, a brand-new lieutenant colonel who had been deployed to Qatar for more than
three hundred days. The boss pulled on his nonregulation-
length moustache as he studied the satellite charts. The
weather was lousy. No, the weather was foul. But the mission
wouldn't wait; they had good intel, a window of opportunity,
and, more, a go-ahead from the boss. The pilots and soldiers

would have flown their choppers though a hurricane to get to this guy.

The ops officer glanced out the window and watched the lightning flash in the predawn sky. "Fifty miles south of here, the weather turns to deep Sierra," he began. "Eighty-mile-an-hour winds. Lightening. Hail. Wind shear. The works. It's going to be a thrill setting down on that boat. So, be careful, men. We all want this guy, but I don't want any of you dead."

The mission commander, a crusty captain who had spent eight years as an enlisted soldier before gracing the officer's ranks, nodded as he studied the weather chart with his boss. He felt his gut crunch. This was what he lived for, and no lousy weather was going to keep him down.

"Once you get to the Straits," the colonel continued, "there is a sudden break in the weather, then another line of storms another thirty or forty miles to the east. A little luck, a little prayer, and it might be clear when you get to the target."

The captain nodded. Pushing the weather charts aside, he picked up a satellite picture, then a dark silhouette outline of the target, memorizing the ship's features that would confirm the ID. The *Jablah* was a small freighter, old and rusted, with double smokestacks, black and red paint, and a squat bridge over a cluttered deck. It flew under a Syrian flag and carried a Syrian crew, but the United States didn't care, at least not any more.

"How many crew members?" the mission commander asked.

"Twenty, maybe twenty-four."

"Will they be armed?"

"Count on it, buddy. They're supposed to be civilians, but some of them are Syrian SSQ forces. Either way, it doesn't matter, the ROE is the same; dead or alive, we want this guy."

"What about the cargo?"

"Don't know, don't care. If you determine the ship is carrying contraband, disable the engine and the navy will move in and impound it after you're gone. But weapons or diapers, the cargo isn't the point."

"But intel has a good bead on the target?"

"Looks like they do. He was spotted boarding the *Jablah* before it left the port in Iran. Looks like he wants to disappear while things are jumping over there. The ship is bound for Syria and will be rounding the Strait of Hormuz by the time you get in the air."

The captain nodded, then glanced to his team leaders. "Anything else?" he asked. All of them stared at him. "Alright then, let's go. I want this scumbag on one of our choppers before the sun shines."

U.S.S. *George H. W. Bush*
South of Oman

A navy Grumman Hawkeye was also assigned to the mission.

The aircraft was heavily loaded with fuel and sat low on her struts, the thick pistons compressed almost full to their stops. The engines whined and the props howled, sending a wash of air over the wings. It was raining hard, and the darkest clouds were still moving in as the enormous carrier, all eighty-nine thousand tons, was turned into the wind. Twenty-foot waves crashed at the bow, sending a cold ocean spray over both sides of the deck, but the carrier rolled with the punches. It pitched up and then down; one hundred eighty million pounds of steel, gas, bombs, airplanes, and men, bobbing and bouncing like a roller-coaster ride.

It was pitch black when the Hawkeye was wedged against the catapult hook. The pilot set his eyes on the horizon and studied the weather, watching the clouds flash with lightning that danced to the water, then he turned to the markings on the flight deck. Steam rose from the catapult engines and was swept back by the wind in contrails that flowed across the grated steel. The cat was set for a forty-five-thousand-pound launch, and the launch officer checked the settings, then gave a thumbs up. The pilot brought up full power and held on the brakes as the two-engine aircraft strained against the cat. He sat back in his seat and advised his crew of launch, then dropped his feet from the brakes and waited for the shot.

Two seconds later the catapult slammed the aircraft forward, sending the turbo-prop-driven aircraft over the bow. It dipped slightly toward the ocean as it cleared the deck, the engines sucking in gulps of cold water that were thrown up in front of the bow, then began to climb gingerly into the dark sky. As the airplane accelerated through one hundred twenty knots, the aircraft commander called, "flaps," and the copilot lifted a small lever near the two throttle controls. The flaps recessed into the wings and the aircraft dipped twenty feet, then continued to climb toward the dark clouds ahead.

The navigator called directions from the back. "Heading 355, Cap'n. The weather scope is showing the worst cells are off our right. If we fly north, I think we can come in from the rear and set up a search pattern behind the first line of storms."

The pilot didn't answer as he turned the aircraft to heading, his weather scope a solid wall of dark green and red. As his aircraft bounced in the wind, the radios were drowned in static from the lightning that flashed off his nose, momentarily blinding him. He hated this. He really did. He knew the danger of flying near such powerful storms. He had a wife and two daughters, and he wanted a son.

His wife would be bitter for a decade if he bought the farm, his government-issued life insurance notwithstanding. But still he turned the aircraft and leveled off at ten thousand feet.

For the next fifteen minutes the crew maneuvered, turning constantly to slide in between the worst cells. Though the sun rose on the horizon somewhere above the clouds, it seemed to get darker as they flew into the heart of the storm. The wind buffeted the aircraft, bobbing it like a cork on the sea, lifting and dropping it with sickening force, and the pilot turned to his copilot, who was looking very green.

"You okay there, Porky?" he asked.

The copilot gulped and swallowed. "Fine, Cap'n, fine."

"Got a hole in the weather up ahead," the navigator said from the back. "Once we get past that, looks like there's a break. I should be able to find the target if we can circle in that."

The pilot pushed up the power and climbed, the altimeter jumping between thirteen and sixteen thousand feet. Five minutes later, the clouds suddenly cleared. "Alright," he said, "take a look around and see what we've got."

The backseater cast his radar down, taking a picture of each ship that was steaming through the Gulf and enlarging it on his screen. Ten minutes later he found it; double smoke-stacks, eighty meters, cruising east through the Straits of Hormuz. Had to be the *Jablah*. He let the pilot know.

The pilot nodded, then got on the radio and gave the combat choppers a good vector toward the target, which was now almost directly below.

The sky had turned from deep black to dark gray as the choppers approached the *Jablah*, flying ten feet over the water and approaching from aft of the ship. The pilots could barely make out the silhouette of the freighter as it steamed around the tip of Oman. Four miles from the target, the second chopper split off, turning forty-five degrees to the right. Glancing over his shoulder, the mission commander checked the ten-man team in the back. All of their faces were determined, though a couple of men smiled.

They were going after Fayesa Amin. It didn't get any better than this!

The second chopper flew to a position sixty degrees off the freighter's right side, then turned toward the target, getting a good broadside look. The two pilots studied the freighter as they drew near; one even pulled out a picture and held it up to the windscreen, comparing the two. "That's our baby," he said.

The second pilot nodded, then got on the radio. "Bull's-eye," he said.

The mission commander clicked twice. Confirmation of target. The mission was a go.

He turned again to his troops in the back of the chopper. "Two has visual confirmation of the target," he announced over the intercom, and the soldiers stirred anxiously. The pilot glanced at the time-to-target countdown. "Two minutes!" he said.

The assault team leader nodded and gave a thumbs up to his men.

The two U.S. combat helicopters approached the *Jablah* at almost two hundred miles an hour in a perfectly coordinated attack. The first chopper flew up the port side of the freighter, the gunner firing his 50.-caliber guns as it passed. This chopper passed in front of the freighter just as the second chopper came within range, then pulled up its nose almost vertically into the air. The pilot bled off the airspeed as the chopper climbed, then flipped the tail rotor to speed down on the target again. As the first chopper climbed and turned, the second chopper approached from the right, both guns firing forward in a deadly hail of metal and heat. Passing over the bridge, the second chopper shot two rocket-propelled grenades, blowing the bridge apart in an orange fireball.

The helicopters made one more pass, each time firing their weapons at anything that moved on the ship, then came to a simultaneous hover three feet over the deck, one fore and one aft of the smoking bridge. Ten soldiers leaped out of each chopper, firing quickly as they moved through the ship. As the soldiers moved across the ship's deck, the pilots lifted their choppers and circled half a mile away.

It was over in minutes. Fourteen enemy down. *Jablah* dead in the water. The target in custody.

The choppers moved back in position over the burning freighter's deck. Pushing a hooded and handcuffed man before them, a group of four soldiers moved from a metal doorway leading under the bridge. The hooded man was shoved onboard and strapped to the floor and the soldiers scrambled in. The two choppers lifted immediately from their hovers and turned to the west. Flying away from the burning freighter, the mission commander radioed the Hawkeye circling overhead.

"Splash one," he announced.

The Hawkeye pilot clicked twice in reply.

The pilot looked back at the prisoner who sat against the copilot's seat, his legs spread before him, his hands tied with plastic cuffs. He wished for a moment he could take off the hood, for he wanted to see him, this man who had killed so many Americans. Fayesa Amin, one of the most wanted terrorists in the world, sat motionless. He rested his hands confidently in his lap and the pilot noted the dry skin, dirty fingers and rough nails. These were the hands of an outdoorsman, a man unafraid of work. Amin was a soldier's soldier, he could see that from the hands, a man who led from the charge and not from the back lines, a man used to sleeping in tents and living in the undergrounds of the world.

One of the most senior leaders of al Qaeda, Amin had provided the bridge between two important terrorist camps, for he was the nephew of the Iranian interior security minister as well as one of the few surviving sons-in-law of bin Laden. For the past five years he had been working from inside Iran, crafting plans and plotting strategies to kill Americans, anytime, anywhere. But though he was the mastermind of the insurgency operating inside Iraq as well as the architect of the bombing against the U.S.S. *Reagan* and the embassy in Pakistan, Amin had proven impossible to get, for he operated unhindered and protected behind the borders of Iran, untouched and unchecked because of the government support he enjoyed.

But his glory days were over.

It was a new ball game now.

South of Camp Cowboy
Northern Afghanistan

Peter Zembeic shifted uncomfortably on the floor of the tent.

The rain beat against the canvas and the wind blew outside. The warlord Gah smoked in silence, sucking on a thick Pakistani cigarette. He pulled a deep drag and held it, then let the smoke run out of his nose. He hacked once and swallowed, then took another drag.

There was no choice in the matter, the warlord knew it had to be done, and he might as well get it over with. Still, the Afghani chieftain kept his eyes low. He had always liked the American who had made him a rich and powerful man, the king of this valley, the top dog on the pile. But now he was going to lose his cash cow. For this, and other reasons, he hated to see the American killed.

Still, better to please the Great One than to let the American live. Better to prove himself loyal than to die a rich man.

Gah looked at the others anxiously. If they were going to incur the wrath of the Americans by assassinating one of their agents, he wanted to be certain that they killed the right man. So the prearranged signal was simple. Crush his cigarette, this was him, the *Apostle* that they were looking for. Keep smoking, he was a surrogate and they would have to try something else.

Glancing to the al Qaeda bounty hunters, Gah pulled a final drag on his smoke, then crushed out his cigarette inside the tin can at his side.

Peter saw the movement, then a dark flicker in the warlord's eye. The older stranger nodded and Peter's instincts screamed. His back muscles tightened and his neck grew instantly stiff. He shot a look to his handgun, almost eight feet away.

No one moved. The air crackled and the stranger frowned, a fierce and defiant look of contempt. Lashkar Gah eyed the soldiers. What were they waiting for! They had promised they would take him the moment he had signaled them. He crushed his cigarette again, then pushed the ashtray aside. "*Apostle*," he said, "thank you for coming here."

Peter glanced at the chieftain, who smiled uncomfortably, his face stressed and cold, then turned again to the strangers who were staring at him. He looked into the dead eyes of the older man and saw the glint of a killer, someone who hated and was ready to kill. Glancing down, he noted the tiny bulge under the stranger's jacket where he had hidden his gun and his heart drummed like a freight train as his mouth went instantly dry. How could he be so stupid?! So careless! So trusting! A mortal mistake!

So this was it.

It was over.

After years of constant gambles he had finally drawn the low card. He shot another terrified look to his gun lying on the canvas tent floor, then turned to the three Afghanis, knowing they all were armed.

The killer watched him intently through his silky brown eyes. His son moved his hand nervously, dropping it to his side. The warlord leaned back, trying to stay out of the way.

Peter shook his head slowly and cursed at the men. And with that it was over, there was no pretense any more. They had come here to kill him. And they knew that he knew.

The father pulled a small handgun from under his jacket. "Don't move," he sneered, his finger twitching on the gun. He had the sturdy aim of a killer and he held it steady on Peter. He would have shot him right there, were his instructions not clear: *"I want a graphic beheading. And use a dull knife."*

The assassin hesitated and Peter saw his opening. Dropping his hand to his pant leg, he felt the blade that was strapped to his boot. The wide-eyed young one reached under a blanket beside him and pulled out his own gun. The warlord growled and pushed back, moving against the tent wall. The role he played was over. It was now between them.

Peter had only one chance, but he knew which man he would kill. The rage and fear burst inside him like a short stick of dynamite. If he was killed, that was fine, but he would not die alone.

Reacting out of gut fear and training, he snatched the four-inch blade from its sheath and threw it with a snap of his wrist, the motion so tight and swift it was nearly impossible to see. But he didn't throw for power, he threw for accuracy, for the target he was after was soft as a water-filled balloon.

The blade flew through the dim light, flickering once as it turned, and the older soldier fell back in pain and surprise. The blade hit him just above the eyeball, penetrating his skull, and he screamed once in agony before falling limp on the floor. Peter cried like out like an animal, half in rage, half in fear, as he pushed himself over and rolled across the tent floor. The young son looked down at his father and saw the knife blade sticking there. He saw the blood spurting from the slashed socket with each beat of his dying heart, then screamed in panic as he fired his gun. But he shot without aiming, sweeping it across the tent wall, and Lashkar Gah cursed in anger as the wild shots rang out. The young soldier fired again, following Peter as he rolled across the floor. The American reached for his gun while rolling to his knees, his back to the enemy, facing the tent wall. He grabbed his holster and turned it upside down, letting the weapon fall in his hand.

The young soldier knew there was enough time for just one shot more; it was kill now or be killed. He lifted his weapon, his hands shaking, his arm weak as wet twine. He aimed down the short barrel of the weapon while closing one eye. Grasping the warm steel, he pulled the trigger again.

Peter didn't even turn his body before he fired his gun. Twisting, he reached under his left arm and fired from his ribs, aiming behind him out of instinct, experience, and fear.

Dual explosions shattered the air as both men fired their weapons at exactly the same time. Peter felt the bullet pass by him, an electric buzz at his ear, so close he sensed the pressure as it passed by his head. Twisting on his knee, he fired again and the Afghani stumbled back. He heard a grunt, then a moan as the young kid dropped to his knees, holding one hand at his abdomen and one hand at his chest. Deep red blood seeped between his fingers as he gasped for air. His kidneys shattered, his lungs deflated, he gurgled and fell to the floor.

Peter was on his feet before the other man hit the ground. Moving to Lashkar Gah, he started screaming again. The chieftain held a gun in his right hand, but pointed it at the floor. "Who were they!" Peter screamed as he waived the gun in Gah's face. "Who were they, Gah! I want to know who sent them here!"

"They came asking questions. They came looking for you."

"Who did they work for!" Peter screamed as he squinted down the barrel of his gun. *"Those were not regular soldiers! Why did they come for me?!"*

"I don't know, I don't know."

Peter moved his gun and sent a shot a mere inch from Gah's head. The explosion shattered the dim light as a spout of flame emitted from the short barrel. Peter moved the gun and held it right at Gah's mouth. "Are you ready for Allah!" he sneered as he stared down the gun.

"Angra . . . they worked for Angra!" the warlord cried.

"Who's Angra?! Who is that? I've never heard of him before!"

"Angra works for the Master. I swear, that's all I know."

"Is he al Qaeda? Afghani? Tell me everything you know!"

"He does the dirty work for the Master. He works counter-ops. They say he's a devil. I have never met him, never talked to him. There's nothing more I can say."

Peter saw the desperation in Gah's eyes and he knew he was telling the truth. "Angra. Alright then." His voice trailed off. "Angra," he repeated. He would remember the name. He turned back to the chieftain. "I thought I could trust you," he muttered angrily as he lowered his gun.

"There are no friends, here, *Apostle,* you know that by now. But I could have killed you, just like you could kill me. I could have shot you before you even picked up your gun. But I didn't, and you know that. Our debt to each other is paid. Now go! Get out! This is the last time I will see you. This is the last time we will speak."

Peter swallowed and holstered his weapon, then reached down for his coat. He was out the tent and into the darkness before the warlord could clear his eyes.

Boulevard St. Michel, Montmartre
Paris, France

Close to the university where his mistress studied, close to the capital where he worked—but far enough away from his wife—the apartment was ideally located. It was small but beautifully appointed, with mahogany floors, marble counters, and a stunning view of the Church of the Sacre-Coeur and, further south, the Sorbonne. Postimpressionist works from the Orangerie in Monet and Musee d'Orsay were hung in the entry and main hall, beautifully framed and expertly lit. A black fireplace, crackling and inviting, warmed the main room, its yellow flame casting shadows through the French doors and into the bedroom while warming the chill and misty evening air. Though luxurious, with a million euros in updates, furniture, and art, the outside of the apartment was modest and unostentatious, having been intentionally designed to fit in comfortably with the less expensive flats on the block. The brick was old and blackened, and steel bars covered the entry to the front door which, like all the others, was chipped and well worn.

The president of France had just stepped from the shower. He toweled his thin hair, then put on a red-and-gold robe with matching slippers. His mistress was still sleeping, buried under the down comforter that stretched across the iron bed, and only her hair, strands of brown with blond highlights, could be seen above the comforter. The lovely hair fell across the pillow and caught the light from the hall. The president watched for a moment, smiled, contented, then turned for the kitchen where the coffee was brewing.

The man stood in the hallway. The president was startled and cursed, his face draining in fear. The stranger was tall and well dressed in a black suit and tie. He smiled pleasantly. "Good evening," he said in French.

"Who are you!" the president demanded. His eyes shot to the door leading onto the street where Institut De'fense security guards were positioned along the avenue. Behind the apartment were his personal guards, hidden along the back wall, next to the alleyway that led to Ile de la Cité.

The American frowned and took a step forward. "We have a little problem," he said and then slipped into English. "We would appreciate your help."

The president cursed. "What—who are you! What do you want!"

"Simple. We want four men. For now. Others will follow. But for now we would be satisfied with Sheik Khalid Shaikh Mohammed, Abdul Qadus, Abu Rawalpindi, and Iftikhar Khanum. You know these men. You know who they are and you know where they live. We think it would be a good idea if you were to take them into custody tonight."

The president looked confused and then worried. "Get out of here!" he cried.

"Mr. President, you need to understand. Such men will not find safe harbor in your nation any longer. Even as we speak we have tails on them. If you want them safe, arrest them. This evening. Right now. We will give you half an hour, not one second more. If these men are not taken into custody, our snipers will take them out. I promise you, not one of them will live through the night."

"This is not our problem! This is not our war!"

"I believe, Mr. President, history shows you are not adverse to war. What you seem to be adverse to is victory, but that isn't the point. Now we are providing you opportunity to finally take a stand. *S'il vous plait,* take this opportunity to join the winning team."

The president fumed, his face puffing with rage. "I know you," he stammered. "You're with—"

"Of course, Mr. President. You know who I am. Now, sir, I believe you were telling me that you have recently had a change of heart, that you understand the necessity of doing your part. That is fine news. We look forward to your cooperation. And I suspect over time we will have other suggestions on how you might assist. I'll report to my president that you were willing, even anxious, to join in our cause."

The president was speechless. Behind him, his mistress began to stretch in her bed. He glanced back at her and turned away from the door to move down the hall. His eyes blazed in anger, his face flushing red. A purple vein in his balding forehead pumped with every beat of his heart. "Listen to me, you arrogant fool," he hissed. "What were you thinking, following me here! Get out! Tell your president that cowboys are not welcome here. We are a civilized people. This is not how we work."

The American agent reached into his coat and extracted a small CD case. "Is this how you work, Mr. President?" He stepped forward and pushed the CD toward the president.

The French leader stood his ground. "Get out!" he cried.

"I think when you hear some of your conversations we have captured on this disk, you might be more willing to help us. In fact, we are betting you will."

The president kept his hands at his sides, refusing to take the CD. The American smiled and placed it carefully on the table. "There is more, Mr. President. Lots more, in fact. We have video. Documents. Money trails. The whole thing. And we're not talking about some tawdry affair with some student mistress or aide. It appears your wife is the only individual in France who doesn't know about those. This is the good stuff, the bad stuff—the stuff, I suspect, you really need to keep to yourself. We're talking criminal indictments. Some very powerful men, even more powerful than yourself, would really appreciate you keeping your business dealings just between you and your friends." The man glanced at his watch, then turned and moved for the back door. "Twenty-seven minutes, Monsieur President. We want those men in custody. There will be further requirements. I look forward to working with you."

The man turned and left, slipping through the back door. The president waited, listening, hoping for shouts or gunshots from his security guards in the alley. But the misty evening was quiet. Not a sound did he hear. He stood without moving for a very long time, staring at the floor, then picked up the disk and turned for his laptop computer.

Minutes later, he emerged from the apartment, a sickly look on his face. His private car was waiting. He jumped in without a word.

Mudhnib al Auda Presidential Palace
Five Kilometers South of Riyadh, Saudi Arabia

The four U.S. Army Special Forces Delta soldiers watched from the darkness, forty meters beyond the perimeter fence. The Saudi presidential security guards moved behind the chain-link and barbwire, aloof, tired, and clearly uninterested. It was just after four in the morning. Sunrise was a little more than three hours away. The Saudi soldiers were on a normal patrol, guarding one of the two dozen or so presidential palaces the king visited when he had a little time on his hands. Very rarely, however, did members of the royal family come to Mudhnib al Auda. And even as they walked the fence, the guards didn't realize that the King of Saudi Arabia slept inside this palace this night. They had seen the motorcade and entourage, but decoys moved throughout the kingdom all the time, and they had learned that black limousines didn't always mean that the king or his family was near. Truth was, the guards, three of twenty that were responsible for palace security, had long ago ceased to speculate if the king was inside.

But while the Saudi guards didn't know where the king was, the Americans did.

The U.S. soldiers' eyes were barely visible atop the desert floor, their bodies completely buried under a layer of sand. Perfectly camouflaged and deadly silent, they had been waiting for almost an hour for the three guards to pass. The Saudis walked in silence, quietly checking the security of the outer fence.

The first of the U.S. soldiers, the squad leader, slowly moved his fingers over the sand. The adrenaline was pumping, causing a constant rush in his ears. His rifle was already positioned, wrapped in plastic to protect it and buried in the sand, with only the scope and muzzle exposed.

"Okay," he whispered into the tiny microphone at his

throat, his voice no louder than a silent wind. "Lead has the target on the east. White brim hat. Cigarette. Two, take the fat one behind him. Three, you've got the straggler. Four, if we need follow-up, you got it. Copy all!"

"Two." "Three." "Four," the squad leader heard in reply. He moved his head down and peered through his night vision gun site. "In three," he announced, then counted in his mind. There was a faint puff, a flash of smoke, and a nearly silent *thooth*. Behind him and to his left he heard two other silenced shots fired.

The squad leader's target reached to his neck, then fell to his knees. The U.S. soldier heard a gasp as all three men were down. The Deltas didn't hesitate. Bursting from the dirt like some kind of underground monsters, they emerged from the sand and moved toward the fence. By then, all three Saudi guards were lying face down on the ground, their eyes closed, looks of pain and surprise frozen on their faces.

The soldiers, dressed in black camouflage, stood beside the fence. While his team checked their weapons on the downed Saudis, the team leader spoke into his secure radio. "Give me sparks!" he commanded.

"Roger," he heard in his earpiece. "Sparks on the way!"

Five thousand feet above the soldier the drone dove down from the night sky.

The team leader glanced up at the darkness, then cut the fence with black cutters and his soldiers moved through. A lance corporal, the youngest member of the team, moved toward the downed Saudi guards and extracted the tranquilizer darts from their necks. They had all been shot in exactly the same place, at the base of the skull and just behind the ear, almost directly into the main blood vessel that led between the brain and the heart. The Saudi guards would be unconscious for seven hours or so, and a little sore, a little wiser, when they finally woke up.

The Deltas moved toward the inner wall, a ten-foot stucco-and-brick barrier that separated the palace from the desert. Floodlights illuminated along the top of the fence. Along the inner wall, the soldiers knew there were multiple layers of laser motion detectors and audio sensors. Beyond the wall were a host of guards and their dogs. The four soldiers moved into position, pressing against the wall. Overhead, they could hear the soft drone of a propeller. The drone approached from the south and flew over the presidential compound at five hundred feet, doing two hundred knots. As the pilotless aircraft approached, the soldiers pressed against the wall, using the cement to provide added protection against the pulse-energy radiation that emitted from its nose. Although their Kevlar body armor protected their guts and their helmets protected their eyes and brains, they still were anxious to hug close to the wall. Similar to an EMP, but with a more focused beam that cut a three-hundred-yard swath, the pulse energy weapon could be hard on the flesh. Capable of destroying any device that was not hardened to exact specifications, the pulse weapon fried every computer, electronic chip, or transistor in the compound as it passed overhead.

"Radiating," the leader warned his team over their headsets.

As the drone flew over, every light in the compound sizzled, then popped. The electrified wire went down, as did every security detector and sensor. Indeed, every piece of electronic equipment within the compound had been instantly fried from the high-powered energy beam that had been emitted from the bulbous nose on the drone. The Delta's radios, protected by circuits and lead plates, were the only electronic things still operating inside the compound.

One of the Deltas stepped back and tossed a small rock on top of the wall, then fell against the stucco and listened. None of the motion or audio detectors went off. The soldier gave a thumbs up and another soldier threw up a thin nylon rope with a metal hook on the end. In seconds, the U.S. soldiers were over the wall.

They ran toward the east side of the presidential palace where the lawn was lush and green and thick as a carpet under their feet. Their footsteps fell silent. Palm trees and water fountains were everywhere, the fountains silent now that the power was out. A single guard appeared around the corner of the palace, and without breaking stride, the leader shot a tranquilizer dart in his chest. The Saudi huffed, then slumped over with a groan of pained breath. Another guard followed. Deltas Two and Four fired as one and the Saudi went down with a dart in his face and neck. The soldiers heard the soft sound of footsteps behind them as another guard moved across a paved parking lot. "Stop!" the guard screamed in Arabic. All four Deltas turned and fired at the same time. Their four darts hit the Saudi almost square in the face and he dropped like a rock, a muffled thud on the cement.

The team leader turned to the lieutenant. "That boy is going to sleep for eight weeks," he laughed.

The lieutenant smiled, but only barely. The truth was the Saudi might never wake up. The tranquilizer was powerful, and the human body could only take so much.

The Americans turned again for the palace. The white marble, rounded columns, and red-tiled roof loomed enormously before them, an incredible symbol of wealth, power, and prestige. Perhaps the most wealthy man in the world, certainly among the top five, all of the Saudi king's palaces were symbolic of his ego and pride, and the enormous structure loomed before them, the white marble silhouetting the moonlit sky. The Deltas approached at a run, broke through the back door, which was unlocked, and moved through the kitchen. The layout of the palace was just as they had been briefed. The soldiers knew everything—the timing and movement of the guards, what kind of weapons they carried, the location of furniture in the rooms, and where the security stations were located. They even knew which direction the hallway door opened and how many steps they had to climb.

Up the stairs, down the hall, and into the royal bedroom suite. The guards burst through the door. The king of the House of Saud was awake, sitting on the edge of his bed. The U.S. Deltas moved toward him. The king screamed like a girl, a high pitched, whiny sound and held out his hands in a gesture of fear and surprise. The blackened faces of the soldiers blended perfectly in the night and the king saw mostly flashes of movement and human forms in the dark. The squad leader looked as his watch. Two minutes, fifty seconds to get over the wall and into the palace. About what they had predicted. He was pleased with his team.

The leader walked toward the king with a determined look on his face and the king backed away. "Take this!" the Delta commanded in Arabic. He extended his hand, which held a single sheet of folded paper.

The king sat expressionless, too dumbfounded to move, and the soldier thrust his hand forward again. The king reached out for the paper, his palms sweaty and wet and trembling with fear. "What is it!" he asked in a terrified voice.

"Your instructions," the solider replied.

The king shook his head.

The Delta spoke carefully. His message was well-rehearsed, the words having been carefully chosen at a level in the government that was far above him, for the threat he was to convey could not be misunderstood. "Your son, Crown Prince Talan bin Abd al-Aziz, is in England right now," the U.S. soldier said. It was a statement, not a question, though he seemed to wait for a reply.

The king watched the soldier in the darkness, then nodded his head.

"Crown Prince Talan bin Abd al-Aziz is your chosen heir," the soldier continued.

The king nodded slowly. It was his greatest desire to see the crown prince take the throne. A tense silence followed as the king began to understand and, shifting his weight, his body grew taunt.

"The crown prince has many enemies," the soldier went on. "There are lots of men in this world who would bring him down if they could; evil men and hostile governments who are not as refined as we; the Israelis, al Qaeda, the Iranian mullahs—even more."

The threat was ugly and personal, but things were different now. Sitting atop a significant portion of the world's known oil reserves, the king wasn't playing poker with a low hand. He could not be threatened by much, he was too powerful and too rich. But the Americans knew how to hit him in the only place it could hurt, which was the transition of power to the son that he loved.

"You would not hurt him!" the king hissed. "You would not hurt the prince!"

"Of course not, Your Highness. But we might turn our heads."

The king's dark eyes narrowed and he cursed bitterly. The soldier moved toward him and tapped the paper in his hand. "Take out these targets," he said with a frown.

The king dropped his eyes to the paper, and the soldier held a tiny flashlight so that he could see. Reading, the king's lips drew tight and pale. "Al Shabakak!? Nykay babiyan!? These are Saudi sites!" he cried.

"Yes, Royal Highness. You have rats in your own home. You carry a deadly cancer, and it must be removed."

The king lifted his eyes. "These are my own people. Villages in the desert—"

"They are Wahabbie indoctrination facilities and paramilitary training centers. They are the core of the poison that you spread through the world. They are a dead goat that feeds maggots and they must be destroyed. You've been promising to take care of them for going on five years. Now it's time to act. This is your last chance."

The king looked again at the paper. "Jask and Bandar Angorhran are inside Iran!"

"Yes they are, Your Highness. Treacherous times such as these force one to consider one's friends.

The king stuttered, then fell silent again, looking up with dry eyes.

"Work with us, Your Highness, or face the consequences," the soldier said. "You have twenty-four hours." He forced a faint smile.

The U.S. soldier looked away and nodded to his men and the Deltas turned to leave.

Before leaving the room the last guard stopped at the door and looked back, his white teeth shining brightly against the black camouflage paint on his face. "It's been a pleasure to meet you," he said with a smile. "Maybe one night, you know, we might pop in again." He flashed a quick V with his fingers, then disappeared through the door.

The soldiers were over the wall and into the desert again. Two kilometers out in the desert, the American chopper picked them up.

Back in the palace, the king sat on the edge of his bed. He stared at the paper, which he couldn't read in the dark. Seconds later, one of his personal guards burst into the room, an emergency flashlight in hand. The guard moved toward him and the king shook his head. Staring, he considered the paper in his hand.

He had his instructions. And he had no choice.

He would join the Americans or he would be destroyed. His son, his power and wealth, his position in the kingdom, it all hung by a thread. In a matter of seconds, his life had been turned upside down. And now the decision was before him. Which side was he on?

29

Dhahran Air Base
Saudi Arabia

Dhahran is the most modern and well-kept airfield in Saudi Arabia, a nation with many extraordinarily expensive, perfectly maintained, and well-designed aviation posts, for the Saudis spared no expense when it came to air power. They weren't particularly fond of their army—ground battle is too dirty and causes too much sweat—and they knew the Americans would do it for them if they ever got in a crunch; but air battles, and an air force that exuded great power, and power projection were what a military was for. So the Saudis spent most of their national-defense budget (which was not insignificant) on fighters and missiles and their support staff, until they reached a point where, with the exception of Israel, the Royal Saudi Air Force was the most potent and modern in the Middle East.

One of the proudest possessions of the Saudi air force was the latest generation F-15s, the best air-to-air fighter in the world. And they also flew F-16s for the air-to-ground role.

At 1833 local time, just as the sun was beginning to sink toward the barren horizon, the evening sky crackled with the constant sound of jet engines. A total of eighteen fighters took off, all of them with Saudi markings on their tails. The

F-15s were laden with conformal fuel tanks (CFTs), to ex-
tend their range, the Falcons with underwing tanks full of
JP-8. All of the fighters were heavy with full loads of missiles and bombs.

The fighters split into five formations, a mixture of Ea-
gles to provide air cover (the least likely pilots to see real action this night) and F-16 Falcons with a load of bombs under
each wing. The formations all flew east toward Iraq and Iran.
Without refueling tankers to give them gas in the air (a lux-
ury only the Americans could afford) they had to make the
very best use of their fuel, so they climbed aggressively to
almost forty-one thousand feet and set their power for max-
endurance fuel flow. Below them, shadows extended to the
east from the low dunes and rolling hills that made up the
southern tip of Qatar. Then the sun set behind them and
night darkened the land as the fighters flew over the black
and eel-infested waters of the Persian Gulf. Midway through
the Gulf, one formation split south, taking up a heading for
the tip of Oman. The others split into slightly different directions, the space growing gradually between them as they
crossed the Gulf.

Forty minutes after takeoff, the first of the Saudi fighters
began to drop over their targets. The F-16s came in low,
from over the water, screaming at more than 550 knots toward the coast of Iran. The first target, Jask, was the premier
Iranian military-training facility, a location known to train
terrorists from throughout the Middle East. Eighteen miles
out from the target, while still over the water, the four Falcons popped suddenly to almost twenty thousand feet. Six
five-hundred-pound bombs dropped from each of the fighters. The bombs arced upward, powered by their momentum
and speed, then began a graceful parabolic descent. They
weren't the newest satellite-guided bombs, but the older, less
reliable, and less accurate dumb bombs. Still, the target was
large enough, and the effect much the same.

The bombs fell silently through the night as the fighters
turned away. They were already low on fuel, and they
needed to climb once again to max-endurance altitude. Be-

hind them, the bombs began to impact the target. Jask began to smoke, and then flame, as the fires leaped and spread, yellow tongues of flame reaching up into the night.

To the north and south, and along the coast line of Oman, the four other Saudi fighters hit their targets just a few minutes later. Eighteen fighters, five formations, a total of seventy-two incendiary bombs.

As the fighters flew to home base, they passed over another formation of fifteen jets, additional Saudi fighters on their way to their targets too. Behind them, another fifteen jets were in flight.

The first formation landed in the darkness and taxied to the hot pits, where airmen hooked up refueling hoses without the pilots shutting the engines down. While the aircraft were refueling, munitions crews loaded up another rack of bombs. An intel officer ran to each aircraft and plugged into the external mike. As the aircraft were refueled, the intelligence officers gave the pilots their next targets and updated the combat situation throughout the Middle East.

A little more than thirty minutes after landing, the first formation was back in the air. Combat operations continued through the night and the next day as well. Then the Saudi air force settled down for the long haul, reducing the sortie count to sixty a day. It was a war, not a skirmish, and they needed to pace themselves.

As the first fighters took off before the sun had fully set, at a military facility outside of Riyadh Saudi special forces soldiers loaded into the backs of armored personnel carriers and headed into the great barren deserts to the south and east of the city. Their targets where the nest of Islamic and Wahabbie training facilities that dotted the hill country along the Saudi Arabian desert, the portable tent cities run by the Saudi fundamentalist who, with the financial support of the kingdom, had dedicated their lives to the Wahabbie extremism that sprouted so much hate of the West.

Similar scenes were repeated all across the globe—from the side streets in Paris to the outdoor bazaars in Morocco, from the Muslim neighborhoods in London to military and government offices in Pakistan, Oman, and Kuwait. Joint military forces moved through abandoned warehouses and secret bunkers. Soldiers burst into private homes and through the back doors of crowded mosques, rounding up the leaders of various terrorist groups from across the world.

With no real information to move on, only guesses and speculation driven by their worst fears, the U.S. administration made the decision to prepare for overt military operations. They wanted forces in place, ready to go, when (there was no *if*) they located the nuclear warheads.

So the *Ikystans* of the world were suddenly crawling with troops.

In a midnight ceremony inside the Pakistani royal presidential compound, Sardar Akhtar Mengal, the Baluch National Party leader, was quickly sworn in as the new president of Pakistan. Surrounded by black-uniformed special security soldiers, he immediately started signing emergency orders. The border of Pakistan was sealed on both the east and the west, as U.S. soldiers teamed with Pakistani government troops loyal to the assassinated president moved to clamp down on dissident movements across the border. When government troops, some 280,000 strong (including those members of the Balochistan National Movement which, though no friend of the new president, formally denounced the coup), flooded into the streets of Islamabad and Karachi, the tide of battle quickly turned. When the Pakistani government didn't seem likely to fall, most every national leader made their decision and rushed to the new president's side, anxious to ride across the finish line on the winning horse. As the flow of Islamic rebels across the Afghanistan border was stanched, and without the reinforcements they had hoped would come from Iran, the morale of the coup-backed soldiers withered as quickly as a rotten fruit in the sun. After two days of street battles and assassinations, the coup leaders and their followers were forced to withdraw to their safe havens along the Afghanistan border, where they quickly disappeared, melting into the local populace while leaving only pockets of resistance to fight the government troops.

To the west, under direct pressure from the United States, NATO moved their forces to shut down the Turkish and Armenian borders. Though they didn't understand exactly why, the Soviets followed suite, deploying their paramilitary troops to monitor the borders of Turkmenistan and Azerbaijan. Twenty hours later, Afghani soldiers could be seen on nearly every street in Kandahar, many of them American-trained and well-armed. Two navy carrier groups then moved north in the Persian Gulf and military forces were redeployed from South Korea and Japan to the theatre. Many of the U.S. forces in Iraq, barely able to support the mission they already had, were dispersed to locations along the border with Kuwait and Iran. A constant stream of transports and fighters landed at the airports in Kirkuk and Baghdad, bringing fresh reinforcements and tactical air assets to the region.

The American public watched in frightened awe, too stunned to react with anything but silent resignation. Though they didn't know the specifics, it was clear something dangerous and unpredictable was going on, but they had been warned for so long now that most Americans accepted the various possibilities with only silent resolve. Another crisis in the Gulf, additional forces moving into the region, their president taut and snapping, the congress out of sight—no one knew what was happening, but everyone had a guess. They had seen it before and had grown weary of it now. So long as it stayed *over there,* no one planned on missing work.

So, behind the curtain of secrecy, the wild search was on.

As combat forces deployed to beef up the region, CIA paramilitary units and military special ops worked themselves to death, tearing and prodding and searching any location, any place they suspected the warheads might have been concealed. The paramilitary forces working in Iraq were nearly doubled overnight. The same paramilitary buildup took place in Afghanistan and Pakistan. A significant number of military operators moved through the West Bank and the Gaza Strip, aided by Israeli commandos and special tactics teams. Special operators moved openly into Iran, along the northern and western borders, defying the

Iranians to stop them in their search. In Syria and Jordan, the
rules there were the same. *Try to stop us if you dare. But be
ready for war.*

On a quiet Sunday evening, two days after the report
from Shin Bet, the President of the United States signed an
executive order authorizing "extreme measures" to locate
and destroy the nuclear warheads.

NSA Headquarters
Manassas, Virginia

Carrying the presidential authorization in her hand, the
national security advisor entered the NSA headquarters
building, surrounded by three bodyguards and two of her
staff.

There were three primary targets she was interested in.
Rawah was to the west, 275 miles from Tehran, out in the
rolling foothills that defined the border of Iraq. The other
two military facilities were in the very heart of Syria and
Lebanon. Al-Kazimya was just north of the presidential
palace, twelve miles north of downtown Damascus. Makkfar
al Buasayyah was in western Lebanon, amid the houses and
small shops that made up the suburbs that nestled up against
the river on the east Euphrates shore.

"Let's look at Rawah first," the NSA commanded as she
settled into the satellite-control room.

The group of intelligence officers huddled around the
NSA, anxious and nervous that she be satisfied. The satellite
controller tapped at her console. Above the center of the
earth, many thousands of miles out, the newest reconnaissance satellite in the U.S. inventory changed the focus of its
sensors just a few degrees south.

The KH-21 satellite focused its sensors on the outskirts
of Rawah, taking a series of visual, radar, and infrared images of the military compound.

The pictures showed a long cement runway that was lined
by two dozen hardened cement bunkers. Inside the bunkers

were four MiG-27s, the only real fighters the Royal Iranian Air Force had left. On the south end of the field, past the headquarters buildings, hospital, and officers housing, was the weapon storage facility, a small row of air-conditioned, semi-buried cement bunkers. Surrounding the bunkers was a no-man's-land—fifty meters of land mines, strands of twelve-foot electrified wire, and a double razor-wire fence with guard stations on each corner.

The weapon facility appeared to be quiet, with no unusual activity of any kind. A small motorcade of military vehicles made their way through the only gate and snaked along the winding road toward the main bunker. The number and formation of guards hadn't changed recently.

If the Iranians were hiding the nuclear warheads at this facility, they were not letting on. The security around the compound hadn't increased at all.

"Go to the next target," the supervisor commanded after getting a nod from the NSA.

The controller worked the satellite, moving her fingers expertly.

Fifty minutes later, the national security advisor had seen enough. Having spent the morning looking at the targets, she didn't know any more now than she did before. She huffed in frustration, scribbled a few notes, nodded to her aides, then left the building quickly to meet with the president.

Riding in her car, she had a dark sense of foreboding as the questions rang in her mind.

Were they on the right trail? Were they running out of time?

Cram 55
Eighty Miles West of the Es Suweida Weapon Storage Compound
Damascus, Syria

Cram 55, one of the newest aircraft in the special forces inventory, a tilt-rotor aircraft that flew like an airplane but landed and hovered like a chopper, was one of the thousands of assets the United States and her allies had committed to finding the nuclear warheads.

The night was dark. The four marine Osprey tilt-rotor aircraft were in fingertip formation, cruising low as they wound their way through the Lebanon Valley at four hundred miles per hour. As the target came into range, the formation tightened up and pulled toward the flight leader. Inside the guts of the four aircraft, the Ranger teams hunkered against their seats. Each of the soldiers were loaded for war, with combat packs at their feet and weapons resting across their thighs.

The night winds howled, creating severe turbulence that bounced the fat-winged aircraft as they lifted into weightlessness then dropped again suddenly. The anticipation of combat and mountain turbulence proved a messy combination, and inside the lead aircraft the cabin smelled of sweat, spit, and puke. Most of the soldiers had chucked up their dinner, a few had chucked up lunch and their breakfast as well.

"Two minutes!" the pilot in command announced to his flight engineer. The engineer stood, bracing himself against the aircraft's interior walls, and illuminated a small red light on the cabin bulkhead wall. The men wiped off their chins, slapped each other on the backs and checked their gear for the eighth or ninth time. The rear door began to crack, letting in fresh desert air.

The gunners sat ready, their .50-caliber machine guns swinging from side to side in their hands. The moon slipped away, dropping behind the low hills. It was dark, very dark, the darkest part of the night, but night vision goggles turned the night into day.

The commander of the operation sat near the forward bulkhead. His soldiers eyed him anxiously, looked for unspoken clues as to whether they should be scared. The commander faced his men. "Bring it on!" he cried.

The tilt-rotor aircraft began to slow down, their massive turbine engines rotating upward on the tips of the wings. The Rangers stood, triple file, and faced the open door. The roar of the engines was tremendous, and though they had earplugs, most of the men still held their ears.

The weapons storage facility came into view, a two-hundred-meter square wall of cement with semi-buried bunkers inside.

"Two miles," the copilot said. "Five hundred feet."

The Ospreys approached at a shallow angle, the pilot fighting the controls, keeping the heavy aircraft in a steady descent. A spray of enemy gunfire emitted from the north and the door gunners immediately returned fire. The pilot swore and dropped the nose as a small light lurched toward them from an RPG round. The Osprey's Gatling guns fired—six thousand rounds per minute—their tracers lighting the sky. The four Ospreys touched down and the Rangers belched out.

The firefight was over in minutes. Fifteen Syrian solders dead. Four Americans wounded.

The Rangers spent thirty minutes searching for the warheads. But none were there to be found.

So they loaded their troops and lifted into the night once again. The next search area was on the other side of Damascus, a little more than a hundred miles away.

30

The leader of al Qaeda stood on a small outcropping of rock and looked north toward Communism Peak, the highest mountain in the Pamir Range. He stared at the square mountain, looking on the south face. The top of the quadrangle mountain thrust upward at eighty degrees, reaching skyward to almost 25,000 feet. A bare wall of rock faced the Great Leader, and the snowline was down to nearly six thousand feet, yet edelweiss and wormwood still covered the base of the mountain, the color of life spreading right up to the ice. From where he stood, the mountain loomed impossibly large, an enormous block of granite pushed upward to create a vast series of valleys and canyons where the feet of great men had trod.

Alexander the Great had given the mountain a name. Parapamisus he called it—*mountain over which no eagle could fly.* And Alexander was not the only great leader to stand at the base of the mount. Tartar hordes once stopped there, and Gengis Khan and Tamerlane. Marco Polo had also traveled these valleys as he detoured to avoid bandits on the Silken Road.

The leader looked west to the top of Tirich Mir, then east,

following the Pamir range, the fist-like peaks that pivoted off the Karakorum, Kunlum, and Himalayan mountains. The leader then lowered his eyes, staring up the valley in which he stood. He could see a distant tower of mortar and rock, one of the watchtowers built by the old Russian army. The valley was quiet. Few men lived here now. Kirghiz nomads, black-skinned men who herded two-humped camels and long-haired yaks, were the predominant tribe that had taken over the valley. The people of Kafir Kalash camped away in the distance to the north, up the small river, beyond where his eye could see. None of the local tribes concerned the Great Leader. They had seen militants and criminals come and go through the years.

The al Qaeda commander smiled appreciatively. This was the perfect location. Ten thousand canyons, rocky, vertical, impossible to search, difficult to drive, with trees in the valleys to cover their movements from either space or the sky, a local population that was hostile to authority, certainly hostile to the United States, and willing to let him come and go as he pleased. Yes, it was an ideal location, even better than their original plan. It had all come together, despite the close call.

As the father of al Qaeda thought of the warheads, a shiver of excitement ran up his spine. Twenty-four warheads! Twenty-four million infidels would die! Die by technology produced by their own hand! He felt nearly godlike; powerful, destined, and unstoppable. He bowed his head, feeling the energy running cold in his veins.

Turning, he walked across the compound toward an ancient farmhouse of baked clay and cement that had been built against the side of the mountain, the back wall butting up against an outcropping of rock. The building was surrounded by huge oak and sycamore trees, ancient, gnarled, with low, sweeping branches and hanging limbs. Pockmarked with bullet holes and shrapnel, one side of the structure had been completely torn down from a long-ago battle with Russian soldiers.

Inside the building, against the rock wall, was a large

steel door, the entrance to a huge underground complex of caverns and caves that had been fortified by the Russian army and used during the war, then abandoned and forgotten after they had quickly withdrawn. The commander of al Qaeda walked through the building toward the cavern door. His soldiers, large men with huge shoulders and bloodthirsty eyes, guarded the entrance to the cave.

The leader passed through the door and walked down a narrow set of stairs that descended sharply until they ended on a rocky platform where small torches provided the light. From there a narrow path descended, dropping further into the mountain. He continued downward. The air was cold and wet and he heard dripping sounds. The tunnel narrowed and the top of the passageway dropped until he had to stoop as he walked. There came a fork in the pathway and the Great Leader turned right. Two hundred paces later he entered the main cavern.

Imad Mohammad was waiting, along with some of the men, standing beside the neatly stacked crates; the nuclear warheads, the great weapons of war. Behind Imad, Angra stood in the shadows, quiet, always watching, his dark eyes smoldering and alive.

Imad turned as his commander approached. "*Sayid,* we rejoice!" he said as he bowed. "What was once lost is recovered, what was once astray, now is found! What had slipped through our fingers is again in our grasp! And the enemy is scattered, searching everywhere for what we have! Indeed, the Great God has smiled upon us today."

The Great Leader nodded dismissively. God had little to do with it, he was certain of that. Hard work and luck were what had brought him success. His men always spoke of God, but he no longer believed, and he didn't do what he did out of love for God or anything else. He did what he did because he hated the United States. He hated their freedoms and arrogance and imbecile way of life. And he hated their influence, especially in his part of the world, their preaching of doctrines he despised to the core.

The only purpose he had in religion was when he used it

to motivate his men. God? Yes, perhaps? Perhaps he smiled above. But a smiling God meant nothing, not a dribble of spit. Now, burned and charcoaled Americans! That was something he could smile about.

The Great Leader nodded arrogantly, his thin lips spreading confidently over his gums. His long face and full beard were but shadows in the dim light, but his eyes seemed to glow from the fire within. "Yes," he answered simply. "They have taken the bait. We sent out a rat and the cat gave it chase. And now the Americans are searching desperately, running here and there, screaming like spoiled children, demanding this, demanding that. *"You help us!"* they are screaming, their snotty noses running red. *"We need you! We need you! Where are our friends!"* And all of it for nothing! The warheads are *here!* The irony is delicious! It almost makes me laugh! From India to the Mediterranean, the imbeciles hunt, and yet here are the warheads, but a few miles from where the search began!"

The lieutenant smiled. It was brilliant, yes, brilliant. The decoys had worked. And now the escaped prisoner was hiding inside the prison walls.

The Great One stared at the dark crates. "Thirty-six hours," he pondered. "That is all that we need. Thirty-six hours we will stay here, then we'll move the warheads north."

His lieutenant's face looked worried. *"Sayid,* if I may, couldn't we stay where we are? We are safe here, protected. Might this be a good place to hide?"

The Great One turned and scoffed. "Safe!?" he scoffed. "We are *never* safe, Imad. They will eventually find us, whether we hide here or there. They will eventually find us, and you know that is true.

"No, the warheads must be dispersed. That is the only way we can ensure that they won't all be found and destroyed. Once they are scattered, the enemy might find one or two, but they will not find them all. And once the warheads are dispersed, then we can plan our attacks carefully. Meanwhile, the Americans must wait, all the time holding their breath, knowing their destruction is imminent but not knowing when or where."

"And let me remind you, my brothers, my fellow sons, even if only a few of our teams are successful, we can claim a great work! An incredible victory! A million infidels dead! Our brotherhood would grow stronger. We would rule the world! We don't have to detonate every warhead to claim victory! Two, five, or ten, is enough!"

The room was quiet as death. The Great Leader lifted his solemn eyes. Five hundred years of occupation. Five hundred years of repression and death. It was time to go forward. The great day was here.

He nodded to Imad. "Give me the target list," he said.

Imad reached into his pocket and pulled out a single piece of paper with the names of twenty-four cities written in Arabic:

London	*New York City*	*Washington, D.C.*	*Houston*
Chicago	*Los Angeles*	*Baghdad*	*Liverpool*	*Seattle*
Beer Sheva	*Tel Aviv*	*Haifa*	*Dhahran*	*Riyadh*
Incerlik, Turkey	*Kuwait City*	*Manama*	*San Antonio*	*Camp Doha*
Boston	*Miami*	*St. Louis*	*New Orleans*	*San Francisco*

American cities. U.S. military stations overseas. The three largest cities in Israel where the Jewish pigs lived. And a few other targets of their enemies throughout the Middle East.

The attacks would come from all sides, across the border with Mexico where thousands of illegals crossed every day, across the Canadian border, porous as any on earth. Three thousand cargo ships unloaded at U.S. ports *every day.* Four hundred seventy-six airports. Ten thousand flights in and out.

Getting the warheads into the country would not be difficult.

The Great One put down the target list and looked at his men, then pulled out a small map. "We will move the warheads tomorrow night," he said while pointing to a small city to the north, just across the border in Tajikistan. "We will send them out in a convoy of three trucks that will move together north, through Pamir pass, then west to the Tajikistan city of Khorugh. From there we will disperse them, assigning one warhead each to our twenty-four teams. Each team will then scatter through Afghanistan, Pakistan, Tajikistan, and Turkmenistan. A few will go north, working their way through southern Russia. Once the teams are dispersed, we will pick up the original plan and attack each of the targets. Preparations have been years in the making. I am confident of success.

The cavern was silent, each man breathing deeply the cool underground air.

"Thirty-six hours," the Great One repeated. "That is all we need. Give me thirty-six hours and we will move the warheads forever beyond their reach. Then we will destroy our enemy. We are *that* close!"

The lieutenant pulled his short beard as he stared at the map. "Yes, *Sayid*, it will work," he announced. "I feel a calm in my soul."

The Great One smiled in agreement as he folded the map.

Angra stepped quickly from the shadows as the group of men started to break up. "And the American pilots?" he asked, his voice lusty and low.

The Great One turned toward him and hunched his shoulders. "Learn what you can from them," he instructed. "Then do what you will. But don't kill either pilot until I am there. I want to look into their eyes and see the life leave them as they pass through the veil."

31

The White House
Washington, D.C.

You wanted to see me, Mr. President." General Abram stood at the president's personal office door. His secret service escort stood behind him and the president nodded the agent away. "Come in, General, sit down," the president said, and Abram walked stiffly into the small room.

"Alright," the president asked him, "what have you found out about my Stealth?"

Abram hesitated. "Sir, I wish I had something for you, but we simply don't know."

"That's not what I want to hear."

"I know, Mr. President."

"What are the possibilities? Where could our aircraft be?"

The chairman pressed his lips. "Syria, Iraq, Iran, or Afghanistan. Pakistan. The Eastern Med. Somewhere short of that target is our most educated guess."

"That's a pretty big chunk of Southwestern Asia, General."

"Yes, sir, it is. But uncertainty such as this is inherent with long-range bomber operations, especially the B-2. They have such long legs, flying missions that take them from one side of the globe to the other. And being undetectable by radar, there is no means of knowing its position or where they might have gone down."

"Is it possible the aircraft was shot down?"

"Possible, but unlikely. There are no weapons in the area that are capable of tracking the Stealth, but still we can't rule it out. We call them golden BBs—random missiles and shells that by sheer luck hit a target—and yes, it's possible a blind missile or lucky Triple-A shell could have brought the aircraft down."

The president's eyes fixed on the window, staring through the bulletproof glass. The Mylar coating, dark and reflective, painted a murkier picture than what was real outside, throwing back much of the illumination from the city lights. The president shook his head. "And the chance of survivors?" he asked sadly.

The chairman thought. If there were any possibility, any possibility whatsoever that the pilots were alive, he would grasp at that straw. But he had to be honest with the president and honest with himself. He took a deep breath. "Mr. President, I am advised by my staff, and I share their opinion, that it is extremely unlikely the aircrew is alive. Ejection seats have emergency beacons our satellites can detect from space, which are automatically activated in an ejection sequence. If either pilot had ejected, we would have known instantly. Additionally, Mr. President, the pilots have personal emergency radios with beacons that are monitored by satellite, as well as having the range and capability to contact our forces in the area. Given this equipment, if the crew were down and alive, we would certainly know. The chance we will find survivors is very close to zero I'm afraid."

"Alright then," the president answered, "let's assume, despite the evidence, the crew is alive. Where do we start to look?"

The general sucked on his teeth. "We don't think the aircraft went down over Syria or Iran," he answered. "For one thing, we have enough space-based sensors keeping an eye on these states that we would get some indication if the aircraft went down—smoke, fire, something would show. Additionally, if any one of these nations had our pilots, they would be wagging them under our nose, probably through their buddies at CNN. Which leaves us northern Afghanistan and Pakistan, the eastern Med, and Lebanon and Iraq."

The president considered. "To search that area would take days," he said.

"Yes sir, it would."

"And it is almost certain the crew is dead anyway."

The general couldn't help but pause before he answered, "Almost certainly, sir."

The president sat back and frowned. "I'm sorry, General. I really am," he said. "But the crew is gone, you know that. It's a knife in my heart, just like it is in yours, but we have to be realistic and accept the truth."

32

Whiteman Air Force Base
Missouri

Col. Dick "Tracy" Kier sat alone in the semi-dark of his office, a single desk lamp providing the only light in the room. He had turned off his phone, actually disconnecting the line, and left his cell phone in the front seat of his car. The door to his office was closed and most of his staff had gone home for the night. He stretched in the dark, rubbing his hands over his eyes, then pulled the zipper on his flight suit down to mid-chest. He stared at the ceiling as the mantel clock struck nine then, reaching into his lower drawer, he pulled out a box of Macanudo cigars, thick, leafy smokes he had carried around for almost twenty-five years. He had purchased the cigars at a little shop in Panama City on his very first deployment out of the States, back when he was a young lieutenant flying F-4s. There was nothing special about them, relatively inexpensive as they were, but the box, worn and faded, had been with him for so many years. The Macanudos had become a ritual he used to mark the passing of time; the births of his children and the deaths of his friends, promotions and failures, accomplishments and good-byes.

He carefully opened the lid. Out of the original twenty,

only four cigars remained. One had been saved for his father, who recently passed away; D. T. would keep that one until the day that he died. One cigar was reserved for his retirement and another to commemorate his last flight. Which left one Macanudo uncommitted.

This seemed like a pretty good time.

He pulled off the wrapper, crinkly with age, then searched for a match, rummaging through his desk drawer. Of course, he didn't have one. He hadn't smoked in fifteen years. He slammed his drawer shut then heard a knock at his door. A young major stepped into the room, the colonel's executive officer, one of the wing's young and rising stars. The exec, dressed in his blues, moved to the corner of D. T.'s desk. He studied the colonel, noting the unlit cigar, then cleared his voice and said, "Sir, they have ordered the rescue choppers at Camp Doha that have been searching the Persian Gulf to stand down."

The colonel looked up. "Yes, I already know."

"They were the last rescue assets tasked to look for our crew."

The colonel didn't answer, but leaned back in his chair.

The major brushed his hands through his blond hair. "I'm sorry, Colonel, but we have just been informed that the legal affairs office at the Pentagon has officially changed the status of the crew from missing to deceased."

The colonel was silent.

"I'm sorry," the major said.

Kier grunted at the condolences. "Still no sign of any wreckage?" he asked.

"No. Nothing sir."

"And doesn't that seem strange to you?"

The young major paused. He knew his boss very well. He knew he was governed by emotion and loyalty sometimes more than by his brain. "It doesn't seem entirely unlikely, sir," he answered carefully. "Losing a B-2 isn't like losing a commercial airliner, with bodies and seat cushions, children's toys and luggage and stuff. A B-2 is a couple of huge pieces of metal, some black boxes, and really nothing more.

I can't think of a single component of the aircraft that would float to the surface if it went down in the sea, and the mountains of Pakistan and Afghanistan are as remote as the moon. So, no sir, I'm not surprised the rescue choppers didn't find any wreckage."

Kier scowled in frustration. "You know, it's just that . . . I don't know, I can't connect the dots. I can't get from here to there. I just don't see how Kill 31 could just . . . *poof,* disappear."

The major was silent. It was pretty clear to him. The B-2 was gone. There wasn't a thing they could do. In peacetime the military lost an aircraft every month or so. In combat it was understood they would lose many more. Sometimes they knew why, sometimes they didn't have a clue. Sometimes they discovered the wreckage, sometimes they only shot blanks. But at some point, you had to accept the facts, count your rosaries, and get on with the job. His boss should be making funeral arrangements, not fighting the obvious.

The two men were silent as Kier chewed on his cigar. "They didn't make it to the Gulf," he said through clenched teeth.

"Sir?"

"I don't think the B-2 made it to the Gulf. Something else happened. They went down before they got to the ocean. I don't believe this crew drove a good jet into the sea."

The major shifted his weight from one foot to the other, cleared his throat and moved forward a step. "Colonel, permission to speak freely?" he asked.

Kier nodded reluctantly. The kid was brilliant, but annoying. Still, he would listen to what he had to say.

"Sir, there are only a few runways in the region that are long enough for the B-2 to land. And we have studied every one. Studied every rock. And what have we found? Nothing, sir, not so much as a whiff of the jet. In addition, NRO satellites have searched the entire area for any indication of impact or fire. There's nothing there, sir. Nothing to give us so much as a shred of hope.

"So it seems pretty simple. We've seen this before. The

crew was on a critical mission and simply pushed too hard, then got themselves into a situation from which they could not recover. They were critically low on fuel to begin with, then ran into trouble. They could have hit severe weather in the mountains or taken enemy fire. The skin of the Stealth had to be damaged, which would have made them detectable to radar, or perhaps they had engine or mechanical problems from the collision with the refueling boom. We really don't know, sir, it could have been many things."

"But they would have ejected."

"Probably. But even if they did, the crew is now dead. We have no sign of survivors, no radio, no beacons, nothing at all. They are gone, Colonel and I'm sorry, but that's what I believe."

The colonel nodded his head almost imperceptibly. "You are right. You are right." His voice was sad, and yet still unconvinced.

The major paused a moment, then nodded to the old wooden box. "Sir, forgive me, but you know it is true. That's why you broke out the cigars."

Kier stared at his Macanudo, then at the floor. The major relaxed, his stiff shoulders becoming less square. "Sir, we need to start making arrangements," he said.

Kier lifted his head.

"A memorial service, sir, and a million other things. It will take several days to complete legal actions for the next of kin. There's a lot to do now that we have moved from missing to deceased."

Kier waved his hand. "Take care of it," he said.

"Yes, sir." The major turned and walked for the door, then paused to look back at Kier. "At least Colonel Bradley and Captain Lei didn't leave families behind," he said in a soft voice, trying to comfort his boss. "There are no children. No spouses. It could have been worse."

Kier thought of his friends and the missing warheads, then shook his head no.

The major was wrong.

It could not be worse.

CIA Headquarters
Langley, Virginia

Doctor Washington's assistant was waiting for him in his office when he returned from the White House. "I've got a message from Zembeic," he said hurriedly.

"Where is he?" Washington asked.

"Back in position at Camp Horse."

"Did he report anything from his meeting with Gah?"

The deputy shook his head. "Said it was uneventful. Said he'd tell you about it someday."

Washington shook his head anxiously. He had heard that line from Peter before. "I'll tell you about it later," meant "It didn't go very well."

He thought in silence as he dropped his wet overcoat on the back of his chair. "What are you hearing from the team in the mountains?" he asked.

"They still can't get in position. Too many bad guys around, and it's making travel impossible. Right now, they are two valleys west of Tirich Mir. But they are seeing multiple army trucks on the road leading to the mountains. Al Qaeda and Taliban soldiers. It sounds like they are everywhere."

"Okay, fine. What else?" he demanded.

"The team is awaiting your instructions. What do you want them to do?"

Washington thought a moment. "Tell them to bug out," he said. "There's no reason to stay there. The warheads are gone. Then get me transportation to Pakistan. And I want something fast. Tell those guys I'm coming over to see what's going on myself."

33

Angra walked into the cell. It was dark—cold and damp, with the musky odor of rot. Three guards followed him in, while another held the door open, allowing light from the hall to illuminate the dark interior.

Tia hunched in the corner, her face white with dread, her mouth dry from dehydration and fear. She watched Angra carefully as her heart pounded in her chest. Since she had been taken captive, she had not said a word, not so much as a whimper, not so much as her name, which had infuriated her captor and excited him at the same time.

Angra nodded to one of the guards, who shouted down the hall. A tray of food was brought into the cell and placed on the floor; boiled carrots and onions and a thick chunk of dried meat. A wooden jug of water was also placed next to the food.

Angra stared down at the woman. She was extraordinary, yes, perfect in feature and form, but she had to be a harlot, an ugly, filthy whore, or she would never had made it so far in the military, which was a man's world. So he sneered at her angrily, a hungry look on his eye. Tia stared at him defiantly, then dropped her head.

Angra smiled again, his thin face and long beard sagging under his cheeks. Tia saw the craving and averted her eyes.

Angra lifted a narrow finger. "Eat," he commanded her in a gruff voice. He wanted her stronger, he wanted her to have her wits back before he returned. It would be more fun, more of a challenge, if she had regained some strength.

Tia pushed herself to her feet and glared at Angra, then moved for the food. Though she didn't want to, she knew that she had to eat. If she wanted to live she had to regain her strength.

Angra watched her a moment, then turned and walked from the cell. "I'll be back for you," he muttered before he slammed the steel door closed.

Tia looked up and stopped eating, feeling suddenly sick.

Sometime later, he came back, but this time he was alone. Tia shivered in her corner, knowing her time had come.

There were no words to describe what he did to her then. It was far more than torture, far more than abuse, far more than humiliation, torment, or shame. When he was finished, she lay beaten and barely alive on the floor, surrounded by her blood, his spit, and her teeth.

Spent and weary, Angra stood over her and glared down at her face. A few hours, a day maybe, she was not going to live. He had seen enough death to measure its pace. And if she was lucky, she would die before she regained consciousness.

But he didn't want her to die without knowing that she had failed. "Can you hear me?" he shouted as he stared down at her. She moaned and looked away and he knew that she could. "You have failed," he hissed. "The warheads are ours. You are going to die. We'll destroy you. You have failed everything."

34

The VA hospital was a gloomy and boxy building three stories high, with several wings jutting off a main cement and brick concourse that faced a large parking lot. Built on a dirty street in a weary part of the city, the hospital's bland construction blended in perfectly with its downtown surroundings. But despite its depressing setting, the Medical Center was affiliated with three excellent medical schools (Georgetown, Howard, and George Washington universities) and had developed a reputation as a top-notch acute-care research-and-teaching facility. Because of this, VA Washington was considered one of the finest hospitals in the entire veteran system.

Which was great news for those patients who were fighting hard to get better.

But for those waiting to die, it didn't matter that much.

A small hospice had been created on the third floor of the north wing. It was an open bay situated at the end of the hall, and because little medical equipment was needed to care for the dying, six beds had been crammed into the space that normally would have held only four. In an attempt to bring cheer to the room, the walls had been painted deep yellow and blue; but that was years before and the colors had faded. The carpet on the floor was short and stained in places, and the room smelled of disinfectant and soap. Three of the beds in the room were unoccupied, their sheets tight and clean and ready for the next dying man. Norman Allen Zembeic lay in the bed nearest the tinted window, furthest away from the bathroom and hallway door, and though his head was turned toward the window, he breathed deeply in sleep. It had been almost twenty-four hours since he had opened his eyes.

At a quarter to nine, a gray-haired nurse walked into the room. Despite the somber environment, she walked with a light step and seemed to smile easily. She had worked in the hospice for many years now and considered giving care to the dying as her special calling in life, a special calling from God. And she had learned from experience that there were only three things the patients in her care needed: morphine, a little water, and an occasional smile. They didn't need speculation about heaven (they would get the facts soon enough), they didn't need a priest to confess to, all their confessing was done. And they certainly didn't need sympathy, they were far beyond that. But they did need occasional drugs to take the edge off their pain and someone who wasn't afraid to talk about death. In addition, she knew that her patients, though dying, didn't want to live their last days in a tomb, so she threw open the window curtains, then turned to the men.

The nurse moved quietly through the room. Moving from one patient to the next she adjusted pillows, checked their catheters, and brushed back a stray hair. Norm Zembeic's bed was the last one she approached.

Norm was one of her favorites, a humble and likeable guy who always apologized for her having to take care of him. "I'm sorry you have to help me," he would tell her as she helped him eat, or "I'm sorry for the trouble," as she changed his sheets.

"Stop it," she would tell him. "This is my job."

"It's a lousy job."

"Are you kidding! I love it. I get to meet great people like you."

"That's a lot of short-term relationships," he had mumbled lightly and they both had laughed.

That was five days before. But he was slipping quickly now.

During the first few days that he had been in her care, when his kidneys were still functioning and the pain hadn't been so bad, the nurse had learned a little bit about Norman Zembeic. She found out that he had emigrated from South Africa, served in Korea, lost his wife when he was young, and never married again.

"She was so beautiful," Norm had told her with an almost romantic smile. "I loved her more than any man has ever loved anyone."

"But she died when you were in your thirties."

He had nodded his head.

"That's a long time to be alone, Mr. Zembeic."

"Yes. Yes it was. But I think she's been waiting, so it all seems worth it now."

"But what about your son?" the nurse had asked him, forcing an understanding smile. It burned her that Norm's son had never come to see him, never so much as called.

"He's a good man," he had told her. "If you knew him, you would like him, he's a straight-up kind of guy."

"Does he live around here?" Translation: *Why hasn't he come to see you?*

"He's an intelligence officer assigned overseas."

The nurse's voice instantly softened. "Is he in Iraq?"

"Sometimes. Sometimes not. He travels a lot."

"What does he do?"

"I don't know for certain, but he must be very good."

Approaching the sleeping man's bed, the nurse leaned toward her patient and Norm opened his eyes, but he didn't even try to smile as he stared at her face. He was going, she could see that, for she knew all of the signs: His eyes were clouding over and his mouth was bone-dry, and his stomach was extended from all of the excess fluid in his body that his kidneys didn't have the capability to purge any more. She leaned toward him, speaking softly, "Can I get you anything, Mr. Zembeic?"

He stared, his eyes filmy, then slowly moved his lips. "I'm so thirsty," he whispered in a voice filled with pain.

She reached to his bedside table and lifted a small plastic cup. Knowing he was too weak to suck, she put the cup to his lips and he slowly opened his mouth. She only poured in a few drops, but he started to choke and she had to pull the cup back. Putting it down, she grabbed a cotton swab and dipped it in the water, then placed it to his lips. He opened his mouth and she wet his tongue and lips, repeating the process until he was too tired to suck at the swab any more.

His head fell to the side. "Thank you," he said.

"You're welcome, Norm. Can I get you anything else?"

He turned his head and stared at her a moment. "Can you bring me my son?"

She shook her head sadly. "I'm sorry," she said.

The old man looked out the window. "I wish he was here," he was barely able to say. "There are some things I would like to tell him . . ." His voice trailed off.

"Tell me, Mr. Zembeic, and I will tell him for you."

"It's nothing. Really nothing."

"Go ahead, sir."

"I wish I could tell him . . . that I have always been proud."

The nurse reached for his cold hand and held it tightly in hers. "I'll tell him, Norm. I'll tell him. I'll make sure that he knows."

Norman Allen Zembeic passed away at 3:17 P.M. that same afternoon. After falling asleep a little after one, he simply never woke up. There were no final words, no long last looks or tearful good-byes, no holding or crying with his loved ones around him, and no grieving children standing with each other in the hall. He simply went to sleep and slipped away as peacefully as he had lived; quietly, easily, with no fanfare or fame.

When the nurse came in to check on him he was already gone. She stared at him a moment, saying the same prayer she always did, then walked to his bed, turned his head so that he was facing the ceiling, crossed his hands on his chest, gently closed his eyes, then pulled the sheet up.

Taking a step back, she slowly bowed her head, cursing the fact that no family was there. No man should leave this life without someone he loved by his side. No man should ever have to die by himself.

She thought of Norm's son, the soldier, and wondered where in this whole wide world he might be, what he was doing, and why he couldn't come home?

"Yes, Norm, he must be good," she agreed with what the sick man had said. "I'm sure that he loved you. And I'm glad you were proud."

The agency made every effort to contact Peter about the death of his father, but under the circumstances it proved impossible.

Lyangar Airfield
Southern Tajikistan

Col. Shane Bradley hunched in the corner of his cell, naked, confused, angry, and alone. He wrapped his arms across his chest and shivered violently from the cold. He was hungry. And thirsty. So thirsty he thought he might die.

His prison was a cement chamber in the basement, a dank and filthy room that hadn't been occupied in years. There were no windows, no bars, and no hope for escape. The only light was a yellow beam that leaked through the crack under the steel door. As he stared at the light, a huge, sagging spider crawled under the crack and climbed up the wall. Angry rats squealed above him. Bradley looked up to see the flash of yellow teeth, long tails, and glaring red eyes. And he smelled death above him. Something was rotting up there.

Colonel Bradley pushed himself to his feet and took a few careful steps. His throat burned and his tongue felt like sandpaper in his mouth. He took another two steps, then began walking at a slow, steady pace. He had to keep going. He had to keep alive.

After ten minutes, he stopped, feeling achy and weak.

He needed some water or he was not going to survive.

He walked a few minutes, then lay down and instantly fell asleep.

Colonel Bradley woke with a start, his eyes darting wildly around the dark room. The steel door to his cell was suddenly pushed back and three guards, strong, and heartless, stood at the doorway and glared at him. They were all dressed the same; leather boots, tan fatigues and black billy clubs. One of the guards shined a flashlight in Bradley's eyes and the colonel pushed himself to his knees and held his hands up to shield his face. The officer grunted in Urdu and the three men entered the room.

"Water?" Bradley begged them. The men laughed at his suffering. "Water," he begged in a dry voice again.

"He wants water?" The leader mocked in heavily accented English. Unzipping his fly, he urinated on the floor as the other guards laughed and slapped their boss on the back.

"Look at him," the leader sneered, unable to hold his disgust. "Look at this American crawl on the floor." He bent toward Colonel Bradley and spit a wad of phlegm in his face. Bradley reached up to wipe it and the Arab slapped his hand away. "Leave it, American. And stay down on the floor." He towered over the pilot, challenging him. Bradley stared up with dry eyes, the wad of spit on his cheek.

"You will die here, American, alone, in the dark. So don't ask me for water unless you want more of my *harre*. There's more of that, if you want it." The guard started laughing again. "We'll be back for you, American," he sneered as he turned for the door.

"I want to see Captain Lei," Bradley demanded as the men walked away. "You have no right to keep us. We are United States officers."

The Arab stopped and turned back. "Believe me, American, I know who you are." He stared at the pilot, spit again, then shut the cell door.

Bradley crawled after him, lowering his face to the crack under the door. He lay there and listened until he was sure they were gone. "Captain Lei," he whispered, calling out to the dark. "Captain Lei, are you there?"

He turned his head and listened. "Tia, can you hear me!" he whispered again.

But the dark remained silent and he cursed wearily.

An hour later Angra strolled comfortably into the cell, his arms behind his back, his eyes heavy-lidded and dead. Two enormous, bearded guards escorted him on each side. Like the others, Angra was dressed in tan fatigues and black leather boots. A shoulder harness was strapped to his chest with a 9 mm Model 17 Glock tucked neatly inside, a weapon he had taken off a dead soldier early in the Afghanistan war and now wore with great pride, his first spoil of war.

Bradley slumped weakly against the back wall. Angra threw him a thin pair of pants. "Get dressed," he commanded.

Bradley pulled on the pants, then stood, a defiant look on his face. Angra stared at the pilot. "You will kneel in my presence," he commanded.

Bradley shook his head. "I will stand," he replied.

The nearest guard cracked his nightstick savagely across Bradley's knee. The bone cracked and Bradley went down with a groan, bending over and grabbing painfully at his leg before the guard kicked Bradley's shoulder, rolling him onto his side. Bradley struggled into a sitting position and wrapped his arms around his legs as a smear of dark blood soaked through the leg of the thin cotton pants.

Angra knelt beside him. "Are you hungry?" he asked.

Bradley nodded slowly.

"Perhaps thirsty as well?"

Bradley licked his dry lips.

"Hmm . . . yes, I'm sure." Angra brought his face level with Bradley's, looking him right in the eye. The pilot stared at the Arab. His eyes were dark holes surrounded by sagging, red lids and he pulled back suddenly, seeing the dark evil there.

The Arab watched him and laughed. "You see it, don't

you pilot?" he said with a sneer. "You see it in my eyes. I call myself *Angra*. That means 'Satan' to you. And that's how I feel. That's what I feel like inside. I am the devil and I will bring you nothing but suffering and pain."

"My country will not forget us," Bradley said. "They won't leave us here."

"Don't kid yourself," Angra laughed. "They have already called off the search. They have already forgotten. They think you are dead."

Angra paused, giving the colonel a moment to think. "We are going to kill you," he continued in a dreary voice. "But before you die, I really want to get in your head. There is so much you could tell us. So much that we want to know. I want to crawl in your brain and pull all of that precious information out. Now, I suspect you will resist, but you need to understand: There is no hope for you, Bradley, no hope at all."

Bradley looked away. "Where is Captain Lei?" he asked as he struggled to his feet to face his interrogator again.

"She is dead," Angra said simply. "She died a couple hours ago."

Bradley swore and moved forward, grabbing Angra by his shirt. One of the guards swung his nightstick and smashed it into Bradley's ribs. The blow bent him over, and he struggled to breathe. He held his cracked ribs, then forced himself straight once again.

"What were you thinking?!" Angra mocked. "Sending a girl! What did you think we would do! And you say we don't care about *our* women. But do we send our daughters into battle? Do we send them to fight, knowing they will be the first to suffer and die!?

"Now, let me tell you how it is. I'm going to kill you, alright! I suspect your death will be slow, based on what I have seen, but it doesn't matter, quickly or slow, you will die all the same. And before you slip away, before I relieve you of the pain, you will tell me everything that I want to know. You might think I can't break you, but I promise I will."

"You will answer to my country," Bradley mumbled in pain.

"Fool! Stupid pilot! Haven't you heard *anything?* Your country thinks you are *dead!* There is no hope for you, American. You are completely alone. Your fellow pilot, she's dead now, which leaves just you and me.

"I won't lie to you, pilot, or give you false hope. This isn't a situation where if you talk you will live. You are walking dead now. That is the simple truth. But there are some things we need you to tell us, things that we want to know. So here is my offer. Talk, make it simple, and I'll shoot you in the head. You won't feel a thing. It's *bang!* and you're gone.

"But fight me, American, and I will prolong your misery long after you have told everything. You will beg me to kill you. Think about that awhile."

Angra stared at Bradley, then grunted, turned, and walked from the cell. "Give him water," he commanded as he passed through the door. "I want him comfortable when I come back for him."

Sometime later, the guards brought him food and a jug of warm water. The colonel stared in stunned hunger as they shoved the food through the door, then he scurried toward it and shoved a piece of black bread in his mouth.

35

That night the door to Bradley's cell opened again and Angra strolled into the room accompanied by his usual guards. He wore a jacket over his uniform, hiding the gun that was strapped to his chest. Colonel Bradley pushed himself up as Angra walked through the door.

"I want to see Captain Lei," Bradley said.

Angra snorted angrily. "You are so concerned about this woman. What was she to you?"

"I am her commander!"

"She was beautiful, yes."

"She was an officer!"

"You were lovers I think."

"We were soldiers. And I am asking nothing that I wouldn't ask for anyone else."

"She was *your woman*?" Angra snorted, surprise in his voice.

"She was my *responsibility!*" Bradley answered defiantly.

"Ah," Angra mocked. *"I am Captain America. I must protect the women and children!"* He laughed in disgust. "Alright then," he snorted, "I will show you!"

He nodded to one guard, who hesitated until he saw the

look in Angra's eye, then turning quickly, he disappeared down the hall. Bradley heard a door open, then a shuffle, then a soft, dragging sound. He stood anxiously, the bile rising in his throat. As the sound grew nearer, the rage built inside.

They dragged in her body like it was a bag of soiled rags. He looked at her beaten face and nearly screamed out in rage. *What animal could do this!* "Tia!" he cried.

Falling to his knees, he reached for her hand, holding it gently and feeling its cold.

Angra nodded to a guard as he pointed to the corpse. "Get it out of here. Go and burn it," he said.

The guard bent over, grabbed the body and dragged it away.

Bradley drew a sharp breath as he clenched his fists at his side. The three guards moved toward him and Angra stepped away. Bradley stood and turned, then suddenly lunged for the monster, who stepped quickly out of his way. One guard lifted his rifle and brought it down with the force of a bull, but Bradley saw it coming and rolled out of the way. He pushed himself to his feet and faced the three guards again. Angra cowered behind them, then disappeared through the open cell door.

The squad leader stepped forward and pulled out his club. He was a small man with flat ears and hard, empty eyes. "Back down, American," he whispered. "It is not time yet to die!"

Bradley didn't move and the guard swung his club savagely. Bradley took the blow, feeling nothing as something snapped in his mind. *"Come on!"* he screamed wildly. *"Come and get me!"* he cried.

Flat Ears swung again, catching Bradley in the ribs. The pilot's eyes blazed with the fury of a violent and mindless craze. He saw nothing but Tia, her broken body and bloody face. Baring his teeth, he snarled like a dog. He didn't care if he died, he didn't care if he lived. He wanted to kill him. He wanted revenge. *"Come on!!"* he screamed, taking a step for the guard.

Flat Ears fell back. "Get him!" he cried. The other guards moved forward. Bradley rushed the nearest one, catching him on the back of his feet. The guard brought down the nightstick, but it was too late.

Bradley pushed him back, knocking him against the concrete wall. The guard exhaled with a huff of stinking breath and Bradley pushed against his ribs again. He heard the guard curse and felt the primeval lust for first blood. The guard swore and leaned forward to bite Bradley's neck, but Bradley felt his teeth and pushed back, knocking the guard's head against the hard wall, feeling the stinging pain of the nightsticks beating on his neck and back. A furious blow hit his head and he went crazy with pain.

It was killed or be killed! He would accept either one!

He smashed the guard's head against the wall again, blood and saliva splattering over his face. He held the Arab suspended, not letting him fall. The man reached for his pistol and Bradley lowered his shoulder and pushed with all his might. The guard huffed in great pain and Bradley felt his ribs crack. A powerful grip grabbed his shoulder, but he pushed it away. Reaching for the nightstick, he twisted violently, wrenching it from the broken man's hand. The guard moaned and went limp, sinking like a rag doll as Bradley turned and smashed the nightstick into the nearest guard's face, then reached out and slashed his dirty fingernails across his wide eyes. The guard screamed, dropped his club, and lifted his hands to his face as Bradley brought the stick down just behind his ear, feeling a *crunch* as the bone collapsed in his skull. He then turned to Flat Ears, but it was already too late.

Angra emerged in the doorway, holding his gun in his hand. *"Get back!!"* he screamed. *"I will kill you right now!"*

Bradley turned toward him in a fury, his mind numb with pain.

"Get back!" Angra screamed.

Another guard appeared, standing at the open door, a look of great surprise and fear on his face. Angra screamed to his subordinate, who scrambled forward and pulled the unconscious man across the floor. The second guard stumbled forward, still holding his eyes, following the sound of his comrades' voices toward the cell door.

Bradley took a step forward.

"I'll kill you!" Angra screamed.

The colonel eyed him coldly. "I'm ready to die!"

Angra winced and stepped back, reaching for the door. He passed over the threshold and the last guard slammed it closed.

The sound of ringing metal echoed between the cold cement walls. It was silent and dark. Bradley held out his hands in the darkness. They were sticky and wet. He couldn't see the blood, but he knew it was there. His entire body was on fire; every bone, every muscle nothing but throbbing pain. He moved his head slowly, feeling the bloody cuts on his neck, then fell back, almost stumbling, bracing against the back wall as he slowly and painfully lowered himself to his knees.

He didn't realize he was crying until he tasted the salt on his lips.

He knew it was over. They would come back for him. They would come back to hurt him. It was personal now. And the beating he had suffered was nothing compared to what they would do to him now.

Yes, he knew it was over, but he no longer cared.

Then he thought about Tia and lowered his head as he moaned.

36

The commander of the Predator squadron was visibly shaking, his hands constantly moving with nervous energy. Doctor Washington sat beside him, his face sagging from jet lag and the "Pakistani gut," an intestinal virus that savaged most visitors. Outside, the wind howled like a pack of angry wolves, bringing moisture down from the mountain in an early and cold winter storm. Beside the air force major was a six-inch stack of photos; almost a thousand photographs he hadn't had time to go through. To the right of this pile were nearly five hundred minutes of digital video—this backlog despite the fact he had been working twenty hours a day.

"I have fourteen frames you need to look at," the major said as Washington leaned toward the screen. "They were taken on the night that our Predator went down. The area we are looking at is a few miles south of Lyangar, a tiny airfield just over the border in Tajikistan, but you'll have to look very closely, for the pictures were taken from almost ninety miles away."

Washington stared at the images on the computer screen,

which showed a tiny blur in a dark desert sky. A rim around the image glowed almost imperceptibly white.

The major sipped at his coffee, his eleventh cup of the day. Washington grunted as he studied the screen, seeing nothing of interest at all.

The major watched him, frustrated, then typed at his computer, commanding it to enhance the photographs. The MATDIS, or Mobile Advanced Tactical Digital Image Spectrograph—essentially a high-end Dell with a sturdy gray frame and highly classified software—doubled, then tripled the pixels per line.

Washington watched. The image became brighter, but his face remained blank. A tiny wrinkle of white was all it looked like to him.

"Here!" the major said as he traced the outline with his finger. "There *is* something there, moving to the north at a very high rate of speed. And it's also descending, dropping like a rock from the sky."

Washington scowled. It could have been a shooting star. It could have been dust on the lens. It could have been a bird on the horizon or almost anything.

"Can't you see it?" the major exclaimed, tapping the screen with his finger. "Faint tongues of fire blowing back in the sky. And a line of white heat? The leading edge of a wing. Now look at this." He typed again. "When I bring up the radar overlay we get nothing at all! There's something there in the photos, but we get *no radar return*. Now, what else could be out there but not bounce back radar energy!"

Washington's hands shook. "Are you saying . . . ?" he muttered.

The Predator intelligence officer finally smiled and nodded his head.

Three hours later the major sat next to one of his Predator pilots, the former F-16 jock who flew from the back of a van. Washington sat quietly behind them, watching the two men as they worked.

The pilot threw the Predator into a tight left turn, banking it up to forty degrees to circle over the target area for the third time. Lyangar airfield lay twenty thousand feet below him. The skies had cleared, though there were mountain-wave clouds rolling over the peaks to the east, smooth waves of lenticulars formed by the turbulent air. The crew had already searched with the optical cameras, scanning the airfield from one end to the other, but despite all their searching they found nothing suspicious to note. There was only one aircraft on the ramp, an old Chinese YAK, and a herd of white goats grazing on the midfield grass. Two men, local herdsmen, walked behind the goats, moving them toward the taller grass on the east side of the field. A flock of pigeons strutted across the tarmac, leaving scattered spots of white, as an old woman, a goat herder, bathed in a small stream.

The Predator, the voyeur, was watching them all.

The major zoomed in on the hangars, looking through the half-open doors. The pilot hunched his shoulders. "Check this out," he said. The camera looked through the hangar door, catching a glimpse of an old MiG 21. The paint was faded and chipped and dark oil spots stained the hangar floor under the engine bay.

"Yeah," the major answered. The old Soviet fighter was not of interest to him.

"Think it flies?" the pilot asked.

"Probably. Lots of these warlords have old Russian jets."

The major focused his lens on the north overrun, where there was a huge overgrowth. Something about the foliage just didn't look right to him. The trees were too perfect, too uniform, too high. "Does that area at the end of the runway look unusual?" he asked.

"Looks almost like . . . camouflage," the pilot replied.

"Do you think . . . ?"

"I think it could be."

The two men were quiet again.

"But look at the size of that runway! It's too short," the officer said. "There's not a pilot in the world that could land a B-2 down there!"

Washington leaned forward. "Colonel Bradley could," he said.

The two men glanced back.

"No way," the major snorted. "That runway's too short."

"Bradley could land there if it was a choice between landing or dying."

The major grunted again, then shot a quick look to the pilot.

The captain brought his throttle to idle. "I'm going down," he said.

"What do you mean?"

"I mean I'm taking it down."

"Taking us to a lower altitude won't help us see anything."

"I'm not descending to a lower altitude. I'm going to land."

The major looked over, his eyes wide and bright. "No you're not, Captain!"

"Watch me," the pilot said.

The sound came over the first ridge of the mountain, out of the setting sun. It was deep and throaty, a mix of low-throttled engine and high, spinning blades. Then the Predator appeared over a fold in the mountain, skimming across the terrain. It climbed quickly as it turned, seeming to pivot on its wing, then dropped toward the runway and throttled back to land.

The Arab guard was situated in a blind on the west end of the runway, a camouflaged hole dug into the hard ground. He peered through field glasses as the drone approached, his jaw hanging open in a look of fear and surprise. The aircraft lined up on the runway only a quarter mile out, then descended at a shallow angle and touched down with a puff of white smoke. It bounced once then continued down the runway at a very high speed, it's shiny metal skin catching the last rays of sun.

The Predator slowed at the end of the runway, near where three guards were hiding under another camouflage net. They all drew their weapons as the aircraft approached. The Predator came to a stop, the propeller whirling noisily from the back of the wing. The stunned guards watched in silence as a black eye swiveled from side to side. Then the eye stopped, staring at them, less than forty feet away.

• • •

"Will you look at that!" the pilot muttered under his breath.

"What *are* you doing!" the major cried. "Captain, you've got ten seconds to get that bird back in the air!"

"Look! Look!" the captain answered as he pointed at the screen.

The major ignored him. "I'm not asking you, I'm telling you, get that bird in the air!"

"What do you see?" Washington interrupted, placing a calming hand on the major's left arm.

"Look!" the pilot said as he jabbed at the central screen.

The visual display showed a small group of soldiers in dark uniforms hiding under a camouflaged net, all of them watching the Predator with dumbfounded stares. "Those are Taliban soldiers," the pilot cried. "And look: there behind them!" The captain leaned forward in his seat. "When the wind catches this netting: look! There it is!"

The major gripped the pilot's chair until his knuckles turned white. The picture lurched and swiveled as the aircraft turned ten degrees. And there it was: black tires, thick pistons—an aircraft landing gear! Overhead the pilot saw the glint of the thick flying wing. *"There it is!"* he cried. *"We just found our B-2!"*

The soldiers stared at the Predator's black, glaring eye as the evening wind blew, catching the corner of the dark camouflage. "What has the devil sent us!" the nearest soldier whispered. "Is there nothing this Satan cannot see, cannot do!?"

The black eye on the aircraft focused on the soldiers again. The youngest of them flinched, then lifted his grenade launcher to his chest. He aimed quickly and fired just as he closed his eyes.

The RPG knocked the soldier back and acidic smoke filled the air. The grenade hit the Predator at the root of the left wing and exploded with a burst of yellow heat. The fuel in the plastic tanks burst into flames, rocking the aircraft up on her wing before dropping it down and collapsing the landing gear. Smoke and fire enveloped the wreckage in a yellow fireball.

Washington sat forward. "That's the B-2!" he cried.

The captain swore pleasantly under his breath.

Then came a quick flash of yellow light and the camera went black. The three Americans stared in silence at the row of blank TV screens. The drone pilot turned to his commander. "Bingo!" he said.

"What happened to my drone!" the major cried.

Washington slapped both men on their shoulders. "Good work!" he said.

Camp Cowboy
CIA Paramilitary Base Camp/Operations
Northern Afghanistan

Peter Zembeic was asleep in his tent, a small camouflaged rigging he had tucked under an outcropping of rock on the south end of the camp. He woke as he heard footsteps crunch through the light snow outside. He looked up, seeing his tent sag from the light snowfall's weight.

A young sergeant stopped outside the flap. "Sir," he said in a hurried voice.

"Yeah?" Peter asked.

"Got a call from a friend of yours down with the Predator squadron. He wants to talk to you right away."

"Who is it?" Peter asked.

"Doctor Washington, sir."

Lyangar Airfield
Tajikistan

Hours after the beating, Bradley slowly woke up. He lay without moving, wondering if he were dead, but the pain that enveloped his body assured him he was alive. For some time, he didn't know how long, he suffered in the silence of his cold cell, the room spinning in circles, his heart pounding in his ears. Then he pushed himself up and crawled to a half-empty jar of water he had stored along the back wall. Pouring the water over his body, he washed as best as he could, pouring the water over his open sores, then shuffled to a corner of the cell and huddled against the two walls.

37

The president was told immediately when they found the
B-2.

"Any information on the crew?" he demanded in a
hopeful tone.

"Nothing, sir," General Abram replied. "But I can't imagine any scenario where they would have let the pilots live."

The president frowned. That probably was true. And now
there was the aircraft to deal with, but he knew what to do.

U.S.S. *Eisenhower*
Gulf of Oman

When the orders came, the enormous nuclear-powered
aircraft carrier U.S.S. *Eisenhower* turned forty degrees to
the north and put its nose into the wind, preparing for flight
operations. The skies grew darker as the half moon approached the horizon. Jupiter shone in the west, clearly visible, with Mars up above her, a tiny red glow. The bow of the
carrier slipped through the water, which was cluttered with
floating debris from a week's worth of storms. The deck was

still quiet, but quickly coming to life. Combat operations were scheduled for 0115 local time.

The carrier cut a silver bow of water before it as the deck flickered from the multicolored flashlights that were being waved in the air. Above the fantail, helicopter blades began to turn slowly. As the chopper's turbine cores reached a temperature that would sustain the fires within, the rotors turned more quickly, then began to beat the night air. The four-bladed CH-60 hovered over the fantail, then turned into the wind and took off to set up an orbit two miles off the starboard bow. An E-2C Hawkeye—the "eye in the sky"—rolled to the catapult and was attached to the powerful machine. Steam, hot and humid, wisped across the deck, creating a surrealistic backdrop against the glow of jet engines. The Hawkeye pilot stirred the control stick one final time, adjusted his helmet, cinched his oxygen mask tight against his face, held his brakes, trimmed the aircraft for takeoff, and glanced down the deck. Pushing up the throttles, he felt the aircraft shudder expectantly beneath his seat, ready to burst with a climax of power. He turned to the cat officer and held up five fingers, then one to confirm the gross weight, then lifted his hands clear of the controls and pushed his back against his seat. Seconds later he felt it, the mighty catapult piston, a surge of raw power, savage and direct. The catapult shot was unlike anything else one could feel in this life— fifty-one thousand pounds of fuel and steel, hurtled down the runway by an explosion of steam.

The airborne radar control aircraft, heavy with equipment, men, and fuel, slammed down the deck. It cleared the carrier and lumbered into the air. The pilot snapped into action—gear up, turn away from the carrier's course, flaps and slats into the wing, then turn while climbing to heading. The Hawkeye pushed through a thin cloud deck, then flew north and turned its radar on the southern coast of Iran. The low moon fell behind the wall of thin stratus and the gray aircraft disappeared in the increasing dark.

Two S-B3 tankers then rolled down the deck. They too turned north to follow the Hawkeye. As the slower aircraft climbed, the combat control center kept watch, searching and listening for any indication the Iranians knew they were there.

The skies remained friendly. So far, no response.

Finally, one after the other, four F-18 Hornets took to the air. The fighter-bombers joined up as a formation, then climbed to forty-one thousand feet. Under their centerline fix points, each Hornet carried two GBU-31s, two-thousand-pound, satellite-guided bombs. The flight leader set a course that would take the formation toward the border of Pakistan.

Twelve minutes later, the coastline of Iran slipped silently under the combat aircraft. The Hawkeye led the formation for the first two hundred miles or so, then, as the desolate mountains of central Pakistan began to come into view, the airborne warning radar aircraft did one final search, confirmed the intended flight path was clear, then fell back and turned for the waters of the Gulf of Oman.

"Trigger Flight's clear out to two-eighty miles," the Hawkeye pilot said.

"Rog," the F-18 flight lead replied.

"You got it, baby."

"Roger that, Horse."

The Hawkeye turned back for the ship. The S-B3 tankers stayed with the formation as they flew farther north and crossed the Afghanistan border. Fifty-five minutes after takeoff, north of the Rigestan Desert, the four FA-18 Hornets slid behind the Vikings and tanked up with gas, draining every available drop from the SB-3s' fuel tanks. After refueling, the Vikings hauled in their refueling baskets and climbed aggressively into the air. They were getting low on fuel themselves and needed to hit the deck. The Vikings headed back for the *Eisenhower*, where they would reload their tanks and take off again to meet the four fighters on their way back home.

As the Vikings climbed away, the F-18s descended to terrain-following altitude, skimming the flat desert at only a few hundred feet. They crossed over the Helmand River and Zareh Sharan salt marsh, then turned thirty-five degrees east. The mountains of central Afghanistan began to clutter their scopes. They would soon have to climb. Kabul was exactly off their nose.

"Trigger, combat spread," the flight leader commanded over the secure radio.

The fighters spread out across the night sky. Four abreast, they proceeded to target.

The four F-18s flew through a narrow box canyon on the south side of the Panjsh Mountain range. The lead pilot glanced outside, lifting his eyes to the top of the surrounding terrain. Up, up, and up, the sheer cliffs rose on both sides. He simply wasn't prepared for the size of the mountains or their incredibly high peaks. The tops loomed above him, above the reach of his terrain-following radar; the solid line depicting the mountains went straight up and off his scope. He glanced quickly upward, then back at his screen. No way his aircraft could maneuver up the sides of these mountains. But a narrow pass through the mountains was just off the nose.

"Trigger, say status?" he asked over his secure radio.

"Two. Three. Four," was all he heard in reply, indicating everything was in the green.

"Trigger, target three fingers."

Target 120 miles.

"Ready to pop on two fingers!"

Be ready to climb.

Moving his hands through his own cockpit, the lead Hornet pilot armed his two weapons, then began to feed the final target coordinates into his offensive target and acquisition computers. He synched up his system to the nearest seven global positioning satellites to cross-check his position against his internal laser ring gyroscopes. Less than two meters off track. Two meters! He smiled.

The formation leader then asked for confirmation over his satellite link radio. "Boss Man, this is Trigger. I've got a tally on the target. Confirm you want a lay down."

"Trigger 18, you are cleared to lay down."

"Confirm, lay down on Lyangar?"

"Cleared Lyangar," the voice over the SATCOM replied.

"Let's make sure we don't have any friendlies," the number-two Hornet called over the radio to the lead.

"Put the Spy on the target."

"Roger that, boss."

The second Hornet swept the airfield with his visual sensors. "Spy looks clear," he then announced over the flight radio.

"Check my sparkles. Check my sparkles. Make sure we are looking good."

The number-two aircraft pilot looked through his infrared display. He placed his infrared target designator at the edge of the runway and saw the sparkle of infrared light exactly over the target. He confirmed the coordinates, cross-checked his range and azimuth, then said, "Looks good to me, boss."

"Okay, Triggers, I've updated the numbers," the flight lead replied. "I'm sending this information to your systems. Accept it into your machines. We want this to be precise. This ain't horseshoes, boys."

"Two has a good data feed."

Three and Four replied in kind.

"Safire?" the leader asked.

"Negative surface-to-air activity."

The flight leader hesitated a moment, then said, "Trigger's rolling in. Go gig'em Aggies. Let's put on a show!"

A single two-thousand-pound bomb would have been more than enough to destroy the target, but the targeters who planned the attack figured if one bomb was good, then four was much better, and if four was much better then how cool was eight?

Thus, in a demonstration of overkill to a ridiculous degree, sixteen thousand pounds of high explosives were sent down range to the target.

Each of the Hornets popped to release their two-thousand-pound bombs, tossing their weapons almost simultaneously from eight miles out and as they were climbing to twenty-nine thousand feet.

Because the Hornets attacked from standoff range, never

flying over the target, there was no rumble of jet engines or flash of tail lights to give warning to the enemy soldiers on the ground who were guarding the bomber from the attack they thought might come but could do nothing about. From their sentry positions under the camouflage netting, there was no indication the bombs were even in the air. For the briefest moment there was a nearly silent whistle, a sense of compression, then eight shattering explosions split the night air. The bombs detonated one after the other, half a second apart, creating four uninterrupted seconds of fire, heat, light, smoke, and thunder that seemed to split the very rocks underneath the B-2.

The bombs were guided to the target by global positioning satellites in space, so that they hit fifteen feet apart and on a near perfect line. Starting at the left wingtip of the B-2, and walking across the top of the bomber, the bombs hit the aircraft with perfect precision. The ground rocked like an earthquake as the air exploded in flames, the detonations powerful enough to be detected on Richter sensors four hundred miles away.

When it was over there was nothing left, not so much as a thumbnail piece of B-2. The wreckage was scattered for miles and secondary fires burned bright.

38

Peter Zembeic sat on a rough cushion on the cement floor, his back against the adobe wall of the ancient farm house, the only permanent structure inside Camp Cowboy. He wore black jeans and black boots and, as always, his Yankees baseball cap. A laptop sat to his side. Four feet away, his satellite antenna was pointed south, out of the open window. The five-foot-long antenna was thin and wiry, with X-shaped prongs extending evenly from the base out to the edge. On Peter's other side, down by his knee, was his breakfast, a wooden plate of dry bread, goat milk, cheese, and some frozen cherries one of his troops had found near the stream. He ate quickly, shoving in wads of food, while he talked to Thomas Washington on his satellite phone.

"We found the B-2," Washington began the conversation.

"You what!?" Peter cried as he shot to his feet.

Washington explained hurriedly.

"Are you telling me Bradley might be alive!" Peter demanded in a disbelieving voice.

Washington was slow to answer. "Almost certainly not," he replied.

"But you don't have proof they killed the crew."

"We don't have proof of anything, Peter. We found the B-2 and destroyed it. And that's all we know."

"So they might be still be alive?"

"They might be. We really don't know."

The two men were silent. Both of them were thinking the same thing. "If we were to try and go in to get them, it would have to be a covert operation," Washington said as he thought. "We don't have adequate forces to fight our way in."

"Not unless you've got a secret unit somewhere up your sleeve."

"You guys are our only option. The special ops units in Iraq are too far away; we'd have to ferry them south of Iran and then up through the Gulf. Afghanistan has some back-ups, but Camp Cowboy is the closest unit to Lyangar by far."

Peter was silent.

"How long will it take you to get a team in place?" Washington asked.

Peter glanced at a folded map on the floor but didn't pick it up. He estimated the distance to Lyangar, the travel conditions and time it would take to ready his team, then answered. "A day. A little more. And that's *if* we use the Russian Hind to get us into the valley. We'll have to drop off near the pass, then hike in from there."

"Too long," Washington answered quickly. "If the crew's alive now, they'll be dead by then."

"Fine. We'll use the transporter. Have Scottie beam us over, I guess."

Washington's voice soured. "Really, Peter, it is too long. *If* the crew is alive, they won't be much longer."

"Look sir, that's fine. But you have to be realistic. Consider the terrain. It isn't like the desert. There is only one way in and out of that place, a grueling and gut-wrenching climb through the rocks and snow of Vrang Pass. That's it. Vrang Pass is the only way into Lyangar. And the pass will be guarded, which means my team can only travel at night, unless we are willing to get them all killed."

The DDO swore. "There's got to be something, anything we can do!"

"I'll tell you something right now," Peter replied. "No friggin *way* I'm going to sit here. If there's any possibility, any possibility at all they're alive, then I'm going in!"

"Great, Peter. Go in and get the bodies, because I promise you, if you don't get there tonight that is all you will find."

Peter paused. He had been thinking of something. It was a stupid idea, but the agency did lots of stupid things. And there wasn't time to be smart, they needed to act! "I want to try something," he said to Washington.

"What?" Washington demanded.

Peter quickly explained. Washington listened impatiently as Peter went through his plan. "Absolutely not!" he shouted into the phone. "What's that going to buy me, Peter? Best case, another hostage. Worst case, another dead friend. Don't even request it. There is no way I would approve that. No way in this world!"

"But sir, think! If Shane is alive, if either of the crew is alive, how else are you going to locate them before it is too late? We assume they are dead, but we don't know for sure. And al Qaeda will certainly kill them, now that we have destroyed their trophy plane. Whatever their plans were before, there's no way they let them live now."

Washington was silent for a very long time. Peter knew that meant he was thinking, and so he gave him space.

Outside he heard the sounds of his men gathering their gear. The light snow was melting and he heard the constant sloshing of boots. "Also," he finally added, "and this is perhaps the more important thing I could say."

Washington grunted. He was listening. Not enthusiastically, but at least he did not cut him off.

"There is the possibility that the warheads haven't been moved," Peter went on. "I've told you before, but I'm going to say it again, if those warheads had been moved out of the valley, some of my people would have known. We would have had some kind of information. We've thrown around enough money and we have people out there. I think they might have sent out a bunch of decoys, nothing but empty trucks. They might not have moved the warheads at all, at least not yet."

Washington growled impatiently. They had been through this before. "They've been dispersed, Peter. We are almost certain of that."

Peter shook his head, a knot of doubt in his gut. "I don't think so," he answered. "And if the weapons are still in the mountain, this is the only one way we find out. Put the aircrew aside for now. Put our friendship with Colonel Bradley out of the equation and consider only this; if I am successful, I would be inside the compound and as close to the principals as we'll ever get. It's worth the risk we would be taking, if for no more reason than that."

"You mean the risk *you* would be taking."

Peter paused, then answered, "Yes, in this case I mean me."

"So you want me to approve a mission in which you will likely be killed?"

"No sir, I don't. If I thought that was the likely outcome, I wouldn't volunteer. But think of this, Dr. Washington, if we don't find those warheads, a million people will die. It's risky, no doubt, but so is the alternative. And what is one more life if I fail?"

Washington sighed wearily. "No," he finally answered. "I can't lose you, Peter."

"So you won't approve the operation?"

Washington paused, then answered quietly. "You know that *I* can't."

Peter caught the subtle answer. "No, sir, I guess that *you* couldn't. Something like this, one would have to do without permission, one would have to do this on his own."

Washington remained silent.

And Peter knew he had won.

Eshkashem Road
Forty Kilometers West of Lyangar
Northern Afghanistan

Six hours later and almost a hundred miles away, the
wind began to blow down the canyon, moving the tops of the
barren trees and whistling through the rock formations on
the sides of the steep, rocky walls. In the bottom of the
canyon, along the narrow gorge, the road was deeply rutted,
frozen in places, muddy in others, with evergreens and dead
cottonwoods lining both sides.

The Afghani four-wheel drive made its way slowly along
the road. More than once the small truck slipped into the
frozen ruts and spun to a stop. The driver would jam the
truck into reverse, rev the engine, and spin the tires crazily
as he backed up to take another run up the road. A single
guard rode shotgun in the front seat, a customized and well-
oiled BMG AR-15 sitting carefully across his lap. The
guards, security agents for al Qaeda, were on patrol, secur-
ing the outermost perimeter of the security ring. Between
them and their masters, there were at least thirty additional
patrols. The Great One was somewhere beyond Lyangar,
buried in the mountains on the other side of the pass.

The four-wheel-drive truck came around a sharp corner
where brush and low branches obscured the view. Suddenly,
from their right, a shadow emerged and staggered toward
them. One guard lifted his rifle as he grunted in alarm. The
driver jammed on the brakes, bringing the truck to a sudden
stop, where it slipped on the ice, sliding downhill. The
driver cursed and drew his pistol, ready to slam the truck
into reverse.

A man stumbled toward them, then fell in the mud, directly in front of the vehicle. Both guards shouted in surprise
and jumped from the truck, their weapons drawn and ready.

Peter Zembeic looked up with dark eyes. Dried blood
caked both his nostrils and mouth. His beard was matted

with more blood and sweat and his entire neck and face were horribly bruised. Blood had soaked through his coat and frozen on his lapel. The American moaned and rolled over, trying to push himself to his knees, then moaned once again and fell unconscious at the guards' feet.

The two Afghanis stared at each other. An American agent! They had heard rumors, heard of sightings, but nothing had prepared them for this.

The driver lifted his pistol. "Should I shoot him?" he asked.

The other guard grunted and moved forward, his rifle at his shoulder, his bare fingers pressed against the trigger, a hair-breath, an ounce of pressure from firing his gun. The American didn't move. The guard took another careful step forward and kicked the stranger in the side. Peter moaned, but didn't move and the guard kicked again.

The second guard moved forward and bent to his knee. He pulled the coat open, looking for gunshot wounds, then placed a hand to the American's throat, feeling for a pulse. "Whoever did this," he grunted, "he nearly beat him to death."

The other guard sneered. "He must have run out of money. This is what the mercenaries do when the devils run out of cash!"

The two of them snickered as the crouching guard stood.

"What do we do?" the junior man said. Both of them thought in silence, too stupid to realize the piece of intelligence gold that lay at their feet.

The senior guard finally snorted, "Get him in the truck. We'll take him to Angra."

The other man laughed. "Angra. Yes, Angra. He'll know what to do."

39

Air Force One is far and away the most sophisticated passenger aircraft ever built. Though there are actually two identical aircraft—specially-configured Boeing 747-200B's, tail numbers 28000 and 29000—and though every sortie they fly is considered a military mission, the aircraft never carry the call sign "Air Force One" unless the president is aboard.

The four GE engines can power the aircraft almost eight thousand miles, with the option of air refueling giving it an unlimited range, while the crew of twenty-six chiefs, aides, stewards, security personnel, medical staff, and technicians make certain the president and his staff are always comfortable. With more than four-thousand square feet of cabin space, the aircraft is as spacious and comfortable as any executive suite. Beginning at the nose and moving aft, the planes feature a private stateroom for the president, with a small bedroom under the nose of the aircraft, a bathroom, office, workout room, lounge, and executive office suite. Opposite the presidential office is a medical room with a foldout operating table. A main conference room sits behind the infirmary, then small offices for the key staff. Further back are more work areas, another galley (the aircraft carries enough frozen food for thousands of meals), seating areas for Secret Service, then first-class seats for the passengers and press corps. On the third floor of the aircraft, directly behind the cockpit, is the communications and security center. With almost ninety telephones, many with secure voice and encryption, nineteen televisions, various satellite feeds, and ground-communication avionics, Air Force One supports every possible means of communication. The aircraft also incorporates incredibly sophisticated safety measures, including antimissile technology and radar jamming equipment.

Simply put, Air Force One, the safest aircraft on earth, was a fortified flying fortress and one of the few places on earth where the president felt secure and protected.

The aircraft was enroute to Boston, where the president would give a speech to the ambassadors from the EU. It was important to keep with his normal schedule, his staff had advised, afraid of creating a sense of immobilization or panic.

But the truth was they wanted to get the president and his family out of D.C. Just for awhile. Until things settled down.

As the aircraft flew north at thirty-seven thousand feet, the president sat on the edge of his bed, which was positioned at an angle, following the curve of the aircraft's nose, directly under the cockpit. There was another twin bed opposite him on which he had placed his briefcase and personal travel bag. He stared at his hands, lay back on the bed, glanced at the clock on the night stand, then sat up again.

The president felt a growing knot in his stomach. And with every hour that passed it grew a little tighter, a little larger, a little more difficult to ignore.

He stared at the blue carpet in his stateroom while listening to the sounds of the jet. The engines were so far behind him, and the aircraft was so well insulated, that it was almost quiet where he sat, though he could sense the wind moving over the enormous aircraft's nose, the slipstream creating a low *whoosh* that was a subtle and comforting sound.

Moving suddenly, the president made a decision. After

days of consultation and consideration, he knew what he had to do. Leaning to his right, he pushed a button for his steward, and a middle-aged man poked his head in the room. "Will you please find General Abram and tell him I want to speak with him," the president said.

"Yes, Mr. President," the steward replied.

General Abram had hardly left the president's side since the DARKHORSE had been called, and it was only two minutes before he walked into the bedroom.

"Sir," he said simply.

The president nodded to the opposite bed and the general sat down. He had never been this far forward in the presidential suite, and he felt uncomfortable in the presidential bedroom. Sitting stiffly, he kept his back straight and both feet on the floor.

"Sir?" he repeated as the president ran his hands through his hair.

"You know this thing could break wide open," the president said.

The general shook his head. "We won't let that happen, sir."

The president smiled bitterly. "It's funny you would say that. I've heard those exact words before."

The general looked confused and the president explained. "Fourteen years ago this month we lost our first child. You might remember that, Lowe—"

"Of course, Mr. President."

"My son was only sixteen, out one night for a drive with some friends. He was hit almost head-on—I thank God all the time that it wasn't his fault—but none of them were wearing their seatbelts. How many times have we heard that before? But Lowe, I can remember so well the doctor talking to us before he took my son into surgery. 'Is he going to die?' my wife asked him. 'We won't let that happen,' he said. But you know what, Lowe, it did happen. Despite the fact that the doctors gave it an extraordinary effort, despite the fact that they did everything they could, it happened anyway. Sometimes life throws you a sucker punch, and it doesn't matter what you do, you have to take the blow."

The general shook his head more adamantly. "No, sir, not this time. We're going to contain this before it goes any further."

The president narrowed his eyes and placed his hands on his knees. "I don't need to review the situation for you, Lowe, and I don't need to tell you the danger we're in. But I want you to know this—let there be no doubt in your mind. If we are attacked, I will respond. And it won't be tit-for-tat, it won't be blood-for-blood. I won't trade one of our cities for just one of theirs. Overwhelming force has been our conventional-war-fighting doctrine for years, and the same doctrine must apply in a nuclear exchange. So Lowe, I need you to help make this perfectly clear—clear to the enemy and clear to our own staff. They might get in one shot, but that is all they will get, for my response will be so overwhelming there will be nothing left. There won't be a second strike against us. I won't give them a second chance."

Lyangar Airfield
Southern Tajikistan

The sound of heavy footsteps filled the dark night, thug-booted stomps on the wood floors overhead that ran up and down the staircase and thumped down the hall. There were voices, loud voices, calling out in angry commands, and the sound of sliding metal as the soldiers chambered their rounds. The footsteps gathered in the hallway, then halted outside Bradley's door.

Col. Shane Bradley slowly rose in his prison. He gasped in pain from the beatings, but he forced himself straight and faced the cell door.

This was it. It was over. They were coming for him. He was scared. No, this was worse, he was utterly terrified. He felt like a child left alone in the night. He felt foolish and weak for having such fear. "No," he breathed sadly. He was not ready to die.

"Keep your head, Bradley!" he commanded himself. "Be

patient. Be ready. They haven't killed you yet! You're smarter than they are. They will make a mistake."

His cell door burst open and four guards stood there, swinging their black clubs menacingly at their sides. Every face that stared at him wore a fierce, hateful scowl.

Bradley studied the guards. Something was wrong. He could sense it, he could feel it, he could see it in their eyes—a fear and uncertainty that had not been there before. He thought of the explosions he had heard earlier, a series of violent concussions that had shaken the old walls, dropping dust and wood splinters from the rafters overhead. He thought of the light tang of smoke that had drifted from the hall. He watched the guards and wondered, as Flat Ears took a step toward him. "Face the wall!" he said.

Bradley turned slowly. He heard the sound of footsteps, then a low, muffled sound, like a heavy sack being dragged across the floor. He heard more footsteps in the hallway, then the clang of another cell door. A soft cry sounded from the hallway and he started to turn.

"*Don't move!*" Flat Ears screamed and Bradley kept his eyes on the wall. The guards spoke to each other, then he heard his cell door close.

He turned around quickly, his eyes adjusting to the semi-darkness again. Then he gasped and ran forward, dropping to his knees.

Peter lay on the floor. He looked so beaten and broken, Bradley knew he was dead. His face was purple and black and dried blood caked his mouth, and his jacket was soaked from a thin slice across the back of his neck. Bradley stared for a moment, unable to move, a horrified look on his face. For a moment his mind flashed back. Peter looked like Tia, the same crumpled body, the same black and purple face. His heart sank and he turned away as a picture of her body flashed again in his mind.

"Oh no!" he moaned from somewhere deep in his chest. "Oh no . . . oh no . . ." His breath came in sobs. First Tia and now Peter. He cried in frustration, a hopeless catch in his throat.

He leaned over to feel for breath, placing his ear next to Peter's mouth, knowing he would feel nothing but the silence of the dead. He listened carefully, then closed his eyes and rolled a few feet away.

Then he heard a grunt and a cough. Peter opened his eyes and slowly lifted his head. Bradley pulled back and gasped as Peter smiled slyly and winked, then pushed himself up to his knees. Bradley thought he was dreaming. Had he gone insane! He moved away quickly, pushing himself to the wall, his mouth dropping open. "Peter! . . . you're alright! Peter . . . what's going on?"

Peter touched his lip, brushing the dried blood away. "I *knew* this would work!" he laughed with great pride.

Bradley reached out and stammered, "Lay down! You're injured. I thought you were dead!"

"I had to argue with Washington, but I *knew* this would work. Man, I'm telling you, I'm brilliant. I deserve some kind of medal for this."

Bradley stared, then moved toward him, but Peter waved him off, brushing the dirt from his beard. "I'm fine, Shane, really. Isn't it cool. I thought of this gig myself. A couple surgical incisions—my medic helped me with that—some blood smears, some goo, and it looks pretty bad. It looks like I got knifed, but the cuts are barely skin deep. And the bruises are only purple dye injected under the skin. I look like I took a beating, but really, I'm okay."

Peter held out his arms, then opened his shirt to examine his blackened chest. "Man, I might have overdone it," he said as he surveyed the dark skin. "It looks like I hit a Mack truck. But it was the only plan I could come up with to find out if you were alive. I knew if I got myself captured they would bring me here. But I figured they wouldn't be nice, you know, I might get roughed up a bit. So I thought I would save them the effort. A pretty neat trick. They should add this to the field manual. Is this a great idea, or what?"

Bradley stared, disbelieving. "You let them find you!" he cried. "That's the dumbest thing I ever heard of. Do you have *any* idea what they might have done to you!"

Peter didn't answer and Bradley fell back again. "I thought you were dead!" he said, his face turning to ash. "I owe you," he whispered.

"You can pay me in beer." Peter studied the colonel and added, "It looks like you took a bit of a beating yourself."

"I'll live," Bradley insisted. He stared again at his friend. "Does Washington know you did this?"

"Officially, no. Unofficially, he's the one who told me how to mix colored dye to inject under my skin." Peter's eyes darted across the cell. "Where's the other one?" he asked. "That pretty little captain you were with?"

Bradley shook his head slowly, an awful sense of failure descending on him. Peter watched Bradley's face and knew the other pilot was dead. He lowered his eyes, but didn't say anything.

Bradley gritted his teeth in frustration and pounded his fist. From the time his aircraft had taken off, not a thing had gone right! The mission. The warheads. His aircraft going down. Tia had depended on him, and look how he failed!

Then he thought of Angra and what he had done. "I want to kill him!" he muttered.

Peter stared blankly at him.

"I am *going* to kill him," Bradley repeated.

"We're going to kill them all," Peter said.

Peter stood up, moved to Bradley, and lowered his voice. "We don't have much time, boss," he explained. "The B-2 has been destroyed and now these guys are scared. They think someone will be coming to look for the crew. I suspect the only thing they are debating is whether to kill us right now or get us up to the mountains where they can conceal our bodies. Either way it doesn't matter, we've got to get out of here."

The colonel shook angrily. "I'm hoping you have a plan."

Peter smiled wryly, then reached down and started unlacing his boots.

40

The Great Leader stood in the shadows of the old adobe building that concealed the entrance to the cavern. Night had settled over the valley and outside the sky was dark. Looking through the broken window, the leader could see to the east. The moon was rising, but had not yet topped the peaks of the tallest mountain, though its light illuminated the thin cirrus clouds that covered the eastern sky, turning them pale and white.

Beneath him, in the cavern, three technicians worked through their sweat. Each warhead was carefully extracted from its box and put on a metal stand. A blanket of composite fiber material, very difficult to get, impossible to buy, secretly built in a German factory near the northern port of Bremen, was wrapped around the warheads and heat-sealed with electric blowers. The material, a mixture of Mylar, Lenmex, and BHT, would absorb any leaking radiation, making the warheads virtually impossible to detect. After wrapping the warheads, they were then packed into nondescript but reinforced wooden crates.

Up top, outside the building, a convoy of three cargo trucks were waiting, hidden under the trees, their lights out, their engines at idle. One by one the cargo trucks, six-wheeled military vehicles with steel sides and drop-down gates, moved into position next to the back door of the building to be loaded. Eight crates were placed in each truck, a comfortable load.

The leader watched his men work until Imad Naghneyeh approached the commander and bowed. "*Sayid,* the trucks are ready," he said. Outside, more trucks were falling into position to surround the vehicles with the nuclear warheads. Five were open-air troop carriers with fifteen soldiers in each. A couple others had canvas tops, hiding the floor-mounted machine guns. A total of nine trucks were lined up to escort the weapons through the pass.

The Great One pushed himself away from the shadows. All of his men were waiting, watching, hoping he might notice their efforts, hoping for a kind word, anxious to see that his will be done. The commander exited the building and walked past his soldiers, moving toward the first truck. Imad followed and the commander turned to him and asked, "How long to the pass?"

"Two hours. A little more. The roads north are muddy and it is snowing in the highest elevations. Once we get over the Pamir Pass and turn west, back into Tajikistan, the roads get a little better. We will also be descending and the weather will clear."

"Will we make Khorugh by morning?"

"No doubt, *Sayid.* We will be there long before sunrise. Our entire journey will take place in the dark."

The Great One pulled out a brown cigarette and lit it with a paper match. He drew deeply, holding the bitter smoke in his lungs, his face illuminated by the orange glow. "If we can make it to Khorugh, nothing can stop us," the Great Leader said. "The teams are all waiting. Once we arrive with the weapons, they will quickly disperse. Then the Great Satan, with all of his eyes, even he will not find them all."

Imad bowed again. "Yes, *Sayid.* And Allah, Gracious God, may he bless you for this great work you have done."

The commander waited, smoking while he watched the high clouds moving across the night sky. He considered the events in his life that had brought him to this time and place. He placed his hands on the truck, wanting to touch the warheads and feel their power. *One night!* That's all that he asked. One more night of concealment, and his work would be through. If he could deliver the warheads to Khorugh, his life's work would be done.

The Great One finished the smoke and leaned toward Imad. "You understand, my good friend, that you have the greatest mission of all," he said in a low voice as he looked at his friend.

The lieutenant stood straight and the Great One watched his eyes carefully. "Tell me again," the Great One said slowly. He didn't want to test him. He simply wanted to hear.

Imad began. "I will travel alone to southern Russia, crossing the border at Orsk. There I will meet Seleiman Khromtau. He will arrange to have the warhead shipped to Turkey, then Morocco, then via cargo ship to Canada. I will then fly to Quebec and meet up with Mohammad Kebul, who has already arranged for the boat in Quebec. From Canada, we sail south, down the coast, then into the Chesapeake Bay . . ."

The leader nodded in approval.

The lieutenant watched his leader, then went on. "We navigate up the Potomac to Washington, then, as we approach the center of the city . . ." Here his voice trailed off.

The leader listened peacefully, then placed his hand on Imad's arm. "And I will be waiting for you in the bosom of God."

Imad nodded slowly. He would meet his reward.

The Great One took a breath, then glanced impatiently down the road. "Where is that animal you call Angra?" he asked.

Imad looked back and hunched his shoulders. Angra had gone back to finish the American prisoners and should have been back by now. "Do we wait?" he asked timidly.

The Great One shook his head as he climbed inside the truck. "Let's go," he commanded. "He will find his way."

The Leader nodded to the driver and he started the engine. With a chug of diesel smoke, the convoy began to roar up the muddy road.

41

Peter Zembeic pulled his thick boots from his feet. The enemy soldiers had taken all of his belongings—his small pack, his belt, his web harness and its gear (all worthless in the situation he was now in anyway). They had emptied his pockets and even taken his hat.

But they hadn't taken his boots, which was a deadly mistake.

Peter held his right boot and twisted the heel forcefully. Bradley heard a dull *snap,* and the heel fell away. Peter dug with his fingers, then pointed to the door with his chin. "Listen for me. This will take a little time," he said.

Colonel Bradley moved to the door and lowered his head to the floor. He could hear voices above the cellar, somewhere up the stairs.

The group of soldiers congregated around their leader. It was cool in the hangar, but, still, sweat stung Angra's eyes. His face was smudged with dark soot. He had been over to the fires, watching what was left of the burning B-2. It looked like the magnesium and composites might burn for a week. The heat was tremendous and the fire had started to spread, catching on the trees and outbuildings, the dry wood of the old hangars nearly exploding in flames. The fires flickered yellow light through the open hangar doors and the smoke hung low and oily as the flames licked the skies. Angra paid no attention to the fires; Lyangar could burn to the ground, it mattered not to him.

His soldiers waited anxiously as he barked his commands. "The main convoy has already left. We are going to have to move quickly to catch up with them. Kill the Americans, get your gear, and let's get out of here."

Angra peered at his soldiers, about twenty in all. "Any questions?" he asked. No one said anything. "Alright then, let's move!" he cried to his men.

Bradley heard the movement of soldiers directly over his head. He listened to the footsteps, then stole a look back to Peter. Peter had his other boot in hand and was snapping off the heel. "Peter," the colonel pleaded, "we don't have much time!"

Peter ignored him, concentrating on his work. Before him, on the floor, were five pieces of gray plastic and a tiny roll of flesh-colored tape. In the center of the stash were a one-inch razor blade and a couple blasting caps. Bradley studied the equipment. "You hid blasting caps in your boot!" he exclaimed.

Peter nodded. "Yeah. Good thing I didn't parachute in, I guess."

Bradley shook his head as Peter began to snap the plastic pieces together. Seconds later, he held up an Israeli Z-4 Zip Gun. Tiny. Plastic. Easy to conceal. Easy to assemble. Impervious to metal detectors and surprisingly accurate.

Bradley stared at the tiny gun. "Toys 'R' Us?" he said sarcastically.

Peter snapped the last piece, which fell in place with a *click.* "Don't judge a man by the size of his weapon," he said.

"What about bullets?" Bradley asked. "Or do you have the BBs in your socks?"

Peter grunted as he grabbed the tiny razor and undid his

pants. Probing his right thigh with his fingers, he pinched the flesh. He felt the small lumps and squeezed at the skin, then touched the razor to the fleshy part of his inner thigh.

Carefully, slowly, he cut a one-inch incision. He grimaced in pain as the blood soaked his fingers and ran down his wrists. Slicing through the skin and the thin layer of fat underneath, he cut another incision next to the first and more blood seeped through his fingers and began to drip to the floor. Peter squeezed the flesh, forcing the .22-caliber shells from where they had been planted under his skin; then, standing, he held four bullets in his hand.

"Water?" he demanded, speaking through his clenched teeth. He spit out the roll of tape and held both hands to his thigh.

Bradley moved toward him while shaking his head. "I'm sorry, Peter, water's been in real short supply." He tore at his shirt, tearing a strip he could use for a bandage, then twisted the material inside out and folded it in a small square.

Peter wiped his hands clean as Bradley moved to his side. Peter held the incision together while Bradley applied the makeshift bandage and surgical tape. Peter cinched his pants, took the bullets, and started loading the gun. Grunting in satisfaction, he lifted the Z-4.

Less than four inches long, the zip gun had a tiny handle and a thumb-operated firing pin. It held four shells, a recent upgrade from the single-shot Z-1. Developed by Shin Bet's assassination teams, the gun required the assassin to get close enough to get a shot to the head, but if he was able, the gun could certainly kill.

Bradley stared at the weapon. "Amazing," he said. He glanced at the other articles and asked, "I don't suppose you crammed a transmitter in somewhere?"

"No." Peter shook his head. "The ones I had at the base camp were too big and too bulky. There are some special units I could have gotten from D.C. or the field office in London, but I didn't have time to wait for one to be sent out to me."

There was the thunder of footsteps and Bradley moved to the door. A single guard came down the stairway, stomping on the wooden stairs. Bradley pulled away from the door, a wild look in his eye, as Peter shoved the weapon into his pants and held his finger to his lips. "Not yet," he mouthed as he stared at the door. The guard ran down the hallway, moving past their cell. Peter pulled on his boots and pushed himself to his feet. There was a slam of closing lockers, then the guard ran back up the stairs.

Bradley took a deep breath and watched as Peter moved his fingers down the hem of his coat. Feeling the plastic, he brought the coat up to his teeth and tugged on a loose thread. The hem gave way and he carefully pulled out the strand of C-4. Powerful, difficult to ignite, sensitive to water, he peeled back the thin layer of protective plastic and exposed the claylike explosive. Working together, the two men positioned the explosive material and firing caps around the rusty hinges of the steel door.

"We won't need it all," Peter instructed as he tore away half the C-4. "We'd blow out the whole wall if we use everything." Bradley positioned the last firing pin and the two men stepped back.

Bradley looked at the agent. "What's next?" he asked.

Peter shook his head. "I was kind of hoping you had some ideas," he replied.

Bradley dropped to his knees. "Where's your team?" he asked.

Peter shook his head. "Don't know for certain. They might be out there or they might not. It depends on how long it took them to hike through the mountains, the number of patrols they had to go around, that kind of thing."

"You mean we might have to do this alone?" Bradley stammered.

Peter gritted his teeth. "Plan on it," he said. "If the posse shows up, that's good for us; but don't plan on them, Shane. We need to figure out how to get out of here by ourselves."

"Okay! Great! Let me get this straight. There are two of us. We have four shells and a gun I could hide inside a dinner roll. We got a little C-4 and that's about it. Against what? Maybe twenty or thirty heavily armed guards?"

Peter pressed his lips sadly. "You don't have to paint such a discouraging picture," he said.

Bradley swore in frustration.

"Hey," Peter reacted, "I didn't have much time to put this whole thing together, my friend. It wasn't like I could come in here with a couple Uzis shoved down my britches! And remember, ol' buddy, my main objective was to get to you before it was too late. If I had waited to get my team up here, if we had come in with our guns blazing, we might have eventually found you, but you would already be dead. We needed an inside-out job to gain the element of surprise. But if we keep our heads together, we are going to be fine."

Bradley scrunched his forehead. "Four shells," he muttered as he listened to the footsteps gathering over his head.

Peter grabbed his shoulders. "There's something else," he said.

"What's that?" Bradley asked, keeping his eyes on the rafters.

Peter leaned toward him. "I think the warheads are here!"

Bradley met Peter's eyes and gasped. There was a cold burning there. The two men stared at each other and Bradley lowered his voice. "How do you know that?"

"I don't. Not for certain. But I want to find out."

"You think the warheads are here at Lyangar!?"

"Here, or somewhere close."

A mass of heavy boots began to move down the stairs and both of the men lifted their heads.

"But if they're here . . . ," Bradley muttered.

"Then we've got a few options."

Bradley shook his head and Peter took a short step toward him. "Are you with me?" he asked him as he rolled down his sleeves.

The colonel didn't hesitate. "I was sent to destroy those warheads! I'd love another chance!"

"Good," Peter whispered as he moved for the door, "Come on! It's time then. Let's go get in a fight!"

42

Peter checked the C-4 that was pasted in a thin line around the back side of the steel door. The blast cap was embedded deeply into the plastic explosive. A two-inch lanyard, thin as fish wire but rough and easy to grip, extended from the cap and dangled toward the floor. He held the cap firmly, pressing it into the explosive, then looked over his shoulder. "We've got a lot of bang here," he said. "If we're not careful, it's going to blow us through the other wall."

Bradley nodded. Outside the cell the enemy gathered, their voices drifting through the crack under the steel door.

"Do you want to fire the blasting cap or the Z4?" Peter asked, glancing over his shoulder.

Bradley shook his head. "I couldn't hit a moose with that thing if it was standing on my chest! You take the gun. I'd just waste the shells."

Peter moved away from the door and Bradley took up his position with the C4. Outside he heard a deep voice and recognized Angra. He motioned to Peter and hissed under his breath. "There's a general. Five feet eight. Pale eyes. Salt-

and-pepper beard. If you want to find the warheads, we need him alive."

Peter grunted as he examined his gun and checked the four shells.

"How long is this fuse?" Bradley asked.

"Ten seconds."

Bradley swore. "How am I going to time that?" he asked.

"Luck, baby, luck! Or prayer. You can choose."

A key was inserted into the cell door. The gentle clang of the ancient metal tumblers turning fell on their ears. Peter whispered his final instruction. "If you can, get them after they have moved through the door!"

Peter took up a position against the far wall, near the corner, where the concussion would be reflected away from him. Bradley hid behind the door, pressing against the wall. The door began to open. He pulled the lanyard and heard a quiet pop as the timer kicked in. Bending over, he moved toward Peter and pressed his body against the wall.

One—two—three—he counted in his mind as he moved to Peter's side. The door swung violently open with a bone-jarring *clang*. Four guards moved into the cell, black clubs in their hands. Flat Ears stood behind them, his weapon drawn and ready. He sneered anxiously, eager to complete this bloody job.

Four—five—Bradley continued.

He stared at the blast caps, then glanced over at Peter. The tip of the Z4 protruded from the palm of his hand. Three more guards moved into the room, then Angra followed slowly, glaring at the Americans.

Peter stared at the general. Pale eyes. Ugly teeth. This was the one he would let live.

Six—Seven—Bradley counted in his mind.

The soldiers bunched at the door. It was perfect, nearly perfect, and he almost smiled. Angra saw his expression, the look of anticipation, the glare of revenge, and realized that something was horribly wrong. His instincts kicked in. He glanced to the other American. What was that in his hand? A dull glint, a dark shadow. It looked like the tip of gun!

"Nine!" Bradley shouted, then turned his head to the wall.

"Kill them!" Angra cried as he lifted his gun and aimed it at Bradley's chest.

The plastic explosive blew at exactly that instant, the blast and overpressure filling the room with an unbearable wall of fire and black smoke. Bradley gasped at the fire and blinding white light. The air was sucked from his chest and replaced with an unbearable heat, suffocating and painful, the hot gas burning his lungs. His eyes bulged from the pressure and his ears and nose bled. The force blew the steel door off its hinges and sent chunks of steel and cement shooting through the air, as timbers fell from the rafters and pieces of brick fell to the floor. The two nearest guards were blown apart in the blast; heads, guts, and limbs spattered against the wall. A huge piece of the steel door hit another guard in the neck and he fell in a heap, his vertebrae smashed at the base of his skull. And the smoke and dust billowed, became a ball of heat that boiled down the hall.

Peter rolled to his knees and lifted the tiny Z4. He aimed the small weapon at Flat Ears and fired one shell. The high velocity bullet impacted the terrorist square in the face and the Arab gurgled, dropped his weapon and fell dead on the floor. Peter fired three times, each shot perfectly aimed, and three more guards went down, each of them shot in the head. Bradley rolled, grabbed Flat Ears' handgun and fired at the last guard, who fell against the wall, his knees buckling as he drifted to the floor, a smear of bright blood following him as he slid down the wall.

Angra was the only Arab left alive in the cell. He lay on the floor, bloody chips of cement embedded in his neck and ears. Both of his hands were now empty, his gun having been blown from his grip. His eyes, dull and lifeless, stared blankly ahead. The room fell eerily still, except for the dying gasps of a few desperate men.

Angra pushed himself up and looked around in a daze. All of his men were down. Bradley pointed a Glock at his head. Angra tried to swallow, but his Adam's apple caught in his throat.

How had this happened? In less than ten seconds, his world had been turned upside down! In his mind, he relived the brief moments since he had walked into the cell—the explosion, the hidden weapon, the pain, the bloody fall of his men.

He watched bitterly as Colonel Bradley took a step toward him. He waited, expecting to be shot in the head. But the American didn't shoot. Instead, he lifted him by his collar and threw him against the wall. Angra whimpered lightly as Peter moved forward, a leather belt in his hand.

"Kill me," Angra muttered, unable to hide the loathing inside. "Kill me, you whores! I want to die now!"

Bradley stared down at him. "Keep your hopes up, good buddy, and maybe later we will." He scowled at the man who had tortured Tia to death, then kicked him once, hard, on the side of his ribs. Using the belt, he tied his hands at his back.

Peter moved through the room collecting weapons and ammunition. He draped four belts of shells across the front of his chest, then threw another pistol to Bradley, who tucked it in his pants. They waited and listened to the steps pounding over their heads. Peter moved to the door, then into the hall, taking up a position that faced the stairs. Smoke and dust filled the air, burning his eyes. Three guards ran down the stairs. Peter waited until they were fully exposed, then fired three times, hitting each one in the chest. Bradley stepped into the hallway and looked at the soldiers on the floor.

He cocked his head to Peter. "You seem to be a pretty good shot," he said.

Peter shrugged, then moved to the soldiers, liberated their AK-47s, and threw one to Bradley. The door at the top of the stairs opened quickly and a young guard glanced down the stairs. Peter shot once, but the guard pulled back and ran.

"You missed!" Bradley mocked.

Peter looked at him, glum. "I know! I can't believe it." He stared at the muzzle of his gun. "Trade me weapons!" he said as he pointed at Bradley's gun. "This one isn't sighted. I don't miss shots like that!"

Bradley hesitated.

"I'm serious," Peter said. "I don't miss that shot if my gun is sighted right."

Shrugging, Bradley tossed him his weapon, then grabbed Peter's gun.

The two men turned and moved carefully up the stairs, which emerged near the back wall of the hangar. A broken window faced them at the top of the stairs, across a narrow hall, and Peter glanced through the window at the darkness outside. To his right he could see barrels of jet fuel and an old Soviet MiG. To his left, enemy soldiers had scattered their gear. A couple of green army trucks had been pulled into the hangar, and smoke drifted through the air now, low and black.

Somewhere off in the distance they heard a single gun-shot and looked at each other anxiously. Then the hangar grew quiet. Peter motioned to Bradley, pointing to his right, and Bradley moved into position beside him. Then they heard the crunch of footsteps on the wet gravel outside. Peter looked around desperately. They were trapped on the stairs. A sudden thunder of bullets burst through the air and the wall shattered beside him, exploding from the force of the shells. The shots ended quickly. Peter stared at the bullet holes beside him and nearly choked on his spit. His body fit neatly between the holes on the wall. He dropped to his knees. "We've got to get out of here!"

Bradley only grunted. That was obvious. "I'll provide cover," he whispered. "If you can get to the back wall—"

Peter suddenly lifted his finger. "Shhh," he whispered so quietly that Bradley could hardly hear. He peeked around the stairwell and Bradley stood still. Then he heard it—a whistle so silent it barely carried through the air.

Peter cocked his head and smiled as he called out, "Hoss! Is that you?"

One of Peter's Rangers pushed his head above the win-dow sill.

"Hoss, you idiot!" Peter shouted. "You nearly cut me in two!"

The army Ranger smiled sheepishly. "Hey, boss, good to see you. Sorry for the scare."

43

The U.S. Army Rangers, five men in all, climbed through the broken window at the back of the hangar and gathered around Peter and Colonel Bradley. The solders wore thin body armor but no helmets, and were dressed in black-and-gray uniforms, subdued name tags, no rank, and no U.S. insignia. Their faces and hands, even their palms and eyelids, were camouflaged black, and out here, in the open, they moved with exceptional care, their heads were on a constant swivel, their eyes constantly darting here and there.

Outside, there was the sound of occasional gunfire as the other Ranger team routed the last of the al Qaeda soldiers. Most were already dead. A few had slipped away, disappearing into the night, sliding into the shadows, leaving everything, including their weapons, behind.

As the men gathered around him, Peter got right to the point. "What have we got as far as comm?" he demanded.

A black sergeant, the team leader, stepped forward. "We've got a SATCOM, but it would take us awhile to hook up."

"What about a communications link with a Predator?"

"Nothing up there, Peter. We weren't assigned any recon for this op. There's an awful lot going on across Asia, and everyone with a uniform and a pulse is looking for the warheads right now. This rescue is a pretty low priority, I'm sure you understand."

Peter swore, even though it was what he expected to hear. "Alright," he said. "Set up the satellite phone. Get a call to Mother. Tell them the op was a success."

The communications specialist separated himself from the group to set up the phone.

"Okay, boss," the team leader said. "Let's get your crap and get out of here."

"Can't," Peter answered, "we've got more work to do."

The team leader didn't understand. "I thought this was a straight search-and-rescue?" he said.

"It was. Now it isn't." Peter took a small breath and pulled the Ranger aside. "We think the warheads might be near," he explained.

"Here!" the Ranger hissed.

"Yes. And we've got someone downstairs who knows where they are."

The Ranger shook his head. "Peter, are you saying—"

Peter put his hand on the soldier's shoulders and pushed him toward the hangar door. "Gather your teams," he said. "Give me a few minutes. Keep your men away."

The Ranger stared at him a moment, then nodded his understanding and turned slowly for the hangar door.

Bradley stepped forward. "What guidance regarding combat interrogations does your field manual provide?" he asked in a whisper.

Peter frowned. "Not much. It's intentionally ambiguous, leaving open the option, you know, depending on the situation. The local commander has great authority."

Bradley rocked on his boots. In his mind, the situation was extraordinarily clear. "You know what we have to do!" he said calmly.

The CIA officer nodded. "It won't be easy, you know that."

"I don't care any more. Think of the consequences! New York or D.C., or Middletown, USA." The colonel paused and wiped his sleeve on his mouth. "No, it won't be pleasant. We are not that kind of men."

The comm specialist called out as he motioned to Peter. "Your boss wants to talk to you," he said.

Peter shook his head.

"He says *Now!*" the Ranger exclaimed.

Peter stared at Bradley a moment, then turned and ran to the satellite phone and grabbed the receiver. "Yeah," he said quickly into the phone.

"You got them," Washington said, great relief in his voice.

"We got *him*," Peter answered. "The captain is dead."

Peter could hear Washington click his teeth. "Okay, Peter," he said after a pause. "Now get out of there."

"Can't do that, boss. We've got a couple things left to do."

Washington stuttered in objection, his voice rising in anger, but Peter didn't wait to listen. He disconnected the line.

Lowering the receiver, he stared at the floor then turned to Bradley and nodded. "Let's do it," he said, a grim look on his face.

Peter and Bradley walked into the bloody cell. The smell of bowels and death pervaded. Angra stared arrogantly at his enemies as they entered the room. He was angry and humiliated, but he was not afraid. He knew they wouldn't kill him. Americans, they weren't like him, and he was happy for that. "Untie me," he muttered in a loathing tone. "Untie me! I demand that you treat me with respect!"

Bradley stared at him, a deadly cold expression in his eyes. Angra saw the dark look. Never in his life had he seen such a look of resolve.

And for the first time he wondered.

Perhaps he was wrong?

"Untie me!" he commanded, mustering his most arrogant tone. "I demand . . ." His voice trailed off.

Bradley lifted the handgun and took a step toward Angra. The general watched him carefully, then lowered his voice. "I know you won't use it. Your mind games will not work on me!"

The colonel frowned, lowered the gun, and looked away, then wiped a bead of sweat from his face. He glanced quickly to Peter, who nodded, then lifted the weapon again. Without so much as a word, he fired a shot into the general's leg.

The shell shattered the kneecap and blew out the entire bone in the leg, shattering the muscle and sinew into one bloody mess. The Arab cried like an animal, shrieking in pure agony.

The colonel bent toward him and grabbed him, holding his face in his hands, forcing him to look at him while covering his mouth. "Listen to me!" he sneered. "We will not, we can not, sit here and see the world destroyed! You've hidden the warheads and we *have to know where they are!* You have ten seconds to tell or you get another shot in the leg. And believe, Mr. Angra, you will run out of appendages before I run out of shells! Now I want you to tell me. Where are the warheads? We simply *must* know."

44

I t only took minutes to find out what they needed to know.

For all his arrogance and bluster, for all his experience in dealing out pain, for all the horrible things he had seen and the cruel things he had done, for all the times he had laughed when men had cried near the end of their lives, Angra proved to be a most talkative prisoner when the pain was on him. The moment he was convinced that Bradley was not going to back off, he talked and he talked, providing accurate and astonishing detail.

The warheads were in a convoy heading through the Pamir Pass, after which they would turn west to the Tajikistan city of Khorugh. There they would be parceled out to twenty-four suicide teams. By midmorning they would be scattered and on their way for destinations throughout the Arab world. And each team had a target somewhere in the West.

When Angra finished explaining, the two Americans were utterly terrified.

Angra saw their fear, which brought great joy to his face, and he smiled eerily through his pain, taking delight in their fright. "You don't have time!" he choked, his voice hissing in pain. "There's not a thing you can do! Go ahead, call in your bombers! They will be too late!"

Bradley stood over the general. "Do you realize what you have done?" he said, his voice sad and exhausted and extremely fatigued. "Do you realize how many people will die? And not only Americans, but Arabs and Muslims as well!"

Angra stared at him blankly. He didn't care any more. The truth was, he and his brothers had quit caring a long time ago.

Bradley swore, then turned to Peter and nodded to the door. The two men climbed the stairs and walked into the hangar.

"He's right," Bradley said, his voice husky with fear. "We don't have time to launch an attack. We've got the U.S.S. *Reagan* off the Gulf, but it's a two-hour flight. Cruise missiles can't attack moving targets and choppers are hours away."

Peter glanced at his watch. "The warheads will be in Khorugh within an hour," he said. "And once the warheads make it to Khorugh, there's not a thing we can do. They will slip behind a wall of silence, anonymity, and animosity we will never break through. Walking into Khorugh is like going back to the dark ages. I've been there, Shane, it's a bizarre universe where the United States is hated more than their children are loved. We could search for ten years and never find the warheads or the suicide teams."

Bradley stared miserably at the floor, then glanced at the MiG.

He only had one idea.

It was desperate. It was ugly. It was literally suicide. And Peter was going to hate it and would try and stop him no doubt. But unless he had another plan there was simply no choice.

He turned back to Peter. "Do you have any suggestions?" he pleaded. "Come on, you're the hero! Think for me, baby. You've got to have something up there!"

Peter was quiet as a painful look crossed his face. "I'm

sorry," he mumbled. "It's not like . . . you know, we just can't order up a miracle out of thin air."

That was it, then. Bradley nodded. The decision was made. "It's okay," he said slowly, looking suddenly forlorn. He seemed to deflate, his shoulders sagging as he took a deep breath.

Peter took a step toward him. "What are you thinking?" he asked, his face tight with concern.

Colonel Bradley ignored him as he looked around and said, "I need a map. And your men. They're going to have to help."

Peter looked at him, puzzled, then motioned to one of his soldiers, who pulled out a detailed topographical map from his thigh pocket. Bradley grabbed the map and studied it, locating their position, then tapped a spot just a few miles to the south. "See this?" he said, tapping the map again. "Here, where the road intersects at the crest of this hill? There's a small open field, maybe fifty meters south of where the roads form a V."

Peter stared at the map. "I see it," he said.

Bradley thought as he talked, trying to remember the scene in his mind. "The field will be easy to recognize," he continued, "one side is lined with heavy trees on the north, and the south end rolls over the crest of the hill. Can you see it, Peter, here, where I'm touching the map?"

Peter nodded impatiently. "Yes, yes, I see it," he said.

"Think one of your Ranger teams can find it?"

"Of course they can."

"How long would it take them to get up there?"

Peter glanced toward one of the heavy army trucks parked outside the hangar. "Five minutes," he answered, "if we use one of those things."

"Okay then," Bradley said, "let's get some guys up to that field."

"But why?" Peter shot back.

"That's where we jettisoned the B-2 warheads before we landed at Lyangar."

Peter's face remained blank. He didn't understand.

"We'll send out a team for the warheads," Bradley instructed. "Then I need a couple other guys to help me with that jet." Bradley nodded to the MiG sitting near the hangar wall.

Peter hesitated. "You're kidding!" he answered, a raspy catch in his throat. He was beginning to guess what his friend had in mind.

Bradley turned toward him. "No, Peter, I'm not kidding. Here's what we're going to do. We get one of the jettisoned nuclear bombs from the Stealth. We strap it to the MiG, and I go after them."

Peter cried in frustration, "No! Your bombs are safed. There is no way to detonate them once they've been jettisoned!"

"Yes, Peter, that's right, there's no way to override the firing mechanism and detonate the bomb. But I don't need a nuclear explosion, not for what I'm trying to do. Remember Peter, the core of the B61-11 is made up of a thousand tiny pellets of high grade uranium, each of them emitting enough radiation to kill a hundred men. The B61-11 isn't a firecracker, it's a very serious bomb, and the uranium inside it is the purest nuclear material in the world. Can you see it, Peter, can you see what I'm going to do! If I can ram my jet into the convoy, it will create an enormous blast. The pellets inside my warhead will be scattered for miles. In addition, I'm almost guaranteed to penetrate some of the warheads in the trucks. Now think of that, Peter, a MiG flying into the convoy at eight hundred miles an hour—it will be the equivalent energy of a forty-thousand-pound bomb. It will blow my warhead apart, scattering nuclear pellets everywhere. The radiation will be so powerful, every man in the convoy will be dead in two days. And the warheads, the trucks, everything within two miles will be so radiated they'll glow. The area will be a dead zone for ten thousand years."

Peter stared, dumbfounded. "A dirty bomb," he said.

"No, not just dirty, it will be a filthy bomb, friend. This would be a thousand times more deadly than anything al Qaeda has ever envisioned. And a high-g impact on the target is all that we need."

"High-g impact? BS! What you mean is a crash! You're going to go out and find the convoy, then fly into it! It's a suicide mission! I can't believe you're even thinking of this!"

Bradley's demeanor stayed unchanged. "If you have another idea, I'd love to hear it."

Peter remained silent and Bradley glanced down at his watch. "Less than fifty minutes," he said.

Peter's face grew pale and he stepped back, his eyes burning, his lips turned down in pain. "Shane, I won't let you."

The colonel took a quick step toward him. "Tell me, then, Peter, what are we going to do? If you stop me we fail, and a million people will die. What am I . . . who are you . . . what is any one man compared to that! We've got to do something and we've got to do it *right now!*"

Peter didn't answer. He was speechless and pale. "But if you fly into the convoy—"

"The warheads will all be destroyed. They'll be too hot to handle until our grandchildren are dead. Look, Peter, I know it's not perfect, but what choice do I have!"

Peter turned away quickly and Bradley saw the tears on his cheek. "I won't let you, Shane," he muttered. "I can't . . . I won't let you . . . this is not how we work. I could never forgive you. I could never forgive myself."

"I don't need your forgiveness. What I need is your help!"

Peter shook, his head hanging, his hands trembling at his side. "You can't . . . ," he said as he lifted his head. His face was grim and determined, a wild look in his eye.

Bradley's hand moved to the gun he had strapped to his hip. "You *will not* stop me," he commanded. "This is no time for friendship. This is no time to cry. How many times have you seen a soldier blown apart at your side? How many times have you given an order, knowing some of your men would die? This is no different, and you *will not* stop me. This is business, Peter, business, and you will put your feelings aside."

Peter swallowed and looked up. "I will not, I can not help you commit suicide."

Bradley stared at him, angry, then shook his head and

turned away from his friend. Running toward the hangar, he commanded in a loud voice, "Rangers! I say Rangers! Come and gather on me!"

Peter watched the soldiers begin to congregate around Bradley, then turned and walked away from his men.

It only took Bradley a couple minutes to gather and organize the teams. The first team set out in two of the four-wheel-drives. The heavy trucks tore down the runway and crashed through the fence. Turning on the road, they headed south toward the mountain where the B-2 warheads had been dropped.

Another team of Rangers then moved to the MiG. Pulling the chocks, they leaned against the landing gear to push it out of the hangar.

45

Colonel Bradley sprinted to help the Rangers pushing on the MiG, pointing to the nearest soldier as he ran. "There's a mule—an auxiliary power unit, a big, green generator on wheels. Get it. I'll need it to start the jet."

Four Rangers were already heaving against the fighter, grunting and straining against its landing gear. The MiG was a heavy monster made of 100 percent Russian iron and steel. Bradley moved to the aircraft and added his weight. Three more soldiers emerged from the darkness and moved to his side. Together they pushed the fighter across the dirty cement, moving it out of the hangar and a hundred feet down the taxiway.

"Okay!" Bradley shouted. "Some of you get the mule."

Four soldiers went back to the hangar and pushed the huge electric generator to the side of the jet. Bradley ran to the hangar. Against the wall he saw a wooden locker with GENERAL ATTA KAWY stenciled across the front in Arabic. He ran to it and pulled on the door. It was locked. He took his handgun and shot the lock off the hasp, sending tiny pieces of metal spraying through the air. The locker door swung open and Bradley peered inside.

A Nomex flight suit hung in the locker—American, green, well-worn but clean. Nomex flight gloves. A helmet. Bradley stripped to his underwear and donned the flight suit, pulling it on over his boots. Then he grabbed the helmet and gloves and ran for the jet.

The Rangers had the mule running and the power cord connected to the MiG. Bradley climbed into the fighter using the narrow steps built into the fuselage directly under the canopy. He dropped into the cockpit and took a quick look around. The team leader climbed the steps to the cockpit and leaned toward him. "Just got word on the radio," he yelled above the roar of the mule. "They found one of the B-2 warheads. They're loading it up. Will be here in five or six minutes."

Bradley lifted his fist in a celebratory salute. "All right," he shouted. "Now listen to me. This is very important. Back near the hangar door are some steel straps and bolts. Look around for a tool box; there's got to be one in there. When they bring the warhead, bolt it to one of the hard points under the fuselage. You have to be careful to center it or it will affect how this thing flies, and make sure it is secure, we don't want it coming off. But listen to me now. Pay attention to what I say. Before you strap on the warhead you've *got* to remove the nose cone. The nose cone is made of depleted uranium and is designed to protect the nuclear material inside. If you can't get that thing off, the nuclear pellets will be protected from the impact of the crash. You'll need a couple wrenches, but it isn't complicated, there's only six or eight bolts. If you can't loosen the bolts, then break them or find a torch, I don't care how you do it, but do whatever it takes to get that nose cone off."

The soldier nodded grimly.

"Do you understand?" Bradley asked. "It is extremely important the nose cone is removed."

"Understood!" the Ranger shouted. Bradley slapped his shoulder and he dropped to the cement.

Turning to the cockpit, Bradley donned his helmet and strapped himself in, running the old canvas harness over his shoulders and between his legs. He heard the mule engine run up to full rpm and nodded to the soldier at the mule controls. The power kicked on and his lights flickered once, then came on steady and bright.

He studied the cockpit. Everything was familiar. It was like riding a bike. The dials and gauges were old, the MiG-21 was a '70s bird, and the cockpit was laid out differently than an American jet, but the basics were so recognizable he felt comfortable. He scanned the cockpit, the cluster of engine gauges, the flight instruments, the radar and avionic displays. The gauge markings were in Russian, but he didn't need to read them to know what they were; any good pilot would have been able to figure them out. He touched the throttle, set the brakes, then heard shouts from outside and looked up to see a Pakistani truck pull up next to the jet. Five Rangers jumped out and raced to the back, where they pulled one of the warheads from the bed of the truck. The team leader ran up to the soldiers, a heavy tool chest in his hands. He shouted instructions, pointing to the nose cone, and the men went to work. The minutes passed slowly. Each second was an agony and Bradley shifted impatiently in his seat. Five minutes. Then seven. The men worked frantically. A soldier grabbed a heavy hammer and crashed it down again and again and the bolt finally gave, and the nose cone dropped and rolled across the cement. The soldiers stepped aside, showing Bradley the warhead wiring and aluminum core and he shook his hand to them, giving them an okay. Working together, four men carried the warhead and scrambled under the MiG. Bradley felt the jet rock as they cinched the bolts, then watched them scatter from under its wings. The team leader gave a thumbs-up. He was ready to go.

He saluted smartly, then glanced to his right and saw Peter standing in the shadows of his wing. He gave a quick wave, but his friend turned away.

"Peter!" Bradley shouted.

Peter didn't look back, but lifted both hands in despair.

Bradley watched him, then looked down to his cockpit lights. He found the start button, then whirled his finger to the ground troops. He hit the start button and felt the aircraft vibrate as the engine wound up. He watched the rpm gauge move through 20 percent, guessed that was about right, and moved the throttle to the RUN position. The engine didn't fire and the rpm stabilized at 40 percent. "Come on, baby!" he pleaded, "Come on, baby, start!" The rpm wasn't climbing. The engine hadn't caught yet. Then he heard a violent *bang,* and the MiG lurched to the side as a huge flame shot from the back and his fire light flashed. Bradley checked the throttle at idle, jamming it against the stops. The engine shook, and then rumbled, then began a soft whine.

The Soviet fighter was an incredible beast, a huge and sturdy monster of unsophisticated power. Bradley savored the feel of the engine, then motioned to a soldier, putting two fingers inside his fist and pulled his hands apart. The sergeant nodded and moved forward to disconnect the electrical hose. Bradley moved his hands through the cockpit, checking his radios and his navigational aids. He adjusted the artificial horizon, ran the flaps, and checked the flight controls. He checked the speed brakes, searched for the gear handle, and found his takeoff lights.

Then he glanced at his leg where he normally strapped his charts and flight materials. He had none of that now. No maps, no flight plan, no communication cards, and for the first time he realized how incredibly difficult it would be. He was going to take off in a jet he had never flown before, navigate through the mountains, the most treacherous mountains on earth, and search out a convoy on the narrow road in the dark.

He swallowed, then reached up and brought the canopy down. Pushing up the power, the heavy fighter started to roll. He taxied south to the runway and threw the throttle forward and the Iron Maiden shot down the runway and lifted into the air.

Peter watched the MiG disappear and slowly bowed his head as the wind blew around him, cooling the back of his neck.

Then he turned to his sergeant. "Get me the satellite phone," he said. "I've got to call Mother and tell them what's going on."

Shin Bet Auxiliary Outpost
Twelve Miles South of Tel Aviv

The deputy commander of Shin Bet called on Petate's emergency line.

"We've got a problem!" he said as Petate picked up the phone.

"What is it?" Petate demanded, his voice gravelly and tired.

"We've been monitoring the U.S. communications at Lyangar. They sent in a special ops team—your boy Zembeic, it seems—and they've been able to recover one of the pilots as well as a jettisoned warhead from the B-2. And you're not going to bloody believe what they're attempting to do!"

Petate listened intently as he sat up in his bed. "You're kidding!" he muttered as the deputy explained. The Shin Bet commander began to get dressed hurriedly. "What is the probability they'll be able to penetrate the casings of the jettisoned warhead?" he asked.

"Pretty good, sir, from what my guys are telling me."

"Pretty good!? Pretty good!? What *exactly* does that mean?"

"It means, sir, that if the Americans were able to separate the protective depleted uranium nose cone from the nuclear core of the warhead, and if the pilot hits the target, then we're about to have a nuclear event in northern Pakistan!"

Petate felt his heart sink as a rush of blood flushed his head. "How much time do we have?" he demanded in a panicked tone.

"Fifteen, twenty minutes. Maybe a few minutes more."

Petate swore bitterly, then commanded, "Get Dr. Washington on the phone!"

After sucking up the gear and flaps, Bradley pulled the aircraft aggressively into the night sky, standing it on its tail as he accelerated to three hundred fifty knots. It was almost impressive. The old girl wanted to run. Then he saw his fuel flow, and jerked the power back. He had used almost a third of his fuel, just to take off and climb! As he moved higher in the sky, clearing the mountain peaks around him, he rolled the aircraft, testing the flight controls. The MiG was heavy but responsive. The cockpit was noisy, much noisier than any American jet, and the cabin was slow to pressurize, but other than that it was not much different than flying an F-15.

There were mountains all around him, some reaching as high as twenty-five thousand feet. A band of clouds hid the stars and it was completely black; blacker than anything he had seen before, no ground lights, no stars, nothing but a black hole. He felt a surge of panic and jerked the stick back, climbing to twenty-six thousand feet, then looked at his fuel and wiped the sweat from his brow.

Flying to the east, he headed down the Chitral Valley, searching for anything with which he could orient himself. He remembered his charts, which had shown a road heading east, then a split in the mountain range that had to be dead ahead. At the east end of the valley, the main road turned south, heading toward Baroghil. Another road, much less traveled, turned north to the Pamir Pass. He pulled back the throttle as he searched for the road. The clouds cleared, the stars broke through, and the moon gave him light. Off the nose, he saw the pass rising up in the night and he adjusted his heading to line up on the road. The mountains crowded the road, rising steeply on both sides and he could barely make it out, winding snakelike below, a ribbon of black that cut through the snow-covered pass. He would follow the road, then turn north as it wound its way through the pass. Remembering the charts, he pictured the flight in his head. The road would skirt the boundary with Afghanistan, then turn back to the west and through the mountains that led to Khorugh, seventy or eighty miles off his nose.

The truck convoy was covered with mud and brown slush. It had snowed over the pass and the road had proven to be extremely treacherous, with slippery turns and dangerous climbs along almost sheer canyon walls. The snowcapped peaks reached above the vehicles, stretching up to almost up to twenty-five thousand feet, but as the convoy crested the pass and began to descend, the weather had broken to reveal the stars.

The Great One rode in the first truck, watching the road pass silently. The plan was moving forward and it filled him with peace.

As the trucks descended down the mountain, the Great One glanced at his watch. "How much farther?" he asked.

The driver answered, "Forty miles, *Sayid.*"

The Great One sat back. He was almost home, his journey nearly over, his life's work complete.

He closed his eyes slowly.

Soon he would sleep.

The convoy drove almost due west until reaching a point where a narrow gorge ran alongside the road. The Vir River, cold and swift, ran through the bottom of the gorge. The convoy came around a final bend and the road descended gradually, following a path to where the foothills rolled onto plains. Far in the distance, the lights of Khorugh shined through the dark night.

Thomas Washington hung up on General Petate, then picked up the satellite phone. It took him almost three minutes to finally getting through to Peter.

As he listened to Washington, the agent didn't believe what he heard. "You want me to what!" he demanded through the satellite phone.

"Get on the radio. Get a hold of Bradley in that MiG!"

"And what am I supposed to tell him!"

"Tell him to abort! Tell him he must turn around!"

"You want him to abort?"

"Yes! Yes! There can't be a nuclear impact! He must turn around!"

Bradley turned north, and then west as he followed the road, hardly daring to take his eyes off the light ribbon that snaked through the darkness below, knowing there was no way he would find the convoy if he lost site of the road.

The terrain fell away suddenly and foothills began to roll beneath him. He noticed another cut in the earth, a shadow that paralleled the road. That had to be the Vir River. Yes, there it was, the glimmer of water reflected in the moonlight. He pulled back his power and began to descend, leveling out just a few hundred feet above the terrain. Ahead, the lights of the Khorugh suddenly came into view.

Seeing the city lights, his heart slammed in his chest as the reality hit him like a hammer on the head.

He had to be close.

Which meant his time was near.

Then he saw the headlights. They were right off his nose.

The convoy was tight, only ten or twelve feet separating each truck. Their headlights shone in the night, almost directly ahead. Even in the moonlight, Bradley could count the vehicles as he flew overhead. Seven—no, nine. They were all there. He racked the aircraft around and shoved his throttle to the stop. The afterburners lit and he felt the aircraft accelerate, pushing him back in his seat. The wind over the cockpit began to scream and the aircraft began to buffet as she approached the speed of sound. It would require enormous energy to activate the trigger mechanisms on his warhead. And speed was energy, so he pushed up the gas.

Craning his neck over his shoulder he kept the target in sight. Bold. Beautiful. A bright line of lights in the dark. This was it. He would do it. The battle was won. "Yeah, baby!" he screamed as the adrenaline crashed through his body. He felt a crushing rush of well-being. Death, with all its mystery, didn't seem a bad thing to him now. He glanced at his airspeed. Mach 1.1 . . . 1.3. He lined up on the convoy and screamed once again.

He was twelve seconds from impact. Twelve seconds to live.

With a crackle of static, his radio burst to life. "Shane, this is Peter! You have got to abort! Abort the mission, Colonel Bradley. Return to base *now!*"

Bradley stared at the radio. He didn't believe it was true. He stared out the cockpit, suddenly disoriented and confused. He heard Peter's voice again, even more urgent than before. *"Shane, if you hear me, please, I beg you, abort."*

It had to be a trick! He didn't believe it.

He stared at the convoy that filled his windscreen, aiming for the middle truck in the line. The terrain screamed by him almost dreamlike, he was so fast and so low.

The truck filled his windscreen when he heard Peter again. *"Shane!"* his friend cried. *"Turn that aircraft around!"*

Peter laid his head on the old plywood desk in Lyangar's run-down control tower. Twenty minutes had passed since he had made the radio calls. He had not heard from Bradley. He felt sick and dejected and lonely and tired.

Then a soldier grabbed his shoulders and he lifted his head. The sergeant pointed to the east, where the sky was less dark. Dawn would soon be breaking and the sky was growing light there.

Peter looked, then he saw it. The MiG had lined up on the runway and was descending to land.

EPILOGUE

The two men sat around a small conference table inside the inner vault, the most secure area in the headquarters building. The table between them was small and round and the room was nearly bare; white walls with no windows, simple furniture and folding chairs. The air was tense, even strained, but their friendship went back many years; they had been through worse things than this and they would get through this too. Dressed in an open-collared white shirt, General Petate sat upright, with one leg crossed on his knee. The Israeli prime minister leaned forward and scowled, but the Shin Bet director met his eyes with no apology. He would answer his questions but he wouldn't express any regrets.

The Israeli leader could fire him, have him court martialed, or strung up and flogged.

But Petate knew that he wouldn't.

He had done the right thing.

The prime minister sat back and stared in disbelief. "Let me get this straight," he muttered. "You sent the Soviet fighters we captured from Syria to deceive the United States, using the Su-27s to keep the B-2 from destroying the warheads. Then you sent a team of nuclear technicians to the cavern at Tirich Mir, flying them in our Pumas before al Qaeda got there? And you *secretly stripped every warhead of its uranium core!*"

Petate nodded proudly. "Yes, sir. Every one. The warheads are empty. They are now no more dangerous than a drained can of gas."

"And the terrorists don't know?" the prime minister demanded skeptically.

"They have no idea," Petate said. "As far as they know, they have twenty-four operational nuclear warheads."

"Where are the uranium cores now?"

"We used the Pumas to transport them to our destroyer, the *Bethlehem*. They are on their way home now, moving through the Suez Canal."

The PM leaned angrily across the table and pointed a thick finger at Petate. "But why!?" he demanded. "Why not just destroy the warheads? And you'd better think before you answer, and your answer had better be good."

The general leaned forward impatiently. "Think about it, Benjamin," he answered with a stern smile. "Put aside your emotions for a moment and think this thing through! Right now, as we sit here, fat, full, and plump, al Qaeda and their brothers believe they have a bunch of nuclear bombs—bombs they hope to use on us and the West, against you and me and every ally we have.

"How much time, how much effort, how much money and work have al Qaeda and the others dedicated to getting their hands on the bomb? And now that they think that they have them, they will quit trying to get more. Why spend any more money and more effort, and why waste precious time, trying to get or develop a weapon *which they think they now have?* All of their efforts to get nuclear materials will come to a halt. Indeed, we have already seen a reduction in activity in and around Iran's nuclear facilities. And we know more will follow. This will set them back years!

"And now that they believe they have these weapons, they will plan the first attack. But they will take their sweet time, using the infinite patience they have, knowing they will have to be excruciatingly careful, for both we and the United States will be on the highest alert. Then, once they have finally determined their first target, once they have worked so meticulously to put the warhead in place, once they send the command to detonate it, it will be *poof!* Nothing there! A little smoke, a tiny bang, and that's all they will get!

"So yes, at some point they will figure this out. It might be a year, probably longer, I hope it might be five or six, but sometime in the future they will realize they've been duped. But that is time, Mr. Minister, which we buy ourselves. It is time they can't hurt us, and *that's* worth a lot."

The PM nodded slowly while he pulled on his short beard.

"And there's more," Petate added with a satisfied smile, his face showing an eagerness the prime minister had not seen before.

The PM sat forward. "What is it?" he demanded.

Petate shifted in his seat. "When my Shin Bet technicians took the nuclear cores from inside the warheads, they replaced the missing components with miniature tracking devices. Because of this, we are currently tracking the movement and location of the warheads by using our satellites. We can watch the movements of the warheads! Do you understand what that means!? Of the twenty-four warheads, we have a bead on all but five, which we know have been moved to an underground facility outside of Khorugh. Now, think of that, sir! Think of what that provides us! With these transmitters in place, we can monitor and track each of the terrorist cells. Over the next two weeks we will gather more information on terrorist operations than we have over the past fifteen years. We are already building a list of safe houses and contacts, where they cross the borders, what nations give them safe harbor and aid." Petate slapped the table as he talked, the emotion building inside. "Do you understand how important this information could be?" he cried. "Can you imagine what the Americans will give us for information like this!? The potential is astounding. There is no other way to say it, this is a paradigm shift."

The PM sat back and though his eyes had softened, he

still forced a scowl. "And what am I to tell the Americans?" he demanded. "What do you propose I say to our friends?"

Petate looked at him blankly. "I'd suggest you tell them the truth."

The PM swore bitterly. "How!" he exclaimed.

"Sir, they already understand part of what happened anyway. I had to tell them something to keep Colonel Bradley from destroying the convoy before it got to Khorugh."

The general paused and fell silent. How much did he want to say? Did he dare tell the minister how close it had been? He pressed his lips together. He would hold the details for now. "There are a few holes Dr. Washington doesn't understand," he concluded. "And the Americans will come to us for answers; but I think, if we're careful, we can work this through."

"Come to us for answers! That's a bit understated, don't you think! We shot down their bomber! That's three billion dollars right there. And one of their crewmen was killed. What am I supposed to say about that!"

"It was never our intention for anyone to get injured," Petate explained. "We expected the crew to eject and we had our Pumas in position to pick them up when they did.

"But yes, that aside, the Americans will demand some answers from us. And I wouldn't try to play with them or take them for fools. We don't have to spill our guts or hang out our entire load of laundry, but we have to give them enough to keep them on our side. I concede this might be a problem, but not one we can't overcome; for I suspect, Mr. Prime Minister, that when the Americans see the treasure of information we could give them they will forgive and forget. Then we all will move on."

The prime minister hesitated. "They may forgive us, but they have long memories."

Petate cocked his head. "We owe them, they owe us. We do what has to be done. And I promise you, Benjamin, if the roles were reversed, they would have done the same thing."

The prime minister looked away. He knew it was true. "Why didn't you tell me?" he whispered, his eyes shifting to the floor.

"Because this is why you pay me. You pay me to do things so you don't have to know. You pay me to protect you. I was doing my job."

The prime minister sat back and held a deep breath in his chest. "I hate this," he muttered as he let the breath go.

"I understand, Mr. Prime Minister. But it will always be easier if you let me do my job."

The men fell into silence. The prime minister stared at the general and drummed his fingers on the bare table. He started to speak, then fell silent, then lifted his eyes again. "You manipulated the Americans to fight a battle that didn't need to be fought?" he said.

"No!" Petate answered. "That's simply not true. We manipulated them to *fight harder,* but the battle has always been there! We are in this together. Surely they understand that by now."

Arlington National Cemetery
Washington, D.C.

The day dawned cold and dreary, with a band of dark clouds hanging in the low morning light. The grass around the freshly dug grave was wet and long and tiny drops of dew glistened from the tip of each blade. The six-man color guard waited by the grave, their uniforms crisp and pressed, their short-cropped hair bristling from under their caps. The sergeant gave his men one final inspection, wanting them to look perfect before the mourners appeared, then, satisfied, he moved to the end of the line and stood at attention himself. Seconds later the sergeant heard the soft clop of hooves coming up the narrow strip of asphalt that wound through the national cemetery. Glancing to his right, he saw the horses drawing a black carriage with a single bronze casket on its flat and sideless bed. Seeing the casket, he took a deep breath. "Ten-*hut!*" he whispered, and his soldiers drew themselves tight. They looked straight ahead, avoiding the mourners' eyes.

As the wagon approached the fresh grave, the sergeant caught a glimpse of the casket and the Medal of Honor that had been placed on the flag.

Colonel Bradley walked near the end of the funeral procession wearing his formal dark blue uniform while Peter, in a dark suit, walked wearily at his side. The two men stood near the back of the small crowd; this service was for Tia's family, and they didn't want to draw attention to themselves.

There was a short prayer, then a song, then the chaplain's final words. The flag was folder reverently and presented to Tia's mother while taps played mournfully, then the casket was slowly lowered into the wet ground.

Bradley turned away from the grave and wiped a hand across his face. "She was good," he said proudly. "She was as strong and dedicated as anyone I've ever known. She stood up to the enemy. That's all we could ask. And she even liked poker. You would have liked her, Peter, you were two of a kind."

Peter stared at the grave and nodded solemnly. The two men stood in silence a few minutes, then started walking away.

Approaching an intersection in the path, Peter stopped and gazed around the cemetery. "Too many good men are buried here," he said sadly.

Bradley's lips tightened. "Yes, this is sacred ground."

Peter pointed to a row of trees on his right. "My father's buried up there, on the other side of that hill."

"I know," Bradley answered. "He was another good man."

Peter stared a moment, frozen where he stood. "I wish I had been there. I wish I could have told him good-bye."

"You can still tell him."

Peter's face remained expressionless and he didn't move. Bradley nudged him on the elbow. "Come on, Peter," he said.

Peter hesitated, then nodded and the two men walked up the hill.